Tales of the Fiction House

RAJI SINGH

TALES OF THE FICTION HOUSE
The Foundlings
Raji Singh

Copyright © 2012 Raji Singh
First Print Edition, 2013
Fiction House Publishing
www.fictionhousepublishing.com
Contact : a1001tales@yahoo.com

This edition formatted by Charlene Newcomb.
Cover art by Joseph Rintoul,
www.rintouldesign.com

All rights reserved. This book is a work of fiction. Names, characters, places and incidents are either products of the author's imagination or used fictitiously. Any resemblance to actual events, locales, or persons, living or dead, is entirely coincidental. All rights reserved. No part of this publication can be reproduced or transmitted in any form or by any means, electronic or mechanical, without permission from the author.

ISBN-10: 0615814670
ISBN-13: 978-0615814674

For Tenille, Cathy, and Thurston

THE FOUNDLINGS

We are left writhing by roadsides or under trees. We are dumped in trash heaps. We are cradled in now rigor mortised but once tender arms of parents killed by war, plague, inferno, flood, or scores of other tragedies.

We are the foundlings.

Around this big world, we, the tiniest, are the most helpless. We are abandoned to the whims of the elements, animals, sometimes, worst of all, to the wrath of humans.

We come into the lives of others naked, or nearly so. Those other babes and toddlers in our predicament, thousands, maybe millions – no one knows – most never survive.

Sometimes wild animals nurse, feed, protect and raise us as their own.

How do we cope? How do we survive our beginnings then thrive? Through the goodwill of others, by mere chance, but finally and ultimately, by fantasy we spin in our feral yet developing minds. As we grow, unbeknownst to those around us, we retreat to a blissful make-believe of serendipity and lark to keep us sane so we can flourish in a life in which we are given a second chance.

Now cometh our stories and those of whom help and hinder us – our, Tales of the Fiction House. For all those 'WE,' of whom I am one, now do I speak for they have beckoned me to do so -- Raji Singh.

> *'He is no turtle; yet they call him TURT.'*
> Charles Darwin, The Beagle Has Landed,
> page 21, Chapter 19, Verse 23

THE CARPER'S TALE

From the reminiscences of Raji Singh
July 3, 1826

Daylight for just 15 minutes and already summer's heat has dried dew from the Cincinnati pier. A stoop shouldered ancient mariner in an age-cracked slicker gamily trudges the un-ending stretch. Alone. Sunken jaw ratchets, way to below Adam's apple, as he grumbles,
"How long I gonna live?"
These would be the first words my great-great grandfa, four-year-old James Thaddeus Fiction, would remember hearing for the rest of his life. From beneath an abandoned fish cart, he mimics squeakily, "How long I gonna live?"
Mariner looks about, swigs Kentucky stump juice to relieve an aching molar. "Ahh!" He squints curiously down at his fresh-caught carp wrapped in yesterday's <u>Cincinnati Daily Opine</u>.
The boy echoes, "How long I gonna live?"
The singsong reminds Mariner of albatross he heard while sailing around the Cape of Good Hope. He clunks down his

bamboo fishing pole and peers under the cart. "Why, you little carper. You just parrot me?" He reaches for and reels into the sunlight a soot-covered boy still trembling from the night chill. Mariner's knobby knees blink at him through dungaree holes.

A calico butterfly of silver, ruby, and gold had lit on the youth's head. "I see one of my friends been keepin' ya company." Mariner winks at it as it flits away, "happy sailen' Calico." He bends to the boy. "So what's youren name? What you been rollin' round in? And what in the name of Poseidon's ocean you doin' schoolin' here?" Sniff. "Eew! Yer rank as my giant pal Turt after e's swum the Atlantic."

Boy wants to say, "How can you smell me over your owen' self?" Manages only, "Umm…"

Mariner squints at his first catch-of-the-day and grumbles to it. "Likes that one too, I do. Don't think I'll throw 'im back, either."

Boy's face crinkles prune-wrinkly as he flinches; not so much from being level with something looking so like the firebreathing monster of the nightmare he's just awakened from – wild silver hair, blood eyes, warty cheeks and knife nose – but from the sour smell reeking from the pebbly-textured mouth.

Everything before this moment – who he is, where he's from, how long he's been here – is blank, dark as his previously alabaster torso. He wears only short pants with pockets hastily stuffed with childhood trinkets, marbles, tin soldiers, and a spinning top:

> *Escaping bed and building during the fire. His mother ferreted away. Wandering aimlessly. Collapsing here from fatigue. 36 hours have passed. For him it easily could have been 36 days or 36 minutes. The wrenching scars his memory – as happens with foundlings. Yet, after all that, he doesn't fear this human monster.*

"I said, what you doin'…Oh never mind. I start you carpin' and you look like the type'll never clam it." He engulfs the boy's hand in his bony fingers – arthritic from a lifetime of casting nets and setting sails – elevates him, until toes are level with his whale-bone belt buckle; surveys him as he would a catch.

A passing paddle wheeler on the mucky Ohio steam-whistles out a baritone 'ahoy' to the old salt and young dawg. "Let's sail, Carper. My stateroom – she's up the way. I'll get ya cleaned and chowed. Then we can find youren. Unless yer a stray. You stray from the orphanage, Carper? If that be, well...all the more power. Believe me," he rasps, angrily clenching fishing pole, rap, rap, rapping its hard butt against the dock. "Ya stay there an' they'll bugger ya and that's one thing ya don'ts want."

Mariner hardly remembers the dozens of times in Boston orphanages when he was buggered. So clear is the last. He is seven, just finishing off an enslaved fourteen-hour kitchen shift lopping off fish heads with a weighty cleaver:

Grabbed by two cooks; Held by them for the chief administrator's dirty pleasure.

That night, when they sleep in their individual rooms, soundlessly he comes to their beds with the cleaver. The cooks – he whacks off their heads, slick as he would an albacore's head. The administrator – lithely with one swipe – he scales his manhood, leaving him bleating and bleeding to death.

To the sea.

Three times before he is 18, with a grappling hook he keeps in his bunk, he guts men who come for him.

The boy's thoughts are blank. He clutches Mariner's hand as the pair walks: No happy or sad as he looks up into a face equally expressionless as his, only a primitive gratitude for the presence, for the touch of another human.

In only a few minutes Mariner and Carper are at the isolated 'STATEROOM.' A barnacle on the backside of an abandoned warehouse, the ten-by-ten foot wharf-shack juts out over the Ohio. It's built of rancorous vegetable crate-wood. The river's fishy odor is less offensive. Two nose-smudged porthole windows peep out. The oilskin tarp door groans a tired welcome when Mariner moves it. Inside, Carper scrunches his face and breathes cautiously.

One can see the sloshing water between inch-thick gaps in the planked floor. The structure sways like a ship in even moderate knot breezes and this makes it truly home for the Mariner. "I built 'er seaworthy, Matey. Can launch this 'skiff' if I've a mind. Sail away wheres I choose iffa the city starts overtakin'."

Firmly anchoring the wharf-shack are shelved books. They line the walls. Mariner can't read, but pretends. For hours, he will stare at the print and mouth words he believes should accompany pictures.

You stare intently, entranced by the array of Mariner's exotic objects never before this moment have you seen. BOOKS – bound in leather dyed blue, black, and red. The bindings' wild animal pungency – primal; the pulp pages emit sweet, pleasant mustiness of the forest. These soothing scents overpower the wharf-shack's odor. These scents, intoxicating, will draw you under their covers. Soon you will sleep. Dream. All their pages of excitement, knowledge, mystery will awaken a passion for life's grandeur in you that never will dull.

There is no way that at this moment can your child's mind perceive all you feel so deeply. You only experience...

The BOOKS: They begin leaping from the shelves. They slide down Harpoon. Its long face, snaggled with sharp-barbed tooth, is still gleaming with the sweet ardor of some past battle glory. When they reach the floor, BOOKS, in cadence begin marching round a three-legged stool and toward you. 'Hup! Hup! Hup, hup, hup!' In parade. Voices echo in unison, 'JOIN US, CARPER. DON'T LET US PASS YOU BY!'

How do they know your name? Other books are open on rickety stands and on the floor. You smile as an artist's drawing of a wiry pooch 'WOOFS' at you. On the page next to him, a little wooden boy dances clip-cloppity. You want to tweak his funny, ever-growing nose. But, 'Ouch!' You are afraid of splinters.

On the pages of a floored book, a pretty, golden-haired girl in a silver

gown looks down from atop a leafy tree. She reaches for you. She has wings of silver, ruby, and gold. She reminds you of the butterfly that spent the night with you under the cart. You whisper, "Calico?"
    'COME FLYING WITH ME CARPER!' she sings. She swoops down, takes your hand, and off you go go go, landing on the picture's cloudy mountaintop. You lock hands and sing, skip and play ring around rosy, pocketful of posy. Ashes, ashes... all...fall...
    'No! No! You fist your hand in defiance. The fire-breathing monster won't eat me,' your thoughts shout, as you partly remember the nightmare. You blink. No longer do you hold her hand. You're still clasping Mariner's.

    "Ouch! Carper, you got a clam's grip there," Mariner says as he bends creakily and closes the fairy tale book. Butterfly girl winks good-bye. Carper doesn't feel scared or sad. He feels protected by Mariner and this place. He can visit the butterfly girl any time he wants. He will find many joys like her in – BOOKS. Carper will have read and absorbed each one in this dry-dock library before he turns eight. BOOKS. They will become his life.[1]

    "This is Ol Tom, Carper. Ol Tom, this is Carper."

    Ol Tom raises paw in welcome and the boy instinctively takes it.

    "Ol Tom," Carper quietly says.

    "Meow." The sleek, one-eye gray feline looks approvingly over their guest then leaps to his usual perch, Mariner's stooped left shoulder.

---

[1] Little Known Famous Foundling Facts (LKFFF) MOSES: (nicknamed 'Nile's Basket Boy' by his intimates) Ancient publisher. Initiated move away from cumbersome tablets, to innovative strains of lightweight papyrus rolls.
(LKFFF) JAMES THADDEUS 'BLACKJACK' FICTION: aka 'The Carper' 19th century publisher (FICTION HOUSE) and abolitionist. Popularized the now banned (yet still-practiced underground) 'sport' of gloved, Cat Boxing along the Ohio.
(LKFFF) LIL' TOM - alias 'Puss 'N Gloves': First and foremost of the cat boxers. Two of his three gloved, posing posters are known to exist. Hoped for third: whereabouts a puzzle; is considered the "Holy Grail" of the Cat Boxing collectibles. Estimated value if found, in even fair condition – TWO MILLION DOLLARS.

"He likes ya Carper. If he didn't he'd been out the door. He can tell a young sailor who's worth his salt," Mariner says, stroking the cat's glistening fur. Ol Tom is handily the cleanest thing in the wharf-shack. A bed of greasy straw and a seldom-used tub for washing is on one side; a chair that long ago lost its stuffing, the other. Sailor clutter- periscope, scrimshaw, bottled ship, swamps the top of a rotting bureau. Conch shells are all about. Dominating the middle of the room is a bottomless bucket over a hole in the floor – toilet to the river. Surrounding it are piles of corncobs and wrinkly newspapers.

"Ol Tom's a Cincy legend. Fathered most of the cats on these docks, he did. Nears I can tell, not done yet. I reels him in as a young stray, just like I did you. Hiszen' line will one day rule this fairen' city.[2] How 'bout you boy? Got ideas liken that for youren' self?"

Mariner's look locks Carper's; makes Carper feel an equal. As he prattles, Mariner goes to stir bubbling clam chowder he had put on a small coal-burning stove earlier in the morning. He sweeps dried peas off a rickety wooden table. Carper listens to their hypnotizing 'tick, tick, tick' as they spatter to the floor, then 'blip, blip, blip' into the Ohio.

He is in a daze. Barely can he feel or sense as Mariner half-sings – half-bellows. "Time ta swab yer deck, Matey. Gotta be ship-shape for galley call." With a wet washrag he mops the boy clean. Where once was soot, emerges sparkling ivory skin. Where ashen sameness of shape existed, appears definition – lithe fingers, willowy legs and arms, sharp shoulders, carnation pink cheeks reflecting in charcoal-hue eyes. "Handsome lad ya are," he barks, brushing soot from Carper's straight, black hair. Mariner's resolve hardens. "No do-gooders'll get our Carper into an orphanage. Eh, Ol Tom?"

Ol Tom adjusts his-self to his comfort level on Mariner's shoulder and winks good eye, inches from ship-shack master. "Meeeooow."

---

[2] LKFFF: There is a famous marble statue in Cincinnati's main library – a one-eyed cat reading a book. It's been in different locations in the city for over a century and a half. Its origin is unknown.

Mariner ladles two bowls. Carper runs to one, sits, and devours. Mariner layers the <u>Cincinnati Daily Opine</u> on the stove as a chopping block. He whacks off his catch's head and tosses it on the floor. As Ol Tom leaps for it, begins batting it around between bites, the famished boy pushes away empty bowl and begins on the other.

"Eat your fill son. None go hungry here."

Carper pulls a red silk handkerchief from his pocket and wipes his chin. Mariner breathes the silk's sweet perfume. He knows the scent, but from where? Then, as he tosses the carp into a salt bucket to preserve until dinnertime, he notices an artist-rendered picture of a woman in the newspaper. He wipes away fish blood and squints closer at it, then at Carper. He sees the resemblance. Instantly he knows from whence the handkerchief came.

THE TALE OF A LOVE FOREVER LOST

Two nights earlier smoke wafts that perfume scent throughout Cincinnati as inferno guts Madam Rrrose Heather's whurehouse. Naked prostitutes and johns scramble out windows and doors. The lucky ones make it past the temperance posse, over 100 in number who wait with wooden rails, rope, cauldrons of hot tar, feathers. Carper's mother is unlucky. Carper kicks, screams, punches to protect her.

Wrenched from her embrace.

"Don't touch that innocent child of the Lord, you bitch of Satan," an old woman (whom we won't name) caterwauls at the reaching-out, sobbing mother.

Roar of fire and mob deafens Carper.

Knocked-down, almost trampled. He clenches teeth - from the pain of the spinning top's point gouging through his pocket and into his thigh. A man grinds a manure-caked boot into his naked chest, pinning him. He can barely breathe. Although a half-block from the flames, heat burns his face. Men grab his mother's arms, and those of three other women and tear away their nightgowns. Others spit on them. Matrons dressed in black, paint the writhing women with hot tar.

Convulsive screams – veiled by vigilantisms deafening rants.

Carper watches mother and the others as they're trussed to rails. His captor bends, rams demonic face to his. "Spawns of whures get their due too." Slime spews through black-rot teeth. Carper's thoughts cry out, 'Mother, stay with me. Will help you. Dry your tears. Kiss you. Make you feel better. Don't hurt, Mother. Love you.'

A half-dozen police, in pressed blue uniforms, stripes down pants sides, billy clubs upon belts, linger nearby. They turn away horse-drawn carts of firefighters. They tip their tall, round hats, nod placidly, quietly agree, "Let nature take its course. The house is isolated. Nothing more will burn. The chiefs and commissioners will find Madame Rrrose's new garden to pick blooms from 'onst another side of city once she's replanted it."

Faceless mob becomes silent to Carper. He hears only Mother's retching. He slides from beneath stinking boot, to run to her. Before he can rise... trapped again. Helpless, he watches her gentle face. Her long black hair sways midst the violence. She finds him. 'I loves ya, me Bonnie's boy,' her soft shamrock eyes say. Then, her small mouth slips open. Her slender body goes limp.

"Mam-ma, Mam-ma!"

"Shaddup spawn. It's done. You'll visit her in Hell...and soon 'enuf." Carper's captor yanks Carper by the hair, drags him toward an isolated alley where he will 'sacrifice' him to justify his hatreds. He swipes the handkerchief poking from the boy's pocket. "Say, whatta we have here?"

"Leave Mama's things be." Adrenalin rushes. Carper breaks free and scrambles monkey-like up the man's trunk to retrieve the silk from up-stretched hand. Carper kicks at his face, bloodying his nose. As the man wipes away the warmth, Carper mounts his shoulders, seizes the handkerchief, and then leaps. He scurries frantically between the crowd's legs.

Freedom from grief and fear is in the running.

"I'll hunt you down spawn," the zealot shouts. "The Luurd

demands it."

Reverend Ezekiah Bellows, in his mid 20s, thin, clean-shaven, had run from rail to rail to try and stop the madness.

What he naively envisioned a candlelight march, protest of the house, has become lynching. Droplets of tar soil his starched white collar and black suit. He clutches a leather-bound King James – his, one book – the only book he will ever need – 'His' Book – whose lessons the mob's actions blaspheme.

Unheeded go his shouts, "He who is without sin..."

A young woman pulls his arms. She wears a prim checkered dress buttoned just below chin. Her blond hair is a proper bun for a single woman. She WANTS the minister. "You started a good thing for our city, Ezekiah. Now they complete it."

Ezekiah Bellows drops to his knees near the dead victims. "These crosses of shame now do I bear." He clutches scepter King James, and stares aimlessly into clear, starry sky, silently beseeching his Savior for mercies. "I only wanted to scare her from that place of sin. I loved Bonnie. Together we could have walked Your pathway."

Seeing him, midst the public humiliation and torture, Bonnie had mentally pleaded, 'Why, me 'feen' darlin' Ezekiah? Did ye come to hate me that much?' When vigilantes watched curiously, accusingly, from her face to his, he just looked away, denying, as Peter, Christ.

Now he feels the scorch of her skin in his soul, blackening it, melting it irretrievably into molten lava that can only harden to cold stone. He knows he is too cowardly to look at the pale face of the lassie he had visited and paid, for years – "Welcome, feen sweetheart. Rrrose Heather has arranged our special 'ide-away. We'll no be bothered."

There was a six-month period when she would not see Ezekiah. It was during her pregnancy.

He never knew he had a son, hidden within the brothel's inner chambers and loved by all the ladies; a child only Bonnie and Rrrose Heather knew for certain was his, and planned to tell him of when his puritanical hypocrisies might mellow, and he could accept the son.

In the distance – a newspaper artist for the <u>Daily Opine</u> draws all he sees – records, for all time, the ways of hatred.

PART I
THE FICTION LINE

CHAPTER 1

'CALL ME TURT

'For that is what is written on my shell. I too am a foundling. A kind human took me in as a shelling. On new shores, I trumpet my anxious call, then wait, fearing there are no more of my kind to hear. I listen. No answer. With finclaws, I scrape the sand. I sniff. No familial soothing dank pungency to assure me my own were here or still might be in existence? My blare resonates with my melancholy.'

1966

Turt's leathery head, the shape, the size of a football, bobs above the glassy Lindian Ocean surf. He notices that absent suddenly are the screams and strafing of gulls. 'Flyers know things,' Turt thinks, 'something is amiss.'

Octopi carcass oils pucker Turt's tongue as they skim past his beak-snout. Blue water fleetingly shines vermillion then dulls. Clear sky mirrors the change. Turt's sea-senses, honed over the past century-and-a-half, warn of these signs no 'two-legs', humans, could recognize: 'Young Master Typhoon is born, grows beyond the horizon. Snake-sly is he. In a blink, those white-capped fangs will grow deadly. He will devour all who are upon the sea.'

Ordinarily, Turt welcomes riding out a typhoon's rambunctious nature and thrills at their slapdash spirit. Today he is wary. For Turt is on a mission. He shadows a ferry, the <u>Bashri Raku</u>, to protect three passengers, Dr. James Thaddeus Fiction IV, his wife, their four-year old James the Fifth.

They are taking a two-year Peace Corps leave of their free clinic in Cincinnati that treats the city's growing number of Lindian immigrants. They hope to recruit a Lindian – a Dr. Singh – to practice in Cincinnati and help them better understand his people's ways.

Turt has vowed the Fictions eventual safe return to their home half-a-world away.

The family knows Turt is near, though he seldom surfaces. Faithfully, he has followed, down the Ohio, Mississippi, through the Gulf, out to sea. He dines quite nicely on sumptuous scraps the cooks toss overboard, and delicacies that swim too close. Whenever some curious critter queries 'Whither thou goest, Traveler?' he explains, then adds, 'In strange lands, best I follow quietly – lest I end up in two-leg soup served in mine own shell.'

Most of his life, this giant of sometimes land, sometimes sea, has looked after the Fiction line. It started with helping protect the patriarch, the foundling James Thaddeus Fiction, the Carper, 140 years earlier, from all variety of nemesis – man, animal, nature.

At a picnic two years before now, Turt rescued impetuous James V after he stripped off britches and skimmed quietly into the Ohio. Turt slipped quickly from bank, coursing swiftly to the rescue. Submerging, rising, he emerged with the boy fish flopping atop his shell. He delivered James safely to shore, to frantically searching parents who had looked away for 'just seconds.'

Why does Turt do this? Quite simply, pet-to-human dedication: He is a loyal hound-in-armor to generations. Only those animals with the freest of spirit, as Turt, choose this highest form of be-knighted pet-hood. Turt has seen all the Fictions' frailties, foibles, faults, traits that turn humans from one another. Of all pets, only the most loyal fully sense these things, never understand them, always forgive, and make fidelity, as Turt does, paramount. Turt's bond to the three on board has been fused, hardened, and forged through generations.

Humans would call it love.

Turt will not let even the most powerful Master Typhoon pull it asunder.

But the sky reddens, ripples patter the <u>Bashri Raku</u>'s stern – nudging, warning, 'The Sea is MINE.' Belligerence rapidly grows as Typhoon reaches adolescence. Now, waves batter. Wind slaps. 'All in it, or upon it, belong to ME!'

PORTRAIT: A CALM BEFORE THE STORM

Dr. Fiction, in an overstuffed chair in a stateroom, sterilizes medical instruments and inventories medicine vials: Beside him ever faithful hanging skeleton, King Leer. Dr. James Thaddeus Fiction the IV. Scientist YEA. Fashion maven, NAY. Brown corduroy suit, tie, perpetually outdated.

Plumping, loving wife, Imah Fiction, bustles between beds and dresser wrapping keepsakes. She looks a bell in her knee-length dress as the boat's rocking dings her about. Her homespun nature camouflages cool business sense. Without her meticulous oversight of meager donations, their clinic's resources would wither and the good doctor's medical charity would be impossible.

Their eyes meet. 'Do not let James sense our worry over the storm.' To relieve the tension, Imah says, "James' learning Lindian from those at the clinic will serve him well here."

James climbs father's lap, listens only-partially to a tale

meant to distract him from Typhoon's bluster. The air is sultry. He is shirtless, short-pants-ed. His natural tan contradicts father's pale, and mother's strawberry, complexions.

Father takes a gleaming, foot-long Bowie knife from amongst treasured personal items in a wooden travel trunk. "The Carper got this from Old Jim himself, not long before the most famous battle in Tehas history." He lets James stroke the pearl handle and the blade's detailed scrollwork. "As years passed, during Civil War and civil strife, it saved the lives of many a Fiction, Son. Maybe yours, one day."

Imah's glance says, 'I asked you not to bring that.'

Dr. Fiction tucks it away. It's the one item that represents to him daring-do, and adventure.

James imagines seizing Bowie, waving it in the air to challenge the storm he's pretending is an ogre. It's a raging battle. Sweat beads his forehead, sifts through eyebrows, 'plips' onto boldly-thrust chest. The 'plips' are rumbling explosions of imaginary cannons James fires to protect his parents — from the ogre rocking the boat, fomenting earthquakes, tidal waves, and volcano eruptions on the wall paintings of palm-treed islands.

Mother lovingly combs fingers through son's thick black hair. She's remembering her husband's and his fa's and grandfa's years of brooding because they'd never taken time to write down the Fiction stories. This precocious four-year-old has memorized them and repeats most, easy as ABC's.

"No need in worrying any longer, Doctor. You know he'll help you record all the tales." She smiles to her husband and motions to their son's haze of a gaze. "It looks as if we've lost James to his other world, at least for now. Enjoy it Son. Say hello to everyone there for us."

James fends off ogre. Boat steadies.

James' look shifts to an intricately scrolled book-sized walnut box. On the lid are carved, bounding in carved jungle environs, a tigress and pachyderm wearing pants and capes. Father removes it from the trunk and lets him hold it as a diversion from the storm. James' thoughts pivot from the exotic animals, to the stories his father begins telling about great-great grandfa when he was James' age and known as the Carper. So often have these stories beguiled him. Eagerly he enters the chasm of his imagination that is the pathway to Carper.

It is the same journey Turt has seen James re-enact – hundreds of times – as Turt crouched contentedly outside their living room window in Cincinnati.

"...So, that place Mariner called his stateroom, Son...Well, that's not quite right."

James jumps ahead in the story. "Let me describe what it looks like Papa... a carbungle onnay bask-ass-side uh a ..."

"Ahem. That's carbuncle," his mother corrects, mentioning nothing about the mispronunciation for posterior anatomy.

In his thoughts, James is inside the wharf-shack asking Carper. 'Think you'll like livin' with the Mariner?'

In James' imagination, Carper parrots Mariner's voice. 'Cain't rightly say.'

James asks. 'Turt look any different than now? Can you ride 'im?'

'Not met 'im yet. When I do, you'll be first to know.'

The ferry lurches from Typhoon's sudden growth spurt. A porcelain pitcher smashes down from a stand. Flying shards impale Leer. Its rattling is overshadowed by flotsam that is swept from the sea, and missiles into and shatters the porthole. Lightning's sulfur stench permeates the room. Typhoon's cold wind-tongue licks their ears.

Imah plugs the porthole with towels. Father hugs son who quivers, almost cries, because the great ogre is real and returning cannon volleys.

'Don't let the breeze scare you, James,' Carper encourages. 'I'm here, and Mariner'll be along. He knows the sea. We'll protect each other. Just like we always have. 'Member how when you almost drown-ded in the 'Hio? Mariner harpooned that giant catfish 'fore it could 'et ya. We'll do the same to the ogre 'iffen he tries to get ya.'

Calming words are Imah Fiction's elixir for the family.

"We'll be docking in just an hour or so, don't you think Dr. Fiction? Ahh! Nice long baths for us then."

"Quite so, Imah."

She binds the porthole patch with surgical tape, and then makes her son grin. "And a good hose down for Turt, eh James?"

Dr. Fiction, he calms with his methodical consistency and planned routine. He talks to his son as he would an adult. "Mr. Balu Baiku will be meeting us James.[3] He will take us to the village where we will meet Dr. Singh and his wife. I will convince them to go to Cincinnati."

This time the father's cure counters the mother's healing instead of reinforcing it. James' grin turns grimace. Home: its safety, comfort, seems a forever away. Reality replaces the gleeful imagining of showering Turt. James knows the ogre will try to stop them from reaching a new home.

The ogre's jolt sends a dozen butterflies flitting moth-like from the trunk. They encircle James. Dr. Fiction's fortitude is bolstered by memories his fa' and grandfa' have told about Carper. "Remember how butterflies were always near the Carper in difficult times?" he whispers warmly, "Now just look at them about you, Son. Your mother and I will protect you, and Turt will. So, too, will they."

Imah caresses her husband and son. "Such curious creatures, the butterflies. They've not been around other family members. You and the Carper must have a lot in common."

James smiles. Carper smiles back at him. 'We shore do; that's true. As long as you visit me in your imagining, James, I'll always be near.'

A jolt of wind makes the cabin lights flicker. James is sure he is the only one who sees tigress on the box's lid come to life and growl to scare off the ogre. Pachyderm blows to add to the pandemonium.

---

[3] LKFFF: Balu Baiku "TIGERMAN" Introduced traditional exotic, pacifist 'Cat Dancing' to America in Zigfield Follies – 1923. Its introduction led to a growing call for and eventual ban on 'Cat Boxing.' Ironically, Balu came to befriend James' great-great grandfa' in Blackjack's elder years.

TALES OF THE FICTION HOUSE

Dr. Fiction slips the box from James. He opens it so they can peek briefly at the Carper's favorite, leather-jacketed book — six inches thick — filled with endless tales. Carper and his descendents have kept it in shining condition for 140 years.

"We'll partake of it later," he tells James who is anxious to disappear into its magical stories, with Carper alongside to share. "For now we'll pack it away so it's safe."[4]

Before he closes the lid, one of the butterflies, a calico of silver, gold and ruby, her powdery colors flecking off, creating a tiny rainbow curtain that only James seems to see — and peek behind — slips quietly into the box. Peeking back from behind the curtain is Carper, who says, 'Don't worry James — Calico — she'll watch over it as she watched over me.'

Mrs. Fiction cocoons the boxed book in plastic wrap to waterproof it.

A knock on the door. From the other side, "The Captain wants everyone on deck. Just formality. Dr. Fiction, he wants you to br..." The steward's voice quavers. He knows of dangers others don't. "He requests you bring your medical supplies."

---

[4] The book is the 'Book of Carpier': Carpier; 7th century Lindian storyteller-philosopher-saint-foundling. His grand tales lightened the burdens of the poor, oppressed, and sick.

CHAPTER 2

UNSAFE AT ANY KNOT

Turt winces as a collage of purple clouds stabs the <u>Bashri Raku</u>'s wake. He looks for the reactions of the malingering throng on deck. Most are mesmerized by Typhoon's swirling growth spurt and in awe of what they should fear. To Turt, some appear gangly octopi as they bask in lounge chairs, others, sharp, shark-featured as they glide inside the railing. Many are pale oysters, others, dark ink of squid. Although he cannot communicate warning, 'Aye, Captain, stoke your furnace full, for a storm be nigh', Turt refuses to be dispirited.

Tenacity. Persist. He could blare out a Satchmo rift. That would only get them clapping and pointing to the 'jammin' bump' in the drink. They would be distracted even more. 'Two-legs. So unaware are they.'

Turt spies his land family. They forage through their travel trunk. A stowaway butterfly flits out, touches James' forehead, then returns to flutter warning to compatriots of the impending swale. Turt knows, 'Flutterers deliver sanctuaries of beauty and peace, but not always safety. That is for me to accomplish.'

He cranes neck and contemplates the ferry's increasing portside list. His one-creature crusade has extra complications.

The <u>Bashri</u> <u>Raku</u>...a converted, once-mighty corvette, a style of precision fighter ship, is now a puttering, stuttering Corvair, a spruced up rust-bucket meant for 500, carrying a thousand...sumptuous cuisine for young Monsieur Typhoon to devour.

Our crusader cannot see it, but smells it – LAND: Musty forest, damp beach. Those fragrances blend, caressing Turt's nostrils. Though beaked snout forms a perpetual frown that masks his optimism, oblong eyes, unblinking, reveal hope the ship will beat Typhoon to shore.

The tip of Turt's armor shell shows above the burbling surf. Graffiti envelopes his plating, revealing his contact with humans over the past century-and-a-half, but only a fading Poseidon clutching a trident is visible. A dark-soul passenger says, "That looks like our stepping stone to the depths."

Turt paddles against the wake to draw nearer the Fictions. Of what he might do, he is unsure. A taunting tuna, a couple-a-pounder, begins circling Turt, impeding his progress. 'Nighyaw! Nighyaw! None swim quicker than Iiii-yaw!'

'Thou thinkest thou art cool beans,' mocks Turt. Stingray swift, Turt stretches neck. Vise jaw opens, closes. Snap! Chomp! Lick! Gulp! 'Well that's farewell to thee then.' He spits out tail and the truant tuna's nearby school scatters.

Typhoon slithers closer, hisses. Turt stiffens. The sea churns and Turt tastes the elevating salt in the breeze. Often he has observed a typhoon's carnage this forecasts. Even sturdy modern ships would have little hope in such a storm.

Blackening clouds turn day night. Typhoon's taunting tango commences.

Turt purges air pockets within his shell that keep him afloat. He submerges, swims to the ferry, and surfaces beside it. Typhoon escalates from teen rage to manhood's force. Gale winds, screaming, tilt the ferry. Turt realizes he must trumpet warning to alert the two-legs.

Turt extends neck and blasts his trill. Steady chords, the consistent somber of a foghorn but with a carillon's tone, resonate, beatific as Gabriel's herald. It pulls passengers from

Typhoon's trance and helps them briefly forget their sudden fear, petty concerns, and animosities; enables them to look deeply at those they care. Turt is reassured. Humans truly aren't the uncaring beasts many creatures believe.

Typhoon slaps the sea, thundering curses at Turt for purloining his audience. Smug, theatrically temperamental, Typhoon's certain he will control the final act.

Only the Fictions know the meaning of Turt's ominous trumpeting. Last they heard it – at the river nightmare before Turt fetched drowning James. Once again, they're given moments, precious ones, to take son to bosoms; final moments to say, "I LOVE YOU!" Moments spent dreading, but spent together. James squirms, not understanding.

In that instant, the crash and bluster of storm disappears for Dr. James Thaddeus Fiction IV. Mariner appears. He stands defiant against the wind. The Doc always used to know him in his imagination, decades ago, before adulthood's realities. Only now does he recall those childhood encounters.

All the times he envied James for having them. They too were his.

'Doc…Ma'am,' Mariner doffs his grimy sailor's cap. Imah can't fathom Mariner. The storm is deafening to her. She grasps husband and son.

"Mariner. Forgive me all the years I abandoned you."

Imah sees her husband's mouth move, but midst the squall, the only words anyone on board hears are shouted ones.

'Nonsense,' comes Mariner's reply. 'We sailed the ship together. You were just starboard while I be port.'

Suddenly there's another voice, another face the Doctor hasn't heard, hasn't seen for so long.

'You did a fine job with our Fiction line, a humanitarian's job. That is what you were accomplishing on the starboard. We are proud of you.' It's Carper appearing as a boy, but speaking as a wizened elder – as James Thaddeus 'Blackjack' Fiction: Publisher; Abolitionist.

Dr. Fiction reaches out to touch his great grandfa's cheek.

The boy backs away. He says, 'Listen to Mariner. Time is

TALES OF THE FICTION HOUSE

short. I must go to James, but I will be seeing you again, soon. Then we will have forever together to trade our tales.'

Pandemonium erupts around them. Deck chairs, Typhoon's surrogate jaws and fangs, gobble up their occupants. Poles, hoisting multi-colored flags of the seven seas, do Typhoon's bidding. They snap then swipe into ducking passengers. Dr. Fiction holds his wife and son tight. Mariner's words are clear midst it all. 'I'll tell it as it is, Doc. Well do I know these waters. There's little hope for you, your wife, probably anyone aboard.' Mariner puts his arm on James' shoulder. 'But there's maybe a way for the boy. That sea line you carry as keepsake – we both know its strength. Tie it to the trunk's handle.'

Dr. Fiction squints. He knows Mariner sees his doubt.

'A seafarin' man has ways, Doc. Twixt my tellin' how, and youren' deck-doin', and Turt's sea-doin', we can help the boy see another dawn. But yas gotta follers what I tells yas. Iffen we cans beats Typhoon outta one human, even if he's a tadpole 'a one, we'll have conquered him. So let's be at it mate.'

* * *

Well over a hundred years earlier, aboard the H.M.S. Beagle. (In calm waters, safely away from any typhoons) Charles Darwin adjusts spectacles as he writes at his desk in his wood-paneled cabin.

'I met the strangest creature during the third week of our voyage. He had been following us for a good two weeks, as if he knew our plans. We netted him up. He did not fight us. It was as if he was curious about something and wanted aboard.

'Age 25 to 45. Length, beak to tail, 144 cm. Head, the size of my fists together. I wonder how big eventually he will become. Hippo, elephant-sized, or stay the height of a large St. Bernard as he is now. He is shelled, but make no mistake, despite the abbreviated lettering on his shell – T-U-R-T – he is no turtle.

'(There are tales of an island of those like him. They sun by day and at night blare trumpet-like, beautiful seductive music, through their highly intricate larynx. They would be extinct now, if accounts I have heard are true.)

'His feet are finned yet strangely clawed, as those of a large raccoon. He could traverse land – he demonstrated that as he coursed the Beagle's deck – as well as he could swim seas, though not as fast.

'There is artwork on his shell. It is Exquisite! Like those of sailors who are completely illustrated. The artwork on his shell encompasses within an African village motif. Surely, it is the work of the finest of tattoo visionaries.

'Perhaps that is where he was hatched and it was carved in when he was hardly bigger than my thumb. I will go into more detail on that later when I study the ship artist's precise copy. The art may reveal clues to the mystery of his species. (A crewman sneaked onto the deck one night and painted the ship's mascot, the beagle, next to an existing image of a sneering tabby standing erect, his paws poised in boxing gloves.)[5]

'I speculate that this 'TURT' is a creature only thought extinct.

'He stayed with us all the way to and through our Galapagos Island studies. It was as if he were on his own voyage of discovery. Of what I will probably always wonder. He seemed nervous, disconcerted, and maybe even lonely. As if he were the last of his kind, yet, didn't want it to be so, I theorize.'

Darwin's long face wrinkles. He sets aside pen, removes jacket, tie, spectacles, and rolls up shirtsleeves. He stretches,

---

[5] LKFFF: The top cat boxers were most always foundlings - because those, like Puss 'N Gloves, were the toughest of pusses, having to survive the wilds as cute kittens. From alley – to ring royalty. They were treated as top racehorses are today. Carried on the shoulders of a quartet of humans, the combatants traveled to bouts in 'spired edifices', velvet inside, large enough for feline cousin, the tiger. Humans by the thousands lined-up to view the parade of lavish,'cat-sels.'

puts hands behind his head, and thinks. I miss the fellow. Been gone three weeks now. I admire what must be his tenacity for life. For what more, could one ask?

Darwin, exhausted from a day spent in writing, begins to doze. Aloud, but to no one but himself, he says, "Ah Turt. You will probably be around long after I have departed this world. The wonderful adventures you will have that never will I see."

Then, Charles Darwin drifts to sleep and dreams of crossing the Atlantic, blissfully riding atop Turt's shell. And Charles is naked, and loving it.[6]

---

[6] LKFFE: RAJI SINGH - present-day American industrialist. Wall Street Journal headline monikor "THE RAJ" has stuck to him. "The Raj" attracts butterflies, the species Danaeus Plexippus. Exhaustive studies cannot show why. (A curious aside concerning foundlings is that, just as hobos, wrestlers and baseballers, most have nicknames – usually given to them by others. Many modern-day sociologists who study the dubbings believe that, until the subject-foundlings self actualize their existence, nicknames allow for a "transitory apparatus" to bridge fantasy-past to reality-present. Others believe, it's all just a good "kick.")

CHAPTER 3

A TYPHOON'S TALE

Youth's pent-up energy explodes as Typhoon sweeps to adulthood. Waves swamp the ferry's railing. Each strike washes hundreds overboard. Imah Fiction kneels, clutches James. She realizes son and husband are in a different world, one where the ocean is silent. They converse with apparitions.

Carper hugs James and says, 'Don't be afraid. Mariner and your fa know what to do.'

Dr. Fiction thinks, only minutes for us now, maybe seconds. Nervously he ties an obscure 19th century knot around the trunk's handle.

'You remember well the seafarin' ways I taught,' Mariner says. His clothes are as dry as the Fictions are wet. He's swift while their moves are concrete-stiff against Typhoon's force. Dr. Fiction hammers Bowie's butt into the trunk creating air holes. The knife sticks.

'Good work, Doc. The blade'll be the little ship's rudder. It'll keep it on the straight and narrow. Boy'll get more than his fair share of sea, but he'll breathe.' Mariner leans to Imah. 'Time I shove-off. Goodbye Doc...' He doffs hat, '...Mrs. Fiction.'

Imah briefly enters their calm world. She smiles gratefully at Mariner. "Thank you for helping our son." He kisses her cheek, whiskery to her softness, pats James' head, and then is gone. The roar of their world's carnage returns. Carper releases James to parents' final embrace. Midst pelting rain, they lift James into what will be either his transport or tomb.

James flails. All he wants is caressing.

'Be strong,' Carper says. He transforms from short-pants peer of James, to James Thaddeus 'Blackjack' Fiction, dapper in waistcoat, tie, and English-tailored jacket. 'This journey is yours alone to make, but I have a special friend who will guide you.' [7]

James feels his great-great granfa stroke his cheek. Blackjack says, 'May we both have the good fortune to be together again.' He fades away.

So little time now. With one arm, father holds his squirming son in place.

'Don't fight, Young 'un,' comes Molly's whisper in James' thoughts. 'He's doing what's best for you. Remember, when you're alone, your Molly'll be here. Long as you'll allow me.'

Dr. Fiction helps his wife toss out microscope, stethoscope, and medicine from the trunk. They push their confused boy between documents and packing material so he's egg carton firm. Butterflies burrow close to him.

From fear, from wildly racing heart, James drifts in and out of consciousness. He feels his mother's kiss. Father's hard, wet cheek touches his for an instant, but it seems like for a whole life. His breath brushes James' ear. "I love you, Son."

There's a deafening thunder-bust. Son barely hears father, "Obey Turt".

James closes his eyes and drifts into the calmness of

---

[7] LKFFE: Molly Brown, the 'unsinkable', at the London International Cat Boxing Competition days before her Titanic heroics: Kneeling along crowded ringside with 'Blackjack' Fiction who, now in his 90's, is dishing sage advice as referee raises winning paw and they both scoop up their winnings: "We foundlings, Molly, must always be ready to act swiftly if we are to survive. Our instincts demand it." His eyes penetrate hers. "We'll never know the good our deeds may accomplish. Still we do them." Days later, Molly would utilize his advice. Many decades later, tales of those decisive actions, recollected by James, would aid his survival.

imagination.

Dr. Fiction glares out to sea. He knows Turt watches, and, because of their lifelong friendship, he knows Turt can read his expression, 'Deliver James, old friend.'

Turt witnesses the cruelest irony. He sees land crags through the blurred horizon. Humans are so close to safety.

Turt is spun and twisted, but never loses sight of his family aboard the rocking horse of a vessel. The <u>Bashri Raku</u> is breaking with sounds like dozens of cannon blasts at once. Ferrous odors from the ship's coal fuel belch from its bowels. Typhoon's fangs slam the trunk's lid. The force jam locks the hasp. Turt trumpets sad cries as he watches, helpless, as waves catapult Dr. and Mrs. Fiction, and hundreds more, overboard.

The trunk catches, teeters in the railing. Inside it dozens of butterflies swarm to boy's ears to buffer him from Typhoon's shrieks. James hears Molly Brown. 'A ball rolls with the waves, young 'un. You must too.' James *pretzels-up* until his body is round.

Slowly Typhoon swallows the <u>Bashri Raku</u>, savoring the delicacy.

The trunk '*THUNKS*' into the sea and drifts toward the swelling whirlpool. Water bleeds through the air holes. 'Don't let your face rest in it,' warns Molly.

Turt submerges and glides stealthily toward James' little boat, along the way passing passengers who cling to pieces of the <u>Bashri Raku</u>. Typhoon rips away from one another, couples, families in final embrace. They quickly disappear down Typhoon's insatiable swallow.

A thousand, minus one, will die this dark day.

--Now cometh the tale of that one, me, James Thaddeus Fiction the fifth. I, inheritor of all the ills, yet, all the joys, of all foundlings--

'Quick, unfurl yourself,' Molly directs. 'Push your feet and hands into the sides of the trunk.'

You do.

'Good. Now you're a stick, stuck-snug. Only an ogre with

steel teeth could break you now.'

THE TRUNK

Your twisty-tumbly arcade-ride coffin, so noisy. 'WHOOSH, BAM, GRRR, WHEE' *seem to meld into one* 'SHEEE' *quiet sound.*
Dark! Touch head, shoulders, stomach. Feel, can't see.
Tongue. Mouth. Talk. "MAMA, PAPA!" No words to hear. Me. James Fic... You suddenly are lost. Who are you? Who Mama, Papa? You hear Molly. 'This is what you must do now...' You can't find out, what, because, she, too, disappears.
You tumble. Bumpity-bump. OUCH! Put mouth to the splintery hole in the side of coffin ride. Precious air. Suck hard. Ahh! Look through another hole. Water seeps past your eye. You see a giant, shelled creature. Riding him to your rescue are Carper and Mariner, like they did when you slipped to the bottom of the 'bio. Suddenly they're washed away. Remains only the creature.
Carper? Mariner? Who, are they? You forget everything and drift into another dream world. This one you've never been to. In it you are alone. It scares you.

NOW BEGINNITH YOUR DAYS OF DAZE.

Though you will often dream of the giant shell-creature, you even forget that you had a dear friend named TURT. Worst of all, you forget MAMA, PAPA.

CATCH A WAVE

The sea line Dr. Fiction tied to the trunk handle whips out. Turt catches it in his beak-snout, and, heart *thumping* from exertion, he tows his cargo beyond the whirlpool's suction.
Typhoon uses the protruding Bowie-rudder to test Turt. A wave pushes the trunk at him. Bowie's swipe grazes fin-claw. The trunk spins. Knife returns. Turt twists. 'ZIP!' Blade cuts the line. Turt lunges, seizes the length still attached. He turns so his shell '*clangs*' into Bowie. Turt thumps repeatedly,

hammering the blade just far enough that the point is harmless to him, and the handle won't harm the boy inside. Absent rudder, Turt must now do the little boat's steadying.

Typhoon's next challenge, a seventy-footer, is the highest yet of his waves.

Atop it is the safest place, Turt knows. He waits coolly, calmly. When the wave's angle is gentlest, he bows neck, tucks fin-claws and belly-rides to the crest. Typhoon whips, spits, but cannot wrench away the lifeline to the towed trunk, nor dethrone Turt.

Turt '*shell-rides*' the curl. Suave, debonair as he hangs ten, he deflects bodies, boards and banana boxes Typhoon spits-out to sink them. Typhoon's rage is futile.

Turt doesn't know how saturated the trunk is getting. Midst sea's clamor, he can hear little boy rasps but no 'baby' whimpers. 'Yes, this is a true Fiction,' Turt beams.

He knows his canyon-peak precipice is unreachable. He feels he can almost stretch, and tear down Typhoon's curtain of black clouds. He has outlasted, defeated Typhoon.

OLD AGE

Typhoon's waving fangs break and crumble on shore. Turt and trunk slip slide, '*WHEE!*' up the sandy beach. Briefly, all is quiet. As Turt thinks, 'we're safe,' a latent wave strikes. Returning to sea, it seizes trunk and pulls. Sand beneath the trunk erodes. It tips. Turt anchors it by clamping-on fin-claw. Typhoon fails to claim the last human left alive.

AND, AT LAST, DEATH

Typhoon's tides tremble. Rain lessens. Dark clouds lighten. Turt surveys the beachscape. The <u>Bashri</u> <u>Raku</u>'s twisted remains wash up and skeleton the coast. Skimming past is King Leer, rattling dejectedly, as if hoped-for castles had disintegrated into the sand. Turt must get his helpless ward to the safety-cover of nearby woods before quick-moving scavengers – beast or human – might arrive, or nightmare-inducing mangled human remains wash ashore. Turt pries the trunk's stubborn hasp. Don't be too rough. Might tip more, drowning, James. 'Stay still, James.'

OL DOC TURT DELIVERS

After your wild ride, it is impossible to lay quiet. Body aches. Your head bobs in and out of the water. You must leave your womb's sloshing darkness, be reborn into whatever new life awaits you.

Possessing the ingrained passion of all living things ready to take their place in the world, you pound the lid.

Turt hears. He knows there may be only precious seconds to keep James from drowning. He claws, determined as the mother eagle he saw, once-upon-a-time, swooping to protect hatchling.

Your adrenalin burst creates 'SUPER CHILD'. You smash through soggy veneer. Water breaks. Like eaglet from its egg, you crack forth. The moment of your rebirth, the beginning of, YOUR, once-upon-a-time, is, NOW!

The fluid rush tips the trunk. Turt steadies it. He scalpels wider the opening James created. Butterflies, wet-winged but little worse-for-scare, emerge. They flit awkwardly, akin to stumbly drunks. 'One strong shot of cocoon that was!' Turt doesn't realize water slaps into James' mouth, until he hears '*aacking*'. He tilts the trunk to see him.

James shakes. Teeth chatter. He reaches for help, but passes out. Turt rams his fin-claw through the opening. He grabs James by the pants. The soggy wood crumbles as Turt yanks him out. Trunk falls, spewing out its contents. Amongst sopping documents is a faded photograph of Blackjack taken with Molly. 'Don't worry old friends,' Turt vows. 'I'll see him through.'

James isn't breathing. Turt lays him face-up and anxiously massages his chest with fin-claw. James looks so his great-great grandfa when Turt first met him, but Carper was sturdy, pink-face fiery, flourishing in Mariner's care. James is turning the pale of decaying sole, and his lips, sea urchin purple. Eyes disappear up into sockets. Turt has seen all this happen to too many land-creatures before they expire.

'*Gurgles*', bubble from James' chest. Turt rolls him and swiftly 'whaps' fin-claw against his back. A yelping birth-scream echoes out. James is shocked into breathing.

He writhes, 'hacks' water, then cries. Turt rolls him again and licks his chest. Turt's rough tongue is massaging, warm. James' cries lessen. Cheeks begin to regain their glow. Mouth reddens. His black eyes reflect serenity; as the Lindian Sea at its calmest. Blank-faced, James examines Turt, then drifts to sleep. Rain slaps James' face so Turt tents himself above him. Butterflies massage James' forehead.

'Does he remember me?' Turt cries to the flutterers. 'He will. He MUST!'

Rain lessens. Clouds thin. Turt is able to fully-see his surroundings. A nearby forest is a half-hour crawl away. The sand is cold from Typhoon's bite. James requires warmth and Turt's shell is becoming sun-toasted. He slips fin-claw beneath boy. Utilizing beak-snout as cantilever, he gently lifts him atop dome. There, with a thousand miles of sea at his back, Turt can best protect James from beasts. 'Rest, James. We'll travel when you're fit.'

James stretches and looks around. He pats Turt's shell, as instinctively, as lovingly as he has done hundreds of times in the past when he climbed atop him to play. He traces his index finger around the carvings and paintings, then through the four inscribed letters. "TURT," he says contentedly, then, again he sleeps. Turt is happy. The boy may not remember him, but knows his name and trusts him.

After an hour, James awakens, climbs down, and retrieves the sea line from the trunk handle. He remounts and instinctively begins tying, untying the 19th century knots his father taught him. He uses Turt's neck like a hitching post. Turt smiles, 'boy remembers a family pastime.'

Turt jerks his beak-snout. He senses movement behind the ship's wreckage. A two-leg's shadow. He's hiding. Watching.

TALES OF THE FICTION HOUSE

Turt considers the suspicious stalker. Slaver? Cannibal? Buggerer?

Turt pries Bowie from the trunk. Clutching it in his beak snout, he holds the blade up to the sun. He vows, 'By your light, Sol, and for the love and memory of all the Fictions, even if I lose my life in the doing, I will keep the boy safe.' So Bowie can't be used against them, he tosses the weapon far into the ocean. He fights, best, bare fin-clawed.

He imagines Carper scolding. "Bowie should be with James."

'Bowie'll sink. But I'll know where to find him when the time is right.'

To the forest — for food, water, safety, new beginnings — the creature, boy, and butterflies, they do parade. None looks back, only forward to adventures yet to come.

But Typhoon's ghost lives, haunting the shelled creature and boy who defeated him. His underwater current seizes Bowie and rolls Bowie back to shore. Typhoon whispers, 'Here. Finish my job.' The stalker sees Bowie's gleam and runs to claim him.

The man raids the trunk for valuables and stuffs them into a knapsack. He removes the wrapping from around the wooden box containing the Book of Carpier. He opens it. Calico flits out. She studies him, and then flies to James. The man bags the Book, its intricately carved box, and Bowie. Cat-sly, he rises to shadow the parade.

CHAPTER 4

1826

Forget the fire, disappearances and deaths – whures, and their cathouse scat this Cincy neighborhood: No blame, only a hero who disavows the whole affair. "The Reverend is most modest," his parishioners smugly agree. Some linger in church, awaiting further guidance. Winsome maidens with mothers arrive at his shuttered home. Visages of being with him; they burn in their thoughts. They leave cake, cookies, pie at his door when he doesn't answer their knocks.

"PLEASE COME OUT AND PLAY, EZEKIAH."

Ezekiah Bellows lies sleepless, in sooty suit, 36 hours after the fire.

'Bonnie. Dear Bonnie. How could I...Oh dear Bonnie, forgive me.'

He's convinced his life is sham. To herald his denial of any worldly pride, his two-room residence is austere; chair, table, bed, bureau stolid as himself, austere oak pedestal for King James. Ezekiah stares at bedroom ceiling cracks. One moment they are Heaven's ivory gates, next, Hell's brimstone entrance.

He's convinced: Father is calling me home to HIS Valhalla. "Father, strengthen me."

Echoing outside, tinged with pseudo-concern, is the bloodlust wail of the zealot who still trolls for Carper. "Spawn, begat by whom Satan whured with. He must be found and raised up to the Luurd."

Ezekiah numbs to the repeating tirade. He counts out the seven deadly sins: gluttony, envy, sloth, pride, covetousness, lust, anger. He feels guilty of all in gaining his conquest, becoming minister to the largest congregation, in *wholly*, Cincinnati.

Bonnie often encouraged him after they made love. "Come 'way with me, *feen* Ezzie. "Ye not be a power-driven man. In a gentler place, ye can minister and do the deeds of your true desires. In such a place we can be truly happy."

Ezekiah whispers now to himself in pretend-brogue, hoping it will allow him to feel once more their closeness: "*Feen* Bonnie lass. Lay in me arms. Always will I cradle ye memory." The Daily Opine shrouds his chest. He refuses to look again, for over the hundredth viewing, at the picture of the woman he loved; helped destroy.

Satan would want him to look again – to take pride.

"PLEASE COME OUT AND PLAY, EZEKIAH."

Instead, he studies a short article about a fire of that same night that destroyed a church, killing the old minister he revered downriver in *Valhalla*, Kentucky; the little town he was born, grew, was born again, and found his FATHER.

"FATHER, your son will return home to become your meager servant and rebuild your temple. Give me strength to never again stray." He prays aloud, drowning the beckoning voice in his thoughts: '...COME OUT...EZEKIAH.' He counters, "Give your son direction, FATHER".

He rises and peaks through shutters at parishioners who have come from church to fetch his absolution, to free their burdened souls. 'Damn us all. I will accept responsibility. I killed Bonnie and the others.' His thoughts swirl. 'What must I do? Leave all behind. Valhalla calls; to Valhalla I will ride one last time.'

His saddlebag, remnant of circuit-riding preacher days: Its

imprint is Jesus' cross. He gently strokes it. 'FATHER, you so loved your SON, You let HIM die for me: I am unworthy.' He recollects the freedom of the trail. Free, once again, he would be. He removes a rope attached to the bag and ties a hangman's noose. He repeatedly tries tossing it over a ceiling beam, but hasn't strength to continue.

Emotions of the deathly night suddenly make this unknown father as tired as his unknown son who is barely a half-mile away in the wharf-shack. Ezekiah reclines on the bed and in seconds is in a calming sleep that temporarily absolves him of all troubles. He sleeps, as son awakens.

Near Sunset.

Carper rises from Mariner's straw bed. One-eye cat, Ol Tom, is gone. Carper looks around. He's barely old enough to reason, yet survival instincts seem to shout comfortingly, 'WELCOME TO YOUR HOME.' Mariner snores in his dingy chair. Crook shoulder is his pillow. Thanks to large doses of the Kentucky stump juice, his sleep is deep.

The imposing heat of summer's day lifts. A sunbeam cuts through a wall crack. It reflects smilingly off snaggletooth of Harpoon. Shelved BOOKS, tired from their welcoming parade, rest snugly together. Against cheek Carper holds Mother's handkerchief – soft, comforting. He climbs Mariner's sea trunk and looks out the porthole. The sun is a reflected red orb in the muddy river. It spotlights Ol Tom. He is standing on hind legs and seems to dance merrily atop the water far from shore. Carper blinks, disbelieving the magic he sees.

Something even stranger occurs, strangely warming, as Carper breathes-in the handkerchief's intoxicating perfume. As Ol Tom catches a fish, above feline appears the face of the most beautiful woman. She has flowing black hair, emerald eyes, and ruby mouth.

'How is me Bonnie's boy?'

"I'm fine." Carper feels invisible fingers caress his cheeks.

'I am in a kind place now. From here I can watch over me boy.'

"Ma…" He can't complete the word, Mama. The memory of her almost returns. He blinks. Loving touch departs, and, with it, the face above Ol Tom. In their place are slender light arms, reaching from the gently rising moon orb, through clouds and the fading sun reflection. Gentle hands push Ol Tom and his catch toward the shore.

The voice returns. 'They'll be calling you by the name of Carper, me boy. Listen to the Mariner. Listen to Ol Tom. From now on I be talkin' to you through them.'

As Ol Tom clutches fish and drifts to a boat ramp the hands fade. Carper presses his nose to the porthole glass. He watches as, oh-so-slowly, the biggest creature he has ever seen emerges from the water. Ol Tom rides on its back, a glistening tan shell looking to Carper like a giant upside-down washtub that, if filled with, could hold twenty Ol Toms. Fin-claws propel it. Tail, the length and thickness of a big rat, drags behind. Pictures – like those in BOOKS – cover shell.

Ol Tom leaps to the pier and the creature follows up a boat ramp. When the fish slips from Ol Tom and begins flopping back home, creature traps it with one leg. With toothless but razor-sharp beak-snout, he bites off the head and swallows it whole.

Carper, frightened by the creature's enormity yet too intrigued to move, clenches the sill.

Creature pushes fish's body toward cat. 'Good catch Ol Tom.'

Ol Tom paws at it. 'Best catches always off shore. Thanks for the ride, Turt. And on your first day back after your voyage.'

'Think nothing 'tuv it.'

'New tattoo, have you?'

'Indeed. Looks like it's from the Leezian' bayou, but I got it in the Gulf of Mexical.'

Turt motions with beak-snout at a grotesque, hastily scratched half-gator – half-man on his shell. The 'he/its' tail and leg meet at trunk that on one side is human skin; other, amphibian leather. Slimy snout eats voraciously into nose and mouth while eyes – one round, blue, other oval, black – peer hungrily, right at you.

Ol Tom's fur rises. He hisses at the tattoo. 'Foe, I presume? Just don't tell me its tale during a full orb.'

OL TOM'S EPIC TAIL

Ol Tom and Turt met on a sea voyage off Madagascar. Cat lost eye battling three ship rats. Disoriented, he toppled starboard from a transport loaded with baled ylang-ylang leaves bound for Paris perfume factories. Turt was trailing the ship for scraps when he heard the '*plop*', the drowning cat screech, and the dreaded "CAT OVERBOARD!" shouts of the crew (for felines are ships' treasured necessities to fend-off cargo-roving rodents).

Proud tail would be last to sink, Tom vowed. 'Atten-Hut': Flagpole stiff tail to the end.

With the help of a giant prehistoric coelacanth Turt had been swimming with, learning about land-ravaging thugs humans call dinosaurs that both his and coelacanth ancestors had known first-hand of, Turt pulled the sopping, but dry-tailed cat onto shell. He kept him there til dawn, with coelacanth leaning flat body to cat, excreting ancient fluids from mouth onto the blank socket to ward off killing infections.

At dawn, the Mariner and other seamen lowered themselves in a johnboat and retrieved Ol Tom. Mariner patted Turt's head, "Thank you me ol mate. But what raised your hackles so much you don't dock with me for two years? That temper a youren' get to you again?"

Turt couldn't quite remember. Some absent-minded comment Mariner made to landlubbers about making a big shell of, not clam, nor oyster, but 'TURTLE CHOWDER!' Count, breathe deeply, slow down even more – Turt vowed he would conquer his nemesis, ANGER! He still had a good many years left, 200 to 250 in two-leg years. That was too long to live with the rage of a mad squid. Anger shook Turt's fin-claw in welcome during his shelling years. It had clutched him, remaining into the end of his second decade.

Mariner patiently endured the stomping, chomping fits that Turt never turned on him.

From the wharf-shack's porthole view, Carper watches Ol Tom and Turt.

'Going to see Angora, a long hair,' Ol Tom, flagpole tail rigid, tells Turt. He arranges the fish in his mouth to take to her. 'A stinking bouquet of fish for Milady': For Tom it never fails.

'I know Angora – you had your way with one in Singapore. The night I had sweet Terry-Pin on the beach. Mariner, he shaved and sweetened that night too – for a land maiden.' Creatures grin testosterone-rich grins at each other. 'Mariner. He in the wharf-shack?'

A TALE OF A CARPER, A CRUD, AND NEAR CARNAGE

Ol Tom trots, forgetting to tell Turt about Mariner's new shipmate.

Turt slowly traverses the dock and disappears from Carper's porthole view. Carper wonders, what he's seen, is it real or pretend? He's still tired. He listens to one of Mariner's conch shells and is lulled to sleep by its ocean.

When he awakens, it is to hissing, and slimy saliva that pellets his cheeks. Turt is inches away. His breath is the rank of the raw fish-head. Turt sees Mariner's crooked recline; thinks him dead; killed by this cleaner, minnow version of Mariner. Turt mentally rages at the intruder, 'I will squish your neck with one bite for what you did.' He lunges.

Carper backs away. Just in time. Turt's jaw 'snaps' shut, where Carper's head, was. Turt climbs the trunk, craning his fat neck to reach for toes and ankles. Carper hurls the conch shell at attacker three times his size. He catches it in beak-snout, '*crunch*', and spits shards. Carper grabs an oar leaning against the wall and strikes Turt's head, once, twice, hard as he can. Stung by the wood's *'thud'*, Turt winces. Before a third hit, he vices the oar in fin-claw.

Carper grits teeth and yanks as he stares defiantly into muddy eyes. "Leggo, you sea crud."

Turt wrenches away the oar and tosses it, leaving the four year old with splinters.

"YEOW!" He fans hands but refuses to let tears come.

'Fighten' little minnow,' Turt thinks with a momentary respect. But he considers how the minnow killed Mariner. He trumpets wildly, shrilly. Carper clasps his ears. The noise hurts so.

The flying oar had struck Mariner's game leg, awakening him. He sees Turt lurch for the defenseless boy. He seizes Harpoon – to fend-off old friend from new. Then, he would calm Turt, as only he knows how; gentle pets, reassurances. Mariner stands and billows-out, "Steady yerselves, gobbies - this vessel ports in neutral waters – we all be mates here." His leg buckles. He stumbles. Harpoon grazes his forehead. Blood gushes. He slumps, losing consciousness.

Turt faces away from the Mariner. He doesn't see what happened. Carper does. Loyalty to Mariner, and a desire to assist, overtakes him. As the creature growls, Carper shouts, "I'll help you Mariner. This sea crud won't stop me."

Turt traps Carper against the wall.

Instinct for survival and the rawest of courage: Carper leaps onto shell; only inches from Turt's head. Turt blinks; surprised by his opponent's bold move. He cranes neck and bites where he sees a leg. Nope. The minnow has jumped away, swift as any minnow of the sea. Turt's snapping was too hard. He trumpets shrilly from the pain. As he turns, sees the bloodied Mariner on the floor, the blare reflecting his rage reaches a deafening crescendo. The wharf-shack rattles as if in gale conditions. Turt lurches beak-snout at the boy who has stopped just briefly to pat the Mariner's reddening, twitching forehead.

Carper turns. He clumsily clutches Harpoon, twice his

height. "Get away stinking monster." He pokes Turt. Turt bats Harpoon with his fin-claw. Carper, grimaces, but holds weapon tightly, challenging creature.

Thrusts with Harpoon. Parrying with beak-snout, neck. If a dock worker peaked through the porthole of the creakily-swaying wharf-shack at this moment, and later described what he saw, even the drunkest salty at a wharf bar would have sooner believed a tall-tale about the Flying Dutchman mating mid-air with a giant mermaid.

Furniture, mugs, dishes smash to the floor. Then instantly, with the burst of mad energy and strength of someone thrice his age, Carper pushes Harpoon between Turt and the floor. With the help of a broken chair to act as wedge, Carper is able, slowly – so slowly at first as he grunts and twists – to pry Turt, screeching and hissing, onto fin-claw hind legs. Turt sways. He almost falls atop Carper. Carper knows he isn't strong enough to topple the creature.

'This is it,' he thinks. 'Be rigid and sturdy, as the wooden boy in the BOOK.'

He releases Harpoon. Turt teeters toward him. Carper braces and runs toward Turt's faded underside shell. As he reaches Turt, he rounds shoulder and bowls into him. 'THUMP!'

'SCREE!' Turt trumpets louder as he falls backward, landing up-shell down, teetering, spinning. Fin-claws flail reflecting full rage.

Carper, his breath knocked from him, drops. He feels the soft hand of the woman from above the river reach for his chest. She rubs. Her other hand strokes his cheek, calming him, parting his lips. She kisses warmly, as if breathing air into him. She cradles him. In this bosom of safety, he begins to breathe. Slowly he rises and strokes blood from Mariner's forehead – gently as the woman stroked him. Bleeding continues. All Carper can think to do is hold a cloth on the gash.

Turt watches Carper help Mariner. A grudging, yet deep respect suddenly begins to grow. He's fought valiant adversaries, tangly multi-legged octopi, cunning, poison-ink shooting squid. He always won, but now...his first defeat — by this land minnow. He studies him. Small hands show the same caring touch as the healer of the sea, the ancient coelacanth. Mariner will live, Turt assures himself. The human minnow will make sure of it.

This would be the first of many times a Fiction would change Turt's life. Beginning now, be it a slow beginning on a long voyage, is the end of a life of rage. From now on Turt would not let it prevent him from being part of this quirky, but caring, wharf-shack crew.

CHAPTER 5

THE TALE OF THE TELLERMAN: THE EMPEROR OF THE LAND OF IMAGINATION

Precious, Honored, Caring Reader: Those who wisely and wistfully purchased this book; and of course those 'uuthers of youuu' who 'borrowed' from a friend; hopeful, when you finish, you too may be inclined to obtain a copy for your collection. I ask this only because as James Thaddeus 'Blackjack' Fiction's, the Carper's, great-great grandson, though for me it is a hobby – albeit one cathartic – publishing for profit lines my blood.

In the swirl of insanity that often is 'merchantry', publishing is not my line. Matters little to these tales what is. Accidently did I trip over the doorstep of, and into the corridors of business. Here I wander; but not bound to empire building as are most tykes who grow into tycoons. Anytime I want, my butterflies, they fly me away to another realm – Imagination.

...that said... GREETINGS, WELCOME.

My rebirth on the Lindian shore begins my foundling story – in magical places and mystical times. Those times, that year 1966, are far away, yet they are always in my thoughts.

BEGINS THE TALES FROM THE LINDIAN WOODS

'Fill me,' tummy shouts. You squirm. You 'stre-e-etch' upward for hanging food as you ride atop your ferry-creature.

Creature must sense your thoughts. He rams a tree with his shell. An equally hard shell, hairy, big-as-your-head, drops. 'CRA-ACK' he snaps it open with fin-claw, offers you half, and you both drink its milk and eat its sweet.

'Happy tummy!' You squint into this new world the creature leads you and your butterfly-entourage, into the isolated one of the foundling. You still don't want to leave your old world.

Close your eyes. Maybe sleep will bring it back.

So now, as I sit in my glass-walled tower office – almost forever-there butterflies about me, even more migrating through the skyscape stopping to flit 'hello' – join me. Let me to be your guide through foundling plights, joys, fantasies. Let me share the aching passion of all foundlings, to discover just who we are, by becoming the many others we are not.

Forgive me if I disappear into the tales, and sound like others; seeming at times to almost become them. It is because our journeys abound with unknown dangers. Chameleon we become. That is how we survive.

When any creature is born, they possess an innate sense of identity. Being reborn into this world as a foundling is just the opposite – you don't know who you are. Your harrowing experiences purge you of identity.

> Ye might be Bristol bloke."Blimey, you don't bloody well say, mum."
> Or Cayanne – with a chorus of bayou gatahs howlin' in the distance.
> "Mon Cheri! Wellllcommmme! Paddle yer pirogue to my swamp. But, do so at yer own reesk."
> Maybe you are Lindian. "To you, young SAHIB, I say.
> Your Goddess Nardesha, blesser of foundlings – She will be with you, no matter where you journey.

TALES OF THE FICTION HOUSE

Even if you hail from the mighty state of mind
that is Tehas.
"Well podnah, ya don't rightly know who you are, so you
very weill could be any of dem wranglers.
Who's to say?
Ya've no waya' knowin'. No siree!"
You could be pirate, preacher, pauper, prince, or, any
of those just mentioned. Maybe, in them, you will
recognize yourself.

Sometimes we foundlings talk like you. We blend in so well...now you see us, now you don't. So when you hear our tales, who, indeed, you may ask, is the teller?

Pirate? "It be walk the plank for me – if I were
to tell who's tellin'.
Aye, need to know basis, Matey."
Preacher? "Lord Bless you for asking. But sinner I
be if I were to reveal..."
Pauper? "A poor humble servant, only be I, my liege. It is
not of my station to say; say I, humbly..."
Prince? "How dare you approach my throne to ask
what may not be told.

"You say you are Raji Singh – sitting high and mighty at your desk, relating the tales, while in commerce making the fortunes. But Raji Singh is only whom you have chosen to be. You do not truly know. The waves – they have swept that knowledge from you. But, but... come close, for only a moment; that I might whisper a hint..."

Now, Dear Reader, more importantly, Dear Buyer, Thank You for spending time with us – whomever, we might be. Please! Allow your imagination to soar with us.
Say I, Goodbye to James Thaddeus Fiction the fifth. Hellllooo to... well, you will see.

It is now my sublime displeasure to introduce you to –

LIMERICKIN' LEEZIANA GOVERNOR LONG – 'HUEY THE KINGFISHER'

ruminating on his nostalgic return to boyhood bayou roots. (I leave to him the dishonor of introducing the nemesis to our Fiction line, Lazarus Bontez 'Laza Bones Thibidioux.)

"See purty buttahfly - see dem flits.
Onst our snouts by mistakes, they sits.
Gulp, yum! Ah so coloricious we would glow;
me 'n gatorhoodhood frien' Thibidioux-
as dey twitter downst into our belly pits.
"...*Huey's* the name. *Long's* the game. I know yez heerd ah me from zee heestory books. But zee heestory never tell yaz – I come, outta, de bayou. 'N I do mean OUTTA; all a leathery-skinned, four-legged and crawlin'; a hunnerd years 'afore zey claims I even born into humanhood.

"But wait, hold on now, you ain't heerd a *Thibidioux* afore thees? Well leh me tell yaz – and you can bank it – eez the most vicious, venomous, villainous, vengeful of vagabonds...

"...Eeeda sell me downs the bayou quicker den we could gulp a buttahfly.

"Eez got secrets – dark ones unknown to hewmane or beast – stole from the far side a Hades' gate. Eez conjured 'em from Norleens to Zeenzeenatti. Eez got powers that taint 'raught for no hewmane nor beast be possessin'. You'll meet 'im. When you do you'll be wishen you hadn't.

"Damn that Thibidioux, all to Hades. Still, can't help wishen' I be him – crawlin' in heez hide, havin' the best a both humanhood 'n gatorhood."

* * *

Charles Darwin examines the carving of Thibidioux; the half-man – half-gator on Turt, just after he's first introduced himself to Turt, and Turt is brought onto the Beagle's deck. Darwin interrupts his conversation with the ship's artist to comment to migrating butterflies resting on Turt's shell before continuing their travels. "I have heard of humans-creatures similar to this. Legends, undoubtedly. Still, best you flit clear of any you might encounter."

Butterflies' unheard flutter, 'From such encounters we have learned. We do not fear. Too important is our job of protecting foundlings we find – be it on the bayou, in Cincy, or Lindia.'

THE BUTTERFLIES

In royal raiment we come to you Carper, and you James.
Our flutters say, 'We are here for you foundlings.
We light by – fly by you.
(Maybe, one day, you too.)
What can we do for you?
Quietly bring pleasure and peace.
Protect you, in this world of ugly, of beast,
That, the gentleness of our beauty may,
For a moment, help you subdue.

THE TALE OF THE BEAUTY

James sleeps atop low-riding Turt. Butterflies sway above them – a Renoir umbrella gaily shading the boy. They barely see in the vine-twisted distance what Turt cannot. It is the stalker: He is cagey, blending so with the Lindian Woods underbrush. *'Human, or beast?'*

Late afternoon heat and humidity marinates woodland oils with the drifting-in salt of the sea. The mixture rains down, basting the youth's skin. 'The boy is a tasty treat for creatures,' Turt knows. He keeps vigilant for sharp-talon flyers, fanged crawlers and the most dangerous – Lindia's *'claw-paw'* – the Tiger.

Turt maps war plan: 'I can yank cane-spears, and hurl them

from beak-snout; from fin-claws propel cannonball-boulders; into streams, drag, submerge attackers.' Turt remembers his last battle defeat – by James' great-great grandfa. 'That long ago, Carper?'

James awakens. He scoops the dozens of images on Turt's shell into his thoughts. They become his stories, and he's escaping into them to survive his turmoil.

He's Poseidon. Shelled creature is his chariot. They glide through blue waters, pulled by a dozen long-mane seahorses. He clanks shell with trident, pretends the sea line he tied around the creature's neck is his reins. "Giddyap. Keel to the aft, gobs. Don't let yer riggings twine." He repeats a gibberish argot of his fa imitating Mariner. He remembers fa's words, but not the man.

Turt cranes his neck, smiles, thinks of his own one-way foundling conversations with imaginary two-legs, creatures, things.

TALE OF OUR HERO'S FIRST GRANDIOSITY

You swiftly pilot your chariot. At just the right moment, you reach to rescue fair mermaiden trapped by a giant squid. 'Myyy Hero!' She kisses your cheek. You blush. Squid's in pursuit. You raise hand. YOU control the sea. Squid is vanquished – as Typhoon in real life couldn't be.

...You reach up. "TA DAA!" You save infant dangling from a palm tree on an isolated island.

...And now, you battle a half-man – half-gator who is readying to chomp a golden-skinned, golden-haired boy dressed in chaps and Stetson. He looks familiar. The golden boy glares defiantly at gator-human whose teeth spark every time he snaps his snout.

"Run," you shout.

Golden boy looks at you. 'I'm from Tehas. Don't run from nothin', podnuh. If you remembered me, you'd be knowin' that. Well, maybe one day you'll remember me, and everything else.'

This image of yours, of where the golden boy reside, is strange. It's not a swamp, where you'd find a gator. It's the middle-of-desert, beneath a giant cactus. You know you've been here before, but when? You know you should be wary, so you rein your thoughts back to reality.

James unties the sea line, the reins, plays with it a while. It's a confidence booster and loneliness shoo-er. He pockets it, and then he hugs Turt's neck. Turt senses James' fear and trumpets low. Like a cat's purr, his shell vibrates.

He knows, by the loosening grip, he has calmed James.

Soon it will be dark. Turt knows he must deliver small fry to humans. He can care for him – assure survival by teaching him the *'way'* of the wild land-life: *'See James: How you can trap a shrewd lizard in the same hole that you collect rainwater.'*

Or, the *'way'* of, just-as-wild, lake-life: *'Now James, now! Grab the fish. Good. A Trumpeter such as me uses beak-snout to clip the head and fin. You can use a sharp rock. A creature eats it raw. But for you, see how it sizzles and cooks on black rocks in sun's heat.'* So many things to teach, so tiniest tyke could know more about surviving than any adult two-leg.

Turt's thoughts are all broad smiles as he thinks of the wonderful moments together they could share. But, from a lifetime of observation, he knows of the invisible barriers twixt two-legs and other creatures. Never, should it be breached. Those who do make the cross-over from person to animal, or animal to person, those like Thibidioux and Huey Long, they are hideous and monstrous to both worlds –

– Half-humans/half-beasts:
You live LONG in the shadows and on the fringes,
bleached of any human kindness – any animal pride.
You enslave, abuse and betray your own,
in your futile attempts to become even more of both.
You may fracture, mar and deface the beauty which is life.
Never can you destroy it.

Though these crossover interlopers possess the physical beauty of both worlds – human, animal – they encompass fully beast-nature of both. This makes them hideous to look at because the sages of the ages are correct in their simple rages…"Beauty is only…", 'But oogly – oogly it traverses all de way to dem bones. (More precisely, to de soul.)'

So Turt is determined. James must have only the human world. He knows it will be wrenching to give him up to two-leg strangers. Turt has experienced this pain: skimmed brutally away from ma, fa when barely more than a tadpole, then the decades of blinding red anger and hatred of the whole world because of it.

Butterflies flit around Turt. For a moment, their calmness makes him forget that the one following them might be Thibidioux or those of his ilk.

* * *

1826 – THE TAIL OF THE BEAST

'Dem be some high-horsin' questions cummin' from sech a little Carper,' the drawing on the tattered wanted poster disgracing the wharf-shack wall replies when Carper asks, "Why you's got a snout on one side, an angel face on t'other? Skull an' bones earring on one; halo on opposite? 'N why you be comin' round the Mariner's whilst he be sleepin, you alligator-man?"

Carper won't say that Mariner is hurt badly, because it might embolden the alligator-man. Carper stands protectively in front of Mariner.

Words Carper can't read 'LAZARUS BONTEZ ' Laza Bones' THIBIDIOUX – WANTED – PREFERRABLY DEAD!' In smaller print: 'for thieven'; rascalin', hightailen' otherens' slaves, murderin', and in generals, disgracin' 'is breed, of, who knows, asprouted from which seed.'

Carper's unafraid, as the 'he/it' climbs from poster and crawls-walks to him. Carper thinks, 'He'll knock a hole in the ceiling if he stands.' Thin, tapering legs look like gator tails. Spit drools from, almost-snout, of one side of face. Almost-albino mouth on the other is dry. He waggles a knife, half Carper's height, inches from Carper's nose. "Ah ets little Carpers the likes a you for askin' whole lots less.'

Carper crosses eyes to examine the kaleidoscope of jewels

embedded in the knife's handle. "Careful now creature." He squints as he taunts back with trusty, Harpoon. "I might jus' do to you what I did to that sea crud yonder."

Upturned Turt glances around. 'Do minnow-two-legs know of someone existing in the thinness of air that you don't?'

Alligator-man Thibidioux ignores Turt. He reckons about Carper, havin' had a few scrapes with harpoon wielders in the swamps. He skedaddles back up and into poster where he recommences glaring out at the boy. 'We'll meet ag'in, ya lil' Carper, I gar-an-tee. You twon't be so big then, twithout that whale-poker.'

Well, that's Carper's version. That's how the foundling recollects it – serendipity-do's-it, always will. And, in the tell, his future embellishments, will, evermore, swell.

CHAPTER 6

NOW COMES THE TALE OF JAMES' FIRST MUSE

1966 – The Lindian Woods

James has the grandest view as he rides atop Turt: His butterflies play beneath the woodland's vine canopy; treed monkeys screech, pointing at, scrutinizing the foreign flutterers; harmless blue-gold ground snakes retreat to behind bushes when Turt's trip-hammer fin-claws *'CLOMP'* close.

It is at this moment James looks to one side and sees – HER.

She wasn't there moments before. So different then anyone he's ever seen: Feather-laden hat, shoes that button at sides, and slender, not quite petite – so curvy in a rose-printed ankle-length dress. To keep within confines, continuously she boosts sleek bosom. Gleaming in the sunlight and separated by an emerald-jeweled shamrock brooch, those mounds seem, to the four year old, to encompass all of her.

But, 'aah, her face.' Hypnotizing.

"You are so pretty."

'So all the gents say, lad. I'll not blush at the compliment. No innocent colleen, I.'

"What's your name?"

'I be Rrrose Heather, Jamie.' Her R's roll. Saucy brogue sways in cadence with swiveling hips as alongside travelers she tags. 'Comes I from old Cincinnat', via old Ire-land. Your and my bedrooms be adjacent one another, though separated by over a century.[8] Remember blarney tales of me? No? How about of me' friends Mariner, Carper?' James' face is blank.

'Well we'll keep company, handsome, and I'll tell ya'. So one day ya' be all-rememberin'.'

She stretches, tiptoe, for hanging moss. James' eyes widen. She shields bosom. 'Ooh, Lad! They almost leaped out: Can't be lettin' ya' be glimspen', now can I.' She rubs James' mosquito-bit legs with the moss. Cool, soothing. 'Seen me Mariner use somethin' like this for healin'. Works, suren' it does.'

It is similar to the same green substance James has seen in vials in his father's medical valise.

A feeling of joy suddenly brims within Turt. Because, out-of-nowhere he thinks of lovely, ageless, Rrrose Heather: Hasn't seen her in a century. He breathes deep. Her floral scent swells his senses. Though he cannot see her, he is remembering, mesmerized by her sweeping black hair, the forever purplish-pink flower of cheeks from whence came name, Rrrose of the Heather.

Her face is lineless at 18 years or 80, eyes, weepy, smiling all at once. They glow, so blue, emblazoned with curiosity, knowledge, with an impassioned desire to fully partake of life's pleasurable mysteries – which, she has.

Turt, he *feels* her presence, as if she was beside him, painting a heather-garlanded rose onto his shell as she had done so long ago. Though faded, its kiss, unlike so many of the other paintings on him, miraculously has withstood the ravages of sun, sea, and time. He saved her life, or had she, his? Neither really knew which. (But that's adventure for another day.)

---

[8] LKFFF: Where, once was, Rrrose Heather's burned bordello, Blackjack Fiction, not by coincidence, would one day build his publishing house. Many years later, Dr. Fiction would add onto it for his clinic.

Turt hears James talk to her. He trumpets low. Will she hear my greeting?

Turt imagines she pets his head. Her touch is soft, warm.

James feels her fingers combing through his hair. He's reminded of his...

'Your mother, Jamie, nay could she be here. She sent me.'

"I don't remember her, Rrrose Heather." Gentle hands cup his cheeks.

'Poor chil'. Course not. But see her in me. Though we be different – traveled such different paths – deep within, we are alike as twin shamrocks of a meadow. We both be women of the flesh business. Hers was in helping heal it, and me, in bringing it pleasure. Most-importantly, though, oh how we loved, fully. She; you and your fa. Me; Carper and the Mariner. And of course Turt...' She strokes the flower on his shell.

Turt sighs. Thinking of Rrrose lightens his burdens.

'...and I loves' ya', Jamie; and young Master Jamie will come to love his Rrrose. I'll be here when ya' need me. Just as my sister Calico is.' She opens palm. There's Calico. The pretty butterfly flies to and nestles in his hair.

James yawns; so tired – so much to feel.

'Sleepy chil'. Lie down. I'll tell a grand tale where you'll experience what's rosy, and what's not; and be learnin' from the lessons.' She strokes his forehead. He feels the soothing motion of being tucked-in by Rrrose Heather as a blanket of butterflies flutter barely above him. 'Once upon a time...way down in the Leezianna swamps, lived the Thibidioux, Jamie...'

'Who is this Jamie?' he wonders.

THE UNSHACKLING

Nearing dusk. Tryst with Angora over, Ol Tom returns to the wharf-shack, to the dishevelment of human-Carper – creature-Turt, battle. Tom hops onto Turt's shelly-belly, licks, removing the makings of a hairball. 'Looks like the minnow left our mad-Trumpeter askew.' He saunters to Carper. Boy's kneeling, stroking Mariner's forehead that's stopped bleeding.

Cat climbs Mariner's stomach, meows thanks to Carper, and then squints righteously at Turt. 'If the minnow could do what he did to you pal, he can surely help Mariner. So show respect when the time comes. Reach out fin-claw. Congratulate him on his victory, with true animal heartiness. His name is Carper. To you, *Sir Carper*.'

Turt knows Tom's right. He trumpets a gentle herald of agreement. He can do nothing until Mariner awakens and uprights him. He contents himself in being up-shell, down, stares at the topsy-turvy Lazarus Bontez Thibidioux wanted poster, and wonders where he's seen that face. How could he forget such a two-face? If he came upon the human/the thing's lair, he'd roust him/it. He'd claim the reward, not in valueless two-leg money, but in wonderfully sour fish heads. 'Ahh!'

Turt's tries to relax and quell the anger that grips most of his waking moments. *'Breath slow, deep; find peace in your inner shell.'*

He curls fin-claws into an inverted lotus position. Eyes close. Muscles around beak-snout relax. Though shell is confined to wharf-shack, thoughts escape to a particularly-calming hurricane – the proclaimed, 'GREAT,' but really just kinda', sorta'-great, maybe even just okay hurricane of a coupala' years back. He'd happened upon it off the Brownsville coast.

"NO GOOD DEED GOES UNPUNISHED"
(so some say)

Turt's calming meditation returns him to that day.

Remember the churning water. See the sparkling shower of beautiful starfish.

Feel the rumbling of seahorses' swift gallop to safety of their coral corrals.

Turt is connoisseur of riptides, waterspouts, sheer currents, everything twixt and 'tween. These waves today contradict true hurricane nature.

Most hurricane waves want to swallow all. This one spews, as if it's swallowed something abominable; something not human or animal; something seeming not of, or wanted in this world. In one word: THIBIDIOUX. But true natures rarely can be changed, so the hurricane gags down Thibidioux and whatever else that floats. All, but the sly, 'ride 'em til they drop,' Trumpeter. 'Typhoon or hurricane – Feh!' Nothing to Turt!

Turt swims near a sinking ship. Moments before, Thibidioux, (the object of hurricane indigestion,) was swept overboard. A tied tightly-at-the-top waterproof oilskin bag rips from his grasp. Its contents could deliver to possessor wealth beyond comprehension. Not cash, bonds, land grants, jewels, but directions, to the well-hidden cache of a stolen Federal gold shipment.

The hider, a naïve soul, was disposed-of as soon as he brought the map to his fellow thieves. None of the four remaining trusted the other as to its isolated burial site. They split equally the convoluted directions. Floating off in the bag is three of the four map sections. Thibidioux had knife-gutted his partners, bagging the directions as the ship sank. In his back pocket is his section, its ink slowly dissolving.

Turt, feeling uncharacteristically generous from the joi de vivre of riding a rampaging gulf-scape, shimmies beneath two-leg and takes him onto his shell. (At this time in his life Turt cared not a whit for any human but Mariner.) Water rushes deafeningly around Turt. He looks back, barely sees through swirling plankton. Immediately he thinks he's mistaken a two-leg for a four:

Too leathery, and Turt feels clawed, not grasped. Pleas for help – that should sound like gurgling shouts – seem yelps, growls. An alligator? Its flopping to-and-fro sounds are like those he's heard made by gators slapping bayou banks while trying to stay cool.

'Why is it so far out,' Turt wonders. 'Maybe it was onboard, destined for a two-leg's cage, and I'm saving it from bondage.' Turt swells with altruism as he paddles against current to get it to shore. (This random, 'good deed', would haunt the Fictions.)

The clawing into Turt's shell is continuous. 'Alligator way of thanking fellow-creature,' Turt thinks. 'No thanks necessary, good sir.' He is sure it would one day return the favor to another creature. Pride, of being a part of animal-kind, seizes Turt.

The passenger wrenches to Turt's shell. Turt glances back and barely sees. 'Not claw; HAND: But so claw-looking.' With its snout-nose, almost sideways eyes and murky complexion: 'Seems more, alligator.' Never has he encountered such a human/creature.

The clawing Turt feels? With free claw-hand, he/it had pulled a knife and began carving into Turt's shell. (Humans have an insatiable urge to add something to Turt's shell: That, as if in Turt's wanderings, other people would see their message, and, though anonymous, their thoughts-ideas might spread.) The carving doesn't hurt, and, even if Turt wants, he cannot pry loose his passenger.

If Turt could crane his head enough, he'd see what Thibidioux is frantically carving before he would forget them – the directions, from his one-fourth erased map section.

Turt floats ashore; deposits soggy human/creature. Anxious to return to the whirlpools and lose this experience, Turt only looks briefly at the man-alligator – Lazarus Bontez Thibidioux. East profile is hideous, but west, beautiful. Sweeping black hair: It plays on smooth, handsomely chiseled west. Brown hair mat canopies crusty east cheek. Half-nose is stately, Roman, other, is snout-like. Eyes: Left, ocean-blue, right, bayou-mud. East, west, beauty, beast. One hand gentle, other, deformed claw-like. Adonis profile will grow nobler as years pass, while reptilian scaling will continue to crawl over other side.

Thibidioux spits out the gulf and rants deliriously. "I'll keel any 'un who try 'an beat me to the stash. I'll gut 'em 'n mount 'em to a wall." To Turt it's gibberish, but he understands the tone, regrets the saving he's just accomplished, and disappears underwater before Thibidioux can review and recopy what he's carved.

Next day a swelled blowfish nears Turt. It's been coated with glistening cod oil from ship casks smashed by the hurricane. Bloated blow is vitreous, shiny as a hand mirror. Turt sees reflection and examines Thibidioux's cryptic tattoo, a human skull beneath a halo. Above it a blood-dripping dagger, and, *26-10-2-9-4*. Two-leg numbers mean nothing to Turt.

Now he is one-fourth of a sought-after map. The meaning of it would unfold brutally, to Turt, and to those whom Turt cares, as the years unwind.

Alongside the cryptic code is a self-portrait. It depicts such hideousness that Turt wonders: Maybe the graffiti warns future artists, rival culprits, or counter-evolutionaries as is the he/it. The warning: Don't trifle with the he/it.

A SUPERSTITIOUS TALE

"Only one who is truly deranged announces his presence to the world with such a depiction," Charles Darwin tells the Beagle's ship artist when he first sees the Thibidioux on Turt. "Let us only hope our copying it does not bring forth its presence." Tweed suit ruffles and glasses slide down sweaty nose as he and the artist laugh at this superstitious creature-to-human and vice-versa and inside-out theory, that, as youth Charles had overheard an ancient mariner on a London street-corner telling about to another old gob.

Turt looks up at the doubting Charles. 'Must you, too, see; to believe? HE/IT LIVES!'

Charles, deciding he needs a pleasant diversion from the hideous he/it, looks down and sees in Turt's eyes the reflection of his sweetheart Harriet who is so far away, in Cincinnati, in America.

Oh, sweet glow of a young man's secret, budding love.

In his thoughts, Charles touches tenderly Harriet's flowing

black hair and caresses her soft cheeks. Though he sees her loveliness, he cannot rationalize why he dwells on the skull carving. He feels a shiver, though it is sunny out. For hardly a mili-second, belief in silly boyhood superstitions — crossing fingers, pocketing dead crows, stroking dried pigeon toes — return. He blinks them away. Though faith in logic is restored, he cannot help saying to himself: 'Be safe, my Harriet. Evil shall never touch you.'

Ignoring rationality, for luck, Charles pats Turt's shell. For added charm: "If I meet a female of Turt's kind, I shall name her after you Harriet: I'll bring her along, so my Turt may have a Harriet, too."

Turt nods. 'I know well your Harriet, Charles. She told me of your voyage. No worry, sir. My friends watch over her. Harriet is the reason I have searched you out Charles. Now, if only I could communicate the reason; maybe you could help me; and I, you.'

CHAPTER 7

JUNGLE VOYAGERS (Whom will you encounter?)

The yellow of setting sun, the orange of rising moon, intersect, briefly exposing James' stalker to the butterflies. Shudders...Flutters... 'Is it animal? Human?' Butterfly ancestors had been around the bayou when Lazarus Bontez Thibidioux was born, hatched, or both. Stories of his brutality abound. 'Could he/it, still be walking/crawling the land after so long a time? Could he/it have spawned a he/it even more treacherous?'

Butterflies helmet inches from your head – as if determined to join Turt in combat. You sense their caution. You tense, from fear. Maybe that is why Rrrose Heather returns. Maybe she never left, and, only now, needing to see her again, you do.

'Be puttin' aside your worries, Jamie,' Rrrose says. 'Look way up. See those two.'

You squint into the sky. The sun and moon are both out.

'They've come to introduce themselves. One's warmth by day gives you strength and courage. Other's glow of night be offerin' calm and safety. When others leaves ya, or are taken away, they'll always – BE.

'They are the ones a foundlin' always, can be accountin' on. They be the reason, when all seems lost, you'll start findin' four-leaf clovers. So don't be afear a' what the butterflies may be preparin' for. Instead, find simple joys in those always there for a foundling. By seizing and never releasin' this sweet joy – this is how you'll survive, flourish.[9]

* * *

THE TALE OF CARPER GREETING POPPY SOL AND LUNY MUM

Inside the wharf-shack Ol Tom sleeps on Mariner's billowing belly. Upturned Turt sways trance-like midst meditative "AAAHHHMMMSSS!" Carper cradles Mariner's head in his lap, while music and musing meld with his imagination.

'Da da... da da, da... DA! AND NOW: Introducin' – for your wee bit o' pleasure, Carper – that magical duo of the sky – the high-flyin', ever spyin', never cryin' – they leave that to the clouds – POPPY SOL and LUNY MUM.'

As if a gent, meticulously adjusting ascot, Poppy Sol carefully frames himself within wharf-shack's porthole window. Sophisticate Cyclops behind monocle, he peruses the titles of the shelved books. 'Indeed, my good man, your ancient mariner has a fine selection. Harrumphh! Harrumphh! I jolly well say you must study them. Memorize each.'

Carper squints up. The soft pre-eve sky-glow plays gently on his face. Luny Mum appears at the opposite porthole. Her crescent smile grows wider as minutes pass. It is as ivory as Poppy Sol's is a fiery orange. To Carper, it is a loving smile. Carper returns it.

Luny Mum counters Poppy Sol's admonition. 'Oh just, PSHAW, must we sometimes say to Poppy Sol, dearie. He is

---

[9] LKFFF: Sun's warmth; moon's glow. We learn early in our abandonment that we are never alone and so seldom, will we ever be lonely.

always so serious. Nothing wrong in that. But, Carper, mind ye find time too, to take tea, away from the heat of 'is passions. Just unwind in the soft calm 'a me glow.'

Carper basks in Mum and Poppy's light and strokes Mariner's sweaty forehead. The wharf-shack is a *'shh-ing'* hospital quiet.

'Such a dedicated young 'un, eh Poppy. A ray of your shine.'

'Indeed Mum. A rare spot a' tea be he!'

Carper has pillowed Mariner serenely in his lap for the past hour. Already the sense of loyalty – of what is most important and what is right – swells his conscience. He'll look after Mariner for an hour, or forever, if that's what it takes.

Mariner's eyelids flex. Carper cups hands, shading him from Poppy Sol's glare.

Carper glares back at Poppy. "And just how may I be of service to you, sire." Child's words brim with adult authority, precision, with the confidence that this is he, Mariner and Ol Tom's home – and Poppy Sol is just a peek-a-boo who comes visiting, but never stays past dark.

Carper doesn't realize, he has heard those same words – "and just how may I be of service to you, sire," hundreds of times; when Rrrose Heather greeted the peek-a-boos, with their so many different accents from around the world, who visited her girls at her 'house'. They never stayed either. Those words, and everything else from before that night of the fire-breathing monster, are just ashen memories. Yet they have helped form him into boy he is; will help transform him into man he will become.

'Well tut-tut, and cheery-ho' says Poppy Sol. 'Aren't we just the brashest polishings on one of me walking sticks I call *lightning*. Don't get me wrong me little ray. I quite like that in you. Indeed yes. Mmm hmm, yes. Whaat ho. Indeed I do.'

Carper, from on the other side of his back room play areas at Rrrose Heather's, has heard all kinds of voices, experienced all variety of attitudes; from rich, poor; Oxford educated, cracker imbecile; scalawag, honor-bound; demon, holy...

...the holy – especially that of one particular voice – so like his own; but deep, adult. It is an animal-scared voice, but one that is kind, quietly preachy about strangers of long ago. Adam, Eve. David, Goliath.

It turns wild, loud, sometimes almost hateful when it blurts out the word "TEMPTRESSES" then the names "Salome, Delilah, JEZEBEL! You ladies need not be like them. Follow me from here: And down HIS righteous path." Those words trigger scuffling, hooting, laughs – then the sound of one woman's gently crying voice –

"Please *feen* Ezekiah, don't start this again!" *That* voice – even more familiar – kind, loving as Luny Mum's is now. *That* gentle one disappears.

That deep voice: It steeps, percolates in Carper's mind. Brew there, would it, always. He would hate its bitter; love its sweet. It would caress with warmth; scald with torments. He would never be sure what to do with it – drink in and savor, or spit before gagging on it. And so, wishing it weren't really there, and his hurting would be no more, Carper would come to hate that voice more than he would love it.

Ol Tom awakens and, startled by intruder Poppy Sol entering through the porthole, he hisses, then crawls up Mariner's shoulder and onto his head. He spells Carper by shading Mariner's closed eyes with his tail. Now Carper can shade his own eyes as he looks up and challenges the sun: "So why did you come?" Carper is exasperated that Mariner isn't looking into his eyes; isn't able to speak to him; isn't stroking him kindly, warmly, lovingly.

'Patience young sire. I am here to let you see that you can look to me in all your hours of cold. Be my sunny boy and you will always be warm.'

Carper rejoins: "But soon you'll peek-a-boo, like always."

Luny Mum stretches out her glow in soft caress as she completes rise from day sleep. Milky and full she has become this eve; supple, soft. 'Dear boy. When Poppy Sol is not here for you – then will your Luny Mum be. By day, Poppy will bring you brightness; that you may see, to accomplish diligently what you must. By night I will deliver the joy and tiredness of the dark that is meant for relaxation.'

Dockworkers going to work continually pass near the wharf-shack unaware of the drama playing out inside the 'barnacle onna bask-ass side.' Suddenly nothing matters to Carper but Mariner. He becomes tearful. "Will he live? He must."

Turt looks over. The aching for Mariner is in the minnow's voice. Turt's only desire is to go and help console him but, up-shelled, he is helpless as Mariner.

'Silly little ray ye are,' Luny Mum says. 'Don't you know? The Mariner will always live: For he has given something of himself to you, and many others. How can he not live on forever?' She tells Poppy Sol: 'Silly human rays. If only they would stop for a moment to realize this. Then will they have discovered immortality, and their fabled fountain of youth, all rolled as one.'

Carper is confused. Poppy Sol puts it simply. 'Do not worry sunny boy. Mariner will live forever. All who have truly lived – do.'

Carper won't re-call the musings of these moments later in life, but their images, their feel, will linger. They will help mould who he is and would be. When he starts to recognize – to remember more than just the impression, he will look skyward, though not really knowing why.

Poppy Sol, slipping slowly from the porthole as Carper strokes the scab on Mariner's head, says, 'Here's a cheery-bye present for you.' A laser-like burst of his light scorches Mariner's face. The scab begins to disintegrate, falling away as dust. In moments, there is barely a shadow of scar. Mariner stirs. Carper hugs him. Ol Tom leaps up. Turt stares over in amazement.

'Good night Poppy,' says Luny Mum. 'I'll stay with them til you return.'

CHAPTER 8

THE TALE OF POPPY SOL, LUNY MUM – 140 YEARS HENCE

James dismounts Turt: No perambulator babe, he. He and his butterfly entourage's journey through the Lindian Woods is no desperate hike, but a strident march, a proud parade.[10]

James valiantly ignores hunger stabs. He spies a solitary earthworm.[11] "You got the last meal, big fella. Now it's my treat." James picks it up, bites in half, shares. Chewy, slides down the throat like spaghetti.

Turt savors it. 'Usually when a two-leg offers me one, there's a hook.' To ward-off the letting-down of guard that lethargy brings, Turt knows he must find more fruit, wild vegetables, fresh water, to replace the *curiously* tangy bulrush berries that have been sustaining them.

Hidden within the forest's twig carpet are razor rocks. They gouge James' feet. His, "ouch, ouch," is answered with '*kaa, scree*,' coming from the leaf ceiling. "Enough!" James '*grrs*'. He

---

[10] LKFFF: We go forth without hesitation into an unknowable world. Promenade with us, if you'd like, and share our only finery – our joy within.

[11] LKFFF: Even morsels we share. Be my guest. Not interested? Well, the creature is bound to be famished.

crawls back onto taxi Turt.

'They'll harden the more you mosey,' Turt wants to assure. He's glad his passenger's back to where he can better protect him. Beacon beak-snout semi-circles: in continuous sniff-out for the two-leg stalker, four-leg meat-eaters, and fanged grass-slitherers. A poisonous web-dweller Tarzans down from a tree. Destination, the mountain that, to an arachnid, is James' nose. Butterflies flutter near. Their breeze drifts spider a few inches away from boy. He bats it – 'WHAP!' over fence of bamboo.

James rubs his scarred feet. Butterflies become medics. Flutters cool burning soles. Pin-thin legs massage them. "AHH!" James reclines; face up.

The forest's damp-plant pungency, mingling with its animal musk, is as smoldering incense. Combining with James' hunger, the mix becomes almost hallucinogenic to him. Slowly he journeys into his satiating world of imagination. Turt happens into a meadow where the grass is shell-high. Poppy Sol is readying for bed. Down he stares. Thousands of his color rays glisten through the swaying blades: psychedelic pinks, yellows, oranges.

"Yes," says James. His tone is placid, yet firm. "May I help you?"

Poppy Sol: 'Tis just you look so bloody-well familiar.'

Luny Mum – rising from east rest: 'Now love. Be minden' your language when you're aboust' an innocent. Be patient. Their parade be goin nowhere fast. 'N that's exasperatin' 'ims.'

'Haarumph! From where do you hail lad. You'll not be from these parts.'

James says to himself, 'So much I can't remember. Him, I do. Like the back of my hand.' He studies his wriggling fingers, dirty nails. 'That is Poppy Sol. She is Luny Mum. But how could I remember them. I know we haven't met.'

So little makes sense midst the dizzying colors.

James tries to show respect, elders and all that, dontcha' know, but his words are edgy. "Why do you care where I'm from. I've heard tell that you'll go, PEEK, then, BOO. And be gone. So what's it to you? You writen' your book?"

'By Jove, I could tell you a thing or two, upstart.' Poppy Sol glares. James squints, doesn't look away. "Feisty one, he, eh Mum?'

'Leave 'im be, Sol. E's been through 'nough today.'

'Aye. That he 'as mum. Full pardons, Lad. It's just – I know your ray, from somewhere.'

"Well Poppy Sol. You have a night in bed to figger me out. 'Cause I can't tell ya."

'I've got it, young sire. 'ow 'bout San Antone? Or Cincinnati? You look like lads I seen there-'bouts. Feisty one in Cincy took shine to sailor dungarees.'

'Quite handsome he was in them,' adds Mum.

Sol blinks as a cloud passes. 'Say, Lad, what's to yer 'liken? Cowboy hats, chaps. Dresses? The quiet golden boy of San Antone; 'e seemed to be in one or the other.

(James' father had spoken often of his great-great grandfa's wonderfully notorious San Antone half-brother – "…gowned gunslinger, turned stetsoned story flinger. That's his story son. He became famous in his day.")

Those memories, tales: They are now just a part of your deep-within thoughts – hidden away until one day you can mine their treasures. And, who are all these people and places Poppy Sol and Luny Mum speak of that you've never heard of, or can't remember? The mix of feelings/desires makes you feel you are on a careening joyride – not the easing comfort atop the shelled creature – at a place in your past as colorful as here, but sweet, cotton candy smelling. The confusion of wanting to return to that carnival of joy in that other life, and sensing you never can, hungrily knots itself inside you.

James crushes shut one eye. With the other, he gives Poppy Sol the 'pop eye' expression of youthful impatience aimed at an adult. James jousts. "Maybe, Poppy Sol, if you saw a boy in a dress, maybe you was lookin' in a pond seein' your own self's reflectin'."

'Ooo, touche', Lad.'

Luny Mum twinkles her delight. So many mortals cower when challenged by celestial forces. This one seems apt to spit into its shining eye. 'Enough jokin' about, Sol, 'e tolt' ya e's not aknowin' where-from he came. If yer so burnin' to know, maybe you ken' 'elp 'ms by doin' a bit 'a yer own rememberin.'

Mum's sly crescent widens. James cannot see her motherly pride of him. The reason: Poppy Sol's own delight in the upstart now paints the sky bright azure.

Glistening red nimbus clouds frame this celestial portrait – a Lindian gothic painted indelibly into James' thoughts. For a moment, he thinks of another time when he looked up to a similar skyscape. There were voices, adult, like Poppy Sol and Luny Mum, telling him:

(his gushing parents on the Ohio River bank, hugging tight to his wet body after Turt saved him) "The world is yours son. All this. And the heavens too. You've been given a second chance. So use it fully." In a cavernous part of his thoughts James barely remembers his eyes popped wide as he stared into *that* vast skyscape as he does now into this one, and hears his own voice replying. "Yes Mama. Yes Papa. I will."

A breeze arrows the nimbus clouds past Luny Mum. James listens as she speaks kindly to Poppy Sol, just as the ones he called "Mama, Papa" spoke gently to one another. 'Here's who 'e reminds ya of Poppy Sol. Think back. Long ago. To old Cincinnati. That Carper the Mariner reeled in. Ponder. Once you do, you'll see this one's a PIP – jus' as ims' was a PIP then.'

'Harrumph! Well I'm blithered, absolutely blithered.'

The meadow disappears as Turt enters a grove. 'Sweet dreams be always yours, Lad,' Luny Mum lulla-bye's. Turt looks about, sensing the duo's comforting visit, that, he too, as a foundling, knew well. James waves farewell to them as forest cover reappears. Time and again they will peak through the leafy ceiling to check on him.

A breeze wafts a lace of scents Turt and James' way, from sizzling meats dripping into someone's campfire. The fragrance doesn't tantalize beak-snout buds, but Turt knows it does human nose-buds. James' stomach growls. Turt decides instantly: Head right to the glow when it appears. No way to know if who is there be a marauder or good-heart. The risk must be taken. James requires sustenance. Just could be that the, *just right*, two-legs await them.

Hunger tires James. He half-sleeps – half-daydreams about the other boy Luny Mum told of. James imagines him his twin – at least in appearance. Maybe he exists; is somewhere. This thought will remain always, will sustain his mind, as food does his body. He begins searching for the boy in his imagination's darkest crevices and deepest chasms. But it is in imagination's brightest corridors where he finds him:

"THE CARPER!" James shouts, rousing himself. Name's familiar. Just why, he doesn't know. Turt looks up. 'James is remembering,' Turt hopes, joyously thinking of his once-wharf-shack-adversary. Turt is tired too. He tries to keep from blinking. 'Plough forward.'

Though Poppy Sol and Luny Mum continue to peak through branches, James thoughts of them depart. He thinks about the boy...

THERE HE IS! – striding beside Turt, in sailor dungarees, loose shirt. He has a small nose, sharp chin, pale cheeks, and eyes hungry for life.

It is as if the reflections of mirrors James has looked into have come to life.

'Hi ho, fellers' says Carper, patting Turt's head. Turt senses him.

James disembarks Turt and holds out his hand to shake that of new mate. "What's yer name?"

'Carper. What's yers?'

James' thoughts are blank. Embarrassed. "I...I... don't know."

Carper grins, not maliciously. 'You'll get one, when the right person finds you. If you don't like what you're called, you can call yerself other.'

"You a gobbie...?"

'Well, no. But I suppose yer meeting me during the time I dressed like one.'

In James' imagination, he nor Carper ever let go of the

other's hand, and now, hand-in-hand, they walk, run, play: along splintery wooden river piers, through forests, into dark, secret places only the two of them know; places in the mind where foundlings can protect, entertain, console, cheer one another in the hours of doleful loneliness or playful serendipity. James knows he will always have a friend in... already the name sweeps from his memory... and he'll be a helper, and confidant – even when all the others he conjures wane, set, or disappear and others take their place only to, to one day disappear. They climb onto Turt. Carper reaches into James' pocket.

Despite Turt's peacemaker purr – 'Now boys play nice,' a little boy spat commences. "Hey! Whatcha' tryin' to steal," shouts James.

'Nothin'. Nothin'. Just gettin' what you probably forgot you had that we'll be needin.'

James sees Carper slip out the long string, the life-saving sea line. He *had* forgotten.

'Tied around Turt's neck, it'll make it easier to hold onto for where we're bound.'

"Where's that?"

'You'll see.' They tie an old fashion knot, together. 'Friends again?'

"Mmm hmm; friends," James says.

Rustling in the woods. Both look over.

To James' query, "What could it be?" Carper says, 'High-time I be taling about Lazarus Bontez Thibidioux. Lots a dangers in forests, deserts, swamps, cities, and country-sides that you gotta keep your eyes peeled for, but he's the biggest threat of all. Those of his ilk, you're plain apt to meet 'em anywhere; doin' anything. I had me the misfortune to greet Lazarus firsthand. There's a reason he's named 'Lazarus', taken from a book Mariner had. He returns from the dead, not only once, but again and again.' He's half gator – half man.'

James listens intently, anxious to meet Thibidioux, yet fearing the greet.

CHAPTER 9

Every few seconds thousands of watching eyes join Luny Mum's crescent smile. They turn the sky bright as the campfire Turt approaches. Turt sees clearly the back of two bushy-haired heads – two men sitting, facing the flames. He easily discerns their attire. Unlike most two-leg scavengers, all ratty-tatty, akin to the creature-scavenger, the vulture, they are natty, neat as a gentlemanly wild Turkey.

Turt senses they notice his rustling '*scooch*', but seem too immersed in a whispered conversation to be concerned. So, if he a swift bandit had been, Turt considers, they're throats already'd be slit. James is unaware of the human presence. He travels his other world.

('How do we survive our beginnings…by fantasy we spin…')

To try and forget Carper's scary tale of the half-gator – half-man monster, in your thoughts you whoop 'HI! HO!', imitating Carper. You mentally mimic with cowboyish 'RIDE 'EM,' the San Antone lad Poppy Sol talked about. Carper sits beside you atop the shelled creature. You clench one another and hold dearly to the sea line and the creature.

The creature's suddenly flying like a glider plane.

Carper shouts, 'Hang onto him. He'll always take you where you need to go.' He whisks you both up, over the forest, jets you through tight mountain passes. Scrubby bushes whisk your shoulders. 'WHEE!' He skims you above rushing rivers. His round belly bounces along the white caps like a skipping stone. Icicle water stings your cheeks.

'WHOA!' reverberates in your thoughts, but you really wanted such a joyride — to escape temporarily the ache from hunger and absence of contact with others.

The imaginary cold awakens you to something even colder — REALITY — and, to the shadowy camp you enter; to the strangest sight you've ever seen — a two-headed, three-legged, four-armed he/it turning from firelight's glow, scampering-shuffling to you, sweeping you up and into many arms. You've no time to react, except to squirm and shout, "HELP", to the kindly shelled creature that already has helped you so much. He's snapping, snarling.

Nimble legs dance quickly away from your protector's beak-snout. Your butterflies assail the identically round faces. To no avail. You're scared because you've deluded yourself into believing,' this must be the gator/human Carper told tale, or maybe it's a croc-cousin.' You look about for Carper. Carper'll know what to do: Carper's gone — swept away by reality.

Everything you are now feeling is real. Still, it SEEMS fantasy.

"Meir ching, abas (I've got you)," one of the heads says. "Tayan de abat (Hold him tight)" is the other's reply.

They speak Lindian, a language you know well as your own. When you say, "What are you MONSTERS doing to me," first instinctively in English, then Lindian, their eyes cross and they begin speaking, not English, not Lindian, but gibberish.

"Ter wi ne spe. Spiliwi."

They carry you to campfire and place you on a rock. It will take at least a minute for your protector to reach you. Together, they say,

"Young man. No monsters are we. With our human heads high we walk the land."

You hear the hurt your words have caused them. It rises from so deep within that it must come from a lifetime of hurts. It will be a wound you will remember all your life; one you vow never again to inflict. No monsters are they, you realize as the campfire sheds its light. Yes, their bodies are misshapen, fused, and they stoop, but their stern looks show their pride.

Conjoined twins Rau and Rue, in their fifties, move sprightly as any twenty year old. They're identical – long, staring faces, calculating eyes, furrowed foreheads – but they try so hard to be different; for who wants to be thought not only as, "just 'nother face in the crowd", but "a 'nother of the one right alongside it." Rau is black bearded; Rue red-cheeked: Rau garlanded with gold necklaces, bracelets, rings; red Rue, plain as rain. Rau wears a black satin, Lindian-style *dhoti* shirt – red satin for Rue. In-common silk pants, more of the black, more of the red, are neatly pressed.

Their attire makes James tremble – more thoughts of the two-face Carper had described. Should he try escape? Couldn't, even if he tried.

Slowly charging Turt contemplatively puzzles, 'They're not two, two-legs. They are one, three-leg? Yes, one. No, two. Common leg gives an extra *spri-i-ing* to their step. They knew we were here. They discussed us in a language known only to them; a communication cocktail existing with both animal and human twins only the other knows.'

Turt can't understand their English, their Lindian, or their cocktail, but he comprehends language better than does the best human linguist. (Pickering, Higgins: PSHAW!) He hears emotions and flawlessly translates. But these two – joined in one:

Are they good? Slaverers? Boogerers? Turt usually knows a human by how they express emotions. He senses now something of the Mariner – the good. Even Mariner, kind one moment, could, the next, slit the throat of one he deemed bad. That's often the two-leg way, Turt knows. But the boy must have nourishment only humans may provide. So, he must trust.

THE TALE OF RAU AND RUE, AND TURT AND YOU

All four rubbery arms lithely swing. Simultaneously they deal steamy soup, bread, cut vegetables and pungent tea onto a folding table before James. Their service set is sterling silver.

Rau sprinkles Lindian rose petals on a tray for James' butterflies; petals this North American species have never seen. They are striped orange and black, more tiger-ear point than round-ish, and tasting so like the cherished milkweed of their native lands. Rue tosses advancing Turt a smoked fish.

Turt prods and sniffs: Untainted.

"We travelers must be friends. We must look out for one another," the brothers say. One is speaking English, the other Lindian. Before serving themselves they bow, chant. "Dearest Nardesha, may this bounty build new friendships." All eat heartily. James gorges. Rau places hand over spoon to steady his pace. Rue wipes his cheeks. Turt's wariness of them lessens. He flips the fish in the air to cool it as he nears the fire.

Rau and Rue are foundlings too: Coincidence? Fate? No. Being foundlings have led them to the nomadic life. Here is their story:

After the worldwide ban on Cat Boxing, one of its many wily former promoters seizes opportunity for a new gambit in 12-year-old Lindian street urchins Rau, Rue. He chomps beetle-nut, wipes sleeve of faded *dhoti* over red teeth: "You fresh sprigs; you box office gold. No, TWO ways about it – pardon a pun. Audiences will line three abreast to see you box."

Pugilists they become. They are good, ravaging all comers. Wealth and fame from spectacle is fleeting: Manager absconds with their winnings. The traveling ring brought them to city of their birth, and, for what all Lindian foundlings pray, "Praise Goddess Nardesha," reunion with their mother, she whom in an instantly regretted fit of woe, was shamed into abandoning her 'monsters' at an orphanage gate.[12]

---

[12] LKFFF Rau and Rue will become international celebrities by fluke a decade after meeting James and Turt, when, in their 60's they return to the ring. 'Duking diplomacy' it will be called by an American President. 250,000 spectators crowd a Lindian arena – two billion worldwide watch on television as Rau and Rue sequentially fight and KO half-dozen behemoths half their age. The event will accomplish what the shuttling emissary of the President had predicted – opening the lucrative Lindian market to the rest of the world.

The brothers dote over James. Turt's close enough now to see their eyes. They are those of dolphin, not shark. They reflect warm wisdom not cold calculation. Though different from any humans he's ever seen, Turt speculates, 'could they be the ones to watch over James on the journey I've planned for him?'

As Turt's traveled with James, he's mapped James' future. The plan is vague, as is any animal's, when planning for their foundling human. What's different for Turt, from other animals? He has a definite and final destination for James: A specific and special place where James, one day, will re-unite with his Fiction past.

Turt stops near Rau and Rue. They nod, respectful, while their hazel eyes communicate to one another. 'Do you think the boy is the lone survivor of the ferry wreck Rue?'

'Undoubtedly,' Rau says, stroking beard. 'Shelled one is delivering him to civilization.'

'Creature as hero,' speculates red Rue. They communicate with their eyes for a long while about the travelers. During infancy, Rau and Rue developed this *silent talk* by tapping into shared nerve impulses. It kept the crib-mates from rolling together, bonking heads.

Meal completed, the brothers draw water from a barrel on their horse-drawn wagon of teakwood, custom-widened to accommodate their conjoined width: They are successful traveling salesmen. They bring for their guests; finger bowl for the human, pan for creature, and a wet sponge for butterflies.

James studies the wagon's canvas cover – painted with soft blue images of the many-veiled Goddess Nardesha kneeling in prayer. Carpier, patron saint of Lindian foundlings, sprinkles rose petals at her feet. Butterflies drape Carpier's shoulder. Carpier, depicted with a much-lined face is full-grown – still two feet shorter than five footers Rau and Rue. His look is as those of the butterflies: Calm.[13]

Carpier's image comes to life, for James alone, and says. 'So, you have decided to come across vast seas to visit me. Just as another boy, who looked just like you, chose to do long ago; a boy whose name sounded so like mine, yet, he is related to thine.'

James begins to ask what this riddle means when Carpier says. 'Do you not remember me? Shh! Do not answer. Long have I ridden with the brothers. Maybe it is time for change. Maybe I should ride now with you. Would you like that? Shh! Do not answer with words.'

James smiles. Rau and Rue wonder why. They've never lacked companionship, so they've never slipped into a foundling world's make-believe to find it.

RAPSCALLION RAU AND RUE

Confidence in their uniqueness bred from years of quiet confiding and prompting, attracted a near cult following of curiously romanticizing women. No day passed when their passionate adult hungers could not be satiated. Alas, they married.

Not one wife each, two.

All live in different, desolate villages hundreds of kilometers separated; dozens of rivers, mountains, other villages between them; dozens of children among them (ironically no twins), midst dozens of years of multiple-marriage bliss. Rau's first wife and family don't know of second, or second, first: same scenario, Rue. Each family is well provided for, loved, content to have father and spouse for a month or so each year, thinking the other time is spent in traveling, selling, and

---

[13] LKFFF: 'Dwarfism by trauma.' Charles Darwin writing in THE BEAGLE HAS LANDED: 'I have seen many such cases of it in the kingdom of animal. Might there also be human examples? Tales of the ancient Lindian, Carpier, grown but to lad-man, point to the physical possibility of it. Over and again such stunting has most certainly been proven to exist, at least mentally, in, unfortunately, far-too-many adult humans.'

spending time with brother's family.

Their business is procuring rare jewelry, at one-fifth value and quickly finding buyers at twenty times it. The process utilizes either their silent communication or personal language. At bazaars, auctions, roadside stands, they relay to each other when to bluff, or when being bluffed. They rarely fail: thus a styling life and most royal of homes for families.

ALAS, ACHILLES

Despite an astute understanding of human desire, Rau and Rue possess the same weakness as most: not knowing, when, is enough – of money, possessions, of always going.

When does accumulation, and travel, stop; living, begin?

For Rau and Rue this question is bigger than for most – because of their sharing of a hip that, from, springs forth a single limb. If one brother dies, other, soon, will follow. And so, as they and their new companions dinners settle, they sink into a too familiar topic, 'some solution, any solution' to this constant quandary of theirs – via their private language.

"Bangay may tor besso."

"Calla, Nardesha."

"No tu me senti calla, Nardesha."

Their musical words lullaby James. He lay by the fire.

Carpier signals to his cape of butterflies. They animate. They leave the wagon's canvas and mix with their foreign counterparts. In appearance, the only difference is, the Lindian butterflies have more silver streaks in their wing, but their sounds are so different. Where James' entourage flutter is as soothing heartbeats, Carpier's are sitar twitter, melodic, hypnotic.

As James drifts to sleep, he watches butterflies making acquaintance. Turt is listening for revelations of intent in the tone of the brother's private language.

"Only Goddess Nardesha knows our fate if the leg gives out," Rue says.

The emotions of the words say to Turt, 'They have

discussed this subject many times.'

Rau strokes the pants of their in common leg. The shoe on the foot of that leg is custom-cobbled, imported alligator leather, and matches the left and right shoes.

Rue strokes his beard. His complexion reddens. "I say, we keep the travelers. They have no other place. The boy can be our *'fetch-it'*; creature, a *'tote-it'*."

Turt tenses.

Rau glares at his brother. Their faces are inches apart. "You speak of slavery, Rue. Think how many circus masters tried that with us but we outsmarted them."

"No! No! Rue. We'd be doing them a favor. No better life could they have than with us?"

"Slaves, Rue? We've seen many horrors in our lives. We vowed never to take such paths."

"He is foundling as we Rau. We will teach him the trade. He will learn easily, for he would understand our ways, as could only a foundling. He would be the son our circumstances will never allow us to take into the business. That's truly, what we've always wanted. Then he would eventually take over, and we could finally be able to spend more time at homes. That's always been our secret dream. Admit it brother. I am not afraid to."

"As a slave Rue," Rau says grabbing brother's shoulders, shaking. "No good could come of that. It would make sweet Nardesha weep for all foundlings who must be allowed to choose their path."

Turt squints. He is certain the emotions are ominous for him or James. He edges closer to James and begins thinking of ways to flee the fleet-footed duo.

CHAPTER 10

1826 – THE TALE OF A GOLDEN BOY'S FIRST BLISS

At an isolated military outpost due south 'a San Antone, way north a' the Re-al Grande', smack dab in the burnin' eye of a Tehas desert:

Wishin' he war not prisoner in the cloister-like bedroom of austere living quarters, sittin' qui'at and lonesomey at his little boy's desk; but wishin'-blissin' he could make, cool escape, to any-whar' long as its many-a-gallop away, is three year and 364 day old William.

'You can call me 'Dollar Bill',' he ventures boldly as he confronts an imaginary six-gun wielding culprit. William is 'Golden Boy' to loving stepfather Captain Golden; Willamina, to more-than-a-tad overbearing mater. With pen, he repeatedly stabs the frilly housedress she makes him wear – miniature of the one in which her bony frame rattles about. In his mind anger rages war against *any* surrender, "Dollar *Bill* am I!"

Margaret appears at her son's open door. Smoldering eyes burn him. "Stop that Willamina. Or you will have no outdoors for a week."

The threat works.

She kneels, envelops him in, *'so-tangly, cold, BRR!'* arms. William stiffens. Her demeanor changes too quickly, too unnaturally.

"Oh Willamina, we are too much the same to always fight. We could be like twins, you and I. By the time those blond locks grow to your waist, you will see," she says, as so many times she has. "I love you so Willamina." She puts hollow cheek to his full, as so many times she has. Sour to sweet. Blech! He always tries to pull away. She traces fingers along son's earlobes, and combs them through the fine ringlets of hair sweeping his shoulders.

Her hot breath imprisons him. He wants to shout, "Captain Golden loves me, you don't." Instead, he puffs, "If you love me you'll let me cut my hair like the Captain's."

"A haircut for my sweet Willamina? Unthinkable. Oh how your 'REAL' father, Reverend Bellows would preach against these tresses." Margaret's smile is lemon. "Satan's strands." She imitates and thrusts fist upward, as Ezekiah does King James.

Margaret was, as so many other women in the congregation, drawn to his man-ness by the power of his pulpit words. Unlike others, she succeeded in seduction – right behind that bastion oak pulpit. She hated him afterward because she was in a 'no-cuts' line for his affections- behind a deity and one of 'Rrrose Heather's whures.'

"Thankfully Willamina, Reverend Bellows doesn't know of you. So I can raze out any of his hypocrite blood running through your vessel. I will incise every last vestige of him from you, if that's what it takes. But I won't talk about Ezzy anymore." Then she rants on for five minutes more.

William watches her face turning the red of beet. She stands statue rigid. He stares up at her no-stop mouth, wondering how she can talk without taking breaths; hoping that she'll just keel over and be forever, *'shh'*, because her body will have deflated like a pumpkin after an unexpected freeze. William hears no sounds. Long ago, he stopped listening because her tirades never change.

'Yech! Phew! Wish I could gallop away from you.' Since he cannot,

he does what he always does to cope: wriggles into the escape of story world. In his thoughts, he scribbles a rootin'-tootin' tale about dastardly Snake-eye Sam. Margaret had taught William to read. He has taught himself to write – to shed his skin, for at least a while, of Willa...'Yech!' And of the anonymous Ezekiah...'*Phew!*'

Fortunately, William is the only boy on post – no others to make fun of him. The little girls, well he's prettier, with his soft, creamy skin, so they say nothing. No soldier is about to say anything about the 'Captain's *son*'.

"Margaret. Time to go," the Captain shouts from the parlor. "Will our Golden Boy like to accompany us on our adventure?"

"We are buying furniture from traders up from Mexical, Willamina. Like to come?"

'Not looking like THIS' he thinks, shaking his head.

"That's just fine. Cook's here if you need anything."

Hearing the door close and the wagon pull away, William thinks, 'now's my chance.' He sneaks past the kitchen to their bedroom and opens a dry-rotting chifforobe. There it hangs: Tomorrow's birthday presents. His stepfather had hinted of them. Cowboy clothes. Canvas shirt, pants and leather chaps that smell of a longhorn's fresh and wild freedom.

He slips off the dress and into them, taking extra time with the iridescent lizard skin boots and up-turned cowboy hat. He clasps thumbs under big oval belt buckle with the carved-in image of a giant cactus, a twin to the one Captain knows he likes to read beneath.

"You'll be a cowboy, Golden Boy. I'll see to that," often the Captain has told him. "Your mother will come around. I know her. She loves us both. It will just take a little time."

William always hears the pleading hope in his stepfather's voice. He trusts the towering man-god more than anyone else in his world, and believes all he says will come true. Captain Golden can say or do no wrong. How can a little boy know a man-god can be simply weak-willed with a woman, yet a leader of men – brave against any adversary, but cowering with bedmate? (Just one time when he wasn't: She jealously grabs the cowboy duds; readying to shred them with his straight razor. Golden's granite jaw juts when he catches her. "Don't! I won't give in on this, Margaret. If you won't accept it, I'll pack you back to Cincinnati and you can work for Rrrose Heather.)

On the stucco wall is a full-length looking glass. William stares, seeing himself for the first time, not as a girl. His heart races. Palms sweat from the rush of excitement of seeing the sharp-featured boy, sturdy-jawed, wide-forehead, same black eyes he shares with a half-brother in Cincinnati whom only one other person knows of, Rrrose Heather.

William's smile widens. No that's sissy. He flexes. He glares. He tips hat over one eye. He squawks at a skinny figure that slithers in from across the bedroom's threshold and peers over his shoulder. "Yaa. I'm the Golden Boy, Snake-eye Sam. I can kill you off any time I want. By chapter two, I reckon... you're gonna be through." He mentally writes the slimy, rot-smelly character to be sidewinden' up aside him.

'Oh no you don't, Golden Boy. I got plenty a varmintin' left in me.'

Golden Boy sees him in the looking glass reaching round to give him a necktie party, not with rope, but necktie-like fang-fingers.

"I'm too quick on the draw to fall for that, Snake-eye," Golden Boy shouts. He draws trusty pen from pocket. He'd put it there soon as he turned from dainty Willamina to cowpoke William – always have trusty pen in holster. *'BAM! BAM!* Chapter One, instead, you're dead."

'No Golden,' Sam hisses as he coils from the looking glass, '*Sss, Sss.* Not in chapter one.'

"HOO! HOO!" Golden Boy blows at the smoking tip of his mighty pistol-pen. "Cowboy writer. That's what I am. I'll never be you, Willamina. Or you, Ezekiah Bellows." He studies himself – from hat to boots. Something missing. The spurs. He rummages through boxes. Nothing. His stepfather had said that "something most special" would accompany his present. (Over at the stable is the real surprise, a pony, golden as his future rider.) William climbs a wobbly stool to spur-search the shelf. He reaches, catches on a strap to a saddlebag: 'Must be in there.'

Sam springs back to life. 'Don't you go a slitherin'-in where you don't belong Golden Boy. You may not like what you find.'

"I just gotta see the spurs, Sam. See if they're gold or silver. Make sure they match the boots." As he pulls the saddlebag he slips and *'thunks'* to the wood floor.

Comes the Spanish-accented voice from the kitchen. *"Esta bien todo, Guillermo?"*

"Just a riden' a bronco."

"Ninos juegos," the cook laughs. She's busy with supper.

Convoluted maps and papers with strange series of numbers strew around William when the saddlebag's latch slips open. It's the saddlebag, oilcloth bagged during the gulf hurricane that pulled from Thibidioux's grasp. Golden Boy sits among the disarray, momentarily forgetting the spurs. He studies the dagger dripping blood through the halo and onto the skull imprinted on its flap; identical to the one Thibidioux carved into Turt's shell.

Golden Boy begins making up scary tales about the insignia and memorizing some of the maps and numbers, for future story scenes.

Sam admonishes, 'Don't go rememberin' things best be forgot.'

There's a note. 'Meet Thibidioux...' that's a name Golden Boy's never before seen – can barely pronounce. He continues reading '...at noon on the boy's birthday.' He wonders, 'Who's going to meet Thibi...Mother? Father? Cook?'

William hears an approaching wagon. Its wheels, because it's loaded with furniture, crush into the gravel. He knows his parents return. He gathers disarray, puts it into the saddlebag, and replaces it on the shelf. He strips from cowboy and again becomes, with sour clench, Willamina. He runs back to his room to invent a dagger, halo, blood, skull, map, and numbers tale.

CHAPTER 11

Traces of light, lingering in the wharf-shack after Poppy Sol's visit, allow the recovering Mariner to see the results of Carper and Turt's battle – dishes broken, chairs upturned, geegaws strewn. He kicks them to a corner, stretches creakily, and rubs his wound.

Carper, up-turned Turt and Ol Tom watch him.

"It's gone," Mariner croaks, surprised. His spattered blood has dried into his dungarees. Who can tell, from all the other stains? He lights a lantern and peers into Carper's sea-calm eyes. "Come might close ta makin' the final voyage, that I did my young mate." Ol Tom leaps from Turt's underbelly to Mariner's stoop-shoulder. Mariner's peer docks on the feline. "But the Carper doctored me up, e' did, Tom."

As the old seafarer strokes Tom, Carper starts to say, "Wasn't me Mariner. 'It was…"

Luny Mum's blink stops him. 'You're the one started 'ims on recovery road, young sire. Poppy Sol's help only steered the healing. E'll be wantin' no credit, so don't try givin'.'

Mariner interrupts Carper's imagination trek. "I see you and Turt met. Not in the gentlest a' seas, but then agein', Turt rarely swims in calm tides. Not with his glaren'-red anger. Looks like you cooled 'im."

TALES OF THE FICTION HOUSE

Mariner steadies himself with Harpoon, until sea legs flow, and then he uses it as lever to right Turt. "Heave Ho: That' 'e blows!" Turt 'CLUMP-THUMPS,' upright rattling the wharf-shack. Books tumble. Mariner carefully re-shelves them, ignoring other clutter: priorities are priorities. As he and Ol Tom busy about the stove preparing mess, Turt approaches Carper.

Carper seizes Harpoon. Turt bows neck, slides head under boy's arm, nuzzles him with his forehead. Respect for past adversary. It is a gentle meeting as it had been for Turt with a lad called Kunta; Turt's only other human friend besides Mariner. Kunta was from Turt's long ago.

(**Editor's note:** Feeling that the reader already will know a great deal about Kunta, because his artwork is so pervasive, I have asked the writer to save his tale for later.)

Carper stares at Turt's shell: So many curious markings; all within a village motif.

"That's the land Kunta's from, Carper," Mariner says, bringing over stew for humans, and fish for creatures. "Kunta carved it when Turt was a shelling. Might say it grew on him."[14] We'll use Turt for a tabletop and I'll tell you all about 'em..."

Carper hardly hears Mariner as they eat. He's immersed in the parts of the village Mariner hasn't covered with bowls, mugs, and baskets of bread. What he can see: Totems of odd birds; whimsical beasts. Around a campfire, weavers create, and artists paint. A cornrowed, ebony-skin little girl playing in front of a hut winks up at Carper. He waves back, anxious for when the Turt table is cleared and he can visit more of Kunta's land.

"Kunta saved both me and Turt's lifes," Mariner says between sips that whistle through missing teeth. His usually steady voice trembles. "Probably lost his in the save." Turt trumpets shrilly, sadly. The wharf-shack vibrates. "Well, Turt

---

[14] Darwin – from The Beagle Has Landed: 'The village expanded on Turt, eventually encompassing his hard dome. I speculate that such tectonics could not occur on most, or maybe any other species of turtle.'

never gives up hope that he's still around."
You sense their hurt; touch Mariner's hand, pet Turt. For now, you just want, happy.
You look out the dusk-darkened porthole. The brightest red Rose imaginable blossoms in Luny Mum's glow. Gentle vines beckon you. You feel them on your cheeks, not prickly, but smooth, and kiss-soft. Sweet Rose, she's from another season — a summer — but came fall and winter for you, and she wilted. Though the season is really summer, now it is your spring — Rose is again beautiful, and fragrant, and sweet. Clouds suddenly block Luny Mum. Rose is gone. But you know she will always be there for you — just as Mariner, Turt, Ol Tom, and Calico.

Rrrose Heather leaves the pier, smiling, convinced: 'Bonnie's boy is in the right place. Just as William is, with Captain Golden, if not Margaret.' (Rrrose and Captain Golden — old friends — write to each other regularly.) 'One day, when the time is right,' Rrrose vows, 'I will unite the brothers.'

CHAPTER 12

Midnight: So bright is Luny Mum's glow that James awakens. Beside him, Turt feigns sleep and plans their escape from Rau and Rue who are talking near the wagon. James fidgets and stares into the campfire's hot licks to relax. 'That's the spirit,' Turt thinks. 'Try the *CALM-AHMMS*!'

Flames flare. Emerging from them is Rrrose Heather. She pats her reddest-ever cheeks and brushes away cinders. 'Heavens! I don't normally reside in Hades, though it makes Margaret happy to think I do. That old sourpuss needs something in her life to bring her joy.' Rrrose strokes James' hair. 'Looks like you be needin' story-en up, Lad.'

"Shore do."

'Now who is he talking to?' Turt wonders.

"I want to hear 'bout Laza Bones." (140 years earlier Carper's shoutin' that too, to Mariner.)

'Oh no you don't,' Turt wants to trumpet, but can't because Rau and Rue would sense his sleep ruse and know he is observing them. '...Golden Boy and Carper both paid high prices for mixing with Laza. They shouldn't have gotten curious about such things. Neither should you.'

BEGINS THE TALE OF LAZARUS BONTEX '*LAZA BONES*' THIBIDIOUX

"Tis 1800, there 'bouts, early morn. Today Thibidioux chil' to be born.

"Butterflies come and tell me so. 'Come Mama Lucy – time to go.'"

110 year-old healer and midwife Mama Lucy chants these words as she walks sprightly along the bayou road leading to the Thibidioux cabin. Amulet necklaces of critter teeth and bones click together in time to her pace. "13's be wild. Bad tidins' for comin' child. Ups to me to potion the innocent one free."

She cups hands behind back and catches a floating leaf. For luck, she extends ritual by popping it in her mouth, swallowing. "Should be gay – this month a May: But today the 13th, Friday, and twelve plus one crayfish, little pussy, at my door, lay."

Mama Lucy's words that come, seldom, yet sublime, often arrive in singsong rhyme. 'Dems of the bayou forgive her this crime. They know the tragedy that fraught this – her only beget, a son, he, alligator 'et.'

Shoeless, her worm-thin toes wriggle in the dirt. Dress looks a gunnysack containing rattly-bony frame. Never tall, with age she's shrunk to the length of a yard-and-a-third stick, almost as thin. She's pliable, like willow; no dry twigs of arthritis. Easily she carries a 40-pound carpetbag of potions, lotions and cures weighing half herself. Ghost-white hair sprouts sparsely from atop once onion-round head that is now withered, avocado shape. You can't tell if she's white or black because time has blended her skin to a neutral gray. Blind, eyes shriveled pits; she views with eagle vision the world through her senses.

From seemingly nowhere lightening crisscrosses the azure sky, occasionally igniting burbling swamp gas. The explosions are like popping firecrackers. They frizz thick moss swaying from trees. Mama Lucy sniffs the rotten egg smell. 'Yea, do it foretell the fomentin.'

TALES OF THE FICTION HOUSE

"Bad day be born – today's chil' lifelong forlorn." She plans to dose the mother with a tonic of foamed mushroom and boiled spleck to delay birth 'til past midnight, when a new day would bring fresh charms.

Mama Lucy sniffs the air, suddenly dank. "Hundred yards yonder 13 gators dey bask. Dey no hinder my carin'-for task." She doesn't veer: BLIND PERSISTENCE; BLINDING STUBBORNESS! Rouge dust stirs at Mama's feet as she meanders to, then among the lounging reptiles: All are tantinted 8 to 12 footers – biggest in the swamps.[15] Senses tell Mama Lucy that today they scheme as they lounge. She feels their fear and apprehension as they nervously swing open their snouts. Teeth brush her knees. They cry out at her intrusion.

Their instincts – to stave off riling-up two-legs, too much, thus, preventing wholesale gator slaughter – dictates their bayou code: GATOR BRETHREN EAT A TWO-LEG. THEN THEIR RELATIVE BE UNTOUCHABLE. SO, NONE MAY HARM MAMA! This, be their ancient bayou 'way'.

Mama Lucy plucks gently into balmy air – mosquito. She holds it, as New Orleans gentry hold teacup between thumb and forefinger. "Skeeter, take mah blood." She lets it sting, then, bayou-lightening fast, moves her hand and places it near the biggest gator's battle-cratered snout – that of King Creole. King Creole instinctively scissors open, shuts jaw. He snarfs insect cleanly, not touching human finger.

"I trick you, *mah shaz a mio*. My blood; into you, floods, so over your precious code, now hast you strode."

Again, this cunning ancient human who knows him well has tricked him – the KING!

She, who took him in as foundlin' gator, hardly bigger 'n a human finger. He were dehydrated, floppin' down-side up,

---

[15] *Perilous tannicus*: Nicknamed 'Gatemouth Browns', because these muddy-complexioned perils have snouts that thrash wildly as gates in a gale. The swinging produces a twangy bluesy melody. Perilous tannicus live five times longer than most gator breeds, and some bayou folk claim it's because their baby-cry-like songs relieve tension, subdue worries.

hunnerd yards from the bayou. Doctored 'im day n' night; wet-nursed scratchy, wee-toothed beast right alongside own boy 'til 'e could 'et solids: Let 'em both sleep together; raised 'im into a fine young specimen, she did, then set im free in the swamps so 'e could live 'mongst own kind.

N' 'ow 'e repays 'er? By, years later returnin' and 'etten her grown son, his own crib, then sandbox, then pirogue, brother.

Creole snaps, bellows. Slimy reptile saliva spatters Mama's face. She wipes it into a bottle she snakes from pocket. 'I trick double. No'ting a better fixer, den gatah-spit elixir.'

--Poppy Sol reflects philosophically down at the alligator conclave. 'As humans do what they gotta; so to, gators do, but not necessarily what they oughtta.'--

Gators stare warily at their king. Grumbling growls. Some wonder. Should they doubt his ability to deal with the bayou two-legs.

King regains composure. He brings the conclave to order by thumping gavel tail. He needs their full support in their long-planned, REVOLUTION against humans that begins today. He raises tail, proudly, and then dangles it, disgusted. Embedded into it is a squirrel that failed to hustle past with a nut.

Mama Lucy: No longer does she despise Creole for 'etten her only offspring right in front of her 3/4s century past. She began rhymin' – that's how she stays sane. It took Mama nearly half-a-century, '...ta be a realizin', life way-too shoat, to be a grievin' a pirogue cain't no longer float.'

She pats Creole's snout. Though blind, she believes she can see son's eyes in Creole's eyes. Imagined though that *might* be, it's the only vestige of his life she'd ever have. Because of that, never would she harm Creole, she long-ago vowed. 'King be fulla greed. Dat why 'e ate mah seed.'

"I know you be a plannin' somethun', King Creole," says Mama Lucy. "I be keepin' eye on you wif' my soul." She slides a bottle from her carpetbag and sprinkles sparkly contents over gators. She chants, "Grinded den pulverized leather hide 'a gators long gone-away. Let descendents see yer evil fate, if de

humans you, all upon today, tryest to prey."
Gators sneeze, quiver, and shiver, at feeling the dust-touch of ancestors. Some run.

Huey Long, ruthless politico, demagogue in the making – King Creole's top Lieutenant and held back only by King Creole – stops them with a growl that sends treed birds flying. 'Do not let the old witch bad-omen us and stop our revolution. If you do, I will hunt you down. Your fate will be worse than that of becoming your ancestors' powder.'

Gators of the conclave crouch. They fear staying but fear even more, going.

Mama Lucy re-commences trek toward the Thibidioux place – just up the way. Gators mill, always with two on lookout for Thibidioux cousins, uncles who might pass by with glistening explosion sticks deadlier than any razor fang.

THE LEGEND OF TRANSFORMATION

From swamplands near and far King Creole has summoned alligator royalty, Baron Tail of the north, Prime Snout, south, Liege Leather, recently escaped from a two-leg circus. They and the others are here to consider Creole's plan of breakthrough – TRANSFORMATION – from crawler to two-leg- via Thibidioux newborn. Transformation: Elders had talked of its possibility. King Creole and many gators believe the Thibidioux clan once crawled like them, and so that is why Thibidioux hunt them – to keep amenities of humanness to themselves.

TRANSFORMATION: To King Creole and many gators – It is a holy word to be chanted, cherished.

Of all the gators gathered, only the king believes he knows *HOW* to achieve it.

* * *

James trembles, fearing his kindly shelled creature, or Rau and Rue, may transform to something bad.

Rrrose hugs him. 'Don't be 'afear', Lad. No gator, *yet*, swum from bayou to Lindian Woods.'

* * *

To discover that *HOW*, King Creole spied, for decades on Mama Lucy's mid-wifing: Crawlin' quiet onto porches, peering through cabin windows. 'Secret's at the birthen', he's convinced.

No foolin' Mama Lucy. She know he there outside the window during birth times. Yeppers, she know 'bout much as you can 'bout Creole, though nothing 'bout 'transformation'.

Her senses, so attuned with nature, now whisper quietly as she climbs the Thibidioux porch. 'More den just peer in will 'e do today. So for all you Thibidioux, do thee, silently pray.'

Creole watches Mama enter the cabin. He wishes he could have snarfed the old woman. Maybe if they were alone. No. He fears the consequences of tempting the time-honored bayou code: 'Kill relative of two-leg 'et by gator, sacrifice own lineage up ta dat family.'

A RARE TALE OF GATOR-HONOR

Son, Prince Ali, is Creole's only relative. Prince isn't like him – cunning, relentless. He is gentle, though big as fa. At lunch: He grits sharp teeth in contrition even when ettin' catfish. Supper: Begs pardon of otter and crow 'fore they disappear down gullet.

King knows Prince would live up to the 'CODE' and sacrifice himself.

THE CONCLAVE

King Creole returns attention to the agenda Mama interrupted. He bites the alligator beside him, soft, playful – a reptilian form of political back slap. 'Ah, TRANSFORMATION! Just think. Us, in der pirogues. No more crayfish one-atta-time, but whole nets-full we pull in. N' not 'jus' smellin' their jambalaya, but we cookin', ettin'. Their white lightenin', brewin', drinken'.'

King's voice booms. His roving glance locks briefly to each set of eyes. 'We can possess the tiny-shiny discs dey' call coin dat' allow 'em to get what dey' want. Den' our bellies'll be forever full. We'll always have shelter from sky's wrath, its knockin' ice balls, 'n shock-rays, for we'll live somewhere sturdier den' hollow logs: We'll occupy DER' places.'

Snouts flap approval. Their whiny cries are now, more than ever, like those of human infants.

King must have his conclave's unanimous approval and cooperation, to commence his plan of *snatch*, so he conceals the major detail – deception. Once he's transformed, he alone will be transformed, and then – DOMINION –and adulation, though grudging, over all in the bayou, because he'll possess the power that is human blood, that will mix with his cunning king blood.

OL KING CREOLE SINGS NO MERRY OL SOUL

Over the decades, you croon in solitary bayou coves, 'Ah de glories 'a the Thibidioux. Dey can be yours alone 'mongst gators.' Watching your objects 'd desire from afar you drool, as you see yourself a Thibidioux man, rockin' onna' front porch while puffin' pungent brown leaves rolled as fat sticks. Fire-glow at one end scares you none, as it does others gators. 'Oh, sweet billowen smoke! It do tickle de innards.'

When Creole enters the reverie of foundling imagination, he's certain that all the minutia of information he's discovered while spying on Mama Lucy adds up to the formula he foresees: *Snatch, devour whole human infant near the time a birth, den' dat' two-leg will live in you, and you be in him; become ONE.*

King Creole's eventual plan is to reveal this formula to just one other, not Prince Ali, whose compassion is not to be trusted to keep it secret. Prince Ali, a gently sculpted, almost Nordic-blonde-hued reptile would be given the fairest of the gaitresses with whom to mate. They would give the King grandgatahs of the purest blood. Of these would he choose to transform – and eventually replace him.

The Prince never knew how to tell the King that he prefers gators, not gaitresses. No other bayou creature has enough courage to tell Creole either.

Some in the encircled conclave distrust King Creole. The last king, one night, drowned. By Creole, they suspected. King must sway these ones.

A rabbit shoots from brambles. A gator tracks, devours. Occasional herons light on floating logs. Other gators, into the drink, dive. '*Chomp. Gulp.*' A baby's cry drifts from the Thibidioux cabin. It's not the human baby intended for Transformation. Creole's certain that baby is yet-to-be-born. Savvy political wonk residing in Creole's soul instinctively acts. If he doesn't have a baby to kiss like two-leg counterpart, next best, use their squeal.

'He sounds little different from us, don't he, *mon* friends,' Creole stumps. 'Just picture, you, bein' he.' Another chorus of the gators own baby-like cries. King knows he is triggering their covetousness of the two-leg life.

* * *

To James' query, "Would they really harm the baby?" Rrrose Heather evades, 'Transformin's a never-endin' spiral downward, Jamie. Laza Bones' is the proof.'

Turt, head swaying in time to faux snores, eyes barely open, studies the topography he and James would encounter in attempting their escape from Rau and Rue. Ravine is impassable – too muddy is the gully. Stream, *if* deep enough, he and James could just float away.

* * *

Conclave meets for hours. Gators disperse when a Thibidioux passes, then re-assemble. Some mount logs. Circus escapee Liege Leather – twenty years captive – rises six inches so a pesky bee that keeps bumping his belly can reach its hive. That understanding of other kinds, IS, Liege Leather. Naked ladies are tattooed across his hide. When he moves, a foot-long bone piercing his snout pokes at them and they do a hoochy-koochy dance.

'Madness is it, to believe any of what King Creole indicates is possible, just because elders referred to it,' Liege Leather cries out. 'I have been around two-legs more than any. I know their good, and cruelty. The freak they tried to make of me.'

He crawls around and looks each in the eyes, lobbying convictions brutally hardened by enslavement, but tempered by the contemplation such imprisonment allows. 'I will accede to the majority. Yet, heed my words – if transformation is possible – we must create guidelines, so we fashion ourselves after, only, their good. Never must this newfound power be abused.'

Claws of most of those gathered tap logs – respect for sage returned from 'other' world. None is louder than Creole. He peruses each gator's face to see emotions they reveal, exploitable ones.

Baron Tail, named because club tail can crush beaver with one swipe, and Prime Snout, whose sword-point snout impales low flying screech owls, icily object to Liege Leather's pleas.

'Dey kill, eat, hang us to dry,' Prime Snout points.

Baron Tail beats club. 'If we can deliver vengeance, 'den we must.'

'Yea, their injustices are legion,' Liege Leather counsels. 'We can show them better ways. Harmony can again reign amongst us: Just as existed in their Garden of Eden we have heard them sing of from their holy stone bastions.'

Mugwumps hem-haw, straddle logs, their fence of neutrality. Stalwarts hiss 'yea-nay.' Prince Ali looks on Liege Leather admiringly, as a long-lost uncle returned, one whom he can learn from, confide.

Liege Leather shifts from claw to claw. Nude ladies dance. 'Let us see the practical side. There is the magic power of Mama Lucy we can only wonder about, only fear, because of the code. And, the brut power the Thibidioux can use if something misfires.'

With these statements, the fence of neutrality collapses. Mugwumps crawl down to the safety, to terra firma that is Liege Leather's logic.

Baron Tail growls. 'It's loony believin' Liege Leather. 'He's duped. Too many years with the two-legs. They must be destroyed.' Baron's acid allure doesn't sway any gators.

King Creole isn't prepared for Liege Leather influence of so many. He takes over where lackeys fail. He crawls into the bayou, paddles to a protruding tree branch. It is sturdy enough to hold his 300 pounds. This is where he would carry the newborn for the transformation ceremony. He roars, halting the argument. All stare at him. Smoothly he stumps, 'Though Liege Leather be right...' Baron Tail, Prime Snout growl. '...and though I be his detractor – let me mediate and provide compromise that you-all will realize is right and just.'

Creole disagrees completely with Liege Leather; agrees completely with Baron Tail and Prime Snout. Yet those two are future competition. He plans to eliminate them when he transforms. Liege Leather, in a manner is 'almost' human; cries, growls, acts almost two-leg. He knows their ways. He will be a good gator to have close. The others are all incumbents, happy, he knows, to go along with him if they bring home plenty of patronage like two-leg incumbents do for their constituents. Happy too, to emulate their King's fervor for revolution if there be gain for them.

* * *

'Known plenty of high-mightyin' politicians in me day, Jamie,' Rrrose Heather says. Never seen one who wasn't schemin'-plannin' at least three slithers in advance.'

Turt flings a pebble from beak-snout. '*Plip*.' 'Water's not deep enough for swim-getaway. Hmm. Now what? Lindia does have its carnivore cranes. Maybe make a deal with them to fly interference, while we amble in escape? Who you kidding,

Turt? Expect help from world's most untrustworthy flyers?'

* * *

King's next wail is sweet, melodic, but alas, propaganda. 'Hear now *mon* plan...'

Disciples listen, mesmerized as he parlays small details into mighty expectations of the, 'E-Z LIFE,' for each of them, and their families, friends, all gatordom. Cheer-cries emanate from snouts. Ah, connivin' Creole. He keep key provisions of transformin' secret while doin' convincin'. Promises be hollow as the logs he'll see to that most'll forever keep residen'-in.

Creole follows his own, set as stone, oratory rules. 'Nay go 'a sayin' too much. Let yer audience convince theyselves, least-wise let em feel they has.' So, he only briefly continues. 'The Thibidioux, and Mama Lucy, mm-hmm, *mi mon cheri*, they worthy adversaries. But gator wits be sly from bayou liven'. Once transformed – *SLY* – thas' what'll let gator control any two-leg. Thibidioux, Mama, pshaw! They shall be helpless prawns in our claws.'

Creole cuts diatribe even shorter when he looks over and observes Liege Leather.

Never easily swayed, Liege Leather, just, momentarily, is imagining himself on circus bleachers, watching, not caged ringside, being watched.

'Yes, prawns in our...' King Creole sees that covetous thought sparking the look of even the great gatoritarian, Liege Leather. He knows he has duped, pshaw, that be not the right word, CONVINCED, them all. He smiles to himself.

Now – to keep them convinced, 'til dark. 'Cue the Kingfisher,' he decides.

* * *

'Ah, the Kingfisher. Now there be a politico for all the ages, Jamie me lad, says Rrrose Heather.'

* * *

A SUB-TALE – KINGFISHER, HUEY LONG: 'MASTER ALLI-BUSTER'

Ya couldn't slide a skeeter twixt any 'a Huey Long's filibust.

'We gatahs won de bayah' long afore dey' two-legs come encroachin'. Deevine right say it's ours.' Vexing cries be-devil audience. All stares steel to Huey Long's magnetic eyes that seem to look a thousand places at once – all for the purpose of imprisoning listeners. They feel trapped, unable to flee yet they're perversely glad being captives. Through the afternoon the Kingfisher keeps the conclave enthralled with scaly tales of their Leezian'.

'Ya-all should know 'bout that terrible season de uni-horned boars try encroachin'. No?' He creates suspense via momentary silence. Rhythmically he slaps ground with tail 'til dust rings circle his head; years spent developing that attention-vising diversion. 'Well, our ancestors repel 'em; all way down to the gulf; wherest de drown.'

Or: 'All ya can stand ta be reminded about de carnivore cranes the two-legs brungs from far-off Lindia ta winnow out rodents what's rightly a gatah's providence. Dey goes fer our baby gates instead.' Baited gators listen, entranced. All the while Huey Long bobs reed splinter twixt teeth. He tilts snout and spits it into the air. 'Dat's how we stop dem furreign' flyers. Flingin' reed spears from our snouts, groundin' em, permanent. Baby gates: Dey *plip, plop* – safe, right back inta bayah's warm, beckonin' bosom.'

Snouts grasp snouts as alligator tears swell. Claw clasps claw of another. You can see in Huey Long's audience, as each tale climaxes, their tension, apprehension, fear.

All the tales have similar endings. Always a brave leader; cut from the same, sturdy jib-hide, as – 'None other den our great Creole who led the way savin' our swamp.'

Nightfall nears. This is all King Creole wants from his adjutant – to hold their emotions in his claws, keep thoughts

TALES OF THE FICTION HOUSE

off the attack until he interrupts Huey Long 'allibuster' with his own bark of – 'LET'S ROLL!' Until then King Creole stays relaxed by listening to the tales and imagining what kind of two-leg political family could come from such a bag-a-bayou-wind like Huey, if, he, ever transformed to a human.

THE TALE OF GONE LUNA

Before setting, Poppy Sol's sly wink – HIGHLY RISQUÉ, for such an upright bloke – about the hoochy-koochy ladies' gyrations on Liege Leather, sends Luny Mum to tittering, then chuckling, finally, uncontrollably guffawing.

When Luny Mum gets like this, it lasts through the night and into the morn. Of course, ocean tides change. That's just the beginning. There's no stopping her. She's 'GONE LUNA.'

That's what those of the bayou call it. Humans – well with maybe the exception of a Mama Lucy, so attuned to nature's ways, or a Mariner, so keen to changes on the sea – they can't predict it until it's on them. Creatures sense it coming and prepare as best they can, as King Creole does now. He's been planning to utilize it to achieve his aim.

Two dozen of the tightly knit Thibidioux clan fills Bontez and Lizzie Thibidioux's sturdy cabin to celebrate the coming birth. Thibidioux tradition is that all be present to welcome the new. Burning lanterns, shielded by colored paper, paint the parlor and kitchen yellow, red, blue. Rug is up and they dance to screeching violin, and accordion. Celebration merrily rolls through afternoon, into night. Apprehensive mother-to-be may not cotton to the damnable commotion, but this is the Thibidioux way, 'always 'as been'. At least Lizzie has the privacy of boudoir and the comfort of Mama Lucy at her bedside.

Mama Lucy knows the swamp creatures stir. She anticipated 'GONE LUNA.'

Luny Mum – so full in reverie – so orange in giddiness after her friendly tete-a-tete with Poppy Sol: Her glow almost sets ablaze the bayou landscape. She turns ivory. Night feels day. Then inky clouds cloak her. She pushes them aside and reappears, all the brighter.

These variations cause rambunctiousness among wild things. Normally cooperative beaver battle for dams, straight arrow bats narrowly avoid flying into haplessly honking geese, lazing tree snakes spiral branch to branch, miss, clunk to the ground, are spaghetti to creatures higher on the food ladder. So, King Creole's unthinkable uprising against the predator of every creature, 'the wily two-legs', a strike at the gathering of the most heralded of the trapping families; it is even more unthinkable among the Thibidioux. Because, during Gone Luna, alligators and all higher rungs would be feasting on disoriented creatures of lower.

Thibidioux kin – So appearance akin. Thick straight black eyebrows and hair, hollow olive cheeks, long, flat noses, square mouths. Among them, non-blood spouses- occasional blonds, brunets; gently featured and round-faced. All assimilate into Thibidioux way of clothes, cooking, easing living. They drink from fine French crystal, custom-made as jar shapes. It is reminder how they have re-invented themselves after being driven from their faraway homeland.

* * *

"So they weren't once gators, Rrrose Heather?"

'Be goshin' no, Jamie boy. They be from very north of the bayou. Never even did they see a gator afore they arrive. Say, why you tremble so Jamie?' She smothers him in her bosom.

"Afraid for the baby, Rrrose Heather. Will he/she be all right?"

'Don't worry, Lad. Took place long ago. No changin' now. May be scary, but you got to know the truth.' Rrrose wipes sweat from his forehead with her handkerchief.

There's a '*CLANK, CLANK*' from the wagon. Turt can't hear Rau and Rue's muffled conversation; instead, he hears '*click*'.

That sound transports Turt back, a century-and-a-half, to when he was a wee-shelling on Mariner's shoulder. "Ere's 'ow we jail pirates aboard ship," Mariner tells him. It's Turt's first view of what two-legs call, **chains**, '*CLANK*', and padlocks, '*click*'; as Mariner secures a dreg to a mast.

Instantly, the '*click*' tells Turt what Rau, Rue plan for him. Turt smiles wryly. 'Just let them get close enough. A clanking bullwhip will I make of it to provide our escape. *Don't pat yourself on the shell too quickly, you tell yourself. Remember, your adversaries are fleet of wit as well of foot.*'

* * *

Thibidioux women wear their best ankle-length dresses, the men, shiny-new plaid shirts with everyday workpants. Spicy gator gumbo steams from China tureens shipped all the way from New Orleans. Gumbo sweet clover scent mingles with platters of honey-butter glazed crayfish and catfish. The feast spreads over an oak table beneath one of three alligator-hide sheathed walls. On the fourth is mounted alligator faces and snouts used as shelves. They display the extravagances bayou abundance provides – delicate figurines, exotic carvings, pouches of the finest tobacco. Nearby hang jackets, galoshes – apparel of their gatoring trade.

Often, when no one is home, King Creole creeps onto the porch. No other alligator has courage to approach a Thibidioux lair. Creole would look through windows, imagining human heads replacing brethren's snouts. Hatred swelled in him, until one day he decided the only way of defeating the two-leg was to transform and take what is theirs.

A fast bayou waltz commences. 20 year-old Bontez balances a jar of sparkly white lightening in his hand. A lit cigar wags from mouth. Pending fatherhood spikes his emotions. Cheerily he two-steps between partners and twirls them. They tumble dizzily into arms of other partners. Bontez is over six foot, a rail anchored by snappy, alligator-hide boots. Shoulder-length hair sways. Curly beard bounces.

Bontez sings, "I be a foot stompin', crawdaddy suckin', gumbo guzzlin' bayou man." He glances at a shy 13-year-old cousin. She pretends to examine a golden ring in a wall snout. *"Tres bien, mi cher a mio.* Come petite wallflower," say he in thick French-becoming-American, Thibidioux. She curtsies. He smiles. He encircles her waist with free hand, spins her over his head. She squeals, *'WHEE!'* He catches her. She titters, unable to conceal crush on cuz.

"All de ladies twixt Ponchatrain and Fontenot supposin' Sweet Bontez wi' be their hissen, but only darlin Lizzie the love of his life, dizzy for darlin Lizzie, she only gal for him." He winks at Lizzie who is watching through slightly open bedroom door. She lay in iron-frame bed, trying to smile at his frivolity midst pronouncement of love.

"13's glow be a fool husband's – NO," grumbles Mama Lucy, wanting all his attention focused on his wife, so he can better help her on this ominous night.

* * *

'Bontez wants be true, Jamie. But, alas, your Rrrose Heather, she knows. He be, but a man.'

Turt hears the thudding drag of the chain. Though he can't see Rau and Rue because clouds slip in front of Luny Mum, he's ready for battle.

* * *

Bontez hugs his wiry granny. An oversize bonnet hides her face, all the way down to pointy chin. She empties her pipe tobacco. He snuffs cigar, toasts, "Here's to my chil.' May Mama Lucy deliver yet another sturdy-strapper, Thibidioux." He enters the bedroom and kisses his wife. Everyone claps, hoots, stomps. Mama Lucy slips lithely past him and closes the door. Despite blindness, she knows every part of a room where she's delivering.

Lizzie, a glowing 17-year-old anxious for motherhood, is numb from Mama Lucy's birth delay potion, so the commotion isn't too annoying. Her blonde hair haloes the pillow. A thin sheet covers bulging belly and milk-full breasts. Mama Lucy swabs perspiration from Lizzie's forehead. She continues birthing preparations while devising a plan to right everything with the new day, and new omens midnight would bring.

That plan – it foments.

Mama Lucy is calm and calculating, despite sensing that the 13 conclavin' gators are utilizing Gone Luna for sinister purposes. After a having the day to decipher the omens, she's beginning to understand what King Creole plans: FOR SOME REASON, HE WANTS THE NEWBORN!

"13's wild" she chants. She encircles the bed with 13 pinches of fresh moss. Upon each, she places gator teeth and a marble-hard gator eye. It's a zone of safety, if only temporary. Only the most callous gator would traverse sacred ancestor parts. Yet even they would go slow.

With her back to Lizzie, Mama makes a swaddling of clothes. It *appears* to contain an infant. She hides it beneath the bed, next to a usually wall-mounted razor-sharp heirloom sword. It would be right where she needs it; where she could shout out its location to Bontez. Bontez could seize it and protect his wife and newborn if that time came, and, 'iffen the *fool* didn't still have buffonery constipatin' his notions.'

Midst the clamor of celebration, no Thibidioux notices the alligators approaching the cabin. Despite closed windows, Mama Lucy smells acrid hide, hears bellies brush spongy ground. She realizes King Creole at last has mustered courage in the others. The Thibidioux couldn't subdue their savage attack because the parlor's too crowded for their firearms or spears to be effective.

'So many'd die, in a battle try.' She decides not to tell what she senses.

'SUPERSTITION: That be my best heppin' weapon.' Her bare feet brush the sword as mentally she chants. 'Once within expert blades-man Bontez's sight; all gators 'a fright. Bontez you be the key. When time comes, that, must you see.'

Huey Long, alongside Baron Tail, creeps onto the front porch: Even at the battle's onset, Huey Long quietly lobbies – for King Creole's long-term plans. Liege Leather and Prince Ali position themselves at the back door. Only Creole knows, from previous exploration, the door is sealed. Son is in no danger. Liege Leather caresses the frightened Prince's claw, solacing the conflicted adolescent.

Gators station beneath partially curtained windows. Those that lean up can see sidewise, with one eye, into the cabin. Dark out; the Thibidioux cannot see them.

On the bayou, alligators could always smell gator gumbo wafting from cabins. Though the scent was a constant reminder of their nest-mates slaughter, they felt helpless to do anything about it. Now, seeing the walled snouts – of those once caressed, loved – resolve for battle, revenge, hardens. As Creole was certain it would.

Prime Snout is with King Creole at the bedroom window. When Creole looks in he sees the '*peeler*,' is missing from the wall. It was there all the other times he looked. He mentally registers this fact, in case something goes awry.

* * *

Rrrose Heather sweeps her hands in a grand flourish and opens an invisible curtain for James.

Behind it, you peek. "Tha's Thibidioux' cabin."

'Shh, Jamie. The gators might hear you. I'll whisper what next they plan.'

Your eyes widen. Creole is glaring in at pretty Lizzie. Midst Gone Luna's quilt of crazed hues, his eyes seem blood pools, redder than your jungle campfire. Rrrose drops the curtain. Reality returns. Rau and Rue approach. What is the strange thing they carry?

The '*CLANK*' of their chain stops. Turt realizes the brothers have put it down.

What takes its place?
Turt's seen it — the 'convincing apparatus' — everywhere in the Kasbah he traveled. (Turt ventures wherever rumors say another Trumpeter might be.) Many-the-time he's ensconced himself in isolated oases to rest. He's disturbed by caravans seeking a private place to convince the unwilling, to become, for whatever greedy two-leg reason, the 'willing'. Turt knows the ordeal Rau and Rue are preparing for him with it is meant to weaken him, to make the chaining easier.

He breathes meditatively, girding himself for the challenge. Reluctantly he begins moving away from James. He must confront the brothers alone.

* * *

Alligators await the unique sounds of human hatching '*SLAP*', as snout snapping onto goose. '*SQUEAL*', violent last honk. When they're certain the hatched is a '*he*'; no bull-gator at the onset of the 19th century will accept '*she*' as leader; Creole will growl to Prime Snout: 'BREAK THROUGH!'

Tails will shatter windows. Leather-armor-protected warriors will leap through shards. 'CABIN PENETRATED!' Valiantly, two-legs will guide elderly and young door-ward. They'll find Baron Tail growling, Huey Long, huffing-puffing-allibustering; his chicanery mesmerizing human as it does reptile.

It is meant to last just long enough to keep two-legs at bay, until King Creole can overcome old Mama. So easy that will be, he's convinced. He'll seize baby in snout, rush into, and disappear in Gone Luna chaos. Conclave will follow; no two-legs or gators hurt — for now.

* * *

"*No Rrrose Heather. Please, not the baby,*" *you cry in your thoughts, grasping her wrist.*

Turt wonders why James makes a mid air fist. 'As I must

steel myself for my challenge, so too, must you James, from the pangs of sadness. Trust that I will find the right adult for you. We may have to scour all Lindia, but I'll bring you to that he or she.'

You look skyward. "Can't Luny Mum help Mama Lucy?" You silently plead.

Rrrose wipes your tears. 'Luny Mum can't always be a interferrin' in our world, Jamie. That's not her way.' Rrrose whispers skyward. 'But Mum. That isn't always so, now is it?'

Rau and Rue set down on stones beside Turt. They put the two feet tall 'convincing apparatus' near Turt. Rubbery arm-like extensions, meant to suffocate, maybe strangle, brush Turt's shell. Turt breathes deep, calmly empties his multi-channel air pockets. He'll need better breath control than when he swims the deepest seas.

* * *

Mama Lucy feels Creole's stare through the window: 'Sees' his eyes now, as they were then, when he attacked her son – cold clay eyes, with ploughed-deep scratches seeming, perpetually, to bleed. Some in bayou say "...they dat way from ettin' humans." Mama Lucy, hankerin' to slay mood-of-gray, in self-console she always say "...it 'cause some-body saved 'emself, den away from Creole dey sails, after clawin' dem eyes with razor fingernails."

* * *

Your Rrrose Heather: always kind, ever-pragmatic.
'Jamie lad, I'm tellin' ya tales your loved ones taled you long ago. You just forgot. Not trying to scare, but if I do, maybe all-the-better.'

She takes your cheeks in warm hands. Emerald eyes tell you the importance of her words.

'This be a dangerous place, Jamie. To get where you need goin', a little fear'll keep you on the ready. I canna' advise of all the perils since I be city lass. I shan't always be around to help. You must rely on yourself, Lad, by creating your own defense. Turt and the butterflies, they be around to protect, but, many times, only the foundlin' can save his or her-self.'

You blink. Rrrose, suddenly, isn't there. You tense. Turt senses it. He winks – signal to other protectors. Lindian and North American butterflies flutter to your shoulders. The Lindian show tourists how to perform their continent's style of, ever-soft, relaxing massage on you.

You do remember – all Rrrose told – all these years later. It serves you well in the jungle of the business world; dispersing the 'Harrumph!' yes men who dispense useless advice. It served you even more, then, in the business of the jungle – to help you to survive. (Oh, for just another of those Lindian massages during one of those boh-ring meetings.)

* * *

TALE OF THE LONG-AGO WITCH HUNT

So many people disappear in the years after Mama Lucy's son is 'et. Hysteria follows. King Creole is too wily to appear the culprit. Mama Lucy's blamed. Wild accusations! "She hexes," they bellow. (Even isolated swamplands are possessed of their Reverend Ezekiah Bellowses.) "She conjures disappearances! She be jealous of other, FINE women, who have chillen' while no longer can she." A Thibidioux often stops midnight mobs from burning Mama as a sorceress.

Decades pass, and these dark times grow enlightened because of all her healing.

A PETITE LEGEND OF KING CREOLE OF PETITE BAYOU THIBIDIOUX

It begins with the devouring of Mama Lucy's son, well over 250 years before you are reading this book. It lives on to this day. Many say it is true, for they have seen 'IT' – a half-man – half-alligator as they have driven off Interstate 10, and continue south of New Orleans, traveling back roads where cabins, like those of the Thibidioux, once stood. Some are still there. Many say they have seen 'IT' in them- living as HUMAN, howling as BEAST.

'IT' has thick skin and ever-changing eye color. They change, legend says, because 'IT' has feasted on so many humans and absorbed the varieties of their eye pigments – indigo, amber, glistening teal, somber black. Even in these modern times when a human goes somewhere, never returns, this 'IT', said to know so much of human ways that it can't be killed, is accused.

(Oft-times I too, think I've seen 'IT', across the table in boardrooms, or slouching from podiums at seminars. 'ITS' fervent yowls of "... it's a no-brainer people,... it's a win-win situation people..." create zombie followers, 'done-deal' people that trudge forth and spread 'ITS' menacing plague of thought-free zones throughout the land. Oh, oh, oh how I could use a Lindian butterfly massage then.)

THE TALE OF LUCY AND HER SON, LUCIUS

That last day with Lucius Abel, so long ago, Mama re-lives, every day. It takes both King Creole and Big Ali, to pull the strapping 40 year-old from beside her in the wooden pirogue. She bats them with oars. Even in THEIR territory, muddy water, Lucius fights tirelessly. More gators torpedo toward the feast. Otter, beaver scatter. Midst hungered growls, Ali and Creole continually roll Lucius. They can't keep him down. Eyes of the three, they become one, to Mama Lucy.

Lucius breaks Big Ali's neck. King Creole is strongest. His ripping bites tear flesh. Blood spurts from former crib-mate. Mama Lucy sees only the deep turquoise of Lucius' eyes in Creole. Repeatedly she screams. No one hears her in this desolate section of the bayou.

From an isolated realm of her thoughts, never visited, emerges a calming silence. Hysteria vanishes, vision too. Skyward she blankly looks. "Goodbye Poppy Sol and Luny

Mum."

'Only, fare-thee-well, Mama,' celestial forces, in unison, assures.

All is dark. Just one thing she sees – her son's eyes – perpetual eyes. She sees them from his beginning to end.

"He has your eyes darlin' Lucy. We'll call him after you", young husband, now, so-long deceased, tells her.

She holds newborn tight. "And after you Abel. We be so happy – *dans notre paradis de jolie.*" Her man strokes her perspiring jet hair and she feels so proud –

A tiny fragile body has her life in him.

Then she sees Lucius Abel a boy; eyes gleaming excitement when he catches first catfish by hand...

...as groom, determined eyes set on beautiful bride and their new life...

...then as new fa, to a boy destined to be their only child – excited, nervous eyes...

...as his wife and teen-age son are pulled from him during the hurricane; cold, despairing eyes...

...as his eyes now go dim, as Creole pulls him under for the final time.

She sees the turquoise eyes again of the newborn she once so tightly held.

"Sleep tight *mon* chil'."

King Creole surfaces; looks up at her, taunting, 'C' est' la vie, Mama. Will you now curry your favor to your other son, the water dweller,' she imagines him saying. She sees nothing but her blood-son's eyes. For the rest of her life she sees those eyes in '*Cain*' Creole.

Bliss, a kind growing from brutal loss, one that never can be explained, overtakes her. She knows, never again can life be so cruel. Blazing hatred for her son's killer vanishes. She knows she can never harm King Creole because of those eyes. Somehow, in some enchanted unknowable way, beauty of son lives in beast. Those eyes would be envied, coveted, loathed, yet loved.

"Yes, *C'est' la vie*, Monsieur Creole; *mon ami* now rests in yer soul." She stares blindly at the eyes until, unnerved by her will, Creole looks and swims away.

From that time on among animals or humans, Mama Lucy will be the only one King Creole fears. Though he can kill her with one '*SNAP*', he can never conquer her will. It is built of love and is stronger than anything he can comprehend.

The moment Lucius Abel passed and Mama felt his spirit enter Creole's, to stay close to him she learned to sense and think as Creole. Each breath he exhaled she seemed to inhale, and nearly every of his thoughts, she intercepted.

Mama's and Creole's bond — forged through blood and time.

She only realizes, just now, these thoughts taking nearly three-quarters of a century to foment fully, that she alone can deal with the King.

Can't have Bontez present. His buffoonery might endanger all the Thibidioux. Instead, she'll utilize his absence to confuse Creole. No more time to dally. After tonight, there will be no stopping Creole. He, must she, destroy.

"Monsieur Bontez. I need you to hither froe, to Bayou Fontenot." Mama's chin is barely above his belt buckle. They stand at Lizzie's bed. "Bring to me fresh-hangin' moss. Layin' it on baby's chest after birthin ceases breathin' loss."

"Mama, that be hour there, and back. Whyn't I just gather some outside, *oui*."

"No argue, *merci*. Go, *tres joli*."

"I send couzan." Bontez looks to the thick oak door, anxiously, as if doing so would change Mama's mind. Fiddle screeches weedle through the skeleton keyhole. Lanterns on bedroom walls wiggle-waggle with the dancin'. Mama Lucy ignores his request.

Lizzie's smiling eyes dart between husband and midwife. She flinches. Labor starting? Something wrong? She says nothing, so strong her trust in Mama. Bontez doesn't notice. He focuses on Mama Lucy. Mama senses Lizzie's pain and knows her time nears. She strokes Lizzie's furrowing brow, and, glancing out the window, thinks, 'now Creole know it too'.

Bontez mimes bow over violin. "I must stay to musicate my chil'. My fa, fiddle me. His fa him, and his fa,... Can't count back how fa."

Mama Lucy seizes his arm. "You be back in a shake. By carryin' Font moss, into your warms hands, its oils bake. Baby gets all fa's strength transferrin' when I do the layin'. So strapper, if babe be a he, any bad come his way, then bad he be a slayin'." She busies re-arranging potion bottles on a bedside stand to mask her nervousness. "Bontez, don't you worry. Baby, hours away."

Bontez is too frazzled to notice – Mama's rhyming suddenly stops. All in bayou'd realize what he misses – "rhyme die when she go 'n try 'n sell a lie". Baby's really just 20-30 minutes away.

New-fa stubbornness. Bontez won't go.

A realization gels for Mama Lucy: Creole's decades of watching has led him to devise some macabre theory about garnering a newborn spirit, via beast instinct. She devises a way to stop him.

"Your granny's helped me deliver plenty, Bontez. Walk to Bayou Font will keep you fresh for when I need you most, afterward." Bontez still doesn't catch missed rhymes.

"I be fine, husband." Lizzie cups tiny hands on his.

He sees the softest of lines crinkle beside her eyes, kisses them.

"Do what Mama Lucy say, Bontez. She know best. She birthed me. And mon ma, and her ma...Can't count back how fa, ma. Don't forget, *merci*, whilst your granfas fiddlin, fiddlin, Mama Lucy deliverin, deliverin."

From outside the window King Creole watches the human tenderness. He'd felt the smiles that are on their faces now, on his snout, when Prince Ali hatched... That jittery first crawl. As

Ali grew – his feeble first attempts at diving, bumbling at stalking even tiny mice. King Creole had kept his claw on his gaitress's cold claw and tsk-tsked. The thought never touched Creole: 'Have I the right to strip from the two-legs their similar human moments.'

Losing eggs to natural predators and humans hardened Creole more than most alligators. Losing gaitress to a Thibidioux spear wrecked him. Other gators despised and forlorn-ed over losses, they knew it was part of the ruling 'way' – just as with those down ladder from them – fish, fowl, rodent. *C 'est la vie.*

Creole watches the two-leg mates put mouth to mouth then the male depart.

'Strange,' he considers. 'Most Thibidioux males stay for the hatchin.' He communicates to one of the birds around him extracting parasites from his hide that he can't reach. 'Follow him. Return with news of 'thundersticks' and 'peelers' he may be secretly gathering. Or if he is bringing other two-legs.' Bird flies.

Creole looks closer at the egged female. He remembers. 'She is of the Boullaire clan, from far off Bayou Boullaire. She is untouchable. Prime Snout, no that's not right, Baron Tail, yes it was Baron Tail who enjoyed her grandfa. Long 'afore she hatch.'

Only he, among conclave, realizes the fresh-hatch would be untouchable. He'd have to convince them at the bayou ceremony, 'a untouchable's not being slaughtered this night mon friends, only transformed.' Brute strength, the dominating rule at such moments: He'd not hesitate to use either.

After thirty minutes Mama Lucy opens the bedroom door, stomps her foot and shouts. "All Thibidioux – time to go." She ignores the confused protests.

Lizzie pleads, "I like the music."

"Hush awhile, chil'.

Bontez's granny approaches. Even she, Mama Lucy dismisses. "Thibidioux songs always a charm. But *this* birthin' –

just might harm."
Granny nods, yielding to experience.
Creole watches the celebration end. 'What is the cagey one up to?'
As the clan traipses out, the alligators slide unnoticed, beneath the porch.
Second part of Mama's plan complete: Purge the cabin to prevent a Thibidioux bloodbath.
"No matter what happen in next hour, Lizzie-chil', your babe'll be a lovely flower."
Lizzie perspires heavily. The potion's wearing off.
Just minutes til midnight. "Schedule just right. New day's magic in sight."
But Lizzie's ma and grandma had hard deliveries. Lizzie too? Mama Lucy stirs a canister of saskwood ointment. After birth, she'll apply it to Lizzie's privates to stop any bleeding. 'Apply it quick – 'afore Creole tries his tricks.'

Stage 3 of plan: When the baby arrives Mama Lucy will slip the he or she beneath the bed, then drench the pseudo-swaddle in mountain lion musk alligators so hate. This will give her precious moments until *fatal* – stage 4.
Lizzie screams. Parlor granfa clock begins gongs. "NOW! Push chil'. Harder than ever you imagined." To herself Mama says, 'Hold off til 12th toll. New day will allow a new soul.'

* * *

THE TALE OF THE LITTLE 'HUUKA' MAN

Rau strikes a match, igniting the contents of the crowned 'convincing apparatus'. It seems to come alive, a little man with head afire. Rue expertly, he's done it thousands of times, squelches the flame between thumb and finger. Strands of smoke-rise, curly hair blowing in a breeze.
James counts: '1, 2...6, 7...' Eight skinny rubber arms dangle from the little man's protruding water gut. Each arm

has a finger. Rau kisses one. *You see the smoky hair sucked down, through the glassy, foot-long neck. It billows and burbles in his belly. The little man belches, 'Huuka, Huuka.' You watch, amazed. Smoke blows from Rau's mouth. Rue kisses a finger, breathes deep, sighs. He grins and holds one of the fingers to your protector's beak-snout.*

Suddenly keen to Rrrose Heather's advice about being wary, you want to shout to your shelled protector, "Don't kiss it". You decide not to when protector glances over, seems to read your thoughts, signals quietly to you, 'shh', with ever-so-slight nod.

Turt had watched the little 'huuka' men of the Kasbah blowing their tops often enough. He knows how to handle this one. *You breathe the sweet smoke into the air pockets within your shell — so deeply, that Rau and Rue's amazement shows in their widening eyes. They offer you two more fingers. You accept, breathe in even deeper, maybe too much. 'HUUKA! HUUKA!' You're afraid the little man might split his gut. His glass belly erupts in a whirlpool of colors from the herbs, spices and flavorings the brothers have added. You lick your beak-snout. 'Sweet!'*

Molasses masks the hallucinogens they've mixed with the tobacco. Caviar is added bait.

Rau and Rue are connoisseurs of the little man. They usually relax with him after supper. Often they have turned his evils on travelers they think might take advantage of their hospitality, to rob, maybe slit their throats while they sleep. The brothers have spirited tobacco blends to fill the head, to disguise the drugs they use to incapacitate. They dose this giant creature four-fold.

"What wonderful paintings you carriage on your shell, big fella," compliments Rau as he pets Turt.

Rue pets. "Oh to meet the artist who did your carvings. The flow brings out, so strikingly, your sleek deportment."

'Fawning to get me to let down guard: Wasn't just born this century.' Turt feigns appreciation of the flattery by lowering his head. He's utilizing Ol Tom's standard dock tacking against catnappers. They'd tempt with fish to try and snatch and imprison him for months in dank hulls to catch rats. Ol Tom'd sidle dangerously close to slippery bait, snatch it, and flee free.

'Such tact shall work for me too. Theirs is the guard that will be lowered.'

Turt continually inhales smoke. He carefully filters it equally through his multiple pockets so the drugs affect is minimal.

Brothers puff cautiously and remain lucid. Yet, slowly, almost unnoticeably does this intense dosage begin affecting them, and, with Turt's own ruse, of using meditative deep breaths, they too, ever so subconsciously, breathe deeper. They become a little dizzy, sweaty.

Turt analyzes. Some of their ingredients are akin to ones he sniffed coming from Mama Lucy's cabin down bayou way when she conjured her magic. Before he got to know her and was invited in, he'd bank alongside Liege Leather. (This was long after the time of Creole's Gone Luna conclave.) Turt would listen to gatatarian philosophy.

'Sweet freedom, Turt *mon ami*. To find it, more importantly, to appreciate it, at any age, I believe is life's biggest...'

They'd breathe Mama Lucy's offerings and drift contentedly to their own visions of freedom. That long-gone time's discipline, of pacing life's exotic enjoyments, serves Turt well now.

Turt gets a tad woozy, but Rau and Rue become engulfed in the ever-tender kisses.

You are Rau. No, you are Rue. You enter the reverie of foundling imagination. The boy, the creature, they stare. You were always a plural 'you', individuals, separate as day and night. For the first time you are singular 'you'. You Rau, you Rue, sense yourselves as others see you. You despise that demeaning look that shouts: "FREAK!"

Nardesha steps from the wagon. You bow. "Goddess. How may we do your bidding?"

'With this experience, do you understand, my dear Rau and Rue? What is required of you?'

She taps bare foot, as matron at your orphanage did. Nardesha's are the most beautiful feet heavens or earths ever have seen. Long. Sleek. You kiss them. Soft. Sweet. They flow like rivers of wine — a thousand-fold more intoxicating than any huuka kiss. It is impossible to quench your thirst for Her wisdom and goodness.

You look up, yet you divert eyes. "Oh Goddess, tell us of what is required."

'I shall not. What you must discover: It is right before you.' With those simple words, she leaves, not to return to your wagon, but into the invisibility of air.

Carpier steps from the wagon. Into butterfly, Calico, of ruby, gold, silver. HE turns then flies to you. Your heads feel as if they spin. Now as butterfly SHE, she whispers to you. 'Homes you must make HOME. Families; FAMILY.'

"NO. They can never know of the others," you shout.

Calico flutters. 'You must. Nardesha demands it. So too, do your souls.'

You notice shelled creature taking his leave, and taking the boy. You must stop them. You can't rise.

Minutes, hours? Hours, minutes? You don't know which is which. Creature finds your chain and drags it onto himself as a necklace. So dazed are you, you can't stop the slow-moving creature. He appears even slower in your altered state.

Calico become Carpier again, vanishes. Butterflies painted on your wagon come alive. They leave with the North American butterflies. You hear their departing flutters, 'We shall show our visitors our favorite Lindian flowers.'

A new voice, one you've never before heard, whispers from the darkness. "Nardesha, Carpier, your butterfly-protectors; they all now travel with the shelled one and the boy."

You ignore the voice — sinister? laughing at you? — because the meaning of Carpier's message, it becomes clear: Your needs, desires can be easily fulfilled. You begin thinking, not as the deformed, ' you', as others see you, but as an individual Rau, individual Rue, always magnanimous in your concern for others. With the help of Nardesha's graces you are able to muster strength to rise, and stumble about putting food and water containers in a bag. You shuffle to the boy and shelled one before they go too far. Shelled one hisses, then realizes your gesture is in peace. He allows you to place the items atop him.

You return to the huuka man, change ingredient and light it. As you savor it — revelation. Yes! 'Make our houses, into, HOME.' Four families – ONE. *It will be difficult, but you are strong. A terror suddenly strikes you. 'Can it ever be? Are we too late in deciding to do it?'*

This thought comes to you, because, standing over you, staring down is...

...a CREATURE/BEAST three times your size.

You barely see a colossal, growling snout. Was his/its, the whispered voice from the darkness? If so, then he/it knows of the boy. Midst your fright, Nardesha's teachings magnify, are personalized. 'Do not think of yourselves now Rau, Rue. You have had good lives. Think of the boy. Is there some way you can sacrifice yourselves to he/it and save him?'

* * *

Granfa clock strikes 9, 10 11... From the bedroom comes a resounding, *'SLAPPP!'* The barely before midnight – *'GONG'* – cries of new life. Mama Lucy positions her back to the window, blocking Creole's view. She cuts and ties the umbilical cord. Creole tries to see the sex but the shifting shadows of Gone Luna make that impossible.

Mama Lucy strokes clean the infant's radiant skin. She's birthed so many while blind; by touch she knows instantly and precisely each, every look. She can't believe what she feels – the handsomest boy imaginable.

A score of the generations of fa Thibidioux's comeliest features intermingle with generations of the beauty of ma line: From arching, imperial Boullaird forehead to sharp, dominating, Thibidioux chin. Miniscule flaws of ma's and fa's are softened. They mould into an even more striking offspring: Calm, determined flush face, cheeks round, yet with square temples making his looks hail him as helmeted centurion. Mama Lucy feels the broadest of shoulders and steel chest with bellow-like lungs, yet producing quiet breaths, bunny soft. Gentle hands accentuate lean arms. Casually curved pink feet anchor sturdy and long trunk-like legs.

Lizzie's face is pale. Her hands tremble as she reaches for her son.

Mama Lucy, hating what she must do, clandestinely hides

the infant beneath the bed.

Creole is barely able to glimpse the hatchling, a male. He flicks snout in signal. Prime Snout smashes the window and they crawl through. The other gators besiege parlor. Mama Lucy douses pseudo-swaddle with the mountain lion scent and then heaves it. Prime Snout is fooled. He retreats. But Creole, slowly forward he *skanks*.[16]

Lizzie screams, drowning out the gurgles of her baby.

Parlor gators snout-butt and tail-slam the sturdy bedroom door, but can't budge it.

No time for Mama Lucy to apply the saskwood to Lizzie. Lizzie begins to bleed. Midst the turmoil, Mama Lucy doesn't realize it.

As Lizzie tries to rise, Mama Lucy prepares her plan's final stage, her exit – tossing herself into Creole's snapping snout. He'd be unable to stop his snap and he would violate the untouchable taboo. Gators would see her mangled body and halt his vicious scheme. 'Mother, child they be safe. I be permanently with mon son. I be there soon, Lucius Abel – soon's am able.'

Mama Lucy dives at the razor teeth. Creole's quicker than she imagined he could be. He bats her against a wall. "Give chil' Luny Mum's mojo eye power on this her supernatural night of Gone Luna..." Her chant fades as she drifts into a haze. Luny Mum-light glistens against the infant's eyes.

Creole approaches the wriggling hatchling. Animal respect for Gone Luna's power stops him from looking into the small eyes.

Hysterical, Lizzie shouts. "You won't take my baby." Movement causes hemorrhaging. She gropes for the sword, instead brushes her child's soft cheeks. Warmth of touch, of life only minutes before in her, fires her resolve to persist.

Creole snorts, ignores seemingly helpless mother. His stare rests greedily on the hatchling. The beauty Mama Lucy saw in the newborn, Creole witnesses through the eyes of his species:

---

[16] Cayan argot for a stalking gator.

TALES OF THE FICTION HOUSE

sleek legs to propel a dive, sinewy arms for swimming, steel-trap jaw, iron lungs. Creole nobly beholds himself transformed with this 'perfect' two-leg.

Pride swells from what you see next. Along the track of Gone Luna's beam the hatchling moves toward you, King Creole. Shakily he garners strength to choose – YOU.

Wait. Newborn two-legs can't crawl. Is this illusion brought on by Gone Luna fancy? Or, your foundling imagination? No! Gone Luna power must be giving him the ability, truly, to crawl. That is nature's way, so the strongest survive. Your adrenalin rushes, emanating chills from snout to tail, just as when Prince Ali hatched. Your leather hide crinkles from excitement.

It is the eyes. You muster courage to look into them. Gurgles whisper from the tiny mouth, but intense determined eyes speak thunder. 'Our desires are mutual, Creole, our destinies one. You must become I. I, you.'

Doubt again seizes you. Are the eyes, dark and secretive as night, just the innocent ones of all hatchlings. Or has Mama Lucy cast her spell through them so that even a hatchling two-leg may control you, the great Creole. You survey the ancient seer's withered body. To bolster your resolve you rationalize, 'only if conscious, can she mesmerize.'

The hatchling is ready for transformation, you assure yourself. All other concerns disappear. It is as if you are lying within the peaceful, easing mist of the bayou. Slowly you advance on the hatchling. You feel the moist, warm human breath against your snout.

* * *

HUMAN/BEAST leans over Rau and Rue. Barely can the brothers discern the shape of he/its snout midst the smoky huuka man. In their haze of imagination Rau and Rue feel he/its saber teeth. They're sure they'll be eaten because they're too lethargic – done in by the vices of their little man. They sing trance-like praises of Nardesha and try to believe: 'She will pull the he/it from the dark side into Her light.'

Vow after hazy penitent vow they make – 'if only She will pull them into Her light. Never again will we leave our families. Our wealth will be used for only good. The boy and shelled one – We'll see they make it to their destination.' *Such impossible promises you make to try to stay alive. Reality sets in – you will fight the HUMAN/BEAST. You will die, but, hopeful, so will he/it, and the boy and creature entourage will be safe.*

* * *

Love of her newborn son gives Lizzie strength to raise the sword when she grasps its handle. She thrusts.
 Prime Snout roars warning to King Creole. Creole looks up, sees his reflection in descending steel. Turning to escape, he upends the bed-stand. Mama Lucy's healing potions shatter to the floor. 'SSSLICE!" Peeler penetrates Creole's hide, slickly slicing off six inches of tail. Grayish, garish, gatorily fluids ooze from the stump.
 Who would think that its pungency would be that of sweet lavender and thyme?
 Creole bellows a heinous scream that makes the newborn recoil into a fetal ball. So loud a scream, coulda' been heard throughout the bayou for miles – if the cabin weren't built so tight. (New fa Bontez mighta heard, mighta hightail it back, saved the day for his Lizzie and their petite 'un.)
 The parlor's decorative wall-snouts begin to *'snap, snap, snap'* from the vibrating. Parlored gators cringe at the sound of gator misery in the other room, and at the sight of their ancestors seeming to come alive. Gator 'haints' seem to snarl at them, so they hightail on out. They rush to the bedroom window, where they look in to see their 'miserating' King.
 Prime Snout is clawing the sword away from the weakened mother. He flings it across the room. Gators watch, mystified as it, *'twangs'*, sticking into the wall. What gators call the 'PEELER', for the way it so slickly de-skins, is – kaput.
 Reality overshadows Creature reverie. 'No room to fail now. Failure will allow two-leg revenge. It would be swift, merciless. Two-legs would chant:' "THERE BE GATOR STEW FLOWIN' LIKE WATER FOR US NOW TIL THE END A TIME – WE GRR-RANTEE."

Prime Snout pins Lizzie to the bed. Over crawls Baron Tail. He '*snnaapps*' Lizzie once to the head, only to stun — she is untouchable. She goes limp. That is fortuitous, because being unconscious slows her hemorrhaging.

King Creole staves off his shock by dipping stump in the puddled potion.

Mama Lucy awakens, has a hazy sense of what is happening. 'I can save Lizzie if I apply the saskwood.' She tries to move. 'Yo ol bones tied in a, *not*, Mama.' She observes the horror as Creole's jaws scissor-open, inches from babe. She mumbles an incantation: "Give Thibidioux babe the power few humans possess — to control creatures — so he may again feel human caress".

Alligators enter the bedroom hesitantly when they see the hatchling is an untouchable. As with Creole, they believe Gone Luna enchantment allows his eyes speak to them, orders them.

'From this night forward, to I alone, must your obedience be reserved.'

'Surely no two-leg is more befitting the honor of transformation,' alligators rationalize. Hesitantly they put aside their taboo. For, none, before this moment, could ever fathom a two-leg hatchling controlling them. What they cannot comprehend, as Creole has but denies, is the possible hexing of the hatchling's eyes by cagey Mama Lucy, or a vexing, by the seeing-all Luny Mum.

The gators follow as Creole, gently cradling the precious hatchling within his open snout, exits the cabin.

* * *

You blink. Rrrose Heather's back, walking beside you and your shelled creature. Her footsteps are so light, so quiet against the forest's thatch floor; you'd hardly know she's there. Maybe she never left, and you only imagined she did. Doesn't matter. You're just glad she's always near. You ask, "Was it Mama Lucy's hex, or Luny Mum's vex, Rrrose Heather?"

'Next time I be talkin' to either I'll be suren' to ask. But, for now Jamie, let me be impartin' this bit of knowledge of the situation about creature and human nature. It'll serve ye well.'

Nardesha smiles from her heaven, a traveling heaven, traveling alongside James and his muse. Nardesha decides she has watched over them long enough. Her grace, her wisdom, comes through Rrrose Heather she sees, so she departs to assist others.

* * *

As caliph in his sharp-tooth palanquin, babe rides to his coronation. Forming corridor around gator procession to the bayou, emboldened by Gone Luna's magic, are hundreds of small critters, beaver, skunk, squirrel... Snorts, chirps, reveal heady feel of witnessing something never before known in creature or two-leg world:
'A two-leg will become one of us.'

Mama Lucy wills herself to rise. She staggers to the bed. From her apron pocket, she retrieves the saskwood ointment, gently applies it to Lizzie's privates, and chants healing incantations. The bleeding stops. "Sleep, chil'." She adjusts Lizzie's nightgown. Mama knows the name parents had picked for a boy – 'Bontez'. "But, Lazarus shall I call him, if back from bayou, miraculously he might swim." Struggling, she extracts sword from the wall. She's struck from behind.

It's Lizzie, grabbing Mama. New mother's protective instincts drive her. Convincing Lizzie to stay would be impossible. They lock arms, and, leaning on the other, they limp to the bayou. Lizzie takes the sword, angles it over her shoulder.

Alligators flank the muddy bank as Creole, newborn firm in his snout, swims to the ceremonial branch. Gone Luna forces agitate ghosts from the bayou bottom – baby gator skeletons, and bones of eaten two-legs. They float up – eerie icons for this most-unholy ceremony.

As two-leg priests with Eucharist he's observed through stained glass windows, Creole elevates his sacrifice. Luny Mum's glow encircles the newborn. Alligators bark-chant, 'Great Orb. Ordain our deed.' They stop abruptly and whisper when Mama Lucy and Lizzie arrive –

'She has the PEELER. Yet, IT reigns.'

Creole sets the newborn in the crook of the branch, and orders. 'HALT THEM!'

Small bayou critters rustle off. No alligators move. Untouchable two-legs, brave, though helpless amongst gators, are reminders of gator place in life's 'way.' They know they tread, too near to violating their taboo, or chancing a spell cast by Mama Lucy on they, or future offspring.

'I DEMAND YOU STOP THEM!' Creole snaps.

Lizzie enters the water.

Liege Leather is certain she'll be killed if she challenges Creole; and so would in this unique time, would too Mama Lucy. Liege Leather's too far away from Lizzie to stop her, so he hurries to Mama Lucy and clamps her foot with his massive claw while she's still on the bank. He knows he must preserve a truly good two-leg like Mama Lucy, even if it means her casting incantations to destroy him.

For the sake of peace, and survival of gators in the bayou, Liege Leather risks himself. He foresees what none other can – deadly battle twixt two-legs and beasts. If beasts triumph, Mama Lucy is their only hope as intermediary with far-away two-legs. They will arrive, and keep arriving, until they destroy all gators.

Lizzie wades through 'click-clacking', floating bones. She glares at Creole. He's so much stronger than she, but because of her humanness – so above him on the chain of the 'way' – he fears her.

'THEY KILL, EAT, EVEN DECORATE WITH US,' Creole rants seeking the conclave's approval for what he's about to do.

'That is the 'way,' Liege Leather roars. 'We are all, even

them, a part. That cannot be changed Lord King Creole. You must accept it – once and for all.'
'NEVER!'
Lizzie nears Creole. She reaches for her son.
Determined to carry out transformation, Creole turns quickly to seize the precious babe. He slips, knocking him into the water. He's sinking.
Lizzie releases the sword, dives. Luny Mum reflects into the water – to aid mother's search.
Mama Lucy's cannot pull free from from Liege Leather. "Call off this insanity!"
Gone again is her need for rhyming, not only for now, forever. She's reliving the day Creole ate Lucius Abel, and Lucius's eyes first resided in Creole's. She's realizing – that unending day of pain, lasting decades, finally would end. "Rhyming salve. No longer I gotta have. Only concern. Savin' newborn."
Liege Leather holds Mama tight, but now, with reluctance. Lizzie emerges, clutching her gagging infant to her bosom. As Mama Lucy 'sees' from the shore, she senses the bravest of acts. With one hand, Lizzie raises infant above her head, just away from Creole's ratcheting snout. With other she forms fist, rams it at his nostrils. Dozens of finger bones *'crackle'*. No cry, or grimace from Lizzie.
Creole is briefly stunned. Mother and son gain a temporary reprieve.
Luny Mum churns the bayou. The floating bones of creature and human kin cry out as they scrape against one another – an unending concertina scream.
Mum blocks what next comes – by pulling dark clouds to shroud her view.
Lizzie does not feel the single, violent – 'CHOMP!'
No alligator looks away. Sudden disgust, at what they've allowed, binds them to the carnage.
Luny Mum slips back the curtain when the baby squeals. She illuminates him so, that he glows. His heart beats so hard it pounds the water where his dying mother dropped him. He

pushes at her blood. It coats his face crimson. It seems to give him strength to float, to glare, defying the jaws readying to encompass him. Eyes, beautiful bluish-black, seize King Creole's muddy grays.

Creole blinks, revealing the doubt and fear that trembles from the deepest of his animal nature. 'Can it truly be? Can even a two-leg hatchling be superior to the greatest alligator to ever conquer a bayou?'

The magic of Gone Luna makes time on the bayou – STOP – for all – creatures, human and animal.

THE TALE OF THE SPAWN

Though less than an hour old, you know who you are:
The newness of Bontez and Lizzie Thibidioux. You will be called Bontez.

This, you know, because you heard ma and fa say it many times while still residing within the darkness of the warm, secure, bayou within her.

Floating now in similar warmth, but insecure, you know your time so far, barely an hour, has been unnatural and disorder.

Never has a newness even closely lived it.

The gentle females' soft voices told you, while you swam in the bayou of your ma, of the loveliness you would soon encounter.

The strange men with deep voices patted her belly and told you of the grand, good life you had ahead: That, all of it, would be yours.

OH, NO. NOT FOR YOU, you now know. You are as the helpless foundling. You will need to seize all of life you can just to survive.

The seconds ago, that ma disappeared forever from your touch; they pass quickly for adult humans. But for a newness, they are, aside from a few seconds of caressing, all you know of that supposed 'loveliness' of which the females gentled. Already, all the un-loveliness moulds into your being as you float in her redness.

If you live for five more seconds, minutes, or if are lucky enough to live hours, all of this time you shall dominate this un-loveliness that never were you told of.

THIS, YOU SWEAR!

***

The look of the hatchling's eyes changes, enrages, Creole. They burn, brand him, '*destroyer of untouchable.*' Their power over him will be impossible to overcome, Creole realizes. He must kill again, now, to begin transformation. He must make those eyes part of him to be able to control them.

Creole ignores the glare of the conclave. The gators seem comatose, unable to act.

What Liege Leather sees seems to incapacitate him, as no circus cruelty could. Letting loose of Mama Lucy is the only act of gatatarianism possible to him. Gatatarian way, he chooses.

Mama Lucy 'feels' the sword's cool as it penetrates through the water. As she wades toward it she senses King Creole lift the newborn by the head and start to...MADNESS!

The glow of Gone Luna sky suddenly fills with thousands of colors: Millions of butterflies descend. They quilt the bayou with their gentleness. Conclave is stilled, astounded by these newcomers. They hover above Creole. Flutters beckon him to halt his vile act.

***

"Is Luny Mum comin' down to help the infant, Rrrose Heather?" James asks. "Is she pretendin' to be all those butterflies? Like the real ones who help me?" Two butterflies flit by James' ear. Away they whisk a wee bee about to sting.

'Aye. Luny Mum might well be doin' it, Lad. You do the decidin'. After all, this be your tale. I be just the reminder of. Just remember this: No one can explain the 'WAY' of a butterfly's kindnesses. It be one of life's great mysteries.'

Turt looks back at James and sees worry, *scrunch*-lines, around his eyes. 'Stay strong James.'

***

The butterflies? They who led Mama Lucy to floppin'

TALES OF THE FICTION HOUSE

foundlin' gator, Creole, so long ago? Long ago Creole forgot their kindnesses.

Tears streak Prince Ali's snout as he watches his father ignore the flutterers. 'You can still change, father. Stop your cruelty.'

Huey Long grinds back a snicker. No matter the outcome, oh what a tale he'd have to spin. No need to embellish; be the tale 'a his career.

Bayou waters stir. Luny Mum interfering? Sloshing water seems to be a voice emanating from the sky. 'Ye killed the mater. Cannot kill the son.'

Some in conclave heed the great orb. 'She is right, King,' they scream. Even Huey Long joins, but he's seeing opportunities for the future. All of the conclave are swayed by the elevated emotions and now join, 'Cannot kill son.' Jaws snap water as they crawl toward their King.

'Rebellion,' Creole is convinced. 'Deed must be completed quickly.'

Nightmarish cries knife coldly through the bayou as he mangles the infant. 'Not a killing of an untouchable,' he whines to his minions. 'A transforming. To something better. Now begins our entwined destiny.'

Mama Lucy rages, "YOU SHAN'T KILL HIM CREOLE!" She finds the sword and lunges at him.

Butterfly curtain blocks Creole so he can't see Mama Lucy and flail her with infant-full snout.

'*SSSSS*' peeler sings mid air. "THUNK!" It penetrates Creole's neck.

'*SSSSS*' – penetrates deep, as if Luny Mum releases all her pull so centenarian widow may conquer the strongest of males.

Mama decapitates her *swamp son*. Head, '*plops*' into the water. Jaw locks, snaring babe. His cries blend with Creole's final echoed growls of, '*Great Spirit, transform your servant.*'

Gators can't tell, 'are the pleas Creole's or those of the hatchling?'

This is *the* fated moment in the world of alligator; the time they believe – 'TRANSFORMATION', it has occurred. 'Will it help or hinder us with the two-legs?'

Tree critters peak from behind Spanish moss, consider, 'A new regime?'

Mama Lucy pries at the floating snout, but cannot remove the infant's body.

Alligators encircle her. 'Does assassination of the King cancel her 'untouchable' state?'

Prince Ali approaches Mama Lucy. He offers his tail. She takes it. Others back away – maybe from respect for their former King's son.

As Ali glides her to shore Mama's barely able to stroke the small torso through Creole's teeth. She feels gentle lung thrusts of the blood-coated infant: ALIVE! She crawls onto the bank and pleads. "For the sake of all animal and human caring, help me. Nary a one of your hatchlings did I harm when my own son 'et. Give this youngen' the same respect I've always gave yours."

To whom, for gators to look? Glances move quickly past Prince Ali. Some rest on Liege Leather. Others find the always-calculating Huey Long. Guilt, at their indecisiveness.

Prince Ali approaches Mama Lucy. He signals Baron Tail and Prime Snout, with determined eye motions, to follow. They honor son of revered leader, sensing the same power of son as in father. This is the first time it has shown. Baron Tail and Prime Snout take the sides of King Creole's snout, *'PULL!'*

Crimson coated baby rolls into Mama Lucy's arms. Head-to-feet, his one side is gouged, distorted beyond any recognizing he is human. Other side, the one resided safely *between* Creole's teeth rows, is unscathed. Mama Lucy quickly applies a sweet-smelling poultice as she addresses new King, Ali. "Enough killed already, *mon ami*. How long it to take 'fore we live in peace. Let this be its beginning."

'Yes, yes,' Liege Leather agrees in sincere growl.

'Indeed, YES,' Huey Long angles. 'I will aid new King as I did old.' Midst tragedy's haze and Gone Luna swirl, the others briefly forget Long's spiel-binding ways, and they nod agreement.

Mama Lucy warms baby against breast and carries him to the cabin. Conclave pulls Lizzie's body to shore then carries her on their backs to the porch. Each knows, for better or for worse, 'this night will be talked of for centuries.'

Luny Mum stares confidently from her celestial throne. 'Mama Lucy has ways to save the child.'

Huey Long allibusters continuously, 'Creole lives in the child. One day he will reclaim HIS kingdom.' True or tale? Doesn't matter. It is what Huey Long will make certain the alligators believe. His future scheming depends on it.

Prine Ali returns alone to the remains of his fa. He hugs trunk and head, then claws soft soil and buries him. He surveys the bayou beauty that creature and two-leg share. He would never have offspring to enjoy it, but he could assure that others would. He chants a prayer to his gator ancestors, and asks their forgiveness for fa's violation of the taboo. Ali'll not deny duty. His self-less act of appeasing the code would be the healing agent all bayou dwellers could look to, and see how to live in harmony. This is his dream.

He props 'peeler', point up, against a stump, positions himself above it, falls. No gator near the cabin hears the 'SLICE!' through leather hide. His act will be talked of – 'one of honor' – first by Liege Leather, then, others of the conclave, and for generations as centuries pass. It will be the inspiration, which finally, brings gators and two-legs of the bayou together – in peace – in the early decades of the 21st century.

But, now, as the 19th is beginning, gator conclave imagines that Creole lives in the hatchling. News of it will spread quickly in their world. 'HE is our leader. Our wise ones will instruct him in alligator ways when the time is right. He may live the way of the two-leg. By night he will be ours to mould.'

Mama Lucy – her son's eyes resided in Creole long enough for her to 'see' these gator thoughts. Even stranger than their thoughts, is what Mama's thinking, 'Gotta go along – for the sake of future bayou peace. My Lazarus Bontez must be one who is of two worlds – creature and human world.'

As surrogate ma she'd instill humanness into him. Liege Leather could instill a gatatarian way. 'Peace be the reward,' she hopes. 'No other choice. I must go along, or they will seize him for themselves, alone. Leastwise this 'way' there will be some human influence.'

* * *

James cries, "Poor Prince Ali. And baby Lazarus Bontez. How sad. But he still has his fa and Mama Lucy, to raise him, right Rrrose Heather?"

'Someone else be better equipped to tell you about that,' says Rrrose Heather.

COMES JAMES' SECOND MUSE

Her gait kinda' shuffley, but pace spry as in her 90s, Mama Lucy emerges from a chestnut grove. 'Why hello Rrrose Heather.'

'Ello, Mama Lucy.'

Turt looks about and, for a moment, thinks he hears a soft Cayenne cadence. He sniffs, remembers-senses pungent swamp roots brewing. When he visited Liege Leather, they used to luxuriate in the delicate scent as it wafted from the potion woman's cabin. He knows she's here. 'Hiya Mama.' He senses a pat to his head.

Mama studies James' eyes. 'I know our Turt's young rider. Spittin' image of his great-great granfa'.

"Who?" James asks. "People keep talkin 'bout people I don't know, but like I should."

Mama touches Rrrose Heather's cheek. 'So young we both were when we met. You sproutin' from your teens, me, just seedin' into my teen hundreds. But your beauty, Rrrose, forever blossoms.' Rrrose smile is a fragrant blush. Mama turns to James.

'Rrrose Heather used to come see me, all the way over from New Orleans on healin' endeavors – one of her ladies maybe havin' a might problem. Enuf' 'bout ol times. I hear James, you be askin' a heap 'a questions. I figure I'd take a little vacation from Leeziaan' paradise and travel over and do some answerin'.

"Baby Bontez bring bayou peace? Bayou folk and gators keep from eatin' the other for the babe's sake?" James anxiously shout-asks.

Mama Lucy nods. 'Holt on, and you'll do some findin' out. I'll spiel exactly how it came to be that he grew to be the 'Laza Bones'. Thousand times worse than King Creole despite all I, and Liege Leather, did tryen' to prevent it. Your great-great grandfa the Carper put 'im in his place many the time, but the name I gave, 'Lazarus,' – more true a name never could one such as he a have – 'e just keep comin' back from 'is grave. 'E even traipsed here to Lindia once, trailen' the Carper, but the Carper was wise enough to give 'im the slip and traipse back home to tell the tale.'

Puzzled, James asks, "Why'd Carper come all the way here?"

'For what better reason? To find Carpier, a foundlin's patron saint, and Nardesha, a foundlin's Goddess. Only natural for him. I 'xpect you'll find em too.'

James' comfort at that thought turns to shivers because – he looks around quickly – he's imagining what the person/creature Lazarus Bontez Thibidioux might have grown to become, and, could he/it could still be, Laza Bones-'n-it, around here. Ugly and handsome visions appear, evaporate in his thoughts. Only one seems to last – Bontez as a sweet and innocent baby.

"So be he gator, Mama Lucy? Person? Both?"

'Most important thing to know, ya must keep a keen eye for his ilk, the Laza Boneses' 'a this world. No matter what corner 'a this woods, bayou or city you turn onto.'

Turt's remembering, 'Ahh! Crayfish by the dozen Mama tossed me when I swum to visit.'

"What bout his fa, Mama?" James asks.

'Poor young fool fa couldn't take losin' hizzen's Lizzie and 'e traipsed into the bayou and never seen again. Some says e's... oh never mind that James...'

Somethun' even more hideous musta' been his fate, James figures. Hmm!

To Turt, Mama Lucy says to change topics, 'You grew. Cayenne cuisine musta' agreed with you.' She sees the carving Thibidioux scratched into his shell, points at it. 'Fortune. That's what Laza Bones savored.'

James looks over his shoulder. Something/someone moves fast. 'Maybe Laza Bones not so lazy today, follow Mama over from the swamp,' James thinks, heeding both Rrrose Heather's and Mama Lucy's admonition to be continually wary. 'Maybe the, he/it never could snatch the Carper, so maybe he's out for me.'

The four move slowly through the woods: the muses, boy, and critter. Mama does some taling, and then Rrrose does, then James. Turt trumpets. 'It's a nice parade,' Turt thinks. But he's wary. He knows someone/something is near. He senses the, he/it.

CHAPTER 13

"I do believe his species must have an extra sinus cavity. That would make the reverberations for the trumpeting possible." – Charles Darwin, one fine day aboard HMS Beagle, prodding Turt's nostrils with a dip pen and nearing, oh, so close, to getting his right hand nabbed.

* * *

1826

The Cincinnati wharf-shack sways in a light breeze. Close your eyes, you'll think you're drifting out to sea. But Carper's are open and he glares at Laza Bones' wanted poster and Laza Bones glares back. Carper asks Mariner as they eat upon tabletop Turt. "The sweet little baby Bontez really grew up to be that – 'thing'?"
"Yessuh, he did."
Laza Bones 'grrrs,' at Carper, pulls out 'trusty blaubuster' and shoots. 'BAM! BAM!' Flouted barrel smokes. Wharf-shack rattles. Carper ducks. Projectiles '*ziinngg*' off Turt's shell, ricochet with a '*tiinngg*' off wall-leaning Harpoon, deflects straight at Ol Tom, who leaps, 'MEE-OWW-OWW-OWW,'

straight up from Mariner's shoulder.

Mariner just keeps chowin' chowder and talin' tales and explorin' Turt's tattoos.

Turt, he's really only yawning.

Ol Tom, just napping.

"The whoppers we conjure up in our imaginin,' eh Carper," Mariner says. "They make for some right good tellin 'bout to others. Bet yer imaginin' a whale-of-a-tale now."

Carper glances at the poster, board-stiff.

The gunfire is real. It's outside. Old Cincinnati's tower bells begin tolling midnight. People are whooping, shouting, running wildly about.

'AHEM! AHEM!' Thibidioux's alive again and he's prying into the worlds of others. Slyly he grins at Carper. 'After hearin' mah story, dontcha' feels sorry fer me, boy?'

Carper thinks he sees the evil sneer of King Creole on Thibidioux's face. 'Not one bit, Laza Bones. Don't know how you got how you did. Only knows you did. N, that's that. I'll jus be like the Mariner, and ignores yer hair-trigger ways.' Carper refreezes him, and, with little boy impetuousness, glances out the wharf-shack's porthole and becomes transfixed by the doins'.

"Nuf a my jaw-jackin, Laddie," Mariner says. 'Good, the boy's seein' more than what's right in front of 'ims.' He scratches chin stubble. "This tiny ship's not big enough to net in all your thoughts and dreams, hmm Carper."

Carper gazes out the round, 19th century version of a television to the world. Turt joins, then Ol Tom awakens and with his Cyclops eye, he does too. "Well all right," Mariner says, rising to pull a raggedy curtain as if pushing an off button. It barely closes and they continue peeking out. Mariner strokes Carper's hair, pats the nape of Turt's ropey neck, then tickles Ol Tom.

"All that hoopin', hollerin'. It's turned Independence Day, Carper. Country's independence as well as yourens'. Probably the first one you'll remember. What say we make it real tootin' special. Takin' a part in it. Not just watchin'. Yes-sir-ree! 1826

America. This great lands a' enterin' its second 50 years and two of its great makers are still 'akicken: Tom Jeffers... and Johnny Adams."

Mariner takes a wooden crate from his sea trunk. He tosses a glob of matches atop the conical and stick-like contents. "China-man gave me these when I docked Singapore. We'll light up the Cincinnati sky right well to celebrate." He picks up tiny American flags mounted on pencil-like sticks. "I got it Carper. What this stodgy ol city needs is a parade. We four 'll start it. The gaul-dondest' a parades."

That captures Carper, Tom, and Turt's spirit. Carper observes the old salt. Aglow like crystal are his eyes, showing his excitement. It's worth more than any gold.

"Blow the horns and git set. The si-reen, she's abeckonin'. Time to hoist anchor."

Turt trumpets. Ol Tom mews, and Carper claps hands as a seal he'd once seen in pictures.

"All aboard," Mariner orders. Ol Tom leaps on his shoulder. Mariner lifts Carper to his other shoulder then climbs atop Turt. He leans the fireworks crate between his legs and the back of Turt's head. Turt exits the shack and trumpets shrilly, excitedly down the pier then soon, onto a street. Ol Tom screeches as torturously as he would if he were perched on a fence wailing to virginal felines.

Carper sings made-up songs with words he'd heard Mariner say. "America, America, Tom Jeffers and Johnny Adams. America, America. Yessirree we're still a tootin' and akicken'. 50 years and for always."

Crowds gather along wooden sidewalks. They cheer the motley paraders.

You see their faces. They glisten in the streetlamps' glitter and look wondrous with joy. And they are looking at you. Smiling. You know, by a fresh, new, and keen instinct, that you are bringing them this joy. It makes you, the floundering Carper, happy.

Mariner lights fireworks then holds them above his head for launch. *'POW!'* Earth is stinking sulfur smoke, but the sky explodes into a glittering bouquet of red, white, and blue.

You feel more and more of your sorrowful pain slipping, disappearing, into the colors. You hear a soft voice that comes from amongst them. 'Bonnie boy – live forever with this joy you now feel.' Embers from the wilting colors seem soft fingers, wiping your tears of joy.
  More sky bouquets. Onlookers line up behind your fours' parade. Hootin', hollerin', shootin',and fireworkin' continue on down the street. The crowd joins in your child's simple ditty. "America, America, Tom Jeffers, Johnny Adams..."
  You learn from this that if you speak, people will listen to you – enjoy what you have to say.

And, on this day, little does Carper realize – BORN, is a showman.

CONTRAST: Carper's father, Reverend Ezekiah Bellows, in his room – alone, despairing.

The parade, introducing boy to world, exhilarates Mariner. He has chosen so much joy in a life that began so ill fated, yet he considers this his happiest time. Boy seems to have made ancient, young again. Mariner's hopin' he can teach every of life's lessons he's learned, to him.

Ol Tom ignores the fal-de-ral. He's had a lifetime of cheering crowds among the swabbies, every time he's cleared a pack of rats from a ship. Warm milk, an albacore head, and a soft warm feline brought on deck at the next port are the rewards he's craved.

Turt cranes his neck high like a ship's mast. He's the vessel, sailing his friends through an ocean of people. Today, much as for the Carper, this is the beginning of a new life for Turt. The joy he found in old friend Kunta, then in Mariner and Carper, is now suddenly emanating from all those surrounding them. Decades of hatred of two-legs melts away. He suddenly realizes – it seems so simple now – all he has to do is to just let the hatred go, loosen fin-claw and SWOOSH! Forever, his burden – banished.

He blares out his pride of being a trumpeting creature, louder than ever.

As he does, the crowd's cheers for he and his mates, boom.

"INDEPENDENCE FOR ALL."

Turt makes his vow this day – to forever care for the Carper, and for those he cares.

Cincinnati's first annual Fourth of July parade begins with these four – unlikelys. The country will remember the half-centennial – bitter sweetly. On this day, the country-makers Tom and Johnny will die within hours of one another. Cincy will remember it for the shelled ship, its stooped, ancient Mariner captaining it with his one-eyed first mate and the little singing boson.

When the city celebrates the centennial 50 years hence, every blauhard 'tween ages of 15 and 60 will have stories to tell how they or relative rode along. In 100 years, giant floating balloons and wheeled floats will depict Turt, Carper, Mariner, and Ol Tom in the first parade. In 150, at the Bicentennial, Presidents, future Presidents, and also-rans will be seen buttonholing voters – claiming Tom, Johnny and the original 4 paraders all would have supported them.

Turt will be at each of these events – watching from the Ohio River, maybe a secluded park, or, quite conspicuous in the crowds' midst – though quite invisible midst the hundreds of concrete or styrofoam Turt replicas. He always returns. He will be at the next you can bet.

With this first parade Carper's reputation as fixture on the streets and piers of Cincinnati – it is set. No more is he a 'bastaad son-of-a nickel-a-night whure', but, friend to nearly all, with words for them that are listened-to, revered, because he'll have gleaned wisdom at the pulpit of the Mariner.

"This parade, she's far from over. So don't be a leavin' yet," shouts Mariner.

You smile. So do all the parade watchers, who've become paraders.

VALHALLA CALLS

Mariner's exploding fireworks jolt Reverend Ezekiah Bellows from his delirium. His room, candle-flicker dim, *illuminates.* Gunpowder smoke filters in. A hellish sweat, saturating clothes, possessing Ezekiah's body for the past 24 hours, now seems ice; bed, a morgue stone.

"Satan's beckoning brimstone YOU send, Lord. What is your want? Blood?" Ezekiah shudders from the damning words. He offers apology-deal. "I shall accept unconditionally YOUR dictate." He foresees grand martyrdom. "I shall be eternally with Bonnie in the lush, rolling paradise that is Your Valhalla. I'll hear her voice in the flowing waters of the Ohio there; and feel her touch in the breeze rustling through the leaves of the Buckeyes."

Dark decision is set. The exploding brightness of the outdoor's hope cannot dissuade.

He lights a wall-mounted oil lamp, dons jacket, clerics collar, pointed black riding boots. Stored in the corner is his saddle. From around its brass horn, he removes precious lariat he did rope tricks with while preaching-entertaining his congregation...

...Lariat, lifeline to his precious Jesus, ceremonially he would unwind it from a cross at Sunday service. His thundering pulpit voice: "The Lord sayeth, and I beg His liberty to paraphrase. Think of life's road as this rope – atwisten', aturnin', arisen' up to smack ya down. Trust in HIM to keep you safe. Amen Brothers, Sisters."

"AMEN Reverend," his congregation fervently echoes.

"Trust in your Dear Precious Jesus to keep you traveling straight." Ezekiah is an un-curtained puppeteer with dancing fingers. He mesmerizes with body as well as prop. He does loop-de-loops, high-low spins, whooping jumps through the hoops he creates. His boots click the floor.

(If anyone ever saw father-son, together, they'd know Carper's showmanship – it's inherited.)

The congregation's boys and men stare at the snaking jute. Reverend's mischievous eyes charm prettily dressed girls. But, ah the women, single and married, they're entranced by his pelvic gyrations. Only a few matrons feign to recoil, but even they re-visit their youth as everyone springs from pews.

Reverie sweeps the church.

Cincinnati of 1826 is a hotbed to early abolitionism. In a few years, it would attract Reverend Lyman Beecher, his young daughter Harriet and anti-slavery Quakers. Yet now, only Ezekiah Bellows allows free-borns, escaped slaves posing as bought-free, or any man, woman, child with dark skin, to attend one of the city's 'BIG SIX' congregations. Cautiously, many line rear pews. Some settle throughout the cavernous cathedral. Despite this, 'forced integration', as some members claim, collection baskets overflow. The church expands with newcomers, and is biggest of the 'BIG SIX'.

Ezekiah's idyllic youth in Valhalla had taught him to love all, especially the ancient Negro cowboy who taught him the ropes. He was more a father than was his own. Whenever Ezekiah *performs*, he tears, imagining his long-deceased mentor watching him.

Ezekiah says to himself as thoughts return to his room's unbearable solitude. 'It was so easy to get them to follow like cattle after I roped them into the pews.' He regrets his only contrived 'trick', using a series of hidden pulleys, and sometimes a hidden hired helper, to enable him to seem to climb a rigid rope to Heaven. His mentor would have said, "You don't need gimmicks, Ezekiah." Ezekiah was to-bound by his audiences' adulation to stop.

"DAMN THE PRIDE!" He clenches lariat so tight his fingers pale. "Now all those Sundays are gone, GOD, they are gone." He blinks hard, obliterates the mental vision of his gospel rodeo.

He holds King James while noosing lariat and tossing it over a rafter. He places a chair below the hanging halo. Opposing thoughts battle: 'It is sin. No, release.' He washes face in a porcelain basin, lathers, shaves. He presses the straightedge to his throat as he stares at the lined reflection in the mirror. Hands shake. "Is this the way, God?"

A *'THUD'* startles him. He turns. Lariat lay on floor as if it had undone itself to deliver a message, 'NO Ezekiah!' to partner-in-showmanship. Ezekiah weaves this scenario in his haze, instead of blaming rodents, a breeze, or a slipped knot.

There's a break in the crash of parade fireworks outside.

When Ezekiah shouts, "COWARD, DELAY NO MORE", an alley dog, so frightened by the shrillness of the tone, howls, and runs.

Meticulously, as when he wrote sermons, then choreographed the tricks to enhance them, Ezekiah surveys the room, 'So many tools for self-destruction. Boxed rat poison in the desk.' "Slow and torturous is what I deserve." Wash basin. He imagines his head, immersed. "Cleanse my sins." Hunting rifle atop saddlebag. "Deliver myself to Satan as a true showman, with explosion and blood. This way God? That way God?" He asks-demands. "NO! Not even my noose-halo, where my angel might appear, pity me, and lift me to You.

"GOD DAMNS ME FOREVER. FOR NOT CORRALLING MY CATTLE IN THE STREETS TO STOP THE KILLING STAMPEDE!"

Ezekiah combs hair, lifts lariat, stiff, reluctant, thinks of Daniel in den, David against Goliath. Never would he have their courage.

The moment seems eternity. He rewinds lariat and slips it and only one other possession, King James, into his saddlebag. Even in death, he would choose the coward's way, he tells himself. The road to Valhalla is twisting, rocky and perilous with robbers this time of night. He would let either fate or a stranger make the decision. Fate would be in God's hands.

He exits the backdoor with the prized gear. In the stable, he prays yet shrewdly bargains as he saddles steed, "In six hours it will be daylight, Dear Precious. Take me as I journey, or provide a sign that I deserve a new life Valhalla may offer."

HORSE SENSE

Ezekiah had wanted to call his new ride, Jesus, to honor his savior. He considered how some might think it disrespectful to their Christ. So, ten years earlier, Ezekiah as a divinity school new graduate names the lanky, doe-eyed colt, Dear Precious.

Anxious looks embrace when they meet; jittery first-time lovers. Both know instantly – horse sense-human sense – an irreplaceable lifetime companion is present. Dear Precious grows, into a fleet-hoofed equine, 30 hands high. Intense eyes change from curious shades of blue to gray. Ezekiah, while entranced in daily prayer, curries Dear Precious and sees God's universe in those eyes. For years, as a circuit-riding preacher, Ezekiah gads him to tiny churches in isolated hill encampments, and north, along Ohio River border towns. As the night sky, coat is shiny black. Bursts of silver, streak mane, and tail, and appear blazing comets whenever Ezekiah sprints him in the moonlight. Thighs emblazon with a series of vanilla dollops that curve to fetlock and gaskin, looking like the BIG DIPPER, with the NORTH STAR as the brightest spot.[17]

Ride, rider, each learn nuances of the others thoughts and movements. If human and creature could speak to one another, three little words, "Precious Dear Friend", are all, they need utter.

As Ol Tom rides Mariner's shoulder in the parade, he spies Spanish Red, a retired galleon cat now on permanent shore leave. Ruddy-furred Red is busy avoiding the tromping of the two-leg crowd as he lurches for dropped food. Tom's mew is unwavering, direct. 'Get to the stable, Senor. Tell Dear Precious: The padre's parade is passing him by.'' Spanish Red knows all the poop-and-scoop, knows Tom's meaning, doesn't mind doing a favor for the one of the wharf called '*el gato de patron*.' Red wrinkles whiskers and shortcuts over buildings.

TALE OF TOM'S PASSION

Ol Tom is on the windowsill many-a-night when Ezekiah is with the Carper's mother. He knows Carper is the son. Though, Ezekiah sometimes threw a shoe in a fit of temper to

---

[17] "Follow the star, north." Those serendipitous markings are savior-like – near-legend on the slave underground railroad that leads to freedom. "Follow the star. Even on clouded nights, trail Dear Precious."

'scat' him, Carper's mother later 'niced', with warm milk. Tom doesn't care about aiding the shoe thrower, but, so deeply he desires son know a father – no matter how misguided a 'shoo-er' he is.

Tom's thoughts most-always are on his dozens of sons. From A to X, never once has he forgotten a name:

Alvin Alley, his lithely pirouetting dancer; Scrotum-draggin, Bogie, with the humped part; Then there's girlish-soft Stray Ray and his gorilla-ish protector-littermate, Manx Kong.

Tom feels cat pride that from blocks away he distinguishes each ones individual scent and senses their mood by how they crook a hind leg. He comforts them with licks-a-love, but scratches them near hairless as a 'damnable, pampered Abyssinian,' if they don't copycat HIS feline fatherhood ways. He considers the *shoo-er*. 'I'll help look after son til you're ready to be a father. But by your God do it soon or it will be too late for you both.'

Tom hacks: 'Two-legs. Can't handle even a single.'

Parade moves on, at Turt's pace. Some high-haired, come-hither-gowned whures join, moseying the barely-lit streets beside precinct captains they just paid off.

"Air is quite fresh tonight," one of the ladies comments. "That must mean the churchers, for the evenin' 'ave retreated to their smelly *p-u's* of self righteousness."

Leathered dockworkers file behind, singing the seafarer's anthem. "Find me a restin' place for me salty dog, and I'll shows ya a wavin' sea bed." Blimey the Limey, who has a royal blue chameleon riding atop his sailor cap, cajoles in crass cockney. "Come all ye coppers, whures, and harem-minders, les' all pop in a chorus. Aye, finds me a restin' place..." His chameleon turns the gray of Ol Tom and bows to *'gato patron'*.

Ol Tom nods, considers Dear Precious' aliken' for Bellows. 'No accounting for what draws a critter to a two-leg: Or, two-leg to two-leg. He winks his good eye at Mariner and Carper.

Spanish Red relayed all to Dear Precious and then scatted from stable when Ezekiah entered.

Ezekiah strokes horse's neck. For a moment, looking into Dear Precious' eyes, he feels a burning to live. Dear Precious whinnies to him. 'Endure Ezekiah.'

That flame flickers as Ezekiah fastens saddle and laments. "You know the way, Dear Precious. Guide me." He is too dazed to know if he talks to his dear equine or his dear Jesus.

He mounts, rides, and *thinks* he travels down sleepy Canal Way. Instead, Dear Precious gallops onto Hell Street, a quick throughway but one Ezekiah always avoids – all that gambling, liquor, debauchery midst ramshackle storefronts. Both routes lead to Valhalla.

Steed avoids Satan potholes.

Rider cares not that pace is unsafe. He wants only to be, away.

Time becomes Ride's opponent as his taut legs sail. The minutes on Hell seem hours.

The duo is halted – suddenly, by the four-headed parade float. Dear Precious rears up. Ezekiah tightens reins. Despite the pandemonium of the parade, he masterfully controls steed. But, who controls whom?

"Heeya! Getty-up Dear" Ezekiah bellows, no care for events or people around him.

For the first time since they've been together, Dear Precious refuses an order. 'Look at them, Ezekiah. That's why we came this way.' Dear Precious answers Ol Tom's mew-ful greeting with a hoof, '*CLOMP!*' Often he would daze pesky stable mice, makin' pickens easier for Tom. Horse and cat know each other from 'sway-back': Tom would rest on the arc of Dear Precious' back; knead claws, to relieve Dear Precious' soreness from galloping, then curl, and *'purr'* furiously – a vibrating feline massage.

Now, horse blusters to cat, 'you can lead a man to his son, but you can't make him love.'

'If any creature, you can, Dear Precious.'

"Heeya!" No movement. Ezekiah lightens reins. For whatever reason Ride has, Rider knows there is no budging until the way is clear.

Forget it 'Ez; this is Hell Street. (Just let the devilment pass.)

Ezekiah surveys the group: No one from church. No one he recognizes. High on his horse – above them all. He glances at the motley float. Seven eyes burn into his, seeming to beckon, "Join us, Sir". Wetness wells in Ezekiah's eyes as he feels their joy. 'Is this heaven beckoning, or yet another Hell Street temptation?'

Emotions urge, 'Ezekiah, go to them,' but calculating thoughts tether him to stirrups. 'The netherworld is often disguised in such temptation. Just look at Rrrose Heather's. No, do not think about that place. Do not think anything about Bonnie beautiful. It hurts so.' So, Ezekiah only watches stern-faced the frivolity beneath him.

"Heeya!" Prompting fails. Fireworks illuminate Carper's profile. Ezekiah sees Bonnie in him, her smooth cheeks he stroked, brooding eyes beckoning, "come", same dark hair, small but distinct nose, pike chin. Time, for Ezekiah, stops.

To Ride, his Rider seems eerily still. Bedeviled? Like equine of the wild? Dear Precious wishes he can explode the creature-human tower of Babel and say,

"Ezekiah, you are no bad man. I have been trying to train you all these years. All animals change – if only you would have seen Turt over the years. He would have soon bit off the hand of a two-leg as shake it. See the once curmudgeon's joy in humans now. You too can find that contentment, Ezekiah. Start with your son. Let us trot right to them and join the parade. Pull the reins, dear friend. Guide us there."

TALE OF TWO HARRIETS

Dear Charles,

So sad I felt watching that happy shell-float parade. Papa had come to talk to Reverend Ezekiah Bellows

about bringing his ministry here to Cincinnati.[18]
I squeezed Papa's hand when I heard a '*SLAP*'.
It seemed loud as the fireworks –
– A few feet away, probably heeded by only me, a little Negro girl, hit across the back of her neck so hard she lurched forward. I was so terrified, Charles. I stood stiff. I was ashamed of doing nothing to assist her. I cried for weeks. I didn't believe such brutality could exist. If only...I had tried to help her. If only.

Obscure six-year old Harriet Ross – later famously known as Harriet Tubman, was dreamily studying the North Star on Dear Precious' flank, knowing well its meaning, freedom, independence, when *that* '**SLAP**', and then a shout came, "You stupid Minta. Pay attention to biz-ness." The craggy-faced Mrs. Crook, a potter selling her goods, growls at her, "We travel dumb Minta. I've had hires before. I knows what you're thinking. Even try and run and the daylights'll be beat outta ya." (Oh, she will run – over and again, taking a whole peoples' with her.)

* * *

For what is eternity for both, son surveys father, and father, son. Parade, people, animal. All disappear. Only artery-pulsing strings of bloodline exist, as tempered steel, fusing them.

You study the lines on the man's face. Blink. They are gone and he is you. You run hands over your face. You feel those lines. If you looked in a mirror, you know you'd see him. Why?

Man-boy are bound by some thing, some sense unknown – a thing-sense even the most profound centenarian sage as a Mama Lucy can not explain; or scientist Darwin decode; or gatatarian Liege Leather, catatarian Ol Tom, insectatarian Calico can rapture. It's complicated as the universe, yet, simple, as Ol Tom's lick-a-love.

---

[18] "Reverend Bellows looked a shell of a man," Lyman Beecher would later be quoted in the Cincinnati Opine. "It made me unduly suspicious – wrongly so, I must now admit – of the abolition movement. It made me postpone my eventual move to Cincinnati."

Carper is too young to understand what the stern-face man means to him. *Can he see anything of his sad-lost world in you?*

Who can understand a four-year old mind, or what a foundling's imagination conjures?

A few feet away from Mariner's shoulder where Carper rides, father rides Dear Precious. It would take only seconds for Ezekiah to sidle over, lean, take Carper and ride triumphant midst the explosions, the prideful glow of Luny Mum, and the knowing clatter-cheer of critters. Poor Ezekiah, if he were in a right mind, not one hardened by narrow ones of some of his congregation – he's a fool who believes his own bile – he might realize he sees mother in son, and not just an imagined apparition.

'Reach over, damn you, *shoo'er.*' Ol Tom reaches out in beckon, his claws curled safely in. 'Lick him away, slickly.'

'It is up to you now, Ezekiah. Go to him,' whinnies Dear Precious.

Mariner ignites the final rocket. Its red glare and tremor – **'BOOM'** – break Ezekiah's trance. Dear Precious rears up. Ezekiah leans forward. "Hold true my Dear." When Dear Precious settles, Ezekiah reins to ride.

Steed jerks neck. 'Look Ezekiah. See yourself before you, before it is too late.'

TALE OF RAPTURE

Smoke clears, Ezekiah sees himself at the boy's age, nearly naked in only underpants for swimsuit, on a years-ago, halcyon summer day. Belly-down, he looks at his reflection in Valhalla Lake: He remembers the blushing complexion and cherub eyes that he sees in the boy now; feels again the sunray baptism washing over him, then.

A voice. That of his, forever-at-pulpit, fossil parson. "Travel always in the joyful light of your Jesus."

Ezekiah the young is ferried away by a team of white stallions, upward, into chariot-shape clouds. It would become a forever ride from Valhalla toward his Savior.

Tears streak young Ezekiah's cheeks. He runs to the peaceful church, a stucco fairytale cottage with thatch roof and cedar steeple. It seems to float on swaying bluegrass in a calm glen. Inside, he kneels, prays.

If the church hadn't burned, and the parson killed the night of Rrrose Heather's fire, adult Ezekiah could take this boy there. Ezekiah tells himself, 'Make no excuses, Ezekiah. Ferry him away. 'Save him and you'll save yourself.'

* * *

In the Lindian Woods: "Did he steal the boy from Mariner?" James anxiously asks Rrrose.

'I did some wee glancin' Mariner's way, that night, Lad. I could see right off he could see resemblance 'tween fa and son. Mariner grasped the Carper tight. Oh, Mariner'd give him up; if that be what Rider truly wanted. Alas, it be not. You'll understand it all one day.' Rrrose winks coyly. 'Ah 'twas a lovely parade Jamie. I, walking wi' me girls, feathers perked high in our hats. So proud we were, bein' accepted by the, 'fine citizenry', for at least one night. I looked over at your great-great grandfa Carper, and...'

"WHO?"

'...and was hopin' he'd be rememberin' me. He smiled. For those few moments, Jamie, I wishen best for the two of 'em – wee son and high-mighty fa. But I be desiren' it for Mariner too. Everyone, the happy-ever after. But no siree Jamie, I was not goin' put in my two cents worth, and maybe be ruinin' their chances for all times by my forcing. Understand, Jamie? Life sometimes must be takin' its own course.'

* * *

One of Rrrose's girls, a bosomy firebrand with blazing strawberry hair and matching dress, leaves the parade crowd. She approaches Ezekiah. She wags her finger. "Reverend! Don'tcha dare leave. NOT til you've taken responsibility for what you caused."

Memories of the riot return. His face pales. Dear Precious looks sideways, sees Ezekiah's look and whimpers. Ol Tom mews a screech of fright because he too sees. Creatures relate their mutual forlorn and exasperation. 'We tried. Too late for fa. Not for son.' Ezekiah, mortally fearing his hell-presence, reins to ride back to heaven-remembered past. Dear Precious obliges, and in anger gallops toward Valhalla.

Mariner spits on the street, disgusted by the preacher's choice.

THE TALE OF CARPER'S WOE

Carper had seen the rider once before, when Carper peeked out from his room at Rrrose Heather's. The rider, sneaking through the frilly corridors, wore his same look of sad-lost. Ezekiah's eyes dart – afraid of being 'found out'. Something *'thumps'*. Eyes freeze, as a deer in bright lights. Carper had wanted to take the man's hand, and tell him as his mother did with him, "Don't worry, frightened little Deer. All will be right." He couldn't then, and can't now, because, quickly as then, the man disappears. The two, blood bound, never touched, never loved the other. That look, sad-lost, emblazons on Carper's thoughts.

Carper shivers. Mariner discards the fireworks crate, takes Carper onto his lap, and hugs him. Ol Tom coils onto Carper and purrs. Turt marches parade onward. Carper, so steeped in this new stage of life, when the smallest impression shapes a child's nature, begins to, unaware of it, make choices that would guide his life: The first; always staying close to his odd, little, now-family.

Rider's tormented face, turned blissful by memories of Valhalla youth, Carper will remember always. That look of joy, brief, but Carper imagines it to be a joy forever, and he will possess that impression of possible-happiness, always. It will take seed in his thoughts. Ponderings will soften it; striving for it will crack germinate it. With Mariner, Turt, and Ol Tom to cultivate, it will grow mightily, rooting deeply into his humanity. Joy will flourish. New seeds falling from gripping branches, he will sow them for all those around him to cultivate for themselves or, to, just enjoy.

A father's hard-paid-for legacy is passed-on, reaped, unbeknownst.

Strawberry whure pinches Carper's cheek. "You takes care a 'im, you'se 'ears me, Mariner," she says, then pinches Mariner's cheek.

Mariner clicks tongue like the maitre d' at the fine Parisian restaurant where once he splurged. "Moi foine liedy. Only the best for young masta." He returns tweak – to 'er bottom.

"Ooh!" She glance him down, up. 'Hmm! Maybe there's still a lick a salt in the old sea dog. But soak 'im in the river for a few days first.' Her thoughts shift covetously to the boy, but she feels Rrrose Heather's stare – 'whurehouse be no place for him, now, what with mater no more.'

Strawberry kisses boy. Hat feathers tickle his forehead. He smiles, stroking her cheek, finding joy in her sweet smell and bright hair, and a mischievous joy in her jiggling walk. Carper pets Tom, hums along with Turt's trumpeting, gently mimics bawdy tune Mariner lambastes. Carper smiles broadly and begins waving at the crowd.

Carper has discovered what so many others like his father never can in a lifetime: Simply, enjoy.

"Come up see me when yer older, young masta," says strawberry, mid-jiggle. Watching intently, as does Mariner, Carper smiles a widely upturned smile – fa's smile of long ago.

* * *

"So the odd little family lived, ever-aft-ily, happy, Rrrose Heather."

'We'll see, Jamie. After all, who in this world can know only joy?'

"Maybe it be the Carper, Rrrose Heather. Maybe he'll be the first."

Re-appearing from the woods – Mama Lucy. 'Not if Laza Bones can help it, dear chil.'

CHAPTER 14

REVELATIONS 6:18
OMINOUS PORTENT

The road to Valhalla snakes dangerously close to the Ohio River. Sudden current changes strand rowdy catfish on the bank. Listen, you'll hear their slapping- smushing slow-to-hop toads. Frog societal shame – of being waylaid by bottom feeders – is heightened by fear that French trappers will render them into spindly pate-de-fra-frog. Either scenario, their screeching croaks, along with the road's many hazards, often spooks the most seasoned horse and rider.

Nothing detracts Dear Precious tonight. Bucked to full gallop, never has Ezekiah ridden him so hard, and there are three hours more to go.

You vow not to participate in Ezekiah's desire for self-demission. You don't throw him, even when prickly cockleburs you brush against lodge beneath bridle. You crane neck, deflecting low-hanging branches. Thoughts focus on keeping rider's rear in gear, soles in stirrups, and galloping.

After you deliver him safely home, Valhalla's sweet waters you will swill; on its blue-hued grass, you will graze; and to purge the incessant dust you cannot avoid snorting, its moist air of daybreak you will breathe.

Dear Precious is confident he can outrun the rides of highwaymen. But he, or any equine of superior lineage, cannot outdistance the mythical pursuers advancing on Ezekiah Bellows' sanity. For that, it would take Olympus-bound Pegasus, or the spirits of the Valkyrie winging to their own Valhalla.

Except for the fish flopping, frog freaking and Frenchmen fricasseeing childhood ditties in warped Englais-Francais accents, "sacre bleua, more fine leapins for grog grau and fondue..." the only sound Dear Precious hears is his horseshoes' thuds against flint-hard tips of buried, traffic-worn boulders:

They spark – beacons for Ezekiah's pursuers, whom near, ever closer. Their 'rides' burning snorts torch the nape of Ezekiah's neck. His hairline beads sweat. Unseen riders drumbeat-out their demands within Ezekiah's thoughts, *'forfeit your soul.'*

Leaning forward, Ezekiah pleads, "Faster, Dear Precious." To his other DEAR PRECIOUS, "Deliver me!" Ezekiah knows just two options: Reach Valhalla, or perish.

Apparitions, in unison, *'It is time.'*

So steeped in the Revelations of King James, Ezekiah knows his pursuers. He looks and affirms; the skeleton riders of the Apocalypse: 'WAR' on blood-red steed; emaciated 'FAMINE' riding black; crowned 'CONQUEST' upon white; 'DEATH', shrouded in night's shadow astride pale. Ezekiah doesn't know if he is being chased, or has already departed the human realm and now rides with them.

Dear Precious leaps a pothole.

Ezekiah pictures the horsemen's skulls, teeming with worms that spew the dust, 'thou shall returneth'. "Why" he pleads to his DEAR PRECIOUS, "must YOU visit upon me all the miseries of mankind? Is it a test to enter YOUR kingdom?" He vows, 'If it takes eternity I shall pass it.'

Ezekiah imagines pale's rider swipes at him with his sickle. To avoid the blade he bows neck and utilizes trick rides. Grasping the saddlehorn he kicks away stirrups. He becomes a pendulum, swinging freely above Dear Precious. He feels vain pride that he is becoming adept at riding as roping so he stops, kneels on saddleback, and clasps hands as penitent. Two trappers see the trick riding-praying mad man chased by no one. Dear Precious is barely visible. His comet markings glow, and, combining with the ladling action of the Big Dipper that comes with each stride, it appears Ezekiah rides the darkness between comet and stars. The trappers throw their bottle of wine into the Ohio, vowing never again to imbibe; to go back to France, to guillotines, anarchy and other insanities, but at least ones they comprehend.

Dear Precious slides on a patch of goose eggs dropped from a wagon a day earlier. Ezekiah's nearly thrown. Dear Precious prevents it. He skids, at peril of breaking legs, before regaining balance. Ezekiah slams back into saddle. Groin gripping torment: grimacing face shows penance-pain. "Again, God's wrath?" The scream-like shout of contrition makes Dear Precious flinch. He '*NEIGHHS*'.

Ezekiah musters courage to glance one of the riders. Dagger green eyes: They mesmerize. Ezekiah can't look away. Its barnacle-pocked snout-like mouth spits bile at him. It is 'WAR', armor-shelled Turt, brandishing a sword in massive fin-claw. Turt trumpets heinously as he swirls the sword. The creature Ezekiah saw in the parade is in a fit of temper so outrageous that Ezekiah knows the rage would disappear only after blood spills: His own – the blood of retribution for sinning ways. Ezekiah stands on saddle, jumps over sword swipes.

Turt falls back and as Ezekiah sits – one at a time – the other horsemen approach, screeching in tongues Ezekiah cannot understand. He knows they must be castigating him, damning him to share their misery. The dark side of his nature assures he is right.

They push their faces beside his. Sickle-wielding 'DEATH' is Mariner. His sour breath reeks as he mouths incomprehensible words. Then, replacing him, 'FAMINE,' is Ol Tom, his one good eye, a peering mojo, pagan evil to the

Reverend. Claws are ten times their normal length, and they are stanchions swiping at him.

Finally, 'CONQUEST,' on white, is the boy, Carper. Messenger mirroring Ezekiah's joy-filled youth? Offering him the power to subdue his inner demons? No.

Ezekiah imagines he slings arrows. If only Ezekiah might let the glowing side of his nature overcome dark, he could understand, and instantly change the evils of WAR, FAMINE, DEATH, CONQUEST, back to the at-peace, beckoning him, parade faces.

He avoids perceived volley of boy-CONQUEST'S arrows, by utilizing his slyest trick. He kicks loose of a stirrup. With boot entrenched in other, propels himself, and while grasping saddle straps, slides until he's upside-down, against the horse's belly.

Ezekiah would have stayed in that dusty, thudding seclusion but in Luny Mum's glimmer, he spies a coiled rattler ahead in the road. Fleet-handedly he climbs to the saddle as Dear Precious, nonchalant in full stride, twists hoof and kicks fanged-one into the river.

Ezekiah turns – now only three riders. The boy? Suddenly he wants to see his chasteness as it was in the parade. The looks of the others emblazon his thoughts. He knows that if he truly examines their faces, as if they are their souls, he would know it is not the apocalypse pursuing, but the beckoning of human compassion.

Heat lightning flashes. Ezekiah looks ahead. Boy on horse is before him. Light emanates from the saddle, the same light Ezekiah saw as a youth coming from the sky to fetch him in its chariot cloud. "Can it be, Dear Precious? Is white ride my DEAR PRECIOUS, my savior? Will HE lead me to the Valhalla of my salvation?"

A thundering 'CLAP' vibrates through the cloudless sky. Dear Precious *'neigh-screams'*, and then tumbles forward. Ezekiah is thrown, and lands twenty feet away on the muddy bank, atop a bottom-feeder, a croaker, and a two-legger depositing the critters into a sack.

"Sacrebleu," shouts the trapper, squirming free. He forfeits loot, scurries to canoe, and paddles off. Critters skitter to their river sanctuary.

Dear Precious lies still. Ezekiah runs to hug his neck. "What has my heartlessness wrought?" The rigid steel of a rifle pushes at Ezekiah's head. He hears a man say to another. "You were supposed to kill the rider. Only value to us was the ride, idiot. Now we lost both it and the poachins' we'd'a got from the Frenchie."

In the darkness, no one sees your eyes open, close quickly. The projectile nicked your hide. You see the location of the two-legs. Just get a tad closer to my rear hooves, boys.'

Ezekiah leans protectively over Dear Precious. He's beseeching his DEAR PRECIOUS, to spare Dear Precious, when the loquacious of the highwaymen yanks him.

"Rise off the knees preacher. That's it. Now keep those hands snug in *amens.* And high up. So it'll be easier for yer Maker to latch onsta' you after I blaus' one sizeable hole tween yer gullet and gizzard." The jocular wrungs out terbaccy juice from his vermin-infested beard. A foot-long, it looks like rodents could take up residence any day.

His hairless, blank-faced partner, a post of a man, as dumb, scarfs saddlebag and searches fer 'vallerbulls'. He pats Ezekiah and holds out coins. Ezekiah is barely able to see Jocular and the Silent, despite Luny Mum's glint of interest. He smells them. Pigs. Their clothes look like they make a habit of slop-wallerin'.

"Either they don't pay you goody types enough or yer a sly one who hides the widder and uurphun' collection at some bank we tain't had fortune to come across." Jocular jabs rifle into Ezekiah's kidneys for a couple go-rounds.

Ezekiah doubles over, wheezes "DEAR PRECIOUS save these sinners."

Jocular pulls him upright. Ezekiah's sight focuses up, into darkness. Silent glimpses the preacher's eyes. They seem dead. He feels he is beside a ghost. He trembles. He wants it gone. Violence often is an opiate for simpletons, diabolique savants, or just the average blow. He clouts Ezekiah with the rifle butt. Ezekiah falls. Blood oozes from the inch-long gouge on his neck. Toothless Silent smiles: He's staved off his spook.

Jocular keeps 'aspoutin. "Ya see Rev, we businessmen need to show gain for a night's work. Goddam. Cain't rightly stay operatin' off our good looks; 'les we branch into whuren. Don't spose you got tips on that line, though."

Silent makes a sound – a hyena laugh. Dear Precious, fights off a twitch from its shrillness, is able to stay possum.

"So Rev, you gotta prod and duce some commerce to go 'longsides yer non-payin prayin', or we'll have to reduce inventory by one bullet."

Silent slams Ezekiah down.

One cheek riding the trail, 'tother, cragged inward by the push of Jocular's rifle, Ezekiah is forced to speak in almost gibberish. "Gost' only mu' DEA' PRESSUS' faith. Looks like you done kilt mu' 'tuther Dea' Pressus'."

"Now Rev. You may'ent have vallerbuls, but there's a thung ya jus might be afloatin in. That bein', information. You get me?" Jocular eases back the barrel.

"What point are you driving at, good Sir?"

"Good Suh! 'Taint that a good one." Dried mud drops from Jocular's sleeve as he curtsies feminine-like. Silent, hyennas out laughs.

You tense; waiting the moment the two-legs drift near your hind hooves. 'Just trundle on over. You'll get a nice surprise.' You flex legs.

"Point bein', Rev. Is you one of – 'Em?"

Ez inadvertently slips into pulpit tone used to render sinners contrite. "Sir? One of WHAT?"

Jocular rams barrel back to Ezekiah's cheek. "Don't you sass Rev. You can sass the devil, you can sass the demons that ride with 'im. But they ain't nothin' compared to me. So don't you sass 'a me. You know exactly what I mean, Rev. A negra lover. We're bountayin' for runaways. Word has it some a youren preacher ilks a-been-a-helpin-ems. Now there's been one particular buck been leadin' em. Biggest, meanest about these parts. 'N he don't like no white men, I hear. Sake a savin' yer skin from him out here, behoove you tell whats you know."

Ezekiah thinks he's seen the man: Standing in the rear of church, head nearly to the bottom of balcony one Sunday, when a family of raggedy Negroes first appeared. He must have guided them. Ezekiah always remembered him because he was watching more intently than anyone ever had before, his rope sermon. "May know of him. He's a free man, it's said."

"That don't keep certain parties from offerin' a hefty scratch."

"I tell nothing."

You don't know if it's bluff when you hear the braying two-leg's hard, cold blasting stick make an echoing 'CLICK'. Luny Mum helps you see it by quickly glinting against its shininess. You won't chance waiting longer. You hope your hooves are close enough. Swiftly you arc hind legs toward faces. 'THUCK!' You feel soft jaw melt into iron shoe, and repeated 'CRACKLE' – dozens of breaking mouth bones. Silent's moans are oddly pleasurable to your horse sense.

Kick renders Silent airborne. But Jocular, planted firm, shifts upper body. Hoof misses his head and whizzes past.

Jocular keeps his gun on Ezekiah. Ezekiah smiles for the first time in two days, thanking his DEAR PRECIOUS for saving Dear Precious.

In a swift move, taking barely seconds, horse is on all fours ready to rare up and come down on the two-leg. But Jocular's reflexes are quick as his mouth, and biceps strong from robbin' and rampagin' as jaw muscles are from flexin' and flappin'. He grabs horse's reins, harnesses him downward and to one place, so that he can buck out his hind legs but not lift front.

Dear Precious knows the raring-up is useless. It might cause the pig-man to pull the trigger. Quivering, he settles, hoping a new tack awaits for him to render into bacon, the oinking pig.

Jocular's too cunning. The opportunity wouldn't arrive.

Glancing at the landed and now sprawled Silent, Jocular mumbles. "Why do I always pick the dumb ones?" He ponders how to utilize the preacher's pride of horse to his favor. "Feisty stallion Rev, but back to the business of the feisty buck.

You give me the skinny on him, and you get you and yer Deah' Precious' freedom."

DEAR PRECIOUS spurning temptation on Gethsemane: Its inspiration purifies Ezekiah. "I love all men. All are equal." Guilt. 'Why couldn't I have lived those words?' The sense, that probably he will die causes, as a reason unknown as sudden shift of a polar axis, a desire in Ezekiah to live. The yearning for death, midst its imminence, dies.

In living, can he make up for what he allowed happen to Bonnie and the others? It is all a fog of thoughts not quite clear, but yes, living is suddenly even more than a desire. It is need. Yet... this gun points at his head, and now, ironically, he isn't afraid of death as during the last two days when he strove for it.

Somehow, miraculously, maybe because of his prayer for Silent as Silent jettisoned, Ezekiah rationalizes – Silent rises. He looks even more pig; face red sausage, jaw, a dangling snout.

Silent tells hisself he warn't yet licked. He staggers back to the group. He kicks equine's flank. '*CRUNCH!*' Dear Precious doesn't flinch. '*Snaps*', emanate from boot. Silent yanks it off. Throatily he '*oinks*', drops. Shattered bones pierce foot and he wallers in spurting blood.

"Durn idiot. Don't go hurtin what'll be my new ride if the Rev don't come clean. Now git up. Stand guard." He pays Silent no more attention. "It's simple Rev. All ya gotta do is tell the route the buck uses to bring 'em all north."

Ezekiah knows about the 'LINE'. He's heard whispered stories of it from his Negro parishioners, some who've taken it to Cincinnati. Circuit riding the Kentucky side he'd seen too many captured runaways who'd been maimed by 'massahs' with whips, axes, and branding irons. He'll not worry for Dear Precious because he is to 'vallerbul' an equine for them to kill.

Ezekiah's glare locks Jocular's eyes. "I will tell nothing."

Jocular pokes the rifle at him – funnin', plentiful time to work on this 'un. A little body grindin', cuttin', and thought bendin' always greases the skids for squealers. He's certain the preacher's no exception. "Best I jest kill ya now and get to breakin' yer stallion to fit my needs. And if he can't come around, look for him to be joinen' you right soon."

Ezekiah looks skyward. 'Thank you DEAR PRECIOUS for giving me strength to find your way. Though your light shines to me late, I thank YOU for the short time it's mine.' Ezekiah closes eyes; prepares to die. 'Let him be kind to Dear Precious. Give Dear Precious strength if he isn't.' Before he can continue, and ask forgiveness for his tormentors – GUNSHOTS!

Jocular jerks the rifle from Ezekiah's cheek, points it in a half-dozen places, blasting into where it seems the shots come. Silent joins, haphazardly firing as, about, he stumbles.

Experience from rope-ruse Sunday services tells Ezekiah he has in the dark a helper, as sometimes he had assistance with the truly impossible rope trick.

The hidden helper in woods, magically, no, divinely Ezekiah wants to believe, seems many places at once. Ezekiah rolls away from Jocular. As Jocular's attention diverts, his hold on the reins loosen. Dear Precious gallops off. What Ezekiah sees next no one could ever believe, even his parishioners who had seen his 'impossible' trick. Ezekiah doesn't want to believe, yet, here he lay in darkness and is glimpsing it in Luny Mum's glint.

A TALE OF A MUM-LIT NIGHT

'I be tellin ya, Poppy Sol – if you could of been out last night, you'd 'a witnessed magic churned real. From nowhere that rope streaks in, straight as yer rays. Hundred meters long, if it be a meter, I tells ya. It dances hither, thither, before wrappin' 'round the Jocular's belly, not two, three, but FOUR times. Spins 'ims like a top it did. Squeezed every last word from 'ims. Then, after e's done 'im in, rope, 'e, hops, skips right over to the Silent and – PIP – snaps Ims neck, then, just dances ballerina-like back to the woods – bowing all the way. Magic! The likes I never seen, I tells ya Poppy.'

Passengers on the deck of a steamboat puffing the Ohio squint, try to see the melee's outcome. Ashore, Ezekiah is too weak from Jocular and Silent's beating to rise, to protect himself from the shooter/rope-master-magician if he is foe not friend.

Lumbering from the woods, rope coiled around shoulder: a six and a half tall Negro. He wears starch-stiff canvas shirt and tooled leather chaps that declare his artistic bent. He prods with metal-tipped boot, the pigs, both, now Silents. Cowboy, to corpses: "I guess you fellows were asking of me. Here I am, and nice to have made your acquaintance." He gives them no more attention, but gently pets Dear Precious when Dear Precious saunters back.

Ezekiah sees the man's face, lineless, unworried, unlike his own, a face of one not more than ten years older than he is. Curl-brimmed cowboy hat barely contains full, tightly kinked hair, jet, nary an indication of ever graying. No fat is visible on muscled, straight frame and Ezekiah is sure he will look trim and healthy at 80 years, as now. He seems to speak to Dear Precious, via wide, intense eyes – as if assuring equine. Dear Precious stares back, serene, no muscle tick, or tail flick.

The man looks at Ezekiah and, with Dear Precious alongside him, approaches. Ezekiah feels an electric-like charge as the giant grasps his shoulder in massive hand while, in other, holds Dear Precious' neck. He whispers a rhythmic incantation in a language spoken by some Negroes who came to Ezekiah's church.

"*Du-bou-debou, Polara, du-bon.*"

Though foibles of faith and background beckon him to disavow the different, Ezekiah feels the man is using touch, words, to channel serenity of ride to his rider, and, to Ezekiah's astonishment, it is working. He feels power of steed coursing into his body, implanting a calmness he never before knew. Close as he and Dear Precious have been, now, they are closer. Ezekiah looks up. Horse, human eyes meet and he knows the feeling is mutual.

The big man's hand leaves Dear Precious and he lifts

Ezekiah, walks him away from the swine.

"Thank you my dear fellow," he says to Ezekiah, "for not giving away me or those who travel the line. You are as the brave warrior priest of my boyhood village, willing to save others at the risk of losing your own time on this earth. It is my honor to help you in your time of need. It honors all my great ancestors that I meet you, not only the great roper, with a little help from pulleys and hidden people at times," he smiles, "but truly a great, though troubled human."

Close up, Ezekiah sees him clear now. He realizes he is the man below the balcony that one Sunday. He knows everything Ezekiah could or couldn't do with his rope, and, evidently, with his life. The man reaches out his hand to Ezekiah; in the custom of the land he now has lived many years. Ezekiah starts to say, "My name is..." but begins coughing blood.

The man clinches Ezekiah's nostrils between fingers, broad, but lithe-moving from a life of carving, painting, creating. He forces open Ezekiah's mouth, trickles dust from a pouch down Ezekiah's throat. Bleeding stops immediately.

"The bayou Mama's cure. Many survive the line's treachery because of her. You can thank Mama, if one day you're lucky enough to meet her." Their previous conversation continues. "I know your name, Reverend Bellows, and that of your Dear Precious. Legend is his 'star' has led many to freedom when you rode your circuit. We both know, yes, that legend is really fact."

Ezekiah is hearing a voice that is deep and kind to him. "Here let me be of assistance to you good Sir, on your troubled journey." The man takes a bedroll from Dear Precious, helps Ezekiah onto it. He wipes blood from Ezekiah's face with his bandana. "Name, my good sir: It is Kunta."

CHAPTER 15

Through the Lindian Woods Turt plods. He hears flutters and looks about. 'Oh, it's you Calico.'

'Your shell is too hot for James to sleep upon, Turt. I will awaken him.'

You stir when Calico brushes your cheek. Other butterflies canopy between you and Poppy Sol. Their breezin' wings cool you. "I know your name," *you say.*

Calico speaks matter-of-factly, through her antennae. 'As well as you know your own.'

"Yet I can't remember mine or yours."

'One day you will. Say, hop between my wings. Visiting we will go.'

"Who?"

'Someone you know.'

"Oh boy." *You climb aboard. Up, you soar. Your protector, waves his fin-claw,* 'so long for now' *to you and your butterfly. He shrinks to a speck.*

Instantly you arrive at your destination: The carbungle onna the bask-ass side a...

'Go right in. They won't mind.'

"What will I say?"

'Silly. How would they know you are there? You are their future.' *Calico flies off.*

TALES OF THE FICTION HOUSE

The tired canvas door grumps 'welcome' as you move it and enter. WOW! You study intricate scrimshaw; spin Carper's top; explore books, seashells, nets. You joust with Harpoon. You've visited, thousands of times in your imagination, yet you don't know when.

There they are, together: The Mariner, Ol Tom, even your shelled protector — all ageless. And the Carper. Sitting on a stool beside Mariner's chair. Wait, what's that look of his?

THE GLUMS

— is what the Mariner sees in Carper when he stops his story. Crinkly lines of melancholy envelope Carper's face. Ol Tom senses sadness. He leaps — from Mariner's shoulder to Carper's. Licking the boy's cheek caringly, he mewls, 'AHEM, TURT. Little help here.'

Turt breaks his distracted gaze from a fish glowering up at him through the wharf-shack's planked floor. Carper's look mirrors Turt's own sadness, when he thinks of Kunta or of his own foundling-shelling days. Turt trills soothingly and with beak-snout, pets Carper's hand.

Laza Bones Thibidioux reaches from his wanted poster and grabs Harpoon. He points it at you. 'I gotta use for this. I'll be a seein' you in a century or so boy. I'll deal with YOU, then.'

Mariner takes sad Carper onto his lap.

THE GLUMS. Mariner'd seen it among fellow sailors: A blanket of fog that smothers, first mast, then souls. "Keep spirits up mates," he'd say. "Soon we'll port. There ya can breathe agin'." 'Til then, all Mariner could do was keep spinnin' yarns, hopin' some tale'd restart the sweet music of their hearts. For this young mate he'd do the same.

"None of those damnable, blue GLUMS, Carper. I know yer feelin bad. But ya hasta' remember, as a foundlin' ya come from a mighty proud line. Holy Moses! Could say, our likes date back ta times' beginning."

Mariner's words stick, briefly, to Carper's thoughts. Slowly, away they peel. So suddenly, so craw-wrenchingly, Carper feels he is spiraling down — alone, helpless — through a dark tunnel in his thoughts. These are the GLUMS. Mariner's words are a net but Carper slips through. He reaches for Ol Tom's paw and Turt's fin-claw: in vain.

Laza Bones leaps from poster and shifts Harpoon away from you and toward Carper. He pokes at him. 'Git you on down, down, and stays yaz der at de bottom, mon fishboy.'

You try to pull Laza Bones away from Carper but your arms slide right through him.

There is a lil' Carper existing in Carper's mind. Eeensy, so teensy. Carper knows, small though he is, he is mightier than all the bad Laza Bones' of the world. So gently, but oh so forcefully Lil Carper whispers, 'Listen to Mariner. Let his words be your line. Hold tight. Don't fight when he reels you in.'

Mariner's arm encompasses Carper's waist. With other, he flails, animating the story he tells, about Kunta, "even as a little boy, so brave a boy, Kunta saved many lives though enslaved by the worst of GLUMS." In Carper's half-real – half-tunnel world, Mariner's arm seems sword fending off Harpoon. The more he concentrates on Mariner's tale, the further off Laza Bones Thibidioux drifts, until again he's imprisoned in his poster.

Laza Bones poses handsome side out, as if he's Honest Abe on the penny. 'Who me? I wouldn't harm a soul.' He's not fooling Carper, or James. Both know there'll be a next time.

Mariner spins and spins for Carper. Next tale, "Pharaoh's daughter, the beautiful Princess, she discovers baby Moses agrowin' 'mongst the Nile's bulrushes and reeds. He's a mighty foundlin'. Sproutin up, leadin 'is people through torturous deserts to freedom. Still leadin em yet today."

Carper's eyes spark. "Still?"

Mariner nods. "So jus' maybe you'll grow up to do some leadin' of yer own." He strokes Carper's face. His crinkly lines of melancholy begin disappearing. "N' then Carper, there's Romulus and Remus. Foundlin' twins suckled to survive by mama she-wolf in a grassy valley of seven hills. Them boys went on to found the great city, ROME, twixt those hills. I ported there dozens a times. Bee-youtiful' Carper. You'll go there one day."

Carper's eyes spark.

Mariner picks a couple of ratty-tatty books from the shelf and opens them to pictures of 'M' in the bulrushes and 'R' and 'R' at the teats.

Carper's imagination is entree into the pages. Escape to imagination begins washing away the GLUMS. The tunnel begins shrinking, then, zap, like that, disappears.

Carper wades out to meet Moses. Princess lifts the future prophet, but wait – a cratered old gator is sliding their way. His vibrating growls quake the pages. The Princess' delicate gold bracelets and necklace chime as they brush her silken gown. Growl isn't from the gator. His snout is closed. Carper glances out from the pages, to the wanted poster. Laza Bones Thibidioux turns Adonis-side profile and shows his mangled gator side. He's the growler. He peers at the helpless trio retreating to shore.

He snorts, 'Git em ol Uncle. Feast on der bones den toss one out ta yer kin.'

Uncle ratchets mouth, snaps inches from Princess' waist. Her golden belt rips away and tangles in his pointy teeth. Looking victim to an overzealous ancient dentist Unc leaps above water. *'CHOMP!;* Just misses swaddled Moses.

Carper uproots a rigid reed, taller than he is. He parries, thrusts, as he did battling Turt. He realizes what he must do to save Moses, but not the same thing that saved him from Turt. With free hand, he plucks another reed. He slaps Uncle Gator's snout with one while jabbing with the other. Unc winces, but he's a comer.

'Git that Carper, Uncle,' Laza Bones shouts.

Carper lets him get just so close, then rams reed between Uncle's upper and lower jaw. It sticks, holding open snout. Squealing, frightful noises no Princess should ever hear! She covers ears. Carper, to the rescue. To give her majesty time to get away he begins spinning the uncle like a bottle, pushing him to shore. He upends him with the reed as he did Turt with Harpoon. He stands triumphant atop flopping reptile. Poised rigidly with reed he looks a miniature of Mariner's 'Poseidon with trident' picture.

'Curse you Carper,' shouts Laza Bones Thibidioux.

Suddenly Carper finds himself watching from a few pages on as loving wolf mother nurses Romulus and Remus. A galloping gator descends a hill and heads toward the unsuspecting trio. 'Git em Auntie,' shouts Thibidioux. 'Keill the beetch and adopt the boys fer yeren' own. Haul em back to the bayou where dey can be learned the swamp things that'll let em rule the world.'

No reed. No harpoon. Carper knows he must make do. He looks about barren valley. He spies a ropey snake and grabs it. Auntie lunges. He snaps snake like a whip, coiling it around her snout. (Just like Kunta did to save the Reverend at the river, James lauds. Maybe Carper and Kunta met somewhere along the way?) Carper loads Romulus and Remus onto mother's back. She smiles thanks, R & R gurgle, and off to safety they ride.

'GRR,' Thibidioux growls. His teeth chatter as terbaccy stick he chews sticks in his craw. He chokes it out. "Ye's not seen de las a me's, mon fishboy.'

Carper exits the book.

The GLUMS! Gone. But remnants remain. Carper shakes; cries out. "I'm not Moses. Not the twins. You tell me I'm Carper. But I know I'm not. Who'm I Mariner?"

Turt cranes neck so his calming, hypnotic eyes are parallel to Carper's. 'Relax Carper. Breathe slow, deep. Count the twinkling starfish as they swirl.'

Ol Tom purrs, gently slipping his head to Carper's cheek.

Mariner squints. "You have to be someone son. Least for a while. Up to me to help that along, til you can decide who you be. I didn't just pluck your name from the sea. I named you after one of the noblest foundlings of all time, the renowned Carpier of Lindia, a great poet and storyteller who inspired his people. He led them to freedom of not only body, but of spirit."

"Carpier?"

'Carpier?' James, too questions, right along with his great-great grandfa. I know that name.' James stands invisibly next to Carper. Their shoulders rub, but neither feels other.

"Patience. I'll be spoutin 'a the Carpier right soon." Mariner rights up the slouching boy.

Suddenly Mariner begins peering over to the space – where James ain't. He whooshes his hand, right through James.

For a moment, James thinks he can read Mariner's thoughts, 'You be there, but a haint you ain't. I'll untangle that mystery knot.'

Then Mariner continues talk with Carper. "In Carpier you have a great legacy to live up to. But I saw right away when I fished you from under that cart that you got it in you."

Mariner runs fingers over Turt's shell as a sea captain would a globe. He stops at a thin, turbaned man. "I tried my hand at carvin' one time. Carved Carpier, sittin lotus-leg next to Kunta's village. He's tellen 'em tales to make their days go easier since they lost their beloved Kunta to the slavers. He's tellen em, 'Kunta forever resides now with their ancestors in Polaris'."

Mariner looks back over at James. Again, James is deciphering Mariner's thoughts, 'I's sure you taint a haint. Just as sure as I knows you ain't the Carpier; 'cause I knows the Carpier. Say, are you the little Kunta returnin' from his restin-place Polara for a spell?'

You want to break down time barriers and shout the surprise: 'Kunta's growed and alive, Mariner. A ropin','ariling downriver.' Sure wish some way I could let you know that.

A TREASURE FOR THE AGES

Mariner sets Carper atop Turt. "Somethen re-al special to show ya Carper. Of yer namesake. The Mahatma Carpier."

Words tempt. Carper's eyes dart. To keep from bustin' from the anticipatin', he plays fingers across a keyboard that a port of Piraeus pianist had painted onto Turt. Turt thumps tail in time to the beat. Ol Tom knows what's coming. He leaps to Turt's head, taps a little soft paw, swirls, sits. GLUMS, be gone, the two critters reckon to one another.

Probably the most precious item in Cincinnati USA of 1826 is under the bed ensnared within hooks and lures. Mariner takes great care sliding from within the bramble a teakwood box. Its sentry tigress and elephant are on haunches looking fierce. *Yours and Carper's eyes widen when you see the pinhead-size rubies, yellow sapphires and salmon coral adorning the four-legged creatures' two-leg raiment — silk looking pants, cape. The box looks so familiar to you. Why?*

Often, has Ol Tom thought, as, mesmerized by it, moribund with tear-twinkling eyes, 'When into cat coffin finally I ninth, into this quite comfortably I could lay. There eternal nap would be pleasure. No. It is Carpier's home and always shall it be.'

Mariner sets the box on Carper's lap. So heavy! It squashes him, nicely. It is cool, smooth. He touches but quickly pulls back when Tigress growls and pachyderm trumpets, 'Stay back. Only Mariner is allowed entry into Carpier palace.'

Ol Tom strokes wild feline cousin to calm her. 'There, now. This is the Carper. He is one of us and can come and go as he chooses. At any time must he be welcomed within.'

'Maybe one day,' comes reticent growl. Ol Tom hisses. She relinquishes. 'Okay, today.'

Turt, remembering dear friend Kunta carving tigress and elephant to life when his shell was tinier than they, trills to trans-species trumpeter, 'Carpier's palace; Carper's palace. That is the way things will be from now on. Remember my pachyderm friend – I was the one filched your jewels from the pirate chest. I can as easily pry them out if you're not good to our boy.'

Elephant toots compliance. His stubbornness morphs to respect for his jeweler. He and Turt do a little jammin', blaring out a spirited rift, and, all in wharf-shack briefly clap along. Elephant winks his amber eye that encases an ancient fly.

'ENTER THE GATE, MY BOY.'

Reality returns to Carper. Animal guards stiffen. Mariner says, "Go 'head. Snap open erster' to reveal bee-uutiful purl." He steps back, wanting full view of Carper's expression when first he sees the boxed treasure and meets the Carpier.

Millions of pages will publisher James Thaddeus 'Blackjack' Fiction turn during his lifetime. Today, as the Carper, slowly, yet conversely, excitedly, he opens the box's hinged lid, using the same page turning motion. That same motion will be a link to discovering precious new worlds inside and outside his mind. Those worlds will stamp his imagination. Escape, freedom, the bursting forth of wild, of new, of exotic, will all come – with the turn of the page.

Forever, for Carper, later 'Blackjack'; will this be the first page turned.

Carper's eyes mushroom. He is certain that never before has a boy seen such beauty. Carper's side-glance reveals that, from his wanted poster, Laza Bones Thibidioux stares at the box, not admiringly but in a creeping, wanting to steal it, way. Carper hunches shoulders to hide it. Thibidioux growls. Carpier's sentries growl back, louder. Their trumpets and screeches make Thibidioux cower. He mutters: 'Gatah no match fo both tigga n zellaphant. Just wait Bontez. 'Nother day yet to come.'

THE BOOK

"Only Kunta's fine workmanship would do for Carpier's home," Mariner says as he watches Carper stroke the leather cover. A likeness of turbaned, clean-shaven seventh-century Carpier is scrolled into it. He isn't handsome – pudgy nose, round, indistinct face, but his smile beckons. Carper breathes deeply savoring the artifact's musk pungency as Mariner spins stories of its history. "When I be a lad, Carper, 'n first hightailed it to sea, I met an ancient Lindian sailor..."

'Lindia, Lindia, know I that place,' you riddle to yourself.
'Heard once, I, that there is whereto I raced.
I ponder – Did that ancient Lindian sailor know my shelled protector?'

Carper disappears into the book. Beautiful to beholder are the handwritten words in the blackest of Lindian ink. Each letter is art, swaying, as do the blade-shaped leaves of the Lindian fan tree. Even as a four year old, Carper can see it is the loving work of a master. The drawings, hardly professional, but ardent, are equally as loving in their depicting of Carpier's life.

"...that Lindian sailor," says Mariner, "old as the seas 'e was. Knew all Carpier's tales, poems, and proverbs. Afearin' they might die with im, e writes 'em. All night long for months, by torchlight 'e wrote, spun. I listened and gets washed up one side, down the other with 'is inspirin'. So I started drawing what e spun. It's not Kunta art, but I'm right proud of it."

Carper leafs through, listens, and slowly is mesmerized.

"Jus' afore red sky daybreak we're composin' and drawin' on deck – I swear this be Poseidon's honest truth boy. He was gettin' riddy to write, 'THE END', when he sort of lists to port side." Mariner imitates. Carper grimaces; clasps box. "Then the glow of St. Elmo's legendary silvery roll of glowing fire appears starboard. Crew stops everything 'cause no one's I know ever seen it before, or since. Rolls right on board it does, like a blindin' sea wave. Licked and spit fire. Tossed balls 'a flames that sent crewmen duckin' and mast 'ablazin."

Mariner winks at Carper. "But we had plenty water to douse it. Then all of a sudden, POOF, Elmo's gone – just a hoop a smoke to say it ever visited. Then – things really got strange."

James watches Carper's, Mariner's, Turt's, and Ol Tom's eyes, widen.

Laza Bones leans in from poster.

"Whart' comes next wuz, the old Lindian – he just hands me this finished book – never did write, 'THE END', maybe 'cause no book truly does. He just walks through that hoop a' smoke. Disappears. '*POOF!*' Mariner waves arms. "He was suddenly gone. Like the Mahatma Carpier had come for him now that the tales was writ'. Maybe one day e'll come for me now that I have you to look after 'is tellins." That's ways off future I'm hopin'."

Laza Bones grouses, 'Hah! 'N if ya believe ALL THAT, I's some buildable swamp land, 'n a bridge across de Ponchetrain to sell ya.'

You ignore the nay-sayin'; trust Mariner's truthen'.

Carper scrunches eyes, looking for a moment a miniature Mariner. "Maybe the ancient teller was really Carpier," Carper ponders. Mariner merely, 'mm-hmms'. Carper imitates 'mm-hmms'. *You scrunch eyes and mmm, too.*

Something 'thumps' outside the wharf-shack. Turt trumpets. Ol Tom mewls. Carper grabs Mariner's arm. "Don't leave me." He is sure Mahatma Carpier comes for Mariner.

You've other ideas. Laza Bones' minions – up to somethin'.

Mariner wipes Carper's tears. "Hells-bells, boy. I cain't go yet. Way too many tales still ta tells ya. Won't get em all spouted out til YER way into bein' an ol man. Nope, Carpier wouldn't let me go til you mesmerized alla' his book. We've plenty a time. But I'll scope the deck. If I see Carpier 'aswabbin' it, I'll tell him to come back inna hunnerd years." Mariner locks his look to Carper's. "Whatever you hear. Don't come out. Promise!" Carper nods. Mariner exits.

You want to keep Carper company. Can't. Somebody has to help Mariner. You follow. You'll soon wish you hadn't.

It's not Laza Bones you see standing behind Mariner and holding above his head a knife long as a whale's tooth and sharp as a shark's. It slices Luny Mum in two as the man fists it down. Mariner feels a persistent, itching against his ankle.

It's you, kicking, hard as you can, warning best you can across the near century-and-a-half time span. Your shouts, "watch out Mariner," aren't heard.

As Mariner bends to scratch, he sees the knife's glint. He rises, quickly ploughs shoulder into attacker's belly. They struggle. Mariner's breached many a port tussle. He rams elbow into attacker's jaw, continues motion, wishbones arms around wrist, forcing him to drop the weapon. It 'plops' into the Ohio. Mariner restrains him by grasping his throat.

"The devil seed must be offered up," the man rasps. His face is drenched in sweat. He is the manure-booted zealot from the riot outside Rrrose Heather's.

"Les' talk this over", Mariner appeases quietly so Carper won't hear.

"Filth, harboring filth. You'll both burn", spits zealot.

"He's only 'a innocent." Mariner's tone is decisive. Of the dirty days in the orphanage, he's thinking, and of how this sacrifice-driven fanatic is no different from the lecherous administrator.

The man struggles, rants of "sacrificen' up the seed to purify the land".

Mariner has had enough. He wishbones the neck. *'SNAP'.*

Mariner looks to where he thinks you might be standing. "If you're there, forgit what you saw. For the Carper's good, he mustn't know of the vileness aimed his way. Best you not remember either. No regrets for what MUST be done. The buggerin' taught me that."

You watch Mariner plop the body into the river. You watch it go far away. You don't judge, 'cause Rrrose Heather warned you about monsters laying-in-wait like this one who trailed the Carper.

'Hear that *kerplunk*,' demands Laza Bones.

"Didn't hear a thing", says Carper.

'LIAR! I saw ya porthole peeking. You're just forgettin' what ya don't wanna remember. Slick foundlin' trick. Well, no scales off mah hide. But I tell you mon fishboy. You get me that fancy treasure box and I won't *kerplunky* you into the water.' Carper sticks his tongue at him.

Laza Bones clams when Mariner re-enters. *You follow.* Seeing Mariner, Carper smiles mightily. For a moment, he thought Mariner might have walked through Elmo's hoop.

Mariner thinks: Gotta keep a foundlin' glums on the runs. He lifts book and Carper onto lap. "Let's start at the beginning. You gloam the pitchers, n' I'll roam the words.

Thousands of worlds in the words, Carper. Each more precious than gold." Mariner weaves Carpier's stories and sees Carper's look of intrigue. Pride swells in Mariner: The boy thinks he can read.

Turt and Ol Tom notice Mariner's hands begin to tremble. Mariner sits on them so Carper won't notice. Savvy creatures. They sense something fatal just took place; that Mariner has done what all creatures in the wild must to protect ones they care for. For the boy's sake, they assist Mariner in continuing his ruse. Turt takes the book in his beak-snout and places it on his shell as a bookstand. Ol Tom slides his tail beneath pages and turns them for Mariner.

Carper memorizes as Mariner parlays the tales.

As Carper pulls closer to Mariner Laza Bones says to him, 'Marks my word. Der's more en one way ta scales a slippery Carper. You'll find me there when least you expect. N' Monsieur's Carpier or Mariner won't be around to heps.' Laza turns, so Carper can't see leather gator side any more, only the handsome. Carper quivers, realizing the darkness beauty can hide. 'I must remember that,' he tells himself, as Mariner's seasoft voice rolls him back to reality.

Mariner's shaking, stops. "Damnable quivers." Over a lifetime, he's learned to block horrors quickly, so life can proceed. He lifts Carper from his lap and brings a pouch from a cupboard.

Carper: "Whatcha got?"

Mariner: "Somma' Mama Lucy magic powder." He heaps it in his palm and searches the wharf-shack. Turt and Ol Tom tilt heads in wonder. *Mariner stops in front of you and blows it in your face. You cough. He says, "Hah! I knews it wuzzin' you there." You know by the way he's squintin' rytch' through ya, that he can't see, only, somehow, sense you.*

"Who you talkin' to Mariner?" asks Carper.

"Never you mind. This be a conjure only Mama Lucy could help you understand." Mariner squints back to where you ain't. He wraps his arms around where he supposes your shoulder is and leads you to tabletop creature. "Join us. My laps got two sides after all, and you'll be wantin' to see Carpier close up too." Creatures sense something special is happening.

As you sit beside Carper, you feel sad for him because you heard Laza Bones threatening him. If only he had been in the woods to hear Rrrose Heather's advice about being 'beware'. Maybe he'll pick it up on his own, or with the help of Ol Tom, Turt, and Mariner. You know you can't bridge the time/space gap to tell him.

You realize how to help! You start tellin', along with Mariner, to distract Thibidioux from pestering Carper. You don't know how or why you know, exactly, the words Mariner is using.

It's working. Thibidioux growls, and then shuts up. You think, 'amazing! How do I know this story?' Then, just like that, as soon as Thibidioux quiets, you forget the stories, and you join Carper in listening, intently, to them.

CHAPTER 16

Eighth Century: BEGINS THE JOURNEY OF MAHATMA CARPIER

Knows not from where he comes or where he goes. Trembling words from the past, "Walk, don't stop," burn the the four-year old Carpier's thoughts. All else is blur.

Along the Lindian country road he travels. His only baggage is a rolled carpet for napping and a cloth bag once filled with food. A parade of grateful critters, a sharp-teethed mongoose, looking akin to the largest rat you'll ever encounter, a svelte brown fox, and an eye-darting green salamander, helped enjoy his meals. They travel with him now. When his stomach growls, mongoose brings him nuts, fox, fruits; salamander, crunchy but nutritious, but passed on by Carpier, grasshoppers.

His silks, new, days before, are dust-coated. A crevice, where a cherry-size ruby rested, indents his turban. While Carpier and critters napped under a shade tree, a destitute tenant farmer '*sly'd*' the jewel away.

He will parlay it into vast farm holdings he rents out and into wagons and ships to transport the crops his lands produce. For centuries, the thief's descendents will enjoy elegant lifestyles.

Then their castle is ransacked, inhabitants murdered, same fate that had destroyed Carpier's family. Karma…and so the world spins. The marauders. Always they come.

A beloved servant is the person who tells Carpier, "Walk, don't stop," when the marauders arrived in their century. She kissed Carpier's forehead; caressed his marble-smooth cheeks. Shouted orders and terrifying screams, emanating from other palace chambers: They churn in his thoughts. The servant shunted Carpier out the kitchen's back door with the carpet and food. Moments later, a sword sliced through her spinal column. "Walk, don't…"

Carpier remembers, obeys. The mental hurt banishes his other memories.

"Don't go gettin' to far up on me", Mariner says when he sees Carper skimming the pages. "Elst you won't get the wisen' Carpier's got to give."

You join your great-great granfa Carper as he climbs atop Turt. Ol Tom leaps beside us. Mariner sets the open book on Carper's lap and stretches. You tug invisibly at Mariner's arm and point at a drawing of a tree-shaded pond. 'I been there. Just came from that same spot Carpier's at. Rrrose Heather warned me, always be aware in the woods. That why I'm seeing this now? 'Cause it's important I remember?"

Mariner nods to the apparition from the future, as if saying, 'yer steering the right course.'

"Did Carpier ever stop walking?" you and Carper simultaneously ask.

"Fer a spell. But 'e always started up ah-gin."

"Where he going?"

"Journey bound."

"But if he stepped over a cliff, it would end", Carper slyly challenges.

"Nope. He'd soar."

Both you and Carper elevate your arms and pretend to fly around wharf-shack. Mariner waves you in for landing.

Carper: "How could he fly? Wouldn't he drop like…?"

Mariner won't let him finish. "His spirit, his soul'd soar. His carpet's magic. Just like right cheer." He chooses from the shelf a book written in Arabic. He opens to a picture of airborne Aladdin. Carper touches his rug, imagines riding it with Turt and Ol Tom.
You imagine the same thing and tag along.
Both boys: *"Carpier's rug could really fly?"*
"Can't claim it. But when Carpier sat on it, imagined, meditatin'-like, eyeballs scooched backward lookin' all white, as Turt's gets, his spirits'd soar 'cause he had the – TREASURE!"
Carper: "How'd he get the ruby back, Mariner?"
"Twarnt the ruby. When he lost it, he received the true treasure. 'It let his imagination soar. It freed him."
"What was the treasure, Mariner?"

Carpier awakens to critters' warning screech. A dull machete descends. The weapon's wielder, a splintery hag, barefoot, dress grayer than her sparse locks, decides she needs the carpet to rest sore feet on after 16 cane field hours. Never before a bandit, she, but the wool looks so comforting. But, oh those eyes of the boy, gentle as a glassy river, blue as sky. They caress her weak eyes with an innocent love. They take within them her pains, relieving them. She can't stop her motion.
Carpier cries in fear but even his tears sparkle with an innocent, trusting love, reflecting her hates and covetousness, and banishing them.
She wails, almost in prayer, as machete strikes. "Dear Goddess Nardesha, NO! How can I do such evil?" She believes, briefly, that she sees Nardesha's eyes in his. She turns the blade slightly. It bounds off his neck. Blood flows from meaty gash. Carpier's eyes dim. He pales. She hurls machete into the cane and clutches him.

Carper cries. Mariner strokes his hair. Turt and Ol Tom grin critter grins. All critters know the tale of what comes next. Mariner says to excited James, but Carper thinks he's saying it to him since how could he know his four-year-old great-great grandson when he too is only four. "I knew you'd like this story since you've got the look of a Lindian traveler about youren'self..."

Old woman strokes Carpier's gash with water. Instinctively, critters react. Fox licks blood with scalpel-like tongue. Flow slows. Mongoose wraps gash with tail, beginning a slow, knitting back together of capillaries. Old woman kneels, prays, "A miracle sent by Nardesha."

Ol Tom leaps to the planked floor and bounds whip-like around the wharf-shack. Mariner stops story so he and the boys can watch. "Discover me' secret stash 'a nip Ol Tom?" Books baubles and scrimshaw teeter in Tom's wake. An uncorked bottle tips. Whale oil gurgles out.

Tom's screeching meows say, 'Tell Carper about the dance-'a-death, Mariner. All boys must learn of the dance-'a-death. Day'll come when he'll need to know its steps.'

For a moment Tom, sensing he's about to slam into a boy who really isn't there, blinks, 'Does my eye deceive?' The distraction causes him to slip on the oil. He slides to a stop in front of Turt. Onlookers laugh. Cat vanity: Tom pretends it's part of the dance. He rises on hind paws and stretches body straight. Tongue hangs limply below whiskers. He sways, staring trance-like at Turt. Turt feigns being under Tom's spell, by snake-imitating-twisting and contorting neck. Turt trumpets, 'Tell him Mariner. He must know the steps.'

Mariner turns a page and points to the next picture he drew. "Dance-'a-death. One day we all must..." Carper wants to look away, cannot. Intrigue overcomes fear.

The beckoning scent of human blood permeates Lindia's countryside. From behind a fan tree, first a silvery hood appears, then the full rope-like length of a cobra. His dirge-hiss, 'I cannot be denied. Whatever falters here belongs to me,' quiets birds and insects.

Mongoose steps between his compatriots and cobra. Cobra

slithers near. One can see the thousands of years of hatred, rivalry, animosity – instinct about one another passed from endless generations of mongoose-cobra ancestors – by the clouds of smoldering brimstone in their eyes.

Smell the rotten musk of creature adrenalin rising. Moments of tango-like swaying – a beast's challenge to war – cease quickly. Instantly they are on one another.

Mariner's drawing captures perfectly the moment. Carper's immersed, feels like he's there.

You wonder. 'Before Calico flew me to the wharf-shack, didn't I see a hooded one staring at me from behind a tree? Did the beautiful winged one save me by swooping me away?'

Violent shrieks pierce the docile Lindian countryside. Cobra and mongoose constrict to avoid the other's razor teeth or poison fangs.

"Nardesha, give our mongoose strength," old woman prays. She doesn't move, willing to die to protect child surely sent by Nardesha. Fox, bravely, foolishly, streaks out and starts nipping cobra's tail. He catches, but holds on too long. He's whipped unconscious against a stone. Salamander, noticing the gash has started bleeding again, slips to Carpier and covers it with his trunk – to keep other cobras in the area from smelling the open wound.

Turt and Ol Tom recreate the epic battle scene. Half Carper's and James' attention is focused on their playful action; other half can't leave Mariner's equally serious telling.

Over a thousand years passing since the event hasn't dulled the drama.

Stirring dust clouds the warriors. Scowling screams. Do they come from mongoose, cobra, both? Old woman's prayers are chants, "Please, sweet Nardesha. Please…" Comes the loudest shriek, a thud, and the foulest fecal odor. A battered creature emerges victorious.

Ol Tom collapses. Turt puffs up beak-snout – a Shakespearean victor. Mariner applauds. The boys join him. Above Ol Tom, Mariner dangles a smoked sardine. "Rise gallant creature."
Ol Tom snatches it and holds it out to share with Turt. Bow. Sniff fish bouquet.
Mariner lauds, "Wharf-shack thespians don't cotton to bein' rewarded with flowers".
"Who was it Mariner? Who won?"
"Patience, my good audience. Sayeth the Bard: 'Let every man be master of his time.'"

"Thank you Nardesha," old woman wails. She reaches to hug battered mongoose. He skirts away. He goes to check on slowly coming-to fox pal.

Your glance shifts to sneering Thibidioux. He's been silent, but you can tell by his look what he's been up to – rooting for the cobra, silently scheming how he and cobra, if victorious, could pair-up to wrangle vallerbull' box for 'emselves. He exits wanted poster, and slithers to fellow slitherer and begins giving him mouth-to-mouth. 'He lost fair and square Laza Bones,' you shout, grabbing Harpoon, forcing him back to poster.

Throughout battle the salamander has bandaged over Carpier's gash. Salamander turns yellow and blue. Now lavender. Now pink. The pale is shocked from the boy's face. Sweat streams from his pores, salt-white, the smell of ocean. Scared at what she sees and of animal medicinal she doesn't understand the old woman reaches to remove critter bandage. She jerks her hand back. Critter's hot as burning coal. He radiates a smoldering sulfur stench. (It will be twelve centuries before human doctors even attempt this ancient lizard excretion cure.)
Cauterized wound is but a line of dried blood when the salamander crawls off minutes later.
Carpier breaths come easy.

'Beyond a doubt,' old woman knows, 'truly Nardesha's miracle.'
As Carpier sits up, critters' eyes meet his. They're smiling. Old woman gives boy berries from her sack. She feeds some to creatures. Sensing her change, they accept graciously, 'In good hands now, he.'
She senses he's from the overrun palace. "I'll name thee Carpier. For it is the carpet brung us together."
Critters bid farewell – to go their way. Goodbyes are quick because that is the way of beast; a lick to cheek, claw-to-hand, shake. They know, 'with two-leg is where foundling belongs.' As day wanes, into sunset they saunter.

'Goodbye time for you too, James' says Calico's flutter as she slips into the wharf-shack.
"So soon?"
'You shall return often.'
"But I'll miss Ol Tom, Mariner, Carper, and the shelled one."
'You shall have Rrrose Heather and Mama Lucy back in Lindia. Maybe meet up with Carpier? Thanks to Mariner, you shall recognize him now.'
You frown, wish critter-quick farewell to all. Mariner's wink says, 'Looks like your ship's come in. When times right I'll be tellin' the others you were here.'
You have a great idea. You whisper it to Calico. She flutters sly agreement then glides to Laza Bones' poster. You watch Calico spin like a wheel so fast that, FLASH! Thibidioux doesn't know what's happenin'. Instantly he's cocooned, only enough air to breath, and tiny slit to look out.
"That'll keep you from botherin' my friends."
Thibidioux squirms his hand into pocket – fishing for something sharp,' ta cut mah'self free'.
"Happy flyin'," says Mariner to Calico as you board. You cry.
'Brought you here,' Calico consoles, 'not to make you sad, but to teach you valuable ways to survive the woods. Have to get you on your way to LIVING humans, who can care for you.'
As off you go Mariner tells you, "You KNOW the tales. Let your

memory sail free n' find 'em."

"Who you talkin' to Mariner."

"Never you mind, Carper."

Carper squints out the porthole; into Luny Mum's glow. For a few seconds he believes he sees the silhouette of the butterfly that stayed with him the night he was alone. And riding on her...'No, now that's impossible to believe – a boy looking just like me'. It scares Carper and he talks to Mariner about something else. "Carpier never changed his name, Mariner?"

"Some foundlings never do, Carper. It's up to them. One day you'll understand why."

Carpier accompanies the old woman to the cane fields. He's too small for back-break labor. He fetches water. Cobras watch him covetously at the pond.

Carpier's deliveries bring workers pause. He sees the relief his kindness brings. Their grimaces fade, but return with the cane cutting. 'How can I make smiles last longer?' He tells of funny things frogs, crickets, turtles do at the pond: Animal tag, critter piggyback. Carpier is too young to understand the mating ritual. Smiles extend. Workers study Carpier's face. It mirrors nature's peace, calms them, and they take time to relate childhood memories.

Carpier thinks, 'How can I make the calm last – forever.' He begins linking simple animal events into longer, complicated ones. "...and there they were folks, this whole team of crickets, pulling the poor, wounded fish back to the pond – almost slipped into the water themselves."

Sometimes a group gathers to listen. When they leave, smiles remain for long times midst work. Or, grins come – sweet remembering replacing grimaces. Even when they nick themselves and Carper applies water to ease the pain a smile sometimes appears. "I was thinken' about the fish tale you told me, Carpier."

Carpier's smile grows big as the ones he sees on the workers' faces.

Mariner bites off a stick of chew. "Jewel 'e discovers Carper, more precious than the ruby, is COMPASSION. 'N 'e wrapped it up nice in the way 'e learns to tell stories. "That's what we all need – compassion – trouble bein', it comes and it goes with most 'a us."

Log-stiff in mud hut they share is how Carpier finds the old woman. She wears the widest smile. "To die happy is Nardesha's wish for us all. You never know when that time will come," Carpier remembers her telling him. "You've given me joy, Carpier." He wipes matted hair from her mouth, kisses cheek. "*Walk, don't stop,*" he reminds himself. Time to depart.

Campfire remembrances of him crackle. "I liked his retelling of the crab races."

"I, his weaving us under his spell with the battlin' bass story."

An elder cracks a walnut wrinkly as his face. "I spied him midst a beast menagerie like 'e were of them. Surely that's another sign he is the holy one of whom Nardesha spoke."

"NO!" another counters. Though kind heart is his fortunate domain, he is but a foundling. No more, less. Yet never have I met someone so intent on lighting another's burdens."

The walnut cracker splits a shell that nearly snaps the last of two remaining teeth. "I cannot believe what some say. He was too kind to kill the old woman."

Carper purses mouth and shakes head. "Didn't did he?"

"Course not Carper. Those were just rumors – spread by those tryen' to elly-vate' theyselves on another's shoulders – 'a even a young sprigs shoulders. Rumors followed him all his days."

Carpier runs quickly from the village he next comes, barely escaping. People throw stones. They are the old woman's kinfolk; just heard a traveling boy has murdered her. A dozen men seize axes and follow him. "FOR NARDESHA'S

HONOR," they chant.

Carper shudders. Mariner holds him tight, and says, "Be brave and strong as your namesake."
Mariner's book drawings vanish from Carper's thoughts. Replacing them are imaginings – crackling bright – from the inferno at Rrrose Heather's. Carper images the contorted face of the white-collared man. He shrieks, cobra-like. "In the name of the Fa, come here boy."
Instead of the manure-booted man chasing him with a knife, this man-monster pursues, with a glistening cross he swings like a machete. Carper runs because he thinks he'll strike. No mongoose to defend him. He knows if he stands, still, he will lose his dance-a-death.
To save himself from *these* imaginings he plans how he might dive completely into the safety of imagination, into the Book of Carpier, into his namesake's life. Carper clutches Mariner.

CHAPTER 17

You dock your story to give Carper a chance to sponge it all up. Carper's swellin' with the curiosity of a sailor fresh to sea. Hissen's quick fingers trace every line you drew in the Book of Carpier. Yer gnarly fingers — you 'member how oncet they looked like his. You scan 'em over words on the opposin' page as you ready to set sail into the next stormy chapter. You look at yer young mate, and his wantin' to know EVUHTHING' about EVUHTHING' dartin' eyes. You think you know evuh question floatin' in 'is thoughts, and how to answer evuh one.

Careful Mariner. That know-it-all'n. It'll sinks ya 'fore evuh leavin' port.

Turt's dozin'; fin-claws drum-brushin' to a dream. Ol Tom's eye, it's closed. He's pawing the air. Must be practicin' ways ta survive if day comes he loses its seein'. Wharf-shack's so quiet you could hear a snail crawlin'. So why's mah head suddenly crashin' like a northerly squall when Carper asks — agiin'and agiin'.

"Who I be Mariner?"

What kin' you tell the boy — when you don't know who youren' own self be. Best be truthen. HAH! You spoutin' truthen? All the while lookin' at words scribed in Lindian, pretendin' their bein' English, 'n that ya kin' read each and evuh one.

"Can't rightly say who you are Carper. Don't be surprised if ya never know. But see; listen close so you gets me here." Mariner places wrinkled palm over the book's page so he'll

have Carper's attention. Carper catches his sight; holds tight.
"All the stuff about where Ah' mighta' come from, that fretted me all mah seafaren' days. It don't rightly matter. What matters is the here, now and evuhthing you do with it. Take Ol Tom. He goes out, loves his-self up sweet Angorra, but on his way back 'e's always on the lookout for the wharf rats that 'ets the people's grain, or chews up their cherished things. See, get me here, Carper. Pay close..." Mariner pets Ol Tom. Tom meops. "Tom's always doin, and bein' parta' this world. Same with Turt. Jus' look over his shell. All he's done. People and animals he helps, keeps 'ahelpin. His shell pitchures' tell the tales. He'll be here helpin' you long after I'm gone."

Carper looks away from Mariner's rheumy eyes and pets Turt's shell. Mariner sniffs, blows nose with a holey gray handkerchief, and thinks. 'He'll be a seein pitchures' 'a Carpier in a different light from now on. Jus' hope 'e learns from'em what Carpier'd want 'im to.'

Mariner leans, squints into Carper's eyes. "All a matter a takin' part in this world. Our Carpier. He had to fight for is very life just so he could help others."

Mariner turns a page. Carper tenses. Carpier escapes the human mob, but the next drawing shows a dozen cobras surrounding him.

'Gotta abandon ship,' Carper imagines shouting, diving into the page. 'Gotta help Carpier.' Suddenly Carper's in Lindia.

Mariner, he goes right on tellin'-embellishen'.

Carper smells the cucumber odor of the cobras, listens to their flute hiss. They inch nearer Carpier. Carper thinks he hears them speak. 'A useless foundling! Even two-legs want his blood. We'll drain it first.'

'I'm here for you Carpier,' Carper shouts, running toward him. He feels as if a wall keeps him distanced. He feels Mariner's hand hook his. Whoosh! He's reeled back onto Mariner's lap as Mariner turns the page. While in Lindia Carper thought-sure he'd seen the boy who looked so like himself. 'Maybe he needs my help to?'

"Don't worry for Carpier, son. 'E got 'is own special talents

TALES OF THE FICTION HOUSE

and you'll discover yer own when the times right." Mariner strokes his hair, reassuring.

Carper's scheming. 'I know I can help if I get to them.'

"Thing 'bout tellin tales is, Carper, and listenen' to 'em, ya gotta give inta imaginin', if ya want to lose yerself in 'em."

Carper fists hands, closes eyes, and wishes, 'Let my imagination run free.'

Mariner interrupts tellin'. "Don't ever be like some folks Carper. Bland, no imagin'."

Carper's already heeding the advice. He leaps back into the pages, scales the wall, Ol Tom-like, and approaches Carpier.

'STAY BACK!' Carpier shouts.

WHAP!' A cobra tail knocks you. You sit dazed. Whapping cobra pushes cold snout to your nose. 'Later we deal with you, Carper.' A long-in-the-fang old-timer, useless, but for one thing, dead weight, crawls onto your lap. You're trapped.

Carpier says. 'It is I you desire. Leave him.'

'For now we will,' their sly looks say. The dozen cobras resume their advance.

You try to get free by thumping the old-timer's belly. He only rolls over, burps.

You watch Carpier's unblinking eyes. He seems to be looking beyond you and the cobras. To some other world? You're nearly hypnotized by his concentration. You suddenly fear what Carpier could do to you with the power you feel daggering from his eyes. Could he really have killed the old woman? NO! Tattles bring doubt where none should be. You stare into his eyes.

You understand. His dagger ray eyes are not for cutting or gouging, but for gently penetrating. His look warms you. You feel, what Mariner has told you, is, Carpier's TREASURE. Your senses fill with a passion for this fresh-born emotion: Compassion. You realize; One's eyes — their silent glint, or dull, or twinkle or flicker — they mirror what is inside everyone.

Mariner's eyes. They show passion for tellin, helpin'. Ol Tom's, for filanderin. Turt's, for contemplatin'. Even Laza Bones' show a passion — for 'athieven. Dear Precious' intense eyes showed it for his dedicatin' of himself to rider, and rider, for his passion for confusin' himself. You want your own passion to grow. Not yet do you know how hard it will be to keep it alive midst life's turmoil.

The eyes. You start to tear. With your newly realized, compassion, you know why Mariner takes care of you — All the stories in Carpier's book have changed Mariner, made him care for everyone, and you, one of the most helpless, he cares for most.

You begin to shake and sob: Because Dear Precious' rider, who somehow encompasses all of you, whose eyes are — you can't explain how — your eyes, is going further away with each hoof-beat of Dear Precious. He rides from you when he should ride to you. You realize it will always be away from, never, to. But Mariner, he will always be there.

Mariner nets Carper up. "Dontcha be weepy and afearin' fer Carpier. E's got 'isself many a ways a gitten' outta siti'ations like this." Mariner holds the boy tight until the sobs lessen. He understands. Truly. Silently he curses Bellows. Aloud he says — just loud enough for Carper to hear and maybe to chew on the words. "Look after your fragile cargo, Dear Precious. Deliver 'ims to where he needs goin'and what he needs doin'."

'Why's Mariner spoutin' on about the horse and rider?' Carper wonders. He looks into Mariner's eyes and chokes out, "What say, Mariner?"

"Nuttin' boy. Les' get back to see just how Carpier handles the snakes." He turns the page.

Carper stares at the picture of the cobras — inches from Carpier's face. Their passion for blood sucking shows in their eyes. Bodies sway: That's their way before striking. Carpier sways too, meeting all their eyes, all at once, seeming to speak to them through his eyes.

Carper grasps Mariner's wrist. "What he say to 'em Mariner?"

Turt awakens. He and Ol Tom begin swaying cobra-like. They'd heard tale of this event many-a-time. Never tired of it, though didn't rightly believe it all — what with Mariner's proclivity for always doin' changes.

"Cain't rightly tell you his words, Carper. But what he whar' doin' was a charmin' em to 'is ways. Some Lindians develop that power. Manys'-a-time I saw it when I ported there. Carpier though, he had it natural. His concentratin' bein' so strong, no animal or few humans could overcome 'im. No siree. Never used his powers for badden', as some laza bones might. 'Used 'em to grow seed a'compassion 'e planted when he went about tellin 'is tales."[19]

Mariner pushes thumb down, as if he's planting, sweeps arms upward, imitating growth. "N' those cobras followed 'im from then on, apostle-like-protectin'. Almost all cobra of Lindia looked out for 'im. Those that thought the blood of a foundling in their countryside belonged to thems? Other cobras took care of thems right quick – so that be that."

Carper imitates Mariner, scratchin' chin, squintin' – kipe'n his expressin's. "Les' jus do some conjecturin' here, Mariner. If the cobra swears to protect 'im, and the mongoose already did...what's the outcome when the two set a critters – sworn enemies for all eternity – meet up with that same common protectin' goal?"

Mariner pets Ol Tom and scratches Turt's neck as the creatures look at him with askin' eyes, 'Ya, Mariner, how you 'xplain avowed foes for all time – becoming as one?'

Mariner scratches bristly chin – imitatin' Carper, imitatin' him. Genially, "Well Lads, that's a tale for another day. Becausin', 'n don't forget. Carpier's still got the old woman's kin 'a chasin' 'im. 'E, and we gotta deal with that first."

* * *

Almost moonset and barely past sunrise. James rides Turt. Butterflies flit around them. They come to a shrine Turt knows well from his travels: Carpier's marble likeness. A dozen marble cobras bow at the feet. Events of over a thousand years before are depicted here at this the scared place where it's said a miracle happened. Flowers strewn by pilgrims cover the

---

[19] LKFFF: Read the simple, little tales of Carpier in Fiction House's Lore of the Lindian Woods – for adults, adolescents, or children. Carpier meant them for any age. Tales told by Carpier are still being discovered and reinterpreted to this day.

ground. Turt had hoped he'd find a kind human here to care for James.

Poppy Sol observes a stirring in the cane field near Turt and James: Barely visible, the silver hoods of a dozen cobras. They're sniffing the foreign travelers. 'I am quite afraid they be a thousand years removed from the lessons of civility Sir Carpier taught their ancestors. Poor blighters. They crawl and spit when they could do the world honor by marching upright.'

'Quite so,' Luny Mum regrets. She keeps a stiff upper, but Sol observes Mum's porcelain stare shattering, and every shard reflecting her fear for their chaps.

Sol's flickers offer solace. 'Squire Turt, e'll have something up his shell, I dare say. E'll pull 'em through. Remember 'ow we seen 'im 'andle the seas' meanest octopus!'

'Sire. Do remind.'

'The one whoms Poseidon blessed with bonus tentacles.'

Mum's crescent smile widens with hope. 'Ah yes! Quite long they were.'

'Indeed Mum. So long, that when 'ere 'e crawled, 'e kept stubbin is arse on 'em. That makes a beast more 'n a bit contrare'.'

Mum: 'Mean. Indeed. Still, our squire defeats 'ims.'

Sol: 'But with 'elp. You did bloody well bend the rules; turnin' the tides for 'ims favor.'

'Quite so, Sol. Yet ye put shell squire's knickers in a bind because you wanted to better view the melee. Almost blinded 'im with your glare.'

'I regrets.' Gentle pause; silence of a contented couple reveling in their eternity together.

Mum: 'I won't hesitate to 'elp the boy and Squire Turt today – or ever. Iffen need be. Foundlings 'ave it 'ard enough. Ow many foundlings 'ave we watched 'oer? 'Ow many yet will war, poverty and greed allow?' A tearful mist of morning dew forms about Mum.

Sol's rays reach to caress Mum's face. 'I know you'll 'elps Mum. As shall I.'

JUST SECONDS

Cobras charge. Turt twists neck and sees them. James, looking forward, doesn't. Poppy Sol blinks. Time slows, briefly. 'Dash it all! What's extra seconds twixt sky and earth mates?'

Turt scans the stately walnut tree they're beneath; knows what he must do. He breathes deep, hunkers to the ground, exhales a jet of air, and bucks like Dear Precious.

Poppy Sol blinks again. 'Couple more seconds, what say, Mum.? So the extra time'll insure our young friend'll 'ave safe sailin'.'

James jettisons skyward. His expression is a mix of exhilaration and fear. 'Grab a limb James,' Turt trumpets. 'You'll be safe.'

Luny Mum breathes deep – walnut leaves sweep skyward. 'Little extra pull'll do the laddie good. Be damned the gravity of the circumstances!'

Just seconds – for a celestial blink, pull, an earthly buck, and an earth-bound boy rockets skyward.

'Whoosh!' You truly fly. Yet, so much can happen in those seconds where one is born of air and free to observe, all. You see a fang just miss your protector's fin-claw. He pulls back, slaps sideways, pushing away the attacker. Another cobra goes for his neck. He 'whaps' with beak-snout. Snake drops. "Murtilate 'em," you shout, duking the air as others coil and lurch. Your protective netting of butterflies sears itself in two. Half of them watch your flight. Others stay with your protector, confusing, hypnotizing cobras that have never seen this kind of flutterer on their continent. This adds a few more seconds for shelled one's defense of, rocket-boy you.

PUBLISHER'S INSERTION

Dear Reader: The craft of sustaining a multi-page scene over a period of only seconds can prove a wrenching task, though not impossible. In various novels written by William Golden (Golden Boy, Carper's half-brother whose mother dresses him as a girl), published by Fiction House, Cincinnati/Lindia City/Manhattan, the author demonstrates succinctly, methods that must be utilized. Mr. Golden's are used here.

This aside is added not for informational/educational purposes; only as warning and disclaimer so the inexperienced writer SHALL NOT attempt this writing technique at home – at the risk of he or she experiencing confusion, dizziness, possibly nausea or fainting. He or she may try it – with the vicarious or flippant attitude, "doesn't look so difficult".

Please, refer, in all thoroughness, to the Golden writings before any such attempt. Paraphrasing the immortal bard whose works Mr. Golden devoured: 'To be or not to be trying this at home – be ye an untrained professional – is the lark of a fool.'

Seconds to an imaginative four year old can be as years, decades, why not even centuries. To one who is scared, stomach-pitting hungry, and separated from other humans, one second you are in one place, another, you're 1000 or 10,000 miles away.

While airborne for just seconds you travel. You live your idea of what a whole life is. You hear what takes some adults a lifetime to, and experience what others never do.

Your travels take you; first back to Cincinnati, later, to the <u>Bashri Raku</u>.

Scent of aftershave; scratch of worsted jacket. James on father's lap. Within their Cincinnati clinic living quarters. Book is open to Carpier facing the cobras.

"Look at Carpier's eyes, James."

'But who is James,' you think.

"See him watch; knowing all that is around him at every moment. Maybe he commands the cobras through his eyes."

You imitate Carpier. That night you dream. You're surrounded. By monsters- long, ropey, silvery hooded, with icicle teeth. You don't run. You use your mother's broom to protect yourself. '*Whap!*' *Heck, why settle for that. Why not make them do what you want.* '*Whap!*'

Back to Lindian Woods: *You're mid air, watching your protector battling monsters. You wish you were beside him with the broom-sword – Whapping! You can't be, because still you travel...*

...Back to the <u>Bashri</u> <u>Raku</u>: The night before Typhoon; on mother's lap in parents berth.

Book's open to Carpier. "If only," mother says "your eyes were wider, son." *She takes mascara from her pocketbook, darkens the sides of your eyes.* "Look Doctor. He looks like Carpier. Just the way Mariner drew Carpier to look – almost as if he used our James as model."

Father comes over. "Maybe so, Imah. But this is a certainty. James looks exactly like his great-great grandfather at that age... that drawing of him in the Cincinnati paper tucked away in the attic of the Fiction House... all that soot around his eyes from the fire at Rrrose Heather's."

The curtain for the porthole is down, so the Fictions can always look out and see protector-companion Turt. Luny Mum's able to peak in. 'Mm hmm. He has both their looks – that hopeful foundling glow. Three of a kind, the Carper, Carpier and James, yet separated by centuries.'

'Even more do they share,' observes Poppy Sol from other porthole. "The lad, 'e 'as the glint 'a courage that possessed both Carper and Carpier at that age.'

Doctor extracts curtain rod from its brackets and hands it to James. "Twist it, spin it, like you are an acrobat." (No tv or radio to entertain this family – they have books, their thoughts, each other.) *You leap nimbly around the cabin, as if you're on stage doing a soft shoe- mesmerizing an audience. You juggle the rod as a baton. You balance it on nose, on clothes, then somersault and catch between toes.* Parents clap. "Just like his grandfather in Vaudeville," father boasts.

In the, just seconds, as you fly up through the air your senses tell you, narrow as your experiences may be, still you can gather the lessons learned, and use them to help your friend and protector fight the dozens of monsters lunging for his fin-claws.

Will you be able to demonstrate the courage and wisdom others see in you?

A SQUIRREL'S TALE

You feel your protector is communicating with beak-snout. 'Grab!' Human instincts tell you the same thing, so you do. Acrobatically you grasp a limb. Hold tight. What's this? Suddenly a squirrel of silver, ruby, and gold is dancing on your fingers. Bushy tail tickles your neck. Your butterflies don't stop it. "Why don't you stop it?" You musn't pay it attention. Your sight and thoughts focus below. The monsters. From your dream. They've come alive.

Cobras lurch and jump. Turt bats, whaps. Cobras regroup, shuffle back to battle in the stirring Lindian dust now clouding the Carpier shrine. Turt almost rises on haunches; so fast his fin-claws move. Turt's blares and cobras' screams become one. Turt's fishy breath and cobras' toxic venom saturates the sacred site.

You dangle; watch your protector fight for you. Other monster eyes catch yours. They beckon. You lock on one set, another, then, two, three at a time, then, many. They reach – their long trunks sway below your toes. Your sight locks on theirs, freezing their advance on your protector. You remember hearing about a boy of long ago who could do that same thing.

Other monsters come at him. You can't catch their eyes to freeze them. The harder you try, the more you lose concentration on the others. One at a time they thaw, resume advance. You realize your power isn't as strong as the long-ago boy. You fear for your protector. His mighty trumpeting slowly becomes gasps.

Squirrel stops his finger jig. He seems to sense something you cannot. He crawls down your arm and onto your forehead, feeling like a fur cap. Small paws are dark with oil from cracking walnuts. He swipes them across the sides of your eyes, staining them. You see this because his eyes become as mirrors allowing you to see reflection. His face changes into Carpier's face. He speaks to you.

'Where, but at the shrine of Lindia's patron foundling, may a creature be so honored, being allowed the opportunity of helping a foundling.'

Quick as chirps become voice – they return to chirps.

Cobras, that were turning away, lock James' eyes when they see the Carpier swipes. Immobilized. Longer they lock, the more confident James becomes.

He drops to the ground. The cobras rushing Turt skid to stop.

Instant silence. Turt glares at James. 'What are you doing?' With beak-snout, he tries to push James to atop shell. James won't budge.

'Appears standoff. That be a good sign,' Poppy Sol winks to Luny Mum.

Hissing whispers among cobras:
'Could it be Carpier is returned?' They stare.
'Those eyes. Carpier's eyes, has he.'
'No! Pretender, be he.'
'A two-leg cannot pretend that.'
'If mongoose were about, we could ask she.'
Hisses, at the mention of cobra archenemy.
'If one thing cobra and mongoose agree on, it is Carpier's eyes.'
'No mongoose about at this hour.'
'Pity us all if we harm this one.'
'Nonsense,' a malcontent hisses. 'Blood of a foundling is rightfully ours.' Nature of a cobra after such an edict would be to attack. Instead, he slips forward. Others join. The butterflies curtain between Turt, James and the cobras.

Somewhere, a matador with a red cape is vexing a bull. Likewise, butterfly color riles cobras.

Quiet of the countryside is broken by the the treed squirrel's chirps. 'No! No! You foreign flutterers do not understand cobra nature.' Risking achingly poisonous death, he leaps down and onto a cobra's hood; then, from one to another. '*Plinking*' sounds. Before any can snatch him, he bounds toward cane field, chirps confidently, 'Ta daa!' Mid air, he changes direction, jets to a cane stripped from its stalk. Body-force sends cane flying toward James.

Somewhere, a picador mesmerizes with coiling sword. This is the same with cane, cobras.

You think of the curtain rod, as, nimbly, you catch the cane. Butterfly curtain opens. You're unsure why, but even more nimbly, you balance cane first on nose, then toes. You point at each monster as rigidly with it you pose. *Fangs sway beneath hoods. All eyes lock to yours. Theirs' are not fearful, angry, only blank, trained by your stare, maneuvered by your cane. As you push down one hood, all lower, until every cobra drapes the ground.*

Turt's beak-snout is bouncy. Eyes sparkle, showing the pride within his thoughts, 'Carper's mettle shows.' The butterflies flutter behind James – his victor's mantle. Squirrel peaks head from cane field, then scurries into it. Seconds later, from that exact spot, Carpier emerges – same age, height and darkening to the sides of eyes as James. His fingers are stained dark with walnut oils. None, on earth, but James and the butterflies, sees him.

However, from above: 'Appears our foundlings 'as found one another,' winks Luny Mum. 'Only 'opin James gets on as fetchin' with Carpier as he did the Carper.'

'Only 'opin,' Poppy Sol agrees. 'James 'as a long ways yet to go. E'll needs plenty of 'elp.'

Says Carpier as he approaches James – 'Well played fellow traveler. Thou learneth' well.'

* * *

Inside the wharf-shack, Mariner takes Carper onto his lap. Onto Carper's lap he splays-open the floppy Carpier book. "Ready to learn how mongoose and cobra formed their century-long bond?"

Carper's recorder mind is anxious. "It was for Carpier's sake. Wasn't it"

"You learn quick about compassion, Carper. Carpier cares about cobras and mongoose. Cobras, mongoose, see it. So both cares about him: No matter their oceans'-old differences."

Ol Tom leaps from Turt's shell. 'How will Mariner spin it this time, Turt?' Tom dramatizes, by drawing a stern glare into that good eye of his and petting the air. 'I offer paw of peace to all the honorable wharf rats – as mongoose offered claw of truce to cobra fang of compromise.'

Turt offers claw-fin to Ol Tom, but in the form of a gentle rap upside cat's ear. Ol Tom stumbles but keeps airy paw 'arisen. 'Continue,' Turt's eyes tell Mariner. Any dozen of Mariner's versions are fine by him. He knows: The story ALL be in the bringen' together, of he, Ol Tom, Carper, Mariner; and mongoose, cobra; Carper, Carpier. 140 years later, it will coalesce in storyteller James' mind. No matter what the century, for foundlings, together, there is pack safety. There is that serenity of joy, closeness of camaraderie, that emotion animals marvel at, that humans call love.

Mariner adjusts game leg so Carper's lap-sailen'll be smooth. He looks sideways, sees Turt surveying him. "If Turt could talk, Carper, he'd sure be tellin' us what's important in this world. We only learn from critters what we choose. So gleams ye well the lesson to be learned".

Mariner exhales a deep, asthmatic breath. "Here blows the tale, Carper."

* * *

"I know where I've seen you," James says to Carpier.

'Seen whom,' Turt wonders, surveying the Lindian countryside.

A soft breeze mixes dry, grassy scents, giving the area the pungency of fresh-laid hay. Turt notices a dozen or so mongoose. They'd heard the scrappin', came ascamperin' just in time to see James, looking so Carpier-like with those dark walnut-accented eyes that mesmerize mongoose enemy, the cobra. Mongoose'll stay – in case cobras turn on James. Turt knows this because the squirrel has painted James to look, so Carpier.[20]

"Where I seen you was," James says, he and Carpier's eyes level, "was in a book. You was lyin' on your carpet under a tree seemin' to look way offy in the distance."

---

[20] Not in over a thousand years had so many cobra and mongoose in the wild been so close without ripping each other to shreds. Not since the millennium of Carpier.

'Meditating.' Carpier demonstrates. Whites sheet his eye sockets, briefly, and then the pigment quilt returns. 'Perhaps one day your shelled protector will teach it to you.'

"I remember hearing the word, met-i-tatin'," James imitates. "While you was, met-i-tatin', people with clubs and whatnots come upon you."

* * *

Carper shouts as he squirms on Mariner's lap. "It's the ol woman's famlee'. They're gonna kill little Carpier." Carper tenses, readies to leap into the picture to help Carpier.

Mariner holds him in the wharf-shack with his words. "Carpier's got other estraspecial help."

Gnarled crone screeches through crooked teeth. "My sister takes him in, names him. All she gets for it is a too soon time to greet Goddess Nardesha." She leads the rush of villagers who pull knives and mallets from beneath their worn-to-an-oily-shine flour sack clothing. Suddenly they halt. In the boy's eyes, they believe they see the beauty of Nardesha's love.

* * *

"I don't have a name," James says when asked it by Carpier.

'You shall find one. Or be given one soon, I am certain,' says Carpier.

As James is talking to the air around him, Turt notices that one of the reclined cobras begins edging toward his shell. He raises fin-claw to squash it, and then stops, remembering the bringen'- together with Mariner and Carper so long ago back in the wharf-shack. Instantly Turt's glad he gave the slider a moment's reprieve — for the cobra comes in peace. With fangs, he begins gnawing Turt's shell — adding his graffiti — his coiling likeness. (As always, Turt revels in the needle scratch of tattooing that relieves invisible itches within shell.)

'This place is a lovely tribute, is it not, traveler,' Carpier says to James as they walk amongst cobra and their stone replicas at the feet of the Carpier statue. Carpier strokes the cold cheeks of his likeness. James sees his pride swell. He can't say why, but it angers him.

James confronts Carpier. No Nardesha does James see now in Carpier. He chooses to see only a cunning glare. James kicks dirt onto his feet. "Why didn't you help when I needed it?"

Turt, real cobras, and distant mongoose tense and look around: There is no other human, only James – in a fit. A silent, almost reverent consensus drifts among critters, 'We must remain with this new version of Carpier – even at a distance – to help him if a time comes when he can't help himself. We must do this to honor our memory of Carpier.'

Carpier bends to pat dirt back into place and pets a displaced bb-size bug. James doesn't know what to do: Nothing? Apologize? Or frantically shake Carpier. He pushes his face inches from Carpier's. Carpier doesn't blink. For a moment, James believes he sees the spark, and then the fire blazing that someone (his mother) told him is the burning power of Nardesha's love.

* * *

"Demon posen' as Nardesha. That's who this Carpier is," crone screeches to the hesitating mob. "He can't fool true followers of sweet Nardesha." She and some others ready to kill him.

From: behind trees, beneath boulders, under cover of scrubby brush emerge dozens of cobras. They hiss, sway, and encircle Carpier. No fire of Nardesha fills their eyes, only a cold serpentine stare declaiming, 'We are poised and ready.' The mob backtracks slowly, to keep from startling the snakes that they are certain protect a demon.

Carper punches the Book's picture of the mob and shouts, "So the cobras didn't need the mongoose this time, right

Mariner?"

"Just wait," Mariner says, blinking pretend tiredness – at the work of pretend reading. As you grow to be a man you'll see there's no end to the foolhardity even stupenditiousness of humans."

Crone shrieks, "What kinda cowards we be if we let a demon walk the land to kill others like 'e did my sister. We can take his minions. They's just rope with a couple sharp edges."

"Lemmings, Carper", Mariner says. "The crone's peoples becomes like those furry-footed rodents sueyciden' it to the seas. They rushed our Carpier and cobras that crazily." He turns the page. Carper's eyes widen when he sees the massive human glob Mariner drew as human-headed lemmings. He mentally records the picture. In his lifetime, Carper will describe it hundreds of different ways. Always the listener would picture, perfectly, Mariner's rendering.

Mariner continues on, "They might have hurt Carpier too, iffen it twarnt for…"

Carper waves arms excitedly. "I know!"

Tom mewls, 'Me too.' Tail keeps time to Carper's wave.

'Don't I just know,' Turt trumpets.' 'That it's all in the bringen-together.' Turt catches the curiosity in Carper's look. It mirrors a voracious appetite for the banquet of life's adventure.

Carper coo-ly parrots Mariner: "They might have hurt Carpier too iffen' it twarnt for…" He fills in for where he interrupted Mariner. "Iffen it twarnt for – THE MONGOOSE."

Mongoose rampage in from the cane fields. Razor teeth glisten in the sunlight. Snouts open, they attack villagers to protect their foundling, even if it means fighting alongside cobra for the first time ever. Their throaty screeches and drumming tails intimidate foe. Cobras quiver, hiss, and ready for a two-front battle. Carpier's heart thumps so loud it drowns out the noise.

"Ended up hardly a battle at all, Carper," Mariner says. "Mongoose slid past cobras. People skedaddled away, back to their village. Didn't bother Carpier no more. Despite the wisdom he spread, the kindness he showed, joy he brought so many downtrodden with his tales, there was always some looking to skin 'im. But now he would have protectors."

Mongoose and cobra stare at each other, and do a slow dance around one another – confused by their new, aligned, status. The countryside is quiet. Other critters peek from behind cover- no chirps, peeps, croaks, whistles. Slowly all eyes – even those of cobras and mongoose – begin to lock to Carpier's. His stare hold them tight.

"Not enslaven' eyes, Carper," Mariner says. "Freein' eyes. Compassion they saw in Carpier brung 'em together. 'N they followed and helped Carpier for over a hundred years, til the day he died. Only then did their alliance begin to crack." Mariner winks. "He didn't really die, some say, and that to this day he walks the earth wearin' many disguises and helpin' foundlings."

Carper's eyes glisten as he looks out the porthole, hopin' Carpier might be a peerin' in.

"Maybe you, Carper, or someone like you, some future foundlin'll be that powerful in the brungen' together. Maybe you or they'll accomplish what Carpier did with mongoose and cobra. Maybe even more. Course that would be one overflowin' net a' brungs' together; 'cause Carpier spent a century a-nettin' in."

* * *

"You asked why did I not I help you" Carpier says calmly to James. "What makes you think I did not? Maybe I saw to it that you got that cane. He pauses as James fingers the cool rod. "I helped you by showing you that, sometimes, you have the power to help yourself."

Ah, you see the wisdom Carpier invites you to share. Poppy Sol blinks agreement, nudges you with a warm ray, moving you nearer Carpier. 'Lifelong mate 'e can be to you young sire,' says Sol. Treasure such friendships.'

Your anger at Carpier vanishes and a, 'warmth', replaces it. That warmth: There is a word for it, one you've heard often in the past — but never really understood until now — 'compassion.'

CHAPTER 18

Shelled one's in his meditatin' world. Mongoose and cobras mill about the woods, curiously sniffing the other. Allies again? Compassion is king? Carpier watches the butterflies flit about you. He holds out his fingers for them to light on. Gently he pets their wings that glimmer so in the sunlight. Just once before have I seen their kind in Lindia. Do they travel with you from your land?'

"Yes" you beam.

Butterflies sense the admiration coming from the renowned Mahatma Carpier. They circle him, showing appreciation, and then they mantle your shoulders.

'Gentle protectors and guiders have you,' says Carpier. He leans toward them and arcs hands around his ears. 'Do you know what they are saying when they whisper to you?'

Okay, along with him you'll play — because it's becoming fun. "I didn't know they talk."

'Listen close.' He motions you nearer. 'They are telling about a boy who is so like you.'

You hear only flutters.

'That boy is far away: Not only in place, but also in time. He too traveled here, with ancestors of these butterflies.'

You know that the puzzlement of not being able to decipher the riddle shows on your face. You like Carpier, even more, because he doesn't make you feel bad for not understanding. His calm eyes beckon you to enter his

thoughts and feelings.
 'Do you know the most important thing about that boy?'
 Curiosity shivers through you. "Please tell me?"
 'It is; what he means to you.'
 Carpier seems to burrow into YOUR *thoughts, feelings — so he can cocoon with you — so you can enjoy fully the news he interprets from the butterflies.*
 'The boy will become your forever best friend — that's what they say. You, his.'
 In a split of a second it takes you to blink Carpier says, 'Go now, must I, but with you soon I will be.' Then, he's gone.

* * *

Butterflies, taking a break from foundling watch, hover near a torch on the Cincinnati pier. Calico departs, informing them. 'Now that Mariner has Carper all cleaned and rested, I will see if the boy is handsome as mother was pretty.' She glides to, and then slips through a wall crack, and into the wharf-shack.
 Though you, Mariner, Turt, and Ol Tom sit together, only you notice her. The sweet scent of her perfume — it reminds you of a smell you remember but don't know why. That despairing night under the cart with her when you first smelled it, all seems blanked from your memory. One day you'll remember?
 Pretty, pinhead-sized peepers wink at you. Many-colored wings flutter near your face and kiss your cheek. 'My name is Calico. Come along,' you imagine she says.
 Suddenly you're upon her back, flying, through a wharf-shack crack. Into the warm night you glide, swept away swiftly as the rider on Dear Precious was. 'Steer clear of the painted ladies,' that grim rider, entrenched in your thoughts, growls. 'You're on one now. (Calico) Steer clear I warn.' Of course you twont' obey. You never will.
 'Hold tight,' Calico coos. 'I will take you places no boy has been.' Her smile is butter, honey, sweet. She even reminds you of a tender someone: Oh, her sweet touch, and voice. ('Bonnie boy. How I love you.') You feel light — lighter than this creature a thousand times smaller than you. You feel free as you drift above your city so aglow with exploding silver glitters

of fireworks. Last night they were exciting as you watched them while safely grounded to Mariner's lap and Turt's shell. Tonight, flying midst them, they are – ALIVE!
'Do you like this?' Calico asks.
You smile, not realizing your mouth could turn upward so.
'Plenty more to come,' Calico cries out.
These joys of imaginin', that Mariner has told you of, are all yours to do with as you like. Ohh! It's time for a landing. Back, through the crack, you slide. Reality beacons brighter now, sparked so, from just that little imaginin'.
Calico perches atop a book – one whose title, 'Butterflies of the World,' soon you'll be able to read. Printed on the cover are those of her kind with as vivid of hues. Blends in so well, she.
Only you see her – because you know she's there. 'Carper,' says she.
How does she know your name?
'I know a boy I'd love you to meet. One day I'll introduce you. He looks just like you, Carper, though talks not like you. He has met you hundreds of times. Only in your imagination can you meet him – because you came long before him. He can be anyone you imagine him to be because he exists far beyond your time.'
You squint at Calico. Your thoughts focus on her fluttery whispers, quiet as brush strokes. Or do you only imagine you hear? You look over to see if Mariner, Turt, and Ol Tom are listening. No. They are staring into the Carpier Book, entranced.
'SHHH! Let's not disturb them,' Calico continues. 'I, and other, some quite fearful-looking, but of whom you must not be afraid – will guide you to the boy. You must find one another. For he is part of you, and you, him, and forever will you each need the other.'
Was he the boy I thought I saw in the Lindian forest? Mariner interrupts your thoughts as he looks up from 'reading', and, for no reason other than to rest his eyes, he points at Turt's shell – to a recently penciled-in tornado of butterflies.
"A Tehas tornado, looks like to me," Mariner says. "That particular picture's a mystery to me, Carper. Maybe you can decipher it."

* * *

Like a Tehas red-dust devil bursting from the earth, butterflies begin swirling in the Lindian breeze. The butterfly mini tornado mesmerizes James. Their orange and yellow funnel coaxes Turt toward deeper relaxation, as when he rests in the eye of a Tehas devil. Remembrances of Tehas long, long-ago: Meeting the Golden Boy?/Girl? for the first time, midst a roiling devil – an extra-special devil day, for there, too, on that day were butterflies, mixing the swirl into multi-layered violet hues. Remembering most fondly that moment, when he'd met another, to be, lifelong friend, a Golden one, Turt breathes in deep.

He savors *now*, the meditative calm of the butterflies' motion, as *then*, when the boy/girl penciled the butterfly tornado scene onto the semi-buried Turt, whom the Golden he/she at first thought was a rock near the fort, and, was meant for all to draw on. When first Turt awakens, raises head from sand where he's buried himself from the desert's mid-day scorch to see whom tickles-massages him, he hears,

"Oh, pardon me, shelled one. A rock, you, I thought."

'Feels nice,' Turt's contented look, says. Many a creature or two-leg might have thought the sight of a boy/girl as odd. Not Turt. Live and let live.

After petting Turt's snout, Golden Boy says, "While I draw I'll tell you the latest tale I wrote about...*slitherin' Sam the ramblin' man*..."

Turt breathes out – slowly ridding the tension of battling the cobras. Time to get on in his quest of delivering James to just the right human. Turt's learned, in his near century and three quarters, everything takes time, pace yourself and you'll arrive at your destination.

James climbs aboard him. Onward, Turt crawls.

* * *

Before closing the Book, Mariner slips in his place-mark, a

seahorse. It is long dead, none-the-less, neighs 'see ya soon Carper.' Mariner says, "And that's how the famous hundred year peace got goin'twixt cobras and mongoose. Written about in all the history books. You'll see when you get older and reads good as me."

Calico flits over, lands first on Turt's beak-snout, then Ol Tom's ear. Tom mews. Turt trills.

"Where you been off travelin' to, Calico?" Mariner asks. He strokes her wings. "Don't matter. Glad you're back." Ashamed, Mariner thinks of a traveling dandy who stopped by the wharf-shack on his way from Connecticut to Tehas; and was showing off his butterfly collection. 'Mighty glad Calico warn't here to witness me NOT tossing him in the river.'

'Cannot stay,' Calico flutters to herself. 'Just came to check on our foundling. His brother, though, no foundling, is, I sense, in need of help, down Tehas way.' Off she flies.

EPILOG TO END PART I

One day, together, Carper and James will help one another to survive, flourish. But there are those that Carper and James must confront in their lifetimes – before this is possible.

First, there is James' well-hidden stalker: never showing himself since he began following James after the ferry crash. Book of Carpier is in one hand, Bowie in other. He glares out from the forest at James and Turt as they travel. Then there's ever-calculating Thibidioux, ever-watching Carper from his wanted poster. The Laza Bones is thinking of the map section to the treasure he'd scratched onto Turt. 'Re-unite it with the other three sections, then I be celebratin' by slittin' open the creature 'n having the fattest bayou feast any gatah's evuh seen.'

INTRODUCTION TO PART II

July 4, 1826: 50 years – to the day – since the signing of the Declaration of Independence.

As in Carper and Mariner's Cincinnati, for a full week CELEBRATION lights the night skies throughout America. No excitement at a serene Franciscan mission in Tehas terrtory. Deadly will be the fireworks here in a decade. It will boost the adolescent nation into brutal adult reality.

When it occurs, Carper will be at that mission, known, remembered as 'THE ALAMO.'

PORTRAIT OF A MAN WHO IS A LEGEND IN HIS OWN MIND – A TAILORED TEHAS TALE

The travelin' dandy who visited Mariner? Stephen F. Austin. Dashing hero of his day. Emissary of the United States government to Tehas. He spends the night at that above-mentioned mission.

Alone in his cloister. He's busy pinning butterflies. He takes time to fancy-up his bushy sideburns in the window reflection and cruise fingers through his jet pompadour. "The ladies are quite right. You are a handsome so-and-so. Don't you ever die." (He'd be fortuitous to make it to 42 – little more than a decade away.)

Austin thinks aloud, practicing turning a genteel Connecticut accent, he'll never be able to lose, into a lyrical drawl that'll become known as 'Tehan'. "Whah, if young upstarts like this Darwin I've been hearing about are correct, then I must be the top link of his chain."

He slips off custom Abacrombie and Stitch waistcoat and adjusts scholar's pointy collar to meet sharp cheekbones. His reflection winks admiringly. At debutante balls, giggling, gaggles of silly gowned girls always gaze with curiosity at his arched brow. He knows well, that in just the right shadow of candlelight, it makes him look more dangerously primitive, as his ancestral Neanderthal brethren, than the tame, 'sophisti-kate', hominid he is. He uses that physical trait sometimes to charm; other times intimidate, to gain whatever he may covet.

At these 'coming out' affairs are jealous single men in their twenties. They whisper to one another their wonder, "Will that top-heavy ledge-brow of Austin's tip his face into the punch bowl if he leans over". More caustic comments by the world's 'zygomatic-arch have-nots', follow.

One-by-one, as Austin's name arrives on their dance cards, and aware of their beaus'-to-be-stares, but not caring, the young ladies will find a way to remove a white glove, and gad and aghast, 'accidently' brush bare fingers against Stephen F's swelled forehead protrusion.

Outside the window of Austin's Tehas cloister is a female, prettier than all Washington, Boston, or New York deb, truly prettier than Austin ever can imagine his own handsomeness. She observes his vanity. She makes no judgment – because the Calico's of our world have no competition when it comes to the truest inner or outer beauty. If Calico could hate, the reason she would ever have those feelings for him is for what he now does to those she loves.

Luny Mum reaches down, caresses Calico's wings with a soft beam. 'Be strong mi' lady. His kind may never destroy the love radiating from your beauty.'

Stephen F. Austin: Bon-vi-vaunt, patrician, fearless

butterfly collector.

Calico flits and grimaces as she watches, empathizes. 'Ooo, OUCH! He never sticks those pins in the right places.' She looks at colorful friends, vibrant in life, now impaled on a slab and entombed under glass. She is unable to sniff back 'honey-dewy' tears. She slams into the windowpane. 'STOP!'

Austin looks up, stares, ambitiously, right past the simple beauty of Calico only inches away. His sight is on elusive Luny Mum, hundreds of thousands of miles off.

"Cannot collect a moon, but Ah'll always be remembered for collecting me a state. One bigger, grander, than all the rest." Luny Mum glares him down and he glances away.

'All humans are not like him,' Calico hopes. (Carper will one day prove to her, she is right.)

She watches Austin's eyes and tries to communicate, 'Why can't you live with our beauty, if you consider us to be so, and not kill us to live with it. You collect and pin us today. Maybe a Lazarus Bontez Thibidioux and his herd shall collect and pin you tomorrow. "The pinning of the fittest, Monsieur Austin," Thibidioux will growl to you as he does his deed.' Calico closes eyes to memorialize her compatriots as she lights on the glass.

Mind reader of the two-leg, is Calico? For, Thibidioux is, in Austin's thoughts.

Austin speaks aloud – as if he's making a plea to the President. "Appoint me 'terr-torrial' Governor, and if I had three men worth Mariner's salt in his prime, or just two of the Kunta he talked about, I just bet I could control everything beyond the Rio Grande – and within a year – everything else who knows how far north."

Meeting Mariner wasn't by chance. Austin had heard the stories about Thibidioux attributed to Mariner. He visited the wharf-shack to decide – 'which is lore, which true?' Austin reconnoiters, "Won't even have to travel to the bayou to find Thibidioux. He's been sighted lazin' in Tehas. Why, if I could bring myself to approach Thibidioux and his herd..."

Barely hearing the vibration of that name, Calico, having seen and heard all she's ever wanted of Thibidioux,... ("Ah've tried, Lawd Ah've tried to teach dat boy the evils a' wrongen'" Mama Lucy had told Calico when she came checking on foundlings down in the bayou. "And now he's on that eternal search over in Tehas for some treasure he did badden for, and is bound to get innocent people involved and hurt for the sake of his greed.")... Calico opens eyes and readies to fly. She views the worst can ever happen to a butterfly.

As Austin mentions Thibidioux's name, wild avarice overcomes him. He begins ripping wings from those he's not yet entombed. His anger rises because he knows, 'Lo will I have to rely on the likes of whatever rabble Sam Houston or Jim Bowie can muster – if I cannot bring myself to just arch my brow and dance with the devil, Thibidioux.'

To deal with Thibidioux is so tempting.

Austin begins breathing deep, to relax. He calms himself by repeating his Connecticut-stern – Tehas-bawdy mantra: "Keep holt a' your wits – or your enemy will holt 'em for you".

Calico realizes Austin's nature better than he does. She knows how the most powerful SHOULD treat the gentlest. The strength that is her inner beauty allows her to overcome the pain of the carnage she witnesses. She must valiantly carry on as she grieves for those now gone. She leaves to spread the news of Austin's, via Thibidioux, soon-to-be power to control the life and the death of all creatures and two-legs – in a land that will soon become a burning hell.

There is a boy in far-off Cincinnati for whom this information will be vital – because one day it will be a matter of life and death for one so close to him – his half-brother – the Golden Boy whom he is yet to know.

Stephen F. Austin – known to political cronies and future generations as 'Intrepid Terr-torry Taker': Here is an excerpt from the I.T.T.'s now famous original communiqué (on display in the Fiction House Museum) to a Captain Golden – of his personal vision of Manifest Destiny.

'Your charge, Captain. Keep watch on movements and

settlements; and reconnaissance; be certain Mexical does not establish a hold on what will be ours when the Washington dolts finally get up off their collective assets and let loose of their...Can't send that part. Adams wrangled New England from the Brits – Jeffers fanangeled Leezian' terr-torry from the Franks – And I'll join them by entanglen' away Tehas from the Mex.'

Austin disregards the butterflies and begins scribbling notes to give to Golden.

A vision of Golden's boy/girl flashes through his thoughts. "What was the name again: William/Willamina? No doubt, mother Margaret will have him in a dress as beautiful as any gowned debutante", Austin laughs.

* * *

Laza Bones: "You rode out a hurry-cane to get those map sections – You is goina' get em. That all there be to it. You'll keill' anyone getting' in yer way."

PART II
THE BROTHERS

CHAPTER 19

Today is Golden Boy, 'William's' birthday. Into the kitchen, he struts, wearing his stepfather's gifts, pointy boots, chaps, canvas shirt, and cactus-scrolled belt. Red bandana's about neck. He nearly disappears under wide-brim hat. Silver spurs click. 'Willamina' doesn't even touch the dainty knitting kit present mother takes from apron pocket and tries giving him.

"He is just a little boy Margaret." Captain Golden appeases. "You can sew him ceremonial chaps and show them off at the party for Austin."

Margaret, anxious for 'fashionable' Mr. Austin to adorn their parlor, smiles.

This easing of tension gives Golden a rare chance to be firm, so later, he can let William revel at the thrill of riding alone for the very first time. Captain hugs wife and as her face presses brass buttons of his army blues he whispers, "A boy has to make a solo gallop someday. On his birthday makes it extra special. I'll be riding close, Margaret. He'll not be out of my sight."

Captain Golden's horse's temporary limp would later cause him to negate that promise and postpone his liaison – with

Thibidioux.

"SWIFT AS WIND" Golden Boy yelps a few minutes later. Through arid desert, he gallops pony – the other present from doting stepfather.

As his eyes widened, when he first saw the white-splotched roan back in the stable, Margaret ruffled her bonnet, cranked bustle and declared, "Why I declare; just as your real father with that ghastly Dear Precious, you'll spend more time with this beast than me, Willamina."

"Name's Golden Boy", William snorts as he rides the roan. He's memorized mother's rants. She'd beat him with the names Willamina, and that other. 'Ezekiah Bellows this. E.B. that.'

Don't even know the man, but already you hate that S.O.B. E.B. If it were possible, you know Margaret'd hogtie you with her apron strings to keep you from ever leaving her kitchen. All so she could regale you with her misery. 'Won't happen today. Today you ride. Free!' You lean and say into pointed, upright ears, "SWIFT AS WIND, I will name you."

FOUR YEARS EARLIER
(just what went on behind the pulpit)

The Right Reverend Bellows: Alone in his Cincinnati church. Sweat streams from his face after another fiery service. Door quietly opens and closes. He looks up. "Well Sister Truewood. For what do I owe this pleasure?"

Margaret's passions were enflamed by his earlier besotting sermon on God and Gomorrah. She slips behind podium and her preying hands are everywhere on him. Ezekiah's weak willpower is tested; immediately fails.

Rrrose Heather is bringing Ezekiah the fresh news – Bonnie is carrying. Rrrose retreats, quietly closing the door after seeing the entwined duo. Tested but not deterred is Rrrose's faith in her mission – convincing one, rigid as Ezekiah, to accept mother and child. A week later, she sees

Margaret on the street. She observes spark of eyes, glow to skin. She has seen it in too many of her girls. She KNOWS; even before Margaret. But she remains a believer – one day, for Bonnie's sake, and that of her child, the Reverend will be reformed of his sanctimony.

"Good morrow Miss Truewood", says Rrrose Heather, instinctively touching Margaret's abdomen. The board sidewalk squeals as they step onto the same plank. *"Dat spezial' flame of a formin' chil'"* Mama Lucy had told Rrrose Heather of – Rrrose Heather feels it burning beneath the cloth of the prudish housedress.

"Here now whure-mistress, just what do you think you are up to. I am certainly not one of your tramps." Margaret pulls away from the perfumed Madam whose sequined gown reveals oh so much cleavage. *"Belly afire – all you need to know,"* Rrrose Heather remembers Mama Lucy saying, as Margaret huffs to the other side of the street.

THE TALE OF A GENTLE RRROSE FOR TWO BROTHERS

As they, part, Rrrose Heather's calculating is cold: 'Separate Margaret and Ezekiah. How?'

'Captain Golden!' He'd accompany his whuring troops and pay – just talk to Rrrose Heather for hours; relaying his dreams and visions...

'...Captain Golden would be a good, no, great father. How simple would be this matchmaking. He wants a child. Margaret will need a father for hers.' Even easier for this many-a-favor-owed businesswoman; convincing the commanding officer to reassign Golden's unit, not too far afield, so she can keep track of the child...

...When the time is right, unite siblings with one another and possibly with father Ezekiah.

During the next four years, Rrrose waits patiently for that time, prodding it with hinting letters to Golden, appealing to his kind nature to be willing to share the love of the Golden child with Bellows when the right day came. And during Bellows 'visits' to her house, subtle conversations with him, about Bonnie, the good life he could have with her. With her Madam's well-honed wiles, the Reverend's Cincinnati son would have dozens of loving mothers at her house, just as the Reverend's Tehas outpost son would have dozens of equally loving soldier-fathers.

Whenever Golden Boy rides, (so giddy he is, riding alone for the first time) mother's repetitions, nearly immovable from his thoughts, drift away. "Captain Golden's not your real father. He married me, took us both in. Of course, we love him. But never forget Willamina. Reverend Bellows is your father. That man! He took advantage of me – an innocent 17 year old. You'll probably never meet him. I can't even remember what he looks like. Maybe you look like him – maybe not."

Her words are but a drone. They'd be even more so to Golden Boy if he could compare them to the fabulous adventures brother Carper's hearing spun by Mariner in Cincinnati. Golden Boy is sure, if he ever meets the one hella-va-fellow Bellows, he will either horsewhip or gun 'im down; just in case he too might bellow-on so sleepily mellow like mother. *'Ahh, the Captain. He is kind, spins for you Tehas tales, and lets you fire his six-shooter. The Captain loves you. The Captain IS your father. Why can't she see?'*

Captain Golden dismounts, kicks sand in disgust after his horse, Jesse, limps. Boy disappears from view. William knows the desert well as any trooper. 'I'll get a fresh mount and come for you.' Golden thinks of his meeting place with Thibidioux. 'It's a big desert, William. Just ride, and don't stop over at Prick Lily's for a visit, and all will be fine.'

"Spitting, is the boy's likeness to Ezekiah Bellows," would be the comparison of anyone who's seen the upright Reverend riding Dear Precious and who now might see William – broad chin, narrow cheeks, wide forehead – on Swift As Wind. Flowing golden hair and blue-sea eyes belong more to 'step' than 'real'. "Agile as Bellows rides", would be the comparison to Ezekiah as William guides Swift As Wind.

Golden Boy locks boots to wooden stirrups, braces in saddle, and becomes part of his pony's constant motion. "At dawn, after I oat and brush you, I'll write about you, Swift As Wind." Mentally he composes as the desert's salt air blasts his face. 'Chocolate colors streak my pony's milky mane. It swirls from his forelock top to tail tip.' William feels a melding as one – boy-pony, pony-boy. He begins mentally writing the adventure of their ride:

'Troubles brew beyond yonder pass. Innocent, wimmin', helpless chillun' ta be saved fum...um...put that in later.' He stares ahead – as if puffy clouds are words – just awaiten' for him to lassuu' em. He ropes 'em into his description then continues. 'Our hero's face streams sweat. Gritty duds cling to steely frame. Loyal steed's hooves kick burnin' sand. It stings granite-hard hands. To important is task of, 'a savin, for our hero to slow down to don gloves.'

Golden Boy's tries to rein-in neighing pony that swerves to avoid a nest of real-life rattlers.

'SHH! SHH! SHH!' Pony hears every bead in their pods. Already is Swift As Wind enamored with his rider – so quick to form are human-equine bonds, but beast instinct warns, 'Must lighten load and just break away.' Up, he rears. 'Neighs' become screams.

Golden Boy begins sliding off the saddle. Rattlers lurch. Boy is so close to flashing fangs he could touch the white diamonds on the snakes' backs. ('If only...,' James would think in the next century, '...Golden Boy had met Carpier. He could've learned to stare 'em down like I did.')

In a move Ezekiah Bellows would be proud, Golden Boy catches bridle, rotates body around bucking pony, lands standing on saddle. "Whoa. Steady. Keep holt of your wits; or your enemy will holt them for you." (Unfortunately, Swift As Wind has already lost them, and the rattlers are readying to take holt.) Often G.B. has heard the Austin statue speak those words to the troops as they fidgeted and complained about why they were in this desolate post. Those holtin' words, and a half-dozen whure's Austin brought in a next day, always seemed to work.

Golden Boy bends and pets Swift As Wind's withers. Master's touch, voice, barely audible midst hissing and marimba rattle, calms the pony. He prances sideways, safely away from the salivating mouths. As mount sits, he begins to trot, then gallop.

"I'll never do that to you again, sire", ride would like to tell mount. Bond of mutual respect is complete twixt human, beast.

'We come to a nest of scorpions wanting blood.' Golden Boy mentally writes what he sees.

'Watch this,' pony snorts. He kicks, showering them with sand.

"Yahoo!" So excited by their exploits G.B. nearly forgets his writing adventures. Not for long. He spies cobble-skinned lounging lizards. Their marble-sized, roving eyes say – "Go thatta-way. Save the wimmin' and chillun'." He veers pony northward. A bayonet-armed cactus salutes. He returns it.

To escape the staid life Margaret provides, Golden Boy's imagination is vivid as any foundling. He looks up at the make-believe friend he greets every morning from his bedroom window. "Race ya to the trouble at the pass, Poppy Sol. Think you can keep up with me?"

'You're on,' Poppy slyly winks.

NOW COMES JAMES' THIRD MUSE, VINEGARY MARGARET

'Damn you, Poppy Sol. Willamina would be with me yet today if you hadn't agreed to that childish chase,' Margaret is cursing skyward as she steps from the Lindian Woods into the clearing where the entourage of Turt, James, muses Rrrose Heather and Mama Lucy travel.

'Trouble brewin',' James thinks.
Rrrose Heather stops her story about James' great-great granduncle Golden Boy. She glares at Margaret. 'Here now, woman! No need for foul language in presence of a wee youngun'.'
Mama Lucy's heard tales of this woman from Rrrose and Lazy Bones; even Laza Bone's leather half-face would twitch when he told the tales. Mama scoops some pulverized tango-root from her pouch; sprinkles it. James coughs. Turt sneezes. 'Best mon small fry and innocent creature have some magic protectin' from such witchin'.'
Rrrose Heather says, 'Your son could NEVER be, 'with you', Margaret. 'You lost him the day you made him wear silly dresses.'
Margaret's stare is vinegar. She hates Rrrose for the once-upon-a-time controlling of her destiny before she even realized it.

* * *

Poppy Sol glares into shimmering sand. 'Drat the bloody luck of humans.' He sees whom Golden Boy will soon ride right into – brother, Carper's poster-board nemesis the Laza Bones.
Laza Bones Thibidioux: 'Here I be, awaiten' ta meet-up with ya Captain Golden. All a lazin' in buckboard bed, 'neath canopy of stretched bayou gator skins. Don't disappoint me, Captain.'
Thibidioux's famished gator herd, two dozen, along with longtime advisors Liege Leather, Prime Snout, Huey Long, and Baron Tail, lounge around intimidated team horses that barely rest and daren't whinny for water. Thibidioux knows that if gators get too hungry, he can sacrifice-up a bony hag.
'Ah, after lo these many years, taday ya'll get three-quatuhs of the maps and soon the treasure will be yourn'- to allow the grand life yourn' entitled. None 'll be stoppin' ya now.' (Thibidioux had a bead, though, not an exact location, on

Turt's back-map, through gator minions that noted Turt's expeditions in Tehas and bayou country.)

'Drat human fate brought on by the simple chances humans take,' glints Poppy Sol. 'Alas. No other way for 'em to live their time on earth? Cans't 'ide-away in a cave.' Warmly he hugs Golden Boy's shoulders. 'Live your adventure, my young blighter, with no regret.'

'The Golden Boy's hair, be golden as your orb, Poppy, and long as your rays,' often is Luny Mum's reply to Poppy's compliment of, 'His face is ivory as your glow, Luny Mum.' Poppy thinks of this as he squints at the deformed side of Lazy Bones. It is as equally ugly as Golden Boy is handsome. 'Just make it to Prick Lily, Golden Boy. You'll be safe with her.'

Golden Boy leans and whispers to his onward pushing steed. "I've two special friends I want you to meet, Swift As Wind. You'll like them." He hopes the giant shelled creature is there. He knows the other; the desert's tallest cactus – he calls her Prick Lily – has nowhere to wander.

* * *

'ZING!' Muse Margaret's barrage of well-aimed arrow-curses, 'This rabble my Willamina took up with! One's scum from the sea...'can only zing ineffectually off the hard back of Turt – because his thoughts focus on getting his passenger safely along. They miss James completely for he's busy imagining Golden Boy, Laza Bones, Poppy, Luny, and Swift As Wind. They aim directly to the heart of Rrrose Heather because they're meant to demean Rrrose's dear friend...'and that Prick Lily of the desert! No better than one of your whures, Rrrose Heather. Prick Lily and that sea scum are rotters, Rrrose – to the depths of grimy shell and stickery stalk.'

Rrrose has her thorn barrier as a deflector. 'Quite the opposite, Margaret,' Rrrose Heather corrects. "Lily's looking to 'elp your lad, and just you be lookin' at Turt – 'elping your lad's great-great *grand* nephew. You, damnable woman, should be grateful.'

TALES OF THE FICTION HOUSE

Margaret doesn't thank Turt, only continues ZING. 'So, that boy's kin to Ezekiah, too. No good shall come of him then, I grant.'

'You hush,' Mama Lucy shouts, sprinkling more dust onto James and Turt. 'You a fortunate one to even meet the shelled one or this chil'.'

As bickering muses walk alongside he and Turt, James, curious to learn more of Prick Lily, tries being peacemaker by getting them to focus on her. "Tell me about Golden Boy's other friend, Prick Lily?"

Rrrose and Mama Lucy smile, then shift their attentions to their sister of the sand.

LET ME TELL YOU THE TALE OF PRICK LILY THE SAGE

A ragin', sagin' 12 feet tall
Green
Cactus Queen
Prick Lily
Whose wisdoms come
Quite Willy Nilly

To partake of her
East Tehas Wit
Far away Critters
To her desert
Will flit
But not too close...
For fear of being
Pricked Silly[21]

Besides Poppy Sol, another knows Laza Bones' herd is near: The elevated-high, Prick Lily. But she knows how to stop

---

[21] This is the oldest published writing known to exist, of the thousands, by William Golden, 'Golden Boy'. Discovered at the Alamo – It is now on permanent display at the Fiction House.

the boy from riding smack into the gators – by way of a visitor flyin' in. 'Divert the Golden Boy and lead him to me, sister Calico.'

As magical as Lily's communion, is Calico's reply from off in the desert. 'Indeed Lil I will.'

The gulf breeze tips Prick Lily's forever-upright arms. Bastion trunk firmly anchors her. She doffs white, ten-gallon – Doves sail. Lily sings: 'Ya hoo and rippity doo. It'll be a rip-roarin', rootin'-tootin day deep in the heart of Teharoo. For the Golden Boy'll be acomin' to see his big sis Lilyroo...' Lily's emanations spring forth from her prickers, thousands of tuning fork transmitters. Critters, plants and varmints of the territory, their sensations, preened from millenniums of nature's honing, absorb her vibrations. Lavender petals, the shape of fine porcelain dishes, and, just as delicate, forever blossom on Lily. Their lacey antennae-like pistils are her sense-sound receivers.

'Did you meet the Carper, while you were away, Calico?' asks Prick Lily. What was he like? Do he and Golden Boy look alike?'

'So kindred are the brothers, Lily – in feature and spirit.' Calico senses, even from a distance, Lily's smile at hearing the news of the Carper. Calico sees Golden Boy astride pony. She becomes – hundreds of butterflies – and her shifting colors bewitch the duo and they follow.

'Know what today is, Calico?' Lily emanates of *The Great Desert Pilgrimage*.'

'But of course, Lil. On this day, at this hour, for thousands of years, never interrupted. I wish I had ferried Carper here today, so the brothers could view it for the first time, together.'

Luny Mum suddenly seems to glow above the desert, making a rare, full, daytime appearance. She gleams to a just-as-anxious Poppy Sol. 'A parade Poppy. Wouldn't miss it.' Her beam streaks the blue sky, touches, and holds Poppy's warm ray tightly.

'Won't it just give our Golden bloke scads to write about,' Poppy winks. They pay no attention to Laza Bones' howling

gators. The gators are used to seeing Mum only at night. Their sand-caked snouts point upward. They'd love to chomp of moist looking Mum.
    Laza Bones Thibidioux glances at Poppy Sol's location. 'Time ta meet dat oh so pretend-honorable Captain Golden.' *Reaction of your horde is immediate to your order.* "Up on claws. Let's go! Eternal drink'll be ours, AFTER we accomplish mission."
    Deterrents to Lazy Bones' plans waft the gators' way, from afar; in the aromatic form of the scent of Golden Boy's tender flesh and Swift As Wind's soft hide.

    The hundreds of Calicos – they swoop down and light upon Lily – then become one Calico again. Golden Boy watches. He's never jaded to butterfly magic. "Swift As Wind," he says, let me introduce Lil." Colt snorts. Cactus curtsies breezily. The desert is quiet as Golden Boy dismounts, lays, belly down, in the cool, wide strip of shade cast by Lily's trunk. He finger pencils in the sand. 'A ragin' sagin' 12 feet tall Cactus Queen, Prick Lily…' He ponders the next lines, smiles at Lily, then finishes. The words disappear quickly from the shifting sand, but not from his thoughts.
    'Just a tad longer, Golden Boy' thinks Lily, 'and you'll witness a parade few humans can imagine. What a tale of it you'll tell'. Golden Boy searches in the sand where often he's found Turt. No Turt today. Instead, he finds a leather strap. He digs. A saddlebag: the one he'd seen in his parents' room. Why would it be here? He traces fingers over the skeleton markings. Suddenly he's scared and tosses it. It lands, camouflaged by afghan-thick spider webbings, atop Lily's shoulder. Golden Boy forgets it for now. He's distracted by whirring sounds.
    Calico perks antennae. 'Do you feel the vibration Lily?'
    'Indeedy do. 'bout time. I 'xpect you'll be the one to lead em all in.'
    Calico affirms with the flit of a wing, then flies off, to beyond the horizon. Lily beams to her subjects near and far. 'As the heat orb shines his brightness and the night Goddess

honors us with a daytime audience, come all, gather for the royal procession that will transform our desert – into – our Paradise kingdom.'

* * *

'Go Jamie,' Rrrose Heather says. 'I know you be faunchin' ta see what all the desert fussins about. We'll be here when ya get back.' Rrrose lightly pinches his cheeks. 'Just be careful.'
Margaret says, 'You should not let the boy go alone. Paradise. Bah! Look at the bad effect it had on my Willamina.'
Mama Lucy sprinkles powders on James. 'That'll keep Laza Bones away. But Lawd protect *Willamina* from him.' Mama Lucy stamps her foot. 'Dang you Margaret. You got me to be mis-callin' the strappin' lad. Curse you woman.'
Margaret smiles at her small victory.
'Whoosh!' *You skim across time and planet and there you are sittin' on Prick Lily's shoulder, near the saddlebag. Ooh! Don't move about or you'll get one sizeable thorn in your butt. You shout 'hallo.' Nobody answers. They don't know you're there. Wow, look at all the...*
James sees desert creatures streaming to Lily; most timid, like lizards and armadillos, but also copperheads, coyotes, Gila monsters. They surround Golden Boy and Swift As Wind.
Poppy Sol proudly glints, 'See, Mum. Word's spread of our duos bravery. Among even the most vicious of the desert they're welcomed.'
Prick Lily senses Laza Bones Thibidioux's horde trekking their way and begins thinking of ways to protect her golden boy. If only she could take him in her arms – ouch IMPOSSIBLE? – And nurture him the way she wished his mother would. She's sure that would be even more impossible. Though Prick Lily's had many-a-sprout, they soon ran along. This golden human one always returned.

TALES OF THE FICTION HOUSE

LILY'S ROYAL TALE

Unlike Calico, who has the Austin's of the world who might net and collect a butterfly, none yet covets a giant cactus. Prick Lily can trust all, fully, and in turn, is of infinite trust. Creatures convey to Queen Lily their most private thoughts. Passing leaves, migrating birds, deliver news; plants, other cacti, relay messages. She collates, stores all; interprets and disperses desert sage.

Lily achieves near harmony among her subjects through her fanciful mix of cowgirl frivolity and Solomon edicts: 'Coyote territory – north of me; wild hogs, south; all insects are fair game to salamander, and sal, for snakes; snakes for birds of prey – but only if those doing the preying rely first on the dying for their diet. ALL must gather for sunset vigil with others of their kind...'

Stray bulls might charge Lily to challenge desert dominance – only once. "Youch!"

Humans stop and look in awe of her majesty when they wagon by. Those lost in the desert, parched by torturous heat, she provides sustenance by easing the sharpness of lower prickers, allowing them to gouge trunk to suckle her liquid.

James' thoughts: *'Because you sit on Prick Lily's shoulders, you are the first to see what comes. You gasp at the beauty.'*

Great-great granduncle William, at the foot of Prick Lily, his thoughts: *'What all the critters spent the year anticipating, you see, when they do'* – the sky – awash with colors, yellows, ambers, reds. Hundreds of thousands, maybe a million butterflies: Calico leads them.

Simultaneous feelings of both boys: *Your eyes widen. You're fanned by the cool flutters. The parade surrounds Prick Lily. You feel that you and all the critters being swept up into it. You sway gaily, airborne within the hues.*

'Can't wait to tell Rrrose Heather and Mama Lucy about this,' anticipates James.

Great-great granduncle's precious thoughts: *'Any sorrows you*

ever had – they are deadened. *Your world is beautiful, loving as the love you feel from only one human – Captain Golden.'*
    Hostility toward mother and Bellows releases. 'If only you can keep these feelings forever,' you write in your thoughts. 'You must try. No more pain, sadness. Just joy. You're certain the world has chosen you to expose its beauty to others; by writing of it.'
    Magic of the in air parade has you again riding Swift As Wind. Butterflies' flutters thunder louder than any herd of horses. Your steed grows wings and flies you around Prick Lily. You barely see Lily because so many of the paraders circle her. You hear, 'Yahoo, rippity roo...'
    Both boys: *Sweet music is the peacefulness you experience. This all may be lasting for a minute, or five, or maybe an hour. Maybe a year, a century. You can't tell; so lost in your reverie.*
    Then, the music disappears.
    Curdling growls replace it.
    "Where you going?" you shout at the butterflies as they 'whoosh' upward, and critters, suddenly again desert-bound, scatter. You see something in the distance that is frightening as the parade was beautiful: strange, snouted creatures. They're coming your way. Fast.
    The beckoning scent of Golden Boy and Swift As Wind is so overwhelming to the gators they bolt forward, ignoring Laza Bones' rants for them to halt.
    Butterflies swarm back down. Calico hovers beside Prick Lily. 'Their leaving was only ruse to get the small desert creatures safely away, Lily. Now, you and we flutterers will protect our Golden Boy.'
    'To do so we must keep the boy here,' telegraphs Lil. 'His pony cannot outrun them.'
    Golden Boy: *You prepare to gallop off. But the thousands of butterflies glue themselves to you and Swift As Wind. They hold you within Lily's shadow.*
    James: *You try climbing off Prick Lilly to help the boy. Prickers poke: "Ouch!" Luny Mum and Poppy Sol simultaneously say to you. 'Try as you mighten', you canst change the past.'*

    Pony and rider are so tempting to rambunctious gators.
    "Heel ingrates. It ees my way or zee de-skinned way," Laza

Bones warns his flesh and hide hungry minions. He brandishes the foot-long knife he'd used to fashion his gator canopy. "Too many days I spend in theez' hell to get my maps. No-ting must go awry." Gators ignore Laza Bones' and quickly distance themselves from master's rickety buckboard and scrawny hags. "Damn! Zey mus be stopped. Stave zem off til I get there, Liege Leather," Laza Bones roars.

Mesmerizing butterfly colors: The herd sees them as only a garnishment around the meal. Only Liege Leather beholds the beauty. Nose bone bounces as he keeps pace with the others. He growls, 'Devouring of an equine will be forgotten, but not so a young two-leg.'

James' pants catch on prickers. Stuck. He watches as gators easily part butterfly curtain. They snap at Swift As Wind's hooves. He dances sidewise. His whinnies, so-buffered by snarls, seem whimpers. Golden Boy hoists his legs. "You snouters, you won't separate me from my Swift As Wind.'

Liege Leather growls to his compatriots. 'This is Tehas. No bayou code here. We will be hunted down if we as much as scratch him.'

James sees the garishly decorated peacemaker. He silently cheers him.

Liege Leather's look meets Golden Boy's briefly. He sees the pity of so many other young two-legs who, viewing him in his cage, tried not to notice his mutilations. In these eyes, he sees the rare wisdom he'd occasionally notice in those of other young two-legs, communicating, *'your spirit is FREE, no matter your imprisonment.'* As Liege Leather begins pulling gators away from boy and pony, he silently pledges to the two-leg. 'You will survive young one. This, I pledge. Afterward, I beg of you. Tell my story. So all the world will know. No freak am I.'

To allay his fear, Golden Boy begins composing:
'Liege Leather, I will call him. A proud creature is he. Taken from his home by evil ones. He is marked upon, not for joy as with my shelled friend, but to scar, to drag down into the evil

ones' own rotting place in life. He won't let himself be pulled down. Nor will me. Not by these creatures, to devour me, nor by my mother. Mother's dresses will not drag me down and break my spirit.'[22]

Golden Boy strokes Swift As Wind's neck. "See how the pierced one helps us, my pony. Stay calm. He'll succeed."

Prick Lily, abetted by a shifting wind, hurls prickers. Gators howl from the peppering. Butterflies block gator's eyes and nostrils to disorient them.

A gator lunges to bite the pony's leg. It's Prick Lily's trunk instead. He gets a mouthful of six-inch long stickers. The more he spits to expel them, the deeper they impale. Madness, can pain bring! He runs wildly into the desert; to lay bleeding to death, eventually ripped apart, eaten alive by coyotes, then picked by vultures, who, tasting first time far-off bayou delicacy, take a liking. Woe to other Thibidioux gator conscripts in the future. Desert carnivores will pursue them as a precious commodity; even follow them back to the safety of home confines.

* * *

Trudging through Lindian Woods, oblivious to the muses squabbling, Turt begins thinking of the pony he'd heard stories of from Golden Boy. The stories must have been true because, though Golden Boy was a teller of tales, no liar was he. As Turt looks about for dangers, he thinks, 'You made the ultimate sacrifice of a guard creature, Swift As Wind, though you were just a young beast of carry. If in another world we meet, I will tell you so. For your action showed me how I could save James.' Turt's buck up into the tree earlier in the day that saved James – that idea came from, none other than, Swift As Wind.

---

[22] Read 'Liege Leather: My Life and Times with the Two-Legs – As told to William Golden,' Fiction House Publishing House, 1851.

* * *

Swift As Wind believes he is being toppled. Not realizing how deadly his hooves can be, he bucks. Golden Boy rockets skyward, thinks he sees a boy his age on Prick Lily's arm reach and pull him. He lands atop the saddlebag. He blinks. No boy there. Imagined? Suddenly, sweet smelling butterflies hide Golden Boy's body and his scent. Gators are confused.

'Don't leave. We can protect you,' Lily telegraphs Swift As Wind. Too late. Instantly Lily realizes the pony's plan – to lead the gators away.

* * *

Quoted from Golden Boy's THE DAY OF THE CACTUS, Fiction House Publishing, 1852. 'Pony barely made it 100 yards, before they were on him. If only you wouldn't have run, Swift As Wind, maybe Calico and Prick Lily could have helped you too. You did it for me, my friend. I will always believe your unselfish act saved me from what next was to come.

'I can't look at what they're doing to my Swift As Wind. My eyes tear. I peek through my butterfly curtain and look down. Liege Leather is at Prick Lily's stalk: He seems to be communicating to her and Calico. His snout barely moves. He stares up; seems to see me despite my camouflage. He looks at me in the same kind way as Captain Golden. Suddenly he looks away; pretends I'm not here when a buckboard arrives driven by..., WAIT! How can I describe the he/it I am seeing, for this first of many times, and expect anyone to believe, ever again, what I write? "Liar," they would say and close my book. "No such person/thing, human/creature, he/it as you describe could ever exist."

James: *You too, see, but don't believe what you see. What should you do? Fly back to the Lindian Woods to tell Rrrose and Mama of the danger the Golden Boy is in. You could stay, but like Poppy and Luny Mum...can't change the past. But, maybe you can.*

CHAPTER 20

THE TALE OF CAPTAIN GOLDEN'S DREAM (AS VIEWED THROUGH HIS ROSE-TINTED GLASSES)

Blue-uniformed, stately in saddle, he rides. Shoulder-length golden hair crowns ruddy face. Desert sky is a calm vermillion, and its sage fragrance is soothing. 'Tomorrow, all will be in place: Resign my commission; no more Thibidioux or Austin's to bother with; take my family to the California territory; buy a 10,000 acre ranchero, raise cattle; have many children to whom William can tell his stories. One day they will give me grandchildren. I am not greedy: Only selling for a fraction what the maps are worth. Nothing can go wrong.'

Golden doesn't realize. He is being followed.

"WHOA!" Steed, Jesse, stiffens. Jesse's hurt leg needed only a liniment rub; now good as Golden, himself. Golden checks his pocket watch. No choice but to suspend search for William because it's time to meet Thibidioux – below the tallest cactus in all Tehas.

THE TALE OF GOLDEN'S GREED

The saddlebag holding the dream came into his possession by chance. After sweeping away from Thibidioux in the hurricane the oilskin-protected saddlebag was found, a low-witted buck private finds it on the shore. He delivers it to his Captain. Secrecy follows; a pseudo-ceremony in Golden's office. "I present this honor ribbon sent by the venerable Stephen F. Austin."

Golden salutes: "You are a hero. You have captured vital information that will bring Tehas statehood." He awards gullible grunt 10, $100 bills – more money than he imagined exists in his world. At midnight, Captain sends homesick underling packing for the Dakotas where he can embellish details of what brought him the bronze-crested laurel. (Even contrived heroism has benefits. He would be sponsored for and hold political offices and judgeships for many decades.)

THE TALE OF GOLDEN'S FLEECE

Sergeant Miles Peabody curiously watched the future-judge escorted out the back gate by his Captain. 'Golden's demeanor's changed,' Peabody calculates.

In the coming months, Peabody scrutinizes his activities: 'Golden meets with Thibidioux, formerly a pariah to Golden's rule.'

At joint sessions with Austin: 'Golden omits details garnered during reconnaissance missions.' ('A sign he's hiding something from Austin? Maybe Austin's been 'brought in' to form some sort of Thibidioux-Golden-triangle deal?')

'If anywhere on this are the fingerprints of Stephen F. Austin,' Peabody tells himself, 'then real money is involved.' Any way he can, he will find a way to partake of it. To try to discover more information, when Golden leads troops on patrol Peabody begins, 'politely', stopping by Golden's quarters to inquire of Mrs. Golden's welfare; and sometimes have tea.

"Why yes, I'd be honored to call you Margaret, Margaret."

Golden Boy hates him: Louse? Creep? Snake? One day he'll write just the right word for him!

Lieutenant Miles Peabody – He has been the one tracking Captain Golden this day.

* * *

LINDIAN WOODS GOSSIP

'Up to then, Lieutenant Peabody, was just a friend in my time of need,' Margaret dictates.
'Me girls 'ad many such, *friends*,' Rrrose Heather laughs, tapping Mama Lucy's shoulder.

* * *

Straddling Lily's shoulder and hidden by butterfly swarm, Golden Boy peers down at 'Laza Bones'. He mentally writes, 'Who/what, is the he/it? Person/thing? One hand, delicate as a girl's; other, beast-claw. Face, so soft, blue-eyed. No! He/it turns – face is now snout, and leather, like the bodies of the crawlers that now pick their teeth with the bones of my Swift As Wind. I hate you, you whoever-whatever. You are one of them. NO! You have smooth hair and soft face. You are 'he', like me.'
You brush hands over cowboy attire – thankful it's not just a dream that you're free of the dress. You think of climbing down to this person. One considered a he/it surely would assist one considered a he/she as you; protect you from the crawlers. But then 'he' moves again, slow, with such agility, just like the crawlers. You freeze. You can't go to 'it'. 'It' is one of them, and will destroy you. Suddenly, as you squint into the distance you are ecstatic but stay quiet. A rider approaches: It's – Captain Golden.
Golden slips a rifle from his saddle as Thibidioux retrieves his from buckboard.

Golden Boy watches stepfather and 'it' talk in Prick Lily's shade.
"Ive leeved up to my part of the bargeen, Golden. None can say Lazeerus Bontez Thibidiox be a welcher." He opens a box. "10,000 green leaves for yeez on deliveree."
Captain Golden draws a line in the sand with rifle barrel.

"Excavate here, Monsieur."

Thibidioux motions with snout side. Two gators commence clawing.

Huey Long glances at Liege Leather who is looking up now and then. Long thinks he sees the young two-leg when he looks up. 'Don't reveal anything now,' he thinks. 'Be pragmatic and record it for later use.'

Golden Boy hears 'click' of a third rifle and a voice coming from behind Prick Lily. He can't see who it is – but the man sounds familiar. "It's a trick Thibidioux. I guarantee your critters will find nothing." Peabody's bluff – to wheedle in on the deal.

Thibidioux explodes with vicious growls when his gators' clawing reveals nothing.

Golden Boy sees something he's never imagined he would – his father starting to shake, pleading. "I swear. I buried the saddlebag here just this morning."

Who can say why, what happens next: Slip of a finger, red rage, greed? Butterflies seem to anticipate it and block Golden Boy's view. Gunshots rattle the desert-scape. Golden Boy tries in vain to part butterfly curtain. Grief rips and shreds his emotions. He knows what happens when two-versus-one. He hopes Jesse hears his mental warning. 'Gallop away Jesse or you'll be next.' Sand scraping. Distant neighing. 'Jesse got away.'

Dead-of-silence; silence-of-the-dead. Absolute stillness of desert – the numbing irony of unsettled peacefulness: This must be what allows Golden Boy – TO SUDDENLY SEE JAMES! Or maybe it's Calico's magic, or Prick Lily vibrating through the barriers of time – because they know how shaken James is, how horrified is Golden Boy, and it's imperative they have human contact – emotional; physical – even if it's imagined.

Boys are too shocked to cry. That comes later. They wrap arms; hold tight to stop the other from shaking. Cheeks press warmly. They become one, to undergo healing via this desert coming-together miracle. As if he is James' best friend, Golden

Boy pleads-demands: 'Soon you must go back to your own life. I must get through this alone. Please don't tell my mother how the Captain faltered. He was good, to the end.'

A TALE OF RE-BIRTH

Calico too is dying – but, a butterfly's natural death. She lights upon, flutters one last time, where James and William's cheeks join.

She is warm, soft. That sensation travels through both of you; taking away your chills and shakes. She whispers, 'Do not feel sorrow for the dying. They live on in those for whom they cared. Grieve only that they no longer feel life's glory.' She drops from you, onto Lily's arm. Simultaneously you reach for her, hoping to revive her, but she shrivels to a larva, no bigger than a dot. She rolls; catches on a flower near Prick Lily's trunk.

Begins the magic of instantaneous *re-chrysalis* – the domain of Calico alone. Larva morphs to caterpillar, hatching, growing in front of amazed boys; devouring flower. Chrysalis sack becomes big as a worm, absorbs sky's colors, burns with them, then, before a re-born Calico reappears, an image of Carpier shines over the desert; almost out-glowing Poppy Sol.

Golden Boy: *You know why the Carpier you've seen pictures of and read of in BOOKS is here. To show you the glory-a-commencin'-on, 'spite what 'sums call 'glums'. Prick Lily weeps flower-petal tears over your fa, shielding you from the gruesomeness. The he/it and Sergeant don't notice her tears, nor do they notice Calico's splendid newness. They're leavin', along with the rest – to create, you 'spect, a fiendish pact. You vow. You'll see it fails.*

Long-time gone:
36 minutes; 36 hours; 36 days?

Your visitor held you all this time. 'Now we must say good-bye.' It's hard for you to choke out those words. Visitor understands. You blink. He's gone. You hope you'll see him again.

An hour passes. Jesse returns; then Liege Leather. (Horse, gator had met at Thibidioux-Golden palavers. They knew they were the only critter, thing, or human present to be trusted.)

Liege Leather half-crawls up Prick Lily, so snout is near Golden Boy. Eyes beckon, 'Slide down me. Danger is done.'
Golden Boy does. He grasps the saddlebag. Most of the butterflies have continued their migration. Stragglers remain near Golden Boy. They comfort him by massaging his shoulders as he kneels beside fa. They brush-away flowers so son may touch fa's face.
'The glory-a-commencin'-on'll spite the glums, you reassure yourself'.
Jesse approaches, kneels, nuzzles dead Rider. Liege Leather's look says, 'Fa requires a proper two-leg burial. He slithers beneath body, lifts.
With grunting pushes, breath-taking pulls, you help him lift fa onto Ride, behind the saddle. Your vow, 'you'll see that Peabody and the, he/it fail.' Whatever it is they want, you're certain this saddlebag holds the secret. You'll figure out the mystery, and, what they want, you'll have for yourself. They won't look in the same place twice you think, re-burying the saddlebag. You mount Jesse and return to the fort.
As you enter the quarters Marr-grrr-ett's all puffed-up, a-waitin' ta blow – "Golden's dead, Willamina. As a doornail. But that shouldn't affect you, Willamina, because he wasn't your real father. Ezekiah Bellows is..."
Instead, from her sails do you remove that sumptuous wind, by pointing out the window and saying: "I brought fa home to the honorable burial he deserves. After all, didn't he die in service of our country?"
"Right you be," says Thibidioux as he steps from the shadows of the kitchen.
You look around, and see Sergeant Peabody in the parlor, sitting on the couch fa recently purchased. He's nodding agreement with the he/it.
Margaret sits by Peabody and takes his hand. "Good. Makes it all the easier to tell you Willamina. The Sergeant and I will marry. He will be your new...."
"No, you shout. No one will replace Fa." You try to run from the room; are seized, held by cold, clammy he/it. He forces your chin up so you must look at him. His words are,
"I'll be like an uncle to you from now on – my new dear niecie-Willa-meanie," but his eyes say, "Me and my minions'll be keepin' lookout on you. You won't have see-crets from your

Uncle Lazarees Bontez Thibee-dough for too long."
Your silence masks the dialogue of your thoughts, "One of us'll be hostin' a necktie party for the other. *It twon't be you.*"

A SHORT TALE ON THE SPIRITS OF ENTRAPENUARIN'

Splintery planks atop whiskey barrels – that's Laza Bones bar in the courtyard, just outside the door of Margaret's, Sergeant Peabody, and Golden Boy's living quarters. He sells bayou hooch he and his minions buckboard in. With just a nod, Austin awards him the government's liquor concession for all the Tehas outposts. (In not too many years, he'll even have one in the old churchyard of the Alamo.)

The contract also makes Thibidioux America's southwest operative. "It's gov'ment work, Monsieur Thibidioux," codicils Austin, "of relocatin' indigenous, deportin' Mexicals, and transitin'-out settlers – any of whom I decree to be 'disadvantageous'."

For Thibidioux, it's all just ruse, so he can be around to discover more about the maps.

Golden Boy senses it and creates elaborate story scenarios in his imagination to try to link together what's in saddlebag and what's on Turt's shell. Until then, it's, keep a distance from bar bouncers Baron Tail and Prime Snout; rely on nods and winks from Liege Leather when abusive new father's is drunk and looking for him or when Huey Long's spying on him to find out what he might know about where the maps may be hidden.

Golden Boy is aloof and cunning as any character he invents. Whenever adversaries come up with their 'sure-fire ways' to fool him into revealing the maps' location, he outsmarts them. (author note: Ways he accomplished it detailed in <u>G.B. Outwits His Captors</u>: Book IV; 1839.)

CHAPTER 21

A LESSON IN HIS-TURTRY

Birth day: early 1800.

On the beach of obscure Jericho Island, mother Trumpeters lay thousands of eggs. A few hundred hatch. Barely a dozen spidery, thumb-tip size babies survive hungry birds and lizards or a fricasseeing Poppy Sol. Of those, only the Mariner's, Carper's, and Ol Tom's mate, Turt, will survive the pirate raid six months later.

...AND THE WALLS COME 'TUMBLIN' DOWN

"Scour every inch-a-sand, mates. If you value your lives, leave nary a trace of what we've come for," orders Capt'n. He is ragged and rot-smelly as his crew. Bellicose, rum-sot and jabbering they maraud, as their brethren have for the past century, for Jericho's bounty, Trumpeter shell. It will be carved by artists from Seville to New Zealand, into precious jewelry, hair adornments, and fans; fin-claws dried, pulverized by alchemists, marketed as medicines in Singapore; meat, cured for ingredient in gourmet soup shops in Shanghai; eyes extracted, sold in their own juices in glass vials, as aphrodisiacs, from Siam to Zanzibar.

No waste, but fat and heads.

This will be the last raid. What had been a population of

100,000 Trumpeters has dwindled to nigh extinction.

Moses-slow Trumpeters the size of helmets are spirited into gunnysacks. Smaller ones raked into buckets. The giants are nearly rhinoceros-size, equally as armored, some 250 years old. They are upended, split open by the constantly slamming iron rods the dregs waylay across their underbellies:

Mustn't muss 'vallerbull' iridescent shell.

Trumpeters' usual cherubim trill is heinous as they are dressed-out, filleted whilst alive.

Ma pushes Turt, just the size of a human baby's palm, beneath driftwood. It camouflages the tan of his shell. Moments later, *Ma and Fa...'scoop'; they're gone from your sight. Your squint catches Luny Mum's glint. 'Sol and I will look after you, little one.'*

The suffering you witness, etches into your thoughts. You clench beak-snout to keep from crying out. Instinct tells Turt: The harmonious and harmonic reign of thousands of millennia on Jericho by Trumpeters is ending.

LAST OF HIS TRIBE?

Pirates drag plunder to jolly boats. Turt follows. *'Ma, Fa'. You scoot over the acid smell of death that is now the beach. You enter deep water for the first time, and follow the cries of Trumpeters still living. (You've only been in sandy puddles, just preparing for a supervised solo swim.) The beating water slaps at you. You spit briny sea. Ferociously you paddle.*

In the hours it takes Turt to reach the multi-mast ship, the jollys are unloaded, and hoisted to outriggers. The towering vessel seems to Turt, taller than the mountains of Jericho. Its swaying ropes appear inverted rainbows. *You reach for a rainbow, but fin-claws slip off. With beak-snout, you take hold, lift yourself, and shakily tread upward.*

An avalanche is unleashed from a bucket on deck. You're pushed back into the sea. *You resurface amongst the dropped contents — eyeless Trumpeter heads. Can't scream — because death's scent is choking. You climb atop the heads to keep from drowning, but slide off.*

Finally find one you can hang dearly onto...
... It is Ma's.
Anger, hatred, sorrow, roil emotions. You shiver, snap shut eyes.
Despair's blare: But for one Turt's size, that blare is merely "peep".
Pain gives you the strength of an elder. You leap from Ma to the rainbow. You catch, confidently edge upward, toward the creatures the elders called, two-legs. Turt's able to climb aboard and leap, clicking onto an isolated section of the deck. *Your desires cloud what is real. 'You will find Fa. Free him. Together you will destroy the two-legs.'*
You watch two-legs trudge past. They don't notice you. Poppy Sol's hiding you within his glare. Anxiously Luny Mum looks on. You see more heads being dumped, among them, Fa's...
...Your disheartening scream. It is barely louder then a cricket's, but hearing it is the fat-belly cook. His face is whiskered like hairy jellyfish Turt has seen washed onto Jericho's shore. 'Cookie' wears a long, grease-stained apron. He is three-fourths way to besotting on the ship's cache of rum. Mighty big effort for him, to squat and pick up the wriggling little Trumpeter. He holds Turt 'tween thumb and finger. He sniffs as connoisseur; squints as jeweler. "Fine garnishment for Capt'n salad."

Cookie's a gasbag from eating raw cod. The amble down the galley stairs churns his gut and he...*'lets 'er rii-ppe'.* Turt closes his eyes and holds his breath. Turt's thoughts, though shredded by despair, become calm, plotting. *'Even without Fa, you will destroy them.'*

Turt feels a new sensation: Vengeance.

Cookie drops Turt onto a moldy chopping block and shouts, "Kunta, come clean this mess."

THE TALE OF THE LAD WHO BECOMES A LEGEND

Turt hears footsteps, much softer sounding than the ones on the deck. He sees a smooth face two-leg half Cookie's size.

Shirtless, shoeless, only short pants cover bony frame. He is ebony, the smooth color of the stones Turt would sit on and watch rainbows over Jericho. Cookie slaps Kunta, hard – an exploding '*CLAP*' sound to Turt. Turt winces, but sees no reaction by the ebony. A bright color, like the middle one of a rainbow, surges from the smooth face. Turt realizes – the smaller, darker two-leg is also 'enslaved'- a word Turt doesn't yet know, but well understands.
Kunta wipes blood from his nose and cleans the block. The twelve year olds eyes widen when he sees the tiny Trumpeter. When Cookie turns, Kunta grabs Turt and stashes him in his pocket. A goodwill amulet; for shelled ones, maybe cousins to this one, are sacred to his people.
The ship rolls from an errant sea wave. Pots and pans crash down from hooks. Cookie slips, clattering atop them. Kunta steadies himself. He pets Turt for charm – that, he might escape at the next port. Cookie scrambles up and fists Kunta's head for no reason.
"Where in hell's my topping." He searches. Kunta slides a butcher knife into his pants and moves into shadows. Unseen, maybe he'll be forgotten for a while. The knife: 'I cannot use it against another, even one whom considers himself all-powerful, and master, but what if I must?'

Frustrated that he's unable to find his garnishment, Cookie goes the last one-quarter toward inebriation. He collapses. Kunta fingers the knife. "I not want hurt you, Sir," he whispers in the language he's beginning to learn. Freedom from this master would be temporary. The crew must eat – a new Cookie'd be chosen.
Knowing he'll be beaten yet again for no reason when Cookie awakes, Kunta creeps into his hidden sanctuary – a forgotten broom closet that is big enough only to crouch. He lights a candle and says a quiet prayer to ancestors who reside in his tribe's heaven, Polara. He takes Turt from his pocket and pats soft underbelly. Kunta tearfully tells new companion of family from whom he'd been taken.

Turt responds, with a breath-full purr, realizing, from the tone and emotion, the young two-leg's pain of their similar experience.

Kunta's clan: Artisans in their central African village. Ever since he remembers, he has carved sticks into the shape of the creatures that approached his hut. On the closet walls, he has carved wild reminders of home: lion, giraffe, and hippo. With the aid of a candle flame, he explores the menagerie. This eases the treachery, the loneliness of enslavement.

"Turt," he whispers – he can't complete the word he has heard used by the pirates, 'turtle'. "You are my only friend: So do not be afraid of what you are about to experience." He holds Turt in palm; points knife. Turt squirms, thinking, 'this is the end.' Kunta holds blade as an artist caresses brush. He begins carving, more like scratching, into Turt's shell.

Turt enjoys it. Itches within shell are relieved, soothed from without. It feels like the gentling of ma and fa pincer-like fin-claws when they tucked him into the sand at night.

"HE IS MY SAVIOR. HE BAPTIZES ME, 'TURT'."

Charles Darwin doing a ribbing-imitation of his Victorian era minister-grandfa, as the new evolutionary attempts to transcend into Turt's thoughts one bucolic night en route to Galapagos. He speculates about who carved the most intricate of artwork onto Turt's shell.

Charles sits at his desk aboard the Beagle to write, via carrier pigeon mail, his pen pal – the secret love of his life:

'Remember, Harriet, how once you described artwork you saw floating in the Ohio when your papa first moved your family to Cincinnati? My sweetest, you know I believe, not, of things supernatural, yet, the beak-snouted creature now aboard, he WEARS what you described.

'He must surely be he, Cupid's emissary. For, seeing his beautiful adornments makes me think of your beauty that night we perchance to meet at my cousin's party. So beautiful did your jet hair glow when we stepped onto the moonlit balcony. So soft your cheek when my lips…

'No Harriet, I shall say no more of that night, lest your father intercept my bird. I know of how he might react, he a man of the cloth as my granfa'.

'Oh, Harriet, I touch your face in my thoughts, and renew my vow to you. No matter how steadfast are my family's demands, never, never shall I wed my cousin. Yea, I shall save that bliss for, us. Therefore, my dearest, until then, shall we both continue our work and our writing.

Maybe one day we will share the same publisher. Speaking of that Harriet, I do so like your idea of using the saint's name, Thomas, as your avuncular protagonist. LOVE, CHARLES'

'Dear Charles. Your proclamation of feelings sends my heart aflutter. In the years I have lived in Cincinnati, I am never happier than when one of your letters greets me. For the day we are again together, I anxiously wait. Yes, SHH! My papa, and your granfa' must not know of our liaison by air. Yours because of your COUSIN. Mine, for what you BELIEVE; or, do not BELIEVE.

'Oh Charles, I am so happy the creature has ignited desires in you – that until now you seemed afraid to express. Oh, I am so giddy I could just kiss our matchmaker's beak-snout. Dearest here is a writing aside. Indeed, I shall call my protagonist, Tom. LOVE, HARRIET.'[23]

Kunta carves, adding a miniature version of his village life to Turt's shell – thatch roof hut, mother sitting cross-legged and weaving a basket, sister playing nearby with husk-headed

---

[23] Letters recently added to and on display at the Fiction House.

doll, father standing-straight, axing out a totem for Kunta's rite of passage that would never take place. They are just three and four line cuts per figure. All combine in less than an inch square, but even in his candle's shadow, Kunta can see, touch, and even in his mind smell, the home, enslavement made certain he would never again know.

"Always will this be with you Turt." He carves the letters, 'T U R T' near the village. Kunta wipes sweat from brow and tears from eyes. "Home will be with me always when I stroke your shell." Kunta's been awake for over 24 hour. Tired, staying awake is a battle.

Cookie stirs from stupor to search-out his 'boy'. "I 'as 'ad just about enuffa' the loafer."

Kunta knows what that means for him – the same fate as his predecessor – overboard to the sharks. Desperation: 'I might conquer one man, but not a shipload.' Silence. He hopes Cookie has left, so he might escape. Where? As he waits, very still, he drifts to a nightmarish sleep of what may come. A thudding sound jolts him awake. Turt peeks from between Kunta's fingers.

* * *

To escape, briefly the tedium of the Lindian Woods – and Turt's slow pace – James flies from Lindia to Cincinnati. *"Yow! You really can do it now without Calico's help."* You enter the wharf-shack.

'Yo ho!' you imagine Carper shout, and that Carper can magically see you, as Mariner is able. 'Mew, toot,' are Ol Tom and Turt's imagined greetings. Mariner dishes steamy chowder for us humans. Onto floor, he tosses fins, gills. Critters lick heartily.

'Nice 'appy 'ome, eh Sol. Our Carper's found 'is place,' Luny Mum winks through porthole at Carper, and then kisses his cheek with her beam.

From other porthole, Poppy Sol: 'Indeed, Mum. 'appy forever. Soon, so will our woods voyager.' *Poppy Sol hugs your shoulder with his warmth.*

You're glad they, Poppy and Mum, look out for you. You, Mariner and Carper chow atop magical tabletop that's a shell of collages, drawings, markings. You pet the carvings done by the young Kunta.

(Expanded by the growth of Turt's shell, the village environs now cover a square foot.)

Kunta's little sister looks up, shows the boys her husk-head doll, and speaks. They can't understand her language, but pretend. "Come visit us, fellas."

'We will.'

Kunta's father motions for them to peek closer – at the saber-beak bird he is carving into the totem. "When it's finished, we will fly it up and bring you boys down to us."

Knowing that their Kunta may never return, father and sister suddenly look sad to Carper and James – the same way they sometimes, feel. Not now. Reverie of imagination seizes the boys. They smile. It's catchy. Kunta's father and sister loose their glums and join in.

Mariner feels the boy's penetrating orbs shift to his. 'They're probin'to finds out how Turt got 'is mystery tattoos. Gost to reel in some real whoppers for the young uns' to gnaw on.' Between gulps of chowder he says, "Turt, e's sailed the seven seas. No tellin' where 'e comes up wi' so many of 'em tattoos. Not uncommon fer some grateful sailor Turt's 'elped, to sketch out their personal thanks on 'ims'. I can tells ya about plenty of 'em Carper."

Mariner looks to where you're not. "And you too, son. But we'll save that handsome village carvin' you been navigatin' over for last – bein' its so special to Turt 'n me."

You look at Carper. He's gotten used to Mariner talking to air. He thinks nothing 'tuv it.

Both of you boys, your eyes, and fingers climb the mountain near Kunta's village. Your palms sail its river while your thoughts glide over the surrounding Serengeti. You'll go there one day, you tell yourself, maybe together with Carper.

Mariner stares down a glassy fish eye that somehow found its way into the chowder. He picks it, drops it through the planking into the Ohio. '*Plink.*'

"Lustin' for spellbindin' mystery, intrigue – ADVENTURE, 'er ya both?" Mariner points to the intricately inked-in face of an oriental, and commences yarnin'. "That's the landlubbin' ship arteest – warn't had no water sense – got swept into South China Sea when 'e dangled by 'is legs outta' porthole window to better draw a giant spermer. Turt, 'acourse fished 'im to safety."

You both blink. You're dangling alongside the artist. Mist covers your faces. A constellation of twinkling starfish falls upward, from ocean to sky. You reach and catch one that conducts, "All aboard. Have a pleasant trip." ZXIP! You're exhilarated by the freedom of speed and flight as you're ferried. "Where we bound?" you both ask. The starfish says, "Heaven Bound!"

Carper had often heard that voice, faintly beckoning his mother through her closed door at Rrrose Heather's. "Let me take you away from this place, my dear. Together we're, Heaven Bound. You'll be the respected wife of Reverend Ezekiah..."

"Heaven, the eternal playground, your next stop, everyone exit." ZXIP! You both open your eyes – Back in wharf-shack. You look at Carper. He looks so sad.

"Is this Heaven, Mariner?" Carper's eyes become hard yet wet – because his memories always slip away, no matter how much he tries to hold them.

Mariner wipes Carper's tears, and then chases his chowder with a snoot-fulla' Kentucky stump juice. "Why, this certainlee kin be *heaven.* Iffen' you choose it ta be."

"Then I do," Carper says, eyes softening as he looks at Turt, Ol Tom, Mariner.

"Right good fer you. Already you learned what it takes some a lifetime. Some never does."

Mariner says to you. *'Glad you come visit, son. Just getting ready to reveal the doins'a' what went on in the pi'rat ship's galley.'*

Carper interrupts. "How could you know what happened there, Mariner? Turt's here. But looks to me like his beaksnout's sealed, and Kunta wasn't the type to brag."

As they lean on Turt, balancing bowls, Mariner goes all

Mama Lucy rhymy. "Eye-witness spy had I in that galley. Our heroes' feats, did he tally."

Turt ignores human babble of what is decades-old news to him.

Intrigued by what's next to transpire, James shoulders excitedly into Carper, and imagines Carper really knows he's there. Carper imagines too, that a pal's there.

* * *

The thudding that young Kunta and shelling Turt hear is drunken Cookie. He collapses atop the squid he starts chopping. He's in a stupor.

Kunta clenches the knife. 'Never again will I be beaten.' For the first time in the months since enslavement, he has a friend. Even one so tiny provides hope, and courage. He pets Turt, relaxes. In the candle flicker, Turt watches Kunta drift to sleep; sees the protector-claw, the knife, slip from Kunta's hand, and lodge between crossbeams.

Turt crawls up Kunta's willowy arm, perches on his shoulder – a place where he can always see the door. To Turt the door is a flat tree. The difference between this tree and those of Jericho Island? This tree can move. When it does, Turt knows, Cookie will have awakened, entered. Gleaming slicer-destroyer he'll be holding. To warn Kunta, who might be sleeping when that happens, and that he has lost protector-claw, but how?

Turt nuzzles Kunta's skin with open beak-snout – as he so often did slippery beach worms. Then it was just ruse – to coax them out, just enough, so he could, '*clip*', savor. He bites at Kunta. Kunta just smiles, doesn't awaken. Turt looks up and sees how he might rouse him. The drooping areas of the two rounded flaps protruding from Kunta's head; fit beak-snout around them, as he did the worms, bite, hold tight, dangle – as do the golden circles Cookie wears.

Turt scales the nape of Kunta's neck – mighty mountaineer – proud of his feat, as, his way-in-the-future friend Edmond

Hillary, the Sir, would feel when he meets FULL-GROWN Turt relaxing atop Everest. Turt pinches Kunta's hair with *eensy* fin-claws, and hoists himself until he seizes lobe.[24] Turt nuzzles it and Kunta's tense breathing relaxes. It would be decades before Prick Lilly tells Turt of the acupuncture-like healing powers she practices on desert animals, so like the stapling earlobe massage Turt is doing to Kunta now. Kunta reaches up and unconsciously pets his little friend. 'Let him rest a bit,' Turt, thinks.

What comes next seems to happen all at once.

The flat tree eases aside. Cookie enters, gripping slicer-destroyer. Turt chomps, but cannot penetrate the rubbery lobe. Boy's eyes stay closed. Turt's ancient instincts, millennia-in-the-making, overwhelm him. He commences trumpeting, for the very first time: timid trills through clenched beak-snout, hardly a sound, compared to ancestor's vibrating choruses that dislodged coconuts from trees and sent rocks skittering down mountainsides. Startled by the new sounds that emanate from within, Turt almost loses his hold.

To Kunta, the sound is as a sickly bird, just loud enough to awaken him. To Cookie, it is a distracting squeak causing him to hesitate, briefly, enough time for…

…Kunta to open eyes. He sees the descending cleaver. He rolls. Turt clings; dangles wildly.

'Whap!' Cleaver sticks into timber that shivers then splits. Cookie strains to wrench it out.

"Ya lazin' neg. I be loppin' both ya and yez earpiece in two." He blocks Kunta's escape.

Cookie is shoeless, and to Turt, it seems that fat, wriggling worms extend from his feet. For adult combat Turt is unprepared; but he knows how to defeat crawlers. Midst pendulum swing, he lets loose of Kunta. He trumpets wildly – hardly a whistle to you or me – as he flies through the air. The Tarzanian perfect swing lands him, dead center on his target –

---

[24] 'No teeth has this species of which Turt is a member. I shall describe them more to be *spiking cartilaginous ridges*. For now I'll just call them, *teeth*.' Charles Darwin.

Cookie's foot.

Thinking Turt a big spider, Cookie tries shaking him off. With a trumpeting, "AYIIEE", Turt bites the littlest worm. Emotions that Turt is learning today – from the brutalities he's seen – will burden him for decades, will all-encompass his existence. So foreign to the peaceful love on his island are these emotions – *hatred!* They seem to give his jaw extra strength. He penetrates 'worm', grits into its bone. Warm red appears, streaking his beak-snout. "Blech!" But Turt vises even tighter.

Cookie shouts, "Lil baazzard." He kicks the air. Turt clings.

Kunta rolls away, reaches into the crossbeams' narrow crevice, slices fingers, but retrieves the knife. Just then, Cookie *could* have served-him-up, but hatred of the Trumpeter for inflicting such lingering pain causes him to violate a galley's ultimate rule: Never change chop mid-air. He bares-down onto Turt. Sans commonest sense he shouts, "AYIIEE" back at Turt.

Turt lets loose, tucks himself in shell. 'Farewell Kunta. Hello forebears.'

"WHISH!" Inebriation obscures Cookie's perception. *"WHAP!"* He plunges cleaver into his own foot. The five toes, and a few inches, a tad on upward – *sliced off*. They seem to tiptoe away as if they've a separate life, and head out; to maybe find and attach afoot a sun worshiper who might dangle them in a brook to relieve the forever itch the dank galley has wrought.

* * *

Carper and James slip their arms around the imagined waist of the other – so frightened by how Mariner is describing the disenfranchised appendage. When Mariner says, "Thems creepers come to be known as walk-offs. I've one tucked-away...somewheres," their grips tighten. Mariner squints slyly. 'No boy'll resist the seas' intrigue, despite their fear.' "Want me to dock tale, or sail? You mates decide."

TALES OF THE FICTION HOUSE

Both anxiously nod and look over to Turt: So big now, but so little then, yet so brave in wanting to protect his friend. He inspires them. 'We'll be like Turt,' their stares say.

Turt glance says to Ol Tom, 'Wish Cookie was here. This time around I'd snap him in two.'

* * *

Rum opiate masks his pain, so Cookie doesn't immediately realize he's done some lopping.

"Sons-a-bitchen' Trumpeter clawed me." Bedlam. Kunta escapes closet. Cookie wobble-chases him around the galley, swinging cleaver wildly, breaking shelves, slitting grain sacks.

Kunta ducks clear. "I never hurt you, Sir. Why you try and harm me," he shouts in his village language. In the lantern's glint, Cookie sees his foot, now a bloody stump. None on board hears his abrupt yell because he bites tongue before it can resonate out. Kunta holds knife in both hands and points at him. Insanely, Cookie charges. "Please, not want to hurt you, sir."

Too late, Cookie tries to decapitate him. Kunta plunges the knife into bulging gut then pulls it out. A deflating balloon – obnoxious odors croak forth. Cookie's face turns wretched blue. He crumbles and grain spewing from sacks he upends hide his corpse.

Turt looks up from the floor and sees Kunta is shaking. Turt wants to nuzzle him calm.

Kunta glares at the red-streaked knife. He feels it has melded to and become an unwelcome part of him. Only a while ago he had used it to carve his peaceful village onto the shelling's back – for all-the world to see that the love he grew up with is possible, somehow, if they try to make it so. Now, even knowing he could have been killed if he hadn't killed, the feeling that he's defiled all life's learning slices through his thoughts, hurting as much as any knife wound.

Footsteps... of early arrivals for supper. Clutter jams open the closet door. No hiding there. Kunta pockets Turt, and

Cookie's walk-off. Clenching knife blade sideways between his teeth, he springs upward, antelope-lithe, and lodges elbows between ceiling beams. Legs, he swings backward, lodging them. Body's parallel to floor. Safe; long as they don't look up.

* * *

"Ah but there is a place to hide," Mariner tells the huddling boys. "Any mate been on an ocean go-er for long voyages knows it. Kunta, new to the sea, wouldn't. I had me galley spy, remember. That's how I know all what I'm tellin'. Eye-spy long been aboard. He knew where ya could hide out; and '*where*' is where HE were that day – seein' all Kunta and Turt's exploits."

Anxious, for more adventurin', intrigue'n midst memorizin' all the lurid detailin', Carper, and James shout in singsong rhyme: "*Where* be there, Mar-i-ner.*"*

Mariner smiles. 'Hook, line, sinker. Reelin' 'em in. They won't soon forget Kunta's story. I'll extend 'er out tad extra – good for young uns' fancy to be scared up one side then excited down the other. Stouten' their fiber. Make 'em better adults.'

Ol Tom rubs upside Turt – 'How's come you didn't know a spy be watching?'

Peeved at the challenge of his powers to observe, Turt nudges with beak-snout, harder than a friendly cat-pat. 'Oh I knew, Tom. Smelled him, heard the breathing, saw his shadow. I tell you Tom, back then I didn't believe there could be such a thing as a half-creature – half-two-leg. You've seen Laza Bones, so you know there is. Well, this spy of Mariner's – a half-er – didn't squeal us out, but he didn't help us either.'

Turt glares at Mariner, wondering how he could ever be friendly with, what/who to Turt was a sea-going version of Thibidioux.

"Okay then, *Where* was I?" Mariner says to the boys. "Kunta's ahangin' there bat-like…"

* * *

Three shirtless crewmen enter the galley, blinking to adjust from the bright deck. One wears tattered balloon pants, others, dungarees. The tallest, his black hair, six-inch long pikes, scrapes Kunta's belly as he walks under him. Kunta grits teeth against the knife blade. He barely understands their jabbering when they find Cookie. "He drunk? Dead?"

Turt and the walk-off have been sliding slowly forward in Kunta's pocket. They drop, right toward impaling pikes. Turt sees that the quill-head two-leg is the same color as Kunta, not sardine-pink as the others. He looks like the porcupines that rest atop trees on Jericho. No more time for observation because '*PLOP!*' Mid-air, Kunta scoops Turt and walk-off into his palm.

Kunta slips; dangles from legs, only inches behind pirates.

They kick Cookie's fat gut to see if he's alive. A pocket of stale gas explodes from his rear.

Kunta is sure that if the lantern flame burned higher the galley would explode.

Turt cannot decide which is worse: The stench from Cookie, or that of his grimy walk-off. He shells up to insulate himself. Pirates exit the galley for air. Kunta repositions himself.

Quill Head returns, lingers outside the door waiting for the stench to clear. (Quill Head's the one who kidnapped Kunta as the wily boy gathered berries outside his village – "led me on merry chase over hills, dales, entrails," he laughs-recounts often to dreg-mates.) He knows Kunta's capabilities. He's certain Kunta's killed Cookie.

Kunta's a master at holding breath – had trained himself, for almost five minutes at a time, in his village's river. He now has held it that long. He drops to go hide in another part of the ship. He stiffens: Before him – Quill Head.

"Sit, dog: For your beating."

Kunta points knife. "No dog. No touch."

Turt emerges from shell and, from within Kunta's fist, sees what looks like a treed porcupine. Quill Head's face is rough as bark: Arms, legs, oak-solid. Turt can't understand why porcupine glares hatefully at Kunta. Though different sizes, they are the same color. In Turt's mind, they are of the same tribe, as he from the Trumpeter tribe. Why doesn't he stroke Kunta, caress him, as those of 'same' do. Turt is still too young to know; enslavement crosses all lines.

Quill Head rolls Cookie with his foot, sees blood-sheathed gut. "You go too far, dog. Now you die." He lunges to strangle him. Kunta moves back. Quill Head blocks the galley door with sacks of flour, and then seizes Kunta's arm. Kunta pulls free.

Turt sees his friend swipe with knife and slit woody cheek. Sap, of red, flows. Quill Head licks it, laughs, and sways back and forth avoiding thrusts. He toys, as lion with fawn.

Kunta tires, retreats, stumbling on pots. They clatter onto Cookie: A volley of, *BURP!*'

Quill Head backhands Kunta's wrist. The knife flies. Cookie's eruption gives Kunta an idea. Before limbs descend on him, he leaps, above Cookie, comes squashing down.

Last of the gas explodes: Cannon-shots of the 1812 Overture, years before Tchaikovsky composed it. Kunta doesn't breathe. Quill Head is 'ground zero' above crumbled-Cookie's-cutters. He coughs violently. Kunta grabs a lantern from its wall hook, jacks flame, removes glass, and throws it at Quill Head. Kunta lurches for the partial protection of his closet door. He peeks at the inferno and its exploding overture.

Briefly, the galley glows brighter than the ship's deck at noon.

Quill Head shouts, "Dog never challenges master", are in vain because flames overwhelm him. His eyeballs liquefy and drain. Heat he breathes-in cauterizes nasal passages and seems to lick his brain. What can he do but drop, writhe, and glisten? Cookie's gas supply burns off almost instantaneously. After violent shaking Quill Head lies still.

Kunta stamps out the isolated flames that barely singe petrifying oak galley floor. He hasn't time to think about rights or wrongs of the two killings. Seems the worse of them was the killing of one of his color. Yet, Quill Head was the person who forced him here.

He starts to pocket Turt, and then feels the squishy, severed foot end next to Turt's shell. A moment before Kunta would have tossed it. Now he considers it a reminder – he'd have to do most-anything to survive. It's a symbol – of the need to get home where such choices are unnecessary.

He takes a knife, exits galley to find a hiding place in the maze of rooms, corridors, and niches that are the ship's belly. His 'artist' thoughts transfix – on creating a necklace, grand as any ever made in his village. Its centerpiece, his symbol of survival – will be this creeping 'walk-off'. 'Walk off this ship,' he vows, that is what he and Turt somehow would do.

* * *

'Hold on Turt,' Ol Tom purrs. "How'd Mariner's eye-spy, the hid-out creature/two-leg, survive the fire? Wasn't Lazarus Bontez his-self was it – getting another chance to defy dying?'

Turt licks beak-snout. 'Mariner tells it better than me. So hold your hairball, Tom.' (Ol Tom's not all-thatta-curious-cat about the creature/two-leg – he's just goading pal, friendly like.)

James is anxious to tell Rrrose Heather and Mama Lucy about Kunta and Turt's galley heroics, so he doesn't hear the rest of the story. Just like – *THAT* – he's back in Lindia riding Turt. He tries conjuring muses. Only Rrrose shows.

"Mariner had a galley spy, Rrrose," James says. That's how he knew the gowens-on."

'Mariner's spy, say ye?' Rrrose laughs. 'Let me tell about that 'Buzzard' of a spy of his. Turt'll not be interested.' She pretends to put her hands over Turt's ear channels. 'I learned, quick, of the doom the Buzzard be capable of spreading. Turt, he knew it, right off.' Rrrose Heather sighs deep. 'Best ye hear the straight story on Buzzard: Because he had a might powerful affect not only then, on Kunta's and Turt's lives, but later, on your best pal, Carper's'.

* * *

Survive the heat flash. E – Z for Buzzard. He's safely perched on a framing timber in a never-used pantry. When the fire stops, he removes thick, wing-like cape he draped around himself for protection. 'You've escaped tighter cages than this ship,' he tries convincing himself. He'd observed all of Kunta and Turt's exploits, then their disappearance. 'Maybe you can use what you saw to garner your freedom. If I tell how it happened, who'd believe.' Mentally he begins 'heightening' the tale.

* * *

'The Buzzard admired young Kunta and the shelling Turt's bravery, he did, Lad,' Rrrose tells James. 'But make no mistake – he'd throw them to the sharks if it might save his feathers.'
James clutches big Turt's neck. Turt wonders why.
'I'll just *zxip* to ship, warn Kunta, then to the wharf-shack to warn Carper,' James thinks, but only briefly, remembering Poppy Sol's maxim about not being able to change the past. He fists hands. "But I Gotta do somethin'."

CHAPTER 22

Dear Charles,
I'd not have believed, had not I seen. Every year, on the same day at the same time, like swallows returning to Capistrano; upriver the buzzards fly en route to Hinckley, Ohio, where they... Oh Charles, as much as the swallows brighten a sky, the buzzards darken your Harriet's sky. Only your resurrection, Charles, back into my life, will brighten it.

THE TALE OF THE EMBELLISHEN' BUZZARD

From the wharf-shack's porthole Mariner points to a clutch of vultures strafing the Ohio.

"Tis an omen, Carper. They letting us know the main bird – the biggest and slyest of all – soon'll be 'agliden in.'" Boy's eyes widen as he imagines such a monstrosity, since even these are frightful, with their dangling faces looking like chewed-up human lips. Carper's not afraid of the unknown. He's beginning to savor its bliss.

Birds scatter when a steamboat sloshes by.

Mariner spits chew. It arrows through planks, '*kerplunks*' river. "You ken jes bet the Buzzard's on board, preparin' to sky away from revenge-bent pigeons he's plucked. He's always agamblin' on 'ouren's hospitality. Sails in, roosts low a spell, then spreads wing lookin' for fresh scavengins'."

Carper grins; glad he's now part of an 'ouren'. The caring way Mariner treats him, Ol Tom, and Turt, the simple feeling of joy Mariner brought to those gathered for the parade – he's converted Carper to the Mariner gospel of 'livin', lovin', enjoyin' fully'.

"Fer some might-good reasons, Carper, our dear Turt never took 'aliken to the Buzzard. Jus' as soon bite offen 'is forever waggin tongue as look at him. But Ol Tom, 'ees fickle. If Buzzard talons fer 'im a few scraps, Ol Tom'll stick about and claw 'n jaw em. If not, e'll mosey."

An hour later.

Carper looks back out the porthole and within Luny Mum's streaky glint sees the 50ish, squat, splindle-leg old bird Mariner presaged. His black-tailed suit flaps in a light breeze. Stooping slightly forward, he steps sprightly along the pier. Carper realizes why he's called 'Buzzard'. Movement, shape, feature, all fowl his humanness. Beady eyes are dark as raven hair, and close together. Enormity of curved proboscis – it was EVEN BIGGER in his youth – had been carved into its present pointy beak, not by a sympathetic but misguided early 19th century experimental rhinoplasty, but by an irate, blade-wielding fellow five-card stud rogue who took unkindly to Buzzard's bottom deck dealing.

Smelly nickname: '*Buzzard*'; It comes not only from the bird he resembles, but because he hails from Buzzard's Bay, Massachusetts, not far from Mariner's Boston. Buzzard embraces the image, even hones the look and mannerisms – for luck; but mostly for the advantage of distraction it gives him at the tables.

Buzzard carries a fresh card pack, a bottle of jack, the latest edition of the <u>Cincinnati Daily Opine</u>. He glances at the front-page drawing: Parade grand Marshalls Mariner, Carper, and Ol Tom, afloat Turt. Dear Precious rears up in the background.

Buzzard looks to the wharf-shack, and wonders, 'What kind

TALES OF THE FICTION HOUSE

of menagerie will Mariner have with him this go round? What, who, might I have to be sleeping beside?' He and Mariner's conversation when last he'd sailed upriver went something like – "All the years I've known you Mariner and still can't cure you of reeling in any stray that happens along."
"Do you good to try it, least once, Buzzard. Ya might take-a-liken'."
Beak scrunches. "Eck! Look out for the number one Bird. That's my motto."

It was that same way for him a quarter-century earlier in the galley's shadows as he peers out from his pantry hideaway. He grins.
'You really stuck it to Cookie and Quill Head, little negra boy. They got their just desserts.'
He returns to the chore he'd been involved – meticulously mushing gold coins into discarded Trumpeter fat. He's hiding loot from on-the-sly gambling, and filching from drunken pirates. He banks his concoction into the medium-size hollow shells, despising the work but knowing the oily substance is good for his hands and fingers – instruments key to the profession of bluff.
Though a slave on the ship, Buzzard survives, even thrives via his wits. He keeps clean-shaven, nattily attired, but not 'too', so as not to arouse ire of the work-ravaged pirates.
Thoughts race: How to twist accounts of the young fellow-slave's victory; to bolster his own goodwill with the murderous Capt'n – until escape is possible. 'One day I'll strap these shells together and raft away with my bounty,' he half-dreams; half-expects. (*'Eww! That Cookie stinks.'*)
Beak flares: 'Got it!' Practiced blank stare reveals none of Buzzard's cunning ruse centering on the boy. 'That negra'll be my ticket to freedom. Him, and one totally fabricated story about that section of Cookie's foot he took along with him. Hmm: Plenty of time to hone the details.'
Buzzard hears cannon shots, gunfire cracks, and metal clanking of swords. It ends quickly. Now – shouted orders,

scuffling, thumping of crates. Work: Buzzard always strives to avoid it. He perches, waits. When he finally appears on the deck the seizing of a minimally armed cargo ship is complete. He squints into daylight's brightness, sees the conquered ship's crew and passengers. They're forced to carry onboard the last of its bounty of foodstuffs, firearms, various fru-fru.

Capt'n ambles among them, cracks bullwhip and shouts, what every apprentice pirate knows, "Take their clothes, jewelry. What we can't use'll fetch a tidy sum." Prisoners are stripped, lined up, made to trek over an oft-used, but still-springy, gangplank. 'PLOP! PLOP! PLOP!'

Our hook-handed Capt'n wears a patch over one eye, one over missing ear, another over festering hole in neck; yet another around wooden peg-leg as a spare – in case another body part might turn up missing or another fissure might erupt. Though he is sweaty, grimy as all pirates in canvas shirt and pants, alas, it is a lovely, sunny May day, he is doing the satisfying work of his chosen vocation, following in papa's footsteps, and all seems right with the world. That is, until he sees Buzzard, looking frilly and fresh in his tailcoat like he's just emerged, all perfumed, from a whurehouse. Capt'n snaps bullwhip. It cracks, inches from Buzzard's beak.

Buzzard doesn't flinch. "And greetings to you too sir." He knows he can always bluff with his own special bluster if the need be there. That is HIS vocation; and it be well-played.

"I see you fly up when harvest's complete," Capt'n shouts. "40 lashes for the Bird before we reach land: Example to the rest of the crew about shirkers." The scab that crescents Capt'n' cheek merrily dances as he thinks of Buzzard stripped to the waist; tied to mast. He approaches Buzzard, scowling, but turns head slightly, winking, so only Buzzard sees. He'd pleasure-in administering Buzzard's displeasure. But where's the profit? "Hhrrmph!" Capt'n scowls.

Knowing Capt'n is posturing for his crew, Buzzard nods. They've a pact that assures mutual gain. Yet Buzzard keeps reminding himself – whom in their rightness of mind could trust such an oceangoing rat…

TALE OF THE UNWEDDEDS – UNBLISS

...especially one so unstable he's fitted onto the ship's parrot's good leg, a pseudo wooden one, and a needless eye patch, so he'll have a pet he can commiserate with in the melancholy rum hours. Always close-by is this near-wife all call Captain Polly. She stays, only because a small chain prevents flight. "Ahh, my sweet Polly...," Capt'n romances nightly in the moonlight "...forever, and always together, will we be." The pain of his lash has cured her of gnarling out a chunk of his hide when he pets with his cold hook.

TALE OF CAPT'N ROMANCING THE BUZZARD

Buzzard had met Capt'n, for only the second time, late at night – outside a Johannesburg bar: Capt'n shoves the flouted barrel of his Ben Bow twixt those beady eyes. Their first meeting was inside an hour earlier. Buzzard had fleeced him of the ship's payroll.

"Plunderin' from a plunderer be a sin, scalawag," says Capt'n, cocking the weapon. I'm here to help you repent." He marches Buzzard to the vessel. Between singing "Ol wife bring me my ol Ben Bow so I can kill this Carrion crow" he outlines Buzzard's penance – deck swabbie by day – card shark by night; with Capt'n and ol Ben Bow magnanimously allowing him 10% of the winnings, Capt'n commandeering 90.

Nothing can stop Buzzard playing for chance, even with his life. He imbezzels from Capt'n. Slight of hand he amasses a tidy booty – which gets packed into the Trumpeter innards.

TALE OF THE NEAR-WIFE'S JEALOUSY

"SQUACK! ARRGH! SQUACK! Naked ladies aboard. SQUACK! Come see, Capt'n."

Captain Polly thumps pseudo peg-leg onto the ship's wheel.

Captn' doesn't hear. His bad ear is toward her. Captain Polly's a 'love bird', half her mother's macaw. Who knows father's breed? He flew past one night, took advantage of naive ma in the dark of a sultry Brazilian jungle night. Captain Polly's blue and gold feathers, some a foot-long, glistening now in Poppy Sol's glare, must've come from fa because they've none of the red and green of ma.

Beak's a razor, from sharpening on the ship's oak rails in preparation for territorial battle with the 'other bird' the Buzzard – on her ship. However, her reviling of him lessened slowly, evolved to curiosity, then admiration of his independence to be able to fly anywhere he wants onboard. Increasingly, her feelings are becoming that of infatuation. He reminds Captain Polly of the imagined dashing Latin father she's pictured since not long out of her egg.

When she doesn't stop squawking, a crewman shouts, "Capt'n, the Captain Polly wants you to come see what we found."

"Be right there, me dear Captain Polly," Capt'n coos. His stump thumps the deck as he walks past the line of prisoners of many raccs – pleading for mercy. Buzzard follows, avoiding their eyes, realizing what little separates him from them: Within moments, they will be, eternally free. No philosopher he, but for a moment, before blocking the morbid thought, he wonders: Maybe they're the fortunate ones. Quickly he reminds himself, 'no side taking.'

"Well, what 'ave we here?" Capt'n says when he sees two blonde women, around 18 years old. They huddle, protected in the grasp of a black haired Irish lass. She isn't much older.

* * *

Rrrose Heather comforts James. His frown shows his worry for the ladies. 'Aye Lad, the pi-rats try touching us as they oughtn't.' She waves inch-long fingernails in front of him and Turt. James leans back. 'Mother-cat quick, I spring. Their cheeks I scratch. I screech. 'Git away ye dung heaps, or next I

be pluckin' out yer eyes.
'Now Jamie. I could see Captain Polly was green-rage-jealous of other females bein' on her ship. To her credit, I could see her commiseratin'-compassion for us when the touching started.'

* * *

The Capt'n – a fire burns in his groin to tame the wild Irish cat. He cracks whip and stops the violence that usually precurses rape. Capt'n quickly decides: 'All three's pleasure I'll have.'

As this happens, Buzzard feels a cold hand scrape his neck and pull him toward the death line. He looks up and sees the stringy seaman he'd whured with in many a port. "MARINER!"

"No fraternizing," Capt'n orders. His attention stays fixed on the trio of bosoms: 'Captain Polly'll sleep on deck tonight; that be certain.'

"Capt'n," Buzzard interrupts. I was getting ready to give you the bad news. Cookie's not going to be cooking anymore. Seems…"

"Get to your point."

Buzzard explains quickly, leaving out details until he decides how he will spin them to his favor. He starts a vague lie about Cookie and Quill Head fighting, and enters prime story-telling mode. "LOP, there went part of Cookie's foot. *Squish*, in went knife. Cookie crumbles."

Quickly as crew cringes they laugh at Buzzard's melodrama of arm flapping to demonstrate Cookie's demise. Buzzard gyrates and does a toe-tap dance. "Away that foot waltzed."

Mariner watches, knowing, 'the gamblin' Bird's brainen' up somethun'. Whatever it is, the calming hand Buzzard keeps putting on his shoulder means part of it's meant to save him. For this, Mariner, no matter Buzzard's motives, forever would be grateful.

Capt'n frowns. "Going to miss Cookie's braised stingray."

"I've the perfect solution, to our galley problems," Buzzard says. "This one here." He pulls Mariner from the line. "I've eaten his cuisine. He'll make quite a fine…"

"Take him below and set him cooking. No time to waste." Capt'n points to the ladies. "I must interrogate these three. Deliver them to my quarters," he orders his crewmen. They anxiously reach for them, but quickly step back when Rrrose Heather daggers out her fingernails.

She takes Capt'n by the arm; pushes breasts to his chest. "Be truly 'a pleasure accompanyin' ya sire." The other ladies crowd near, following Rrrose Heather's lead. Rrrose's glance catches Buzzard's. Their eyes communicating, 'We'll only survive if we work this together,' is broken when Capt'n queries Buzzard. "What became of Cookie's slave boy?"

Buzzard hesitates — hasn't invented that part yet. "Well…he …Truth be Capt'n, he scurried away. I didn't see where…"

"Never mind."

Mariner glimpses Rrrose Heather. Surely the youngest Madam ever. They'd met when she boarded the now-adrift cargo ship. Old enough to be her father, he wanted to protect her as a daughter, yet he'd become infatuated with her, would give up all whuring if only she asked him to. 'Ah dearest Rrrose. Appears we're spared. Fer each otheren' ya think?'

Mariner's sure the wily wench and her girls will control Capt'n afore Mum rises.

'PLOP!' Carnage-of-plank restarts. Nothing can stop it, Mariner knows. As ladies depart with Capt'n, Mariner plans, 'tween Rrrose, Buzzard, me-self. Surely we'll find a way to escape.

* * *

'You're out early this afternoon, aren't you?' Poppy Sol asks.

Luny Mum grins down. 'Sister Rrrose be the reason. She's humoring things up so Jamie won't be hearin' lurid details. Rrrose's vines always tickle-me-pink, Poppy. Just you listen.'

TALES OF THE FICTION HOUSE

Rrrose Heather jokes to James as she accompanies him and Turt in their woodland journey. 'Captain Polly 'ad more'n just a lassie's crush on the Buzzard, Jamie. Barely did 'e, give she, the least nod. If she wasn't 'achained to the crow's nest, ship's wheel or the railing, I believe she'd 'ave dug claws into his shoulder, never let go. And fight off any human female dare approach 'im. Indeed, Lad, I can attest to that.' She rubs a century-plus-ago healed shoulder scar.

Mum to Poppy Sol; James listening in: 'Rrrose no different from most young ladies; couldn't resist Buzzard's smooth-flyin' ways. Fortunately, she learns fast. After some short dalliances, dealin' with him – all business.'

Poppy *tsk-tsks*, 'Buzzard's gamblin' with emotions breaks him every time.'

Luny Mum flickers, 'I be out that particular night Captain Polly attack Rrrose on the deck.' She winks to James. 'Ah my sweet Rrrose flower, though she'd shed any intentions on Captain Polly's bird before that, she had 'er thorns bared for a fight. Petals flew that night, but feathers flew too.'

James wants to smile, imagining Polly's jealousy, and her not-so-flowery row with Rrrose. He frowns, thinking about his muse being hurt. "If everyone couldn't work together, Rrrose? How could you get away from the pirates?"

Rrrose Heather glances upward, as if acknowledging Mum and Poppy, and thanking them for lighting and enlightening his way. 'Poignant thinken' fer such a little feller, hmm?'

Poppy Sol glimmers proudly, 'Indeed. Shades of 'is great-great grandfa Carper is cast 'is way.'

Madam hugs boy. 'Well, Lad, we was all set – ta be 'aplayin our stormy parts, you might say. But it took the Mariner, with his special mariner wisdoms, to chart us to calm seas by seein' we was sailen' for a common port – Freedom.'

* * *

Sometimes Buzzard's 'bolsterin'-of facts' about the galley slayings takes half the night, three keg-o-grog for the crew, and the length of the ship's deck to soft shuffle over while dramatizing via his half-ballet – half-tragedy. In the coming weeks, Buzzard's embellished versions begin sounding more real than outlandishness. As all *'true'* storytellers, he forgets what truly happened. Even he begins believing his accounting: "Aye mates," Buzzard hedges. "Quill Head, he lifts Kunta above his head and readies to impale him on his spikes." Drunken pirates look up and think they see the imaginary boy. Buzzard pulls hands to his throat. "That Turt, that hound of, *s'hell*, he dives from Kunta's pocket – aims right for Quill Head's bulging jugular. He clamps on, giving Kunta a chance to break free of the porcupine."

Captain Polly, as if she works in concert with the new bird, Buzzard, convinces herself they are becoming a team – at least in her bird's brain. Like a member of a Greek chorus, she sings out "TURT! TURT!" at the appropriate times when Buzzard tells of the lil Trumpeter's heroics. If a parrot could salivate, that's what Captain Polly would do; because she wouldn't mind getting a bit o' taste of that sweet *'terror-pin'*.

* * *

For James, there are never enough questions to ask or seek answering. "If Mariner's in the galley, Buzzard's busy tellin' on deck, you and your ladies are confined to the cabin and who knows where Kunta and Turt are hiding , how could Mariner get you all to working together?"

Rrrose Heather simply replies, 'Mariner SEEMED to be the new Cookie to all. So 'e could be forgotten about by the dregs. He's slowly becomin' Captain of the fate of all onboard. Nary a pi-rat soul be 'aknowin that yet. 'E started by 'avin Buzzard convince Capt'n into letting me and my ladies be his cook assistants when Capt'n wasn't, 'ow gently can I say this, 'bein' busy with us. We Irish lasses damn well could cook too! So doin' that in the meantime at least saved us from the, um, *'brutality'* 'a the rest 'a the crew.'

* * *

Watching Buzzard fly about the deck cawing, crowing, taleing in the glint of Luny Mum, is Mariner. As Captain Polly, he's chained, but with enough slack to ascend galley steps to the deck. Only he realizes Buzzard's gambit: Create legends that will grow even more ominous to keep dregs occupied – so they don't think too much about the women, he, or Buzzard. Not even Buzzard, with his imagination, could forecast, that soon the legends would start coming true.
"Kunta. At first, he's just conniving," Buzzard soft pedals. "But that Turt, an evil, revenge-minded Trumpeter, taught him to be evil as he. So, beware, everyone, of them both."

* * *

James scratches his head. "Where's Capt'n in all this to stop the confusion, Rrrose?"
'POP!' Suddenly Mama Lucy appears beside them. 'I can answer your question for you youngen', though I wasn't there. I knew somethun' about Mariner. See, Mariner be cookin' special-potioned meals for Capt'n, I, years before, taught him to make. Slowly, surely they was debilitatin' Capt'n, thwartin' his Capt'nly duties. Makin' it so Rrrose and her ladies didn't have to bear his friskiness, anymore.' Mariner be poisonin' crew too, but not so much. Needed 'em alive. Ship ken't sail itself without sailors, 'ken-it!'

* * *

Turt peaks from Kunta's pocket one night while Kunta surveys the deck through a rot-hole below deck. Turt sees the villain Buzzard is making of him. He grits beak-snout as Buzzard struts, scurries, and gains glory at his expense.
'THE BUZZARD' – *who's black-feathered flyin' kin ate your shelling friends and relatives on Jericho.* *'THE BUZZARD'* – *who defiled Trumpeter, remains below, behind the 'flat-tree: You hate him; you vow you will, forever.'*

CHAPTER 23

As Buzzard enters the wharf-shack Turt trumpets shrilly. Shelved books vibrate. Carper covers ears. Mariner curses, "Dammit Turt. Either cork yer melodramy or take it to the opry."
Turt quiets. 'Soothing thoughts; starfish at play; the depths' absolute quiet.'
Tranquility's sea buoys him only briefly. Steady breaths become hissing snorts as he glares at Buzzard. This scenario plays whenever Buzzard arrives: Acrimony sans-attack.
Buzzard edges warily to the table. He hands Mariner his bottle of jack, tosses deck of cards to Carper and drops scraps to Ol Tom. Before Mariner can even "welcome-aboard", Buzzard commences. "Now where was I when I left off my story last time I was here?" Carper cracks open the fresh deck, little realizing, this man-bird, these rectangular objects, they would change his life nearly as much as Mariner's shaping of it.
"Let's see. I believe Kunta had just marshaled a herd of whales to torpedo the ship. That drowns a couple dozen dregs. The ladies are knocked overboard. They ride whales' tails safely to the Cape Horn. All-the-while we battle Capt'n and the rest while Captain Polly takes over steering so we wouldn't capsize."

TALES OF THE FICTION HOUSE

Carper memorizes his words midst fiddlin'-fumblin' with the cards.

"There's whales-tales somewhere theres," Mariner says, pouring jack for the pair. He and Buzzard toast. "After decades of tellin', Buzzard, have you, completely, deluded yerself into believen' yer own version?"

Buzzard disregards jibe by perusing <u>The Daily Opine</u>. "I see you gents are local celebrities."

Turt ignores him, and glares at Laza Bones in the poster, who glares right back out. Turt has been trying to decide which of these two non-creatures, but not-really-humans either, he most despises, when something Buzzard caws, grips his attention. "I saw Kunta not long ago. He was looking good. Nothing like that skinny runt he was aboard ship."

'You lying vulture,' Turt blows, hard, loud. Memories of Kunta brings him only happiness. His name on Buzzard's beak is sacrilege. (Mariner steadies a shelf of rattling knick-knacks.)

"I saw him when I was coming up-rive'. I took a break from the table, went on deck to tally winnings. I see Kunta onshore, talking to this very same steed pictured here in the paper." He pokes it. "I recognize the Big Dipper marking the flank."

'Dear Precious!' Ol Tom and Turt simultaneously think.

Mariner crooks eye at Buzzard. 'Story's possible. Why'ud Buzzard hoist Turt's 'ope, only ta stir his bile agiin' him even more. No percentage in that fer a gamblin' man.'

Turt wants so, to believe. Heart thumps in anticipation. 'Kunta, ALIVE! This is too much coincidence, even for Buzzard to invent. I must find out if it is true.' He scooches toward the door, and plans, 'I'll paddle downriver and see for myself.'

* * *

Onto the pirate ship's deck Kunta often sneaks. He must escape the stench and heat of the ship's bowels, or perish. So far he's eaten little, so he comes up to scavenge too. To Turt who rides in his pocket, he whispers, "We'll be together for all time, friend."

Many of the crew claim to have seen Kunta – naked from the waist up and wearing his walk-off necklace. Only Captain Polly, from her perch, really has. She doesn't tattle, fearing the next walk-off Kunta might claim would be from her, and then, her pseudo peg-leg might become a necessity.

* * *

Buzzard shies from the middle of the wharf-shack allowing Turt wide-berth. "Where, pray tell, is HE bound?"

Mariner downs jack, re-pours. "Reckon maybe he thinks somethin'-some-un' in here stinks, Buzzard. N e's hankerin' fresh air."

The complete opposite of Mariner's salty-sea Boston talk is guest's Buzzard's Bay, Mass., nearly 'R-less', accent. He grew into it as a child. As an adult, he'd bluffed-it-up with tones of aristocracy. He gently sips his drink and imperiously addresses Turt. "You should let bygones be bygones, good fellow. Why, if I were to covet a grudge and behave as you, I would have no friends. And the grand riverboat Captains would banish me forever from their vessels."

Turt nudges back the canvas door and blows a grand trumpeting trill directed at Buzzard. Buzzard gentles glass between fingers; considers briefly that the pitch might shatter it. Carper clenches teeth. Turt looks back, sees he is hurting Carper. He stops and lowers his eyes in contrition. He glances at Buzzard, spits out caustic '*HISSSSSSS*', then, is away.

Carper runs to Mariner and hugs his leg – a lobster lock. "Why is Turt leaving us?"

"Don'cha frets small fry." He pries Carper loose, lifts and cradles him to his shoulder. "Turt heads yonder. Always straddles back. Like I spieled earlier, Turt nay takes 'acotton to Buzzard. Truthen be told, only ones probably do are me 'n Ol Tom. We ain't discernin'. We likes all."

Buzzard whispers derisively: "Even that bayou bank *mudder*,

Monsieur Bonteez' Thibidioux?"
Laza Bones' waxy ears perk. 'If I warn't stuck here, I'd...'
"We likes *most-all*." Mariner's blank-face masks hatred for Thibidioux's kind. 'The boy don't need experiencen' the scaly side 'a humanity when livin's so precious. Carper'll never need to meet him.' He mutters to Buzzard: "Laza Bones 'n that piratey Capt'n. Two ersters-inna-shell."
Tears stream Carper's cheek. Pleading eyes find Mariner. Mariner holds him tighter when the boy says, "Turt leaves, and then Ol Tom. Then you, Mariner? Then I have no friends. And be like poor Mr. Buzzard. Sad and lonely."
Buzzard dryly swallows. He flourishes a new silk handkerchief from his vest pocket and wipes Carper's tears. He is consoling, yet miffed at the impression Mariner's given the boy – true, though it is. He says. "Don't listen a minute to him, son. A kind heart like you will always have friends. You can bet on it every time. I know because, fact is, I've plenty."
Mariner raises his hand, signaling a temporary truce in their sport of mutual josh. He sits at the table and takes Carper on his lap. "Jolly him with a tale, Buzzard."

BUZZARD'S BELLES

Buzzard winks. "Let me tell you about not all my multitudity of good friends, just four. Beautiful Georgia belles I call *Spring, Summer, Autumn* and *Winter*."
He takes Carper's deck and repeatedly fans cards diagonally. To Carper they seem a staircase spanning Buzzard's 'wingspan'. One hand is the landing, other the top.
"Picture them son, in gowns of chemise, promenading so genteelly up a riverboat's gangway: *Spring*, awash in the blues and yellows of her season; *Summer*, hot-red. Gentle auburn-*Autumn*, cool *Winter* – snow white."
Carper squints- transfixed. ('Yes, Mr. Buzzard. I see them.' They whisper. '*Will you be our forever friend, Carper?*')
Ol Tom lifts front paw to greet the pretties. Mariner senses the moment's magic. Oh how his cold friend could warm a

young heart, and an old one too. Laza Bones peers over, planning to steal gentle *Autumn*.

Buzzard arcs elbow, as if intentionally blocking Thibidioux's view.

Thibidioux grumbles and scrunches into seclusion.

Buzzard proclaims, "The ladies board the riverboat and come all the way up the Mississippi, then Ohio, to fetch me." The gangway recedes and he forms a continually looping, three and a half feet in diameter circle with the cards – a paddlewheel. Cards '*click*,' '*swoosh*.' "Bet you can hear the paddlewheel slapping the water."

Carper studies the cards and the talon-quick hands. He seems to notice everything around him. He locks it all into his thoughts for future tryin'-of, tellin'-'bout. How, say, when the two men drink, Buzzard takes only a few sips to each glass Mariner finishes. That, though they joust with words the men's looks embrace one another and the sight is like the feeling of Ol Tom softness when he climbs purring onto your lap. How, when Buzzard shuffles cards, voice-inflections and facial-expressions meld becoming-one with spiraling fingers. Carper can't understand how Buzzard does it, but vows he too will learn these tricks, talents, abilities – whatever they are.

(Buzzard could warble his tales for hours during a poker game. He mesmerizes most gentlemen-rubes, and many-a-shark, with his card props, gestures, expressions. As their concentrations flag, meticulously he picks their 'bones' – they, hardly realizing.)

Buzzard lowers paddlewheel close to the floor, and Ol Tom, intrigued, maybe even hypnotized by the Buzzard and his flutter, jumps through it. Carper claps.

"Tom should travel the riverboats with me and perform," Buzzard laughs. "He'd clean up the mice and I the bones."

"Just be sure you clean up this account of your belles," Mariner reminds.

Buzzard *brakes* the wheel: All 52 paddles stack neatly in one quick hand that swerves to meet them. He thinks, 'I'll hasten the story into a five minuter' for the boy.'

"So what were the beautiful belles doing on the deck while I was visiting my friends Mariner and Ol Tom on the wharf?" Carper is glossy-eyed with wanting to know. "Why, they were fanning themselves because it was so hot."

He splits deck and in each hand shuffles the halves between pinkies and thumbs. He forms two fans and sighs, "AHHH" at the cool breeze they create. Carper instinctively repeats, "AHHH". He doesn't know the expression 'audience participation', but he knows it feels good to join in, just like the parade. Mariner, "AHHH's", too. Ol Tom meows a little.

"It was so hot that day on deck that the fine ladies developed a right torturous case of the vapors. So they fanned faster and faster to keep cool."

Buzzard begins fanning so fast that the card faces become a blur of black and red. Ol Tom jumps onto the table to look closer and his whiskers get whisked. "Know what happened next, son?" Without waiting for an answer Buzzard, with quick slight of hand, turns the fans first back into the gangway, then stairs, then quickly into the paddlewheel.

Ol Tom takes opportunity again to jump through. The hoop is so wide, and Carper is so excited that he bounds from Mariner's lap and leaps through too, back and forth: A joy so sweet never would he forget.

"So what happens?" Mariner asks, squinting at the wheel. After seeing this trickery dozens of times, he still tries to figure out how Buzzard's able to keep that wheel spinning and spinning.

"Why, the fine Georgia belles were ringing and dinging because they fanned so hard to stay cool. So hard, they blew away the gangplank and the paddlewheel and launched the riverboat. Why, they fanned so hard they were carried all the way down to the Gulf of Mexical where it happened to be a cooler day."

Mariner grins. "And whats become of those huar' fine fiery ladies you claims as friends, Buzzard?" he spouts in perfect shill form.

Buzzard looks through the wheel and leans down so his face is inches from Carper's. "Want to meet them, son?" Carper nods excitedly.

Buzzard quickly swoops arms and gathers cards back into one hand. One-at-a-time, he lay down the top four on the table: ALL QUEENS.

Carper's eyes widen more. His arms move wildly, like a combination fan, paddlewheel, and gangway. Buzzard motions him to stroke the faces of the beautiful Belles.

"So if they'n care fer ya so much, how's come they aint's with ya now in real life," Mariner lightly taunts. "Thas' what me an Ol Tom hankerin' to know."

"Oh disbelieving man and feline!" Buzzard lifts Ol Tom, pets, and then sets him on the table. Carper simultaneously strokes Tom and the belles. "The cards are real life, Mariner. You must just – Believe! With the faith of a child."

Buzzard swipes his four belle-queens into one hand. With the rest of the deck still in his other he flips the next top card and adds it to them – "THE HEART KING – am I," Buzzard pronounces imperiously. "And I always travel with my BELLE-QUEENS since that incident."

He begins moving the king and queens between fingers and thumb, a slow procession so that one always seems to remain mid-air. "You fellows had your parade, and me, I have mine, right here-and-now."

As promenade continues, Carper pretends he joins it.

Mariner, sympathetically, "See, Carper, they came back to Buzzard. Just because they left, don't mean they don't come back. So don't worry about Turt. Iffen I read it right, Turt's plannin' a fast swim downstream to see if it really was Kunta that Dear Precious was neighing to. Kunta and Turt, they had somethun estra-special. Like you and me."

As he speaks, Mariner's thinking sorrowfully of the boy's murdered mother. Was Carper thinking she'd abandoned him and so would everyone else? Mariner hugs him. Though Carper intently watches the cards, he assimilates all Mariner's said.

"Glums-be-gone. Turt'll return," Mariner quietly says.

'Mood's changed,' Buzzard sees by slightish-of-boy-smile. It makes Buzzard smile. Doesn't know why, he likes the tyke. 'Who'd imagine that the Mariner,' he thinks, as he remembers Mariner's past, 'who could be hard – murderous-hard – as any pirate or beast, would reel in a flounder and choose to school him up.'

'PLOP!' Just then, they hear Turt jump from the far-end of the pier and into the Ohio. The magical spell of the cards is broken and Buzzard knows it. He stops the parade as he sees new glums sweep Carper's face. To a child, the wisdom of rationality is always fleeting when a dear one's return becomes a concern. They hear Turt's 'swishing' as he swims, then the 'SLAP-SLAP' of fin-claws as he submerges and speeds south, faster than any riverboat, except Buzzard's fan-powered one.

Carper runs to the porthole: Nothing to see but Turt's whirring wake.

Mariner limps over, strokes Carper's hair. Feeling sad for Carper, he is too tear-choked, to speak.

Buzzard acts quickly when he sees the glums shrouding them. He sweeps Carper from the porthole, carries him to Mariner's sloppy overstuffed chair, and perches him on his lap. Instinctively, Ol Tom leaps to join them.

Mariner pours, drinks all; pours another – banks it. He is remembering the boy, Kunta, on the ship – all they meant to each other when finally they met: Maybe it was as much as Kunta and Turt had meant to one another, maybe more; because, he thought of Kunta as a son then, just how he feels for Carper now.

* * *

While chained in the galley during the start of his captivity, Mariner begins hearing rustling noises. Though not seeing the stealthy Kunta, he knows it is he, pilfering, to keep from starving. He starts leaving food for him, and fish-innards as a special treat for Turt. He won't meet Kunta for a while, but once or twice, he sees Turt. Eyes meet. A lifetime creature – two-leg bond, though it is beginning, has many obstacles yet to overcome.

* * *

Mariner glares at his jack-o-lantern toothy reflection in his empty glass and dreams, 'Wouldn't it be crackerjack if Kunta really is alive. How I want that!'

Buzzard wings arms around both Carper and Ol Tom. "So maybe Turt has his reasons for rejecting me, son. That does not stop me from admiring he and Kunta's friendship midst the ship hardship. After me and Mariner tell you the stories about what they meant to one another in those bygone days, you'll see how Turt treasures those he cares for. Like you: And would never leave for long; if he didn't *have* to." With those words, Buzzard commences his next dreg-ship story. "It was nigh on quarter century ago when…"

CHAPTER 24

A TALE OF BLYTHE-ABWE:
Kunta's survival quest in the ship's bowels begins.

Turt in one pocket, Cookie's twitchy walk-off the other, for hours Kunta crawls through blue-black darkness. He clenches butcher knife, sniffs: A musty burlap odor – "rats". They lunge – *'SLASH!'* Rodent screams deflate to whimpers. Edging onward, *'schhh'*, cargo stowaways – poison snakes. Kunta rolls. *'SLICE!'* Single serpents become helpless twos. Turt, beak-snout peaking from pocket: He *'snips'* witchy tarantula moving daringly close. Legless, they whither.

Then suddenly: Just picture – you or I a kid again, emerging from a matinee. Not used to the light – we're temporarily blinded. These same sparkling rays rake Kunta's face. Squinting, he gasps, "GLORIOUS!" Turt, though startled by the glow-burst, doesn't retreat to his shell. The 'burst' reminds him of Luny Mum's comforting light that gilded Jericho beaches.

Kunta's eyes adjust. He realizes he's at the bottom of a twenty feet deep shaft. Designed to house a pulley elevator, never installed, it is capped on-deck with a louvered cupola. Morning light streams through.

"We've reached Blithe-abwe, Turt." Blithe-abwe, Kunta's tribe's joyous 'land-beyond', combination Paradise, Shangri-la, Valhalla, where all Kunta's tribe are destined to live forever, together; where light is so golden, artisans may work for all eternity and see results clearer than ever in life. "Here we will be safe, friend, until we may escape."

The desolate floor area six by six.. Turt crawls onto Kunta's knee. Kunta looks around and finds... Capt'n' spare peg-leg. A disgruntled crewman had pinched it. A packrat pilfered it from him. It's just right for Kunta to use to clear cobwebs, but *perfect*, for something else.

On it, in the coming weeks Kunta inscribes hundreds of fingertip-size faces- those of his village 'gone-onto Blithe-abwe'. The more he carves, the hungrier he gets. He dwells in euphoric states. *You cannot believe it. Their faces speak to you:*

"You will survive on the abundance of insects, rodents and serpents in this place, Kunta. Observe your shelled friend. He will show you the parts that may be eaten. The rain that drips in. Find ways to catch it. Drink sparingly."

Kunta's thoughts are solemn, 'With this totem forever will my forebears be with me.' He pets Turt. "By now we are probably thought dead by the dregs, fella." Just the opposite: With Buzzard's continual spinning of the duo into the deadliest of specters, all the spirit, and physical force of the club will be needed – to save them from the repercussions of becoming a legend.

THE DISPUTIN' RASPUTINS OF THE HIGH SEAS (AND THEIR WALK-OFFS)

Buzzard strokes mast-prop then pulls away with a dramatic flourish. "Slick-as-a-badger, gents, Kunta slid down the mast, unseen by all but me. Before I could get here to stop him, he tangled his feet 'round the throat of your unsuspecting mate. Wrung his neck."

Buzzard invents as he tells. By playing-into audience's endless superstitions brought on by the fog and grog-life of the sea, he manipulates them into believers. "Kunta's the cunning deceiver that sliced out the Moroccan's tongue. Fed it to his ravenous Trumpeter, who ingests our languages – to use against humans in the future,' I'll wager.[25] That beak-snouted demon is heartless. So Kunta cuts out the heart of the Algerian for him to devour while it beat."

'A vile, contemptuous evil pervades the ship,' thinks Captain Polly. From her perch, she watches the sallow-faced crew. Their attention never leaves Buzzard who is wending about the deck. Parrot knows she must do something to save herself from the stealthy young badger-human, Kunta, and his shelled beast that her Buzzard warns of: But, what? With leg chained? 'Your only hope, Captain Polly' she tells herself, 'is your dream-lover bird, Buzzard. But... how to woo a human?'

"Kunta stalks," Buzzard rails. "LOPPING more walk-offs for his necklace; PLOPPING his victims overboard. Some of the walk-offs are quick, devious. They escape. BEWARE! These walk-offs gone-feral hate humans. They lie in wait to destroy us."

"What the Buzzard says gotta be true," a pirate belly-aches to the others. It's after lunch. They sit on crates near the railing – so they can vomit. The Rasputin-of-the-word – Buzzard, his sly comrade Rasputin-of-the-poison, Mariner, has upped the dosage – just a smidgen – so that the savvy-to-the-tricks-of-the-sea, dregs, don't notice. They think only, 'the waves are having their way with gullets.' They tremble continuously, and sweat so much that their raggedy limp clothes seem starched from saturating then drying so often.

(The poisons keep Capt'n stupor-fied. The pentad of mutineers know he may prove an asset if alive. One of them always guards him in his quarters turned prison.)

Crew's superstitions beckon irrationality. In their poison-induced hallucinations walk-offs come to life; stalk. They begin believing they sail on what is becoming a ghost ship that may be overtaken anytime by the walk-offs. As Buzzard spins his tale, the dregs mutter vows in a dozen languages, about skirting

---

[25] Morrocan's now a mute, driven mad by the cutting – so he can't relay what really happened; that Mariner's the slicer-dicer.

the mast after dark and keeping near the rail to avoid Kunta.
"That'll never do," Buzzard counters. "Kunta and his fiend straddle the ship's sides, leaping on the unsuspecting." Dregs look warily over the rail, wishing for land- a thousand miles off.
The usually mawkish-squawkish Captain Polly is quiet. 'The monsters'll see I am no dreg. I will reason with them. Teach them the humans' many languages. (Captain Polly knows at least a dozen.) Oh so valuable I can be.' None of Captain Polly's self-assurances quells her horror of, while still alive, being plucked, de-beaked and de-clawed by Kunta and Turt.

When not perusing the deck, flapping and doing his beak jacking, Buzzard's usually arguing in the galley with Mariner about the tactics of their tightly schemed mutiny. But they agree, fully, with the results.
"How'd it get to this?" the crew whispers to each other. "Trumpeter curse, for ravaging their island?" Others think hexing, by a tribal witch in retaliation for stealing Kunta.
Ominous signs of the walk-offs – stinking dried blood trails staining the deck – swell superstitions. A once-tranquil voyage of plunder and pleasure is now, nightmare. "Why's our Capt'n keepin' to quarters? Even at his sickliest, he's stayed the deck wielding his whip. Why's he issuein' orders through Buzzard?"
Buzzard, in this short time, seems to have been elevated to acting Captain. Many pirates are loyal to him – 'only way to survive' – as they struggle to man-the-ship to get close to land.

THE TALE OF MAMA L'S SECRET SLICKENS

Mariner, allowed enough chain to come up for daylight, listens to Buzzard's tales from the galley doorway. Captain Polly watches 'new Cookie' wipe fish blood from cleaver onto his neck-to-knee apron. In futility, she gnaws her chain, wary of the time he might want her for a 'fixin'.
From the first meal, he cooked – it smelled sweet as any Amazonian jungle cuisine. Pirates shoveled it in. When they

spooned some into Captain Polly's bucket, she sniffed, recognizing ingredients humans cannot. (Plants from Leezian' bayou; recipes, come courtesy of Mama Lucy.) Flying over the 'Big Easy' Captain Polly had seen their effect on critters. They went battier than during a Gone Luna. So now, Captain Polly is subsisting on the array of bugs flying close to her perch. '*Oh*,' growls Captain Polly's stomach, '*but to fly free of this ship.*'

Mariner found the slickens – kegs of North Africa's plants, almost cousins to poisonous Leezian' claw-root and twig-lick – during his first day in the galley. "One dasha' claw render evil spirits helpless and raw." Creviced old Mama had 'scienced-up' Mariner in her cabin's kitchen-lab. "Cure most ills. Two dasha' twig cures yer patient of inflictin' dev-ils. Three-'a-each, 'n the de-vil escape; slitheren' inta another ta inhabitate."

Mariner always uses two-and-a-half, insuring deferred insanity. He can't give three to finish the job – crew's needed to get ship to shore. If it appears madness may arrive before land, he lessens the dose. For Buzzard, Rrrose Heather, her ladies and himself he prepares simpler fare. For Capt'n, who killed most of Mariner's dear friends from the commandeered ship, Mariner prepares meals with another cousin-berry – the dung-flower.

"Gaarente-ad'," Mama'll testify. "Tuz cause most-vile hallucinatin', yea inde-ad'."

Mariner looks from Buzzard, who is gruesomely lopping off the end of another tale. He glances at Captain Polly. She imagines he's saying, "Ready to join yer Capt'n, Captain?" She gnaws shackle even more desperately.

TALE OF A SAIL

"Hoist starboard keel. Set jig-rigging north, northwest." Buzzard mangles the orders of the 'silent-Captain', Mariner, rendering them illogical. Doesn't matter; bedraggled crew sails by rote. No doubt, Rasputin-Buzzard steers the emotions of fear; Rasputin-Mariner helms the mayhem triggering it.

TALE OF HOW THE WALK-OFFS 'REALLY' CAME ABOARD

Late at night: Cleaver descends. *'WHAP!'* A piercing scream, *'THUMPS'*, of running. Scream stops with watery *'PLOP'!* Someone yells: "MAN OVERBOARD." In the shadows, Mariner wipes cleaver clean and oysters-out a slimy walk-off from the tip of leather shoe.

All the crew now wears shoes. 'Does 'em little good,' Mariner grins.

From her manacled spot near the helm, Captain Polly quivers midst a new revelation: 'New Cookie's got a key. He can come for me anytime.'

Mariner eases back to the galley and re-shackles himself. He stows walk-offs in the Capt'n' humidor. In a few days, as just another small way to nudge Capt'n closer to insanity, he'll have Rrrose deliver it to Capt'n' new quarters – a cramped dungeon-like room, rancid from 50 years of storing smoked mackerel.

Capt'n sleeps constantly, awakens only to his own screams caused by hallucinogenic dreams of sea creatures devouring him alive – more of the effects from Mariner and Mama's 'slickens'.

THE TALE OF A 'GOOD' LIFE FOR SOME

Buzzard, Rrrose Heather, and the ladies they now occupy Capt'n' plush quarters.

"You'll live with the bloody walk-offs throughout hell's eternity," Rrrose Heather, veiled as fortunetellers Capt'n always visited when in ports, soothsays to him – her personal revenge for what he's done to she and her ladies. She leaves the humidor of walk-offs with him in his dungeon.

THE TALE OF A 'WORSE' LIFE FOR OTHERS

Midst hot-cold sweats, Capt'n removes lid and reaches for a cigar. The slimy walk-offs feel like jellyfish, their stench, worse than the rancid mackerel. He pushes the humidor. Contents spill. His eyes widen as hallucinations spiral into a parade of the moldy gray-green walk-offs tip-toeing to come choke him. Too paralyzed to move, he screams, continuously, *curdling-ly*.

Reverberations echo through ship and shake the mast. Crew looks up at the sails, expecting to see Kunta and his fiend, their arms, and fin-claws stretched in a victory sign to show they now control the ship.

Buzzard swoops from the ship's wheel. What to expect? He is sure he'll find Capt'n, dead.

Captain Polly hops on the wheel to steady the ship as Capt'n has trained her for times when an automatic parrot is necessary. Though she loathes Capt'n, she feels pangs of sorrow. That lasts just seconds. She sings in an ecstatic combination of a half-dozen languages. "Blow the man down, mate. Blow the man down. You gave us time, we blew the man down."

The crew doesn't share her joy. If Capt'n is dead, hope for survival is with Buzzard.

'Who will be at his mercy?' Many silently vow 'to become *his* slave if he protects them from Kunta and Turt.' Captain Polly's had enough of being a chained slave. She has another idea.

Buzzard returns to the wheel, relieved that Rrrose's act of revenge hasn't killed Capt'n. Captain Polly hops to his shoulder, brushes plumage sensually against his neck, gently nibbles ear, coos, "Lover bird. Lover bird. I'll be true to you."

CHAPTER 25

THE TALE OF A BIRTH AND RE-BIRTH

Kunta massages Blythe-abwe's petrifying walls until the oils of his finger soften the wood.

Into it, he carves his village's towering trees and forever flowing waterfall. He depicts his family canoeing its peaceful lake. The strokes, crying out his artist's passions, soon become as an infant's soft breath, as if he's carving new life. He adds his perception of a fully-grown Turt, traipsing into the village. People gather around the Trumpeter, awed. Monkeys and anteaters peek from behind bamboo; their expressions, 'Never have we seen so massive a land-hugger.'

Rhythm of the ocean's pulse, a soothing *'thump-shh, thump-shh'* against stern of the triple-mast square-rigger, entrances Kunta.

Turt, staring intently from the floor, feels admiration for the new life Kunta beckons-forth from the wood, and familial pride, that he can crane his neck and visit Kunta's home, his *Jericho*. He imagines a time when it might become his new home. He'd swim alongside the gentle two-legs. Tears, and a squeaky trumpeting of glum come, 'Will memories of my own *Jericho* fade, vanish without a picture reminder as Kunta has of his home?'

Kunta seems to understand his companion's hurts. "I'll not let you forget, Turt."

What Turt sees Kunta do next eases glums, and flutters heart. With barely a dozen swift-but-sure knife swipes, he adds, frolicking in the waterfall, dozens of Trumpeters. Their beaked faces emblazon into Turt's memory. Because of Kunta, forever may his tribe be with him.

Author's note: 'Blithe-abwe's walls are still intact. The long-ago sunken ship – perfectly preserved for over 150 years by lichen, barnacles, zero light, and moderate temperatures. (Turt swum to visit tribe there often.) The saved paneled carvings by Kunta are on permanent display, alongside Capt'n' peg-leg turned totem – at the art wing of the Fiction House Museum, open daily 8 to 5; (for a nominal admission charge.)

Also, be sure to see our newly renovated, micro-chipped, snapping Alligatormotran of Laza Bones Thibidioux – doing constant battle with…well, you'll see. And while you're there be sure to pick up a jar of James Thaddeus Jr.'s ever popular GOAT SCROTUM JUICE. 'THE, crystal-clear, ever-popular grand elixir for yourself, men, and for mi'ladies man – aged 18 and virile, through 108 and almost to heaven's gate. Its lore is proven – tried and trued – to bolster male FORTITUDE!'

Midst creation's bliss, Kunta repeatedly looks up, coveting the 15 feet of shaft he cannot reach. He envisions there, birds that visit his village. Their freedom to fly home; he envies it so.

KUNTA'S TALE OF LIFE IN THE *'HOLD'*

When our hideaways forage through their nether-world maze, they discover a crawlspace beneath the mess hall. Morsels of Mariner's honey-steamed vegetables, wine-saute`ed grilled meats, heels of his butter-glazed baked breads slip through the planked floor. "Blithe-abwe's manna," Kunta whispers to Turt. Queasiness follows succulent feast. They return to their rudimentary bill of fare, bugs, rats, snakes, and so avoid the poisoning besetting the crew.

Maybe it's coincidence, or biological, triggered by their extreme protein diet – during these weeks boy and beast begin growth spurts: Turt, from being able to be cupped in Kunta's palm, to the size of a big man's fist; beak-snout from hardly bigger than a sparrow's, to that of an eagle; tail from thread, to clothesline. The tiny African village on his ever-shifting tectonic shell: "I wish you could see it Turt," Kunta says. He waves hands upward, out as he describes it. "The campfire flickers, ever higher; the lake swells; and the curing antelope skins *striitch* ever more."

Kunta, it seems, grows a foot. He remains thin, so the tunnel crawling isn't affected.

Sometimes, as Turt rides his widening shoulder, Turt must 'in-shell' himself to keep from scraping, *'ouch!'* his head on low rafters. If Kunta had a mirror, he would see a boy's face becoming a young man: Nose broadening, cheeks hollowing, chin, and forehead effusing prominence.

Our growing boys need vitamin C. Who has it? *Ourrr* pirates.

THE TALE OF THE VITAMIN C WARS

Scurvy of nature, nurture but not nutrition, these pre-Linus Pauling health adherents of the high seas, but much-less pacifist, from necessity are well-versed in their need of citrus.[26] In their sleeping quarters, they store and keep close-account of what they commandeer from other ships.

"What the devil goin' on," shouts a dreg – drunk, delirious from Mariner's drugging – when he enters sleeping quarters and sees Turt nosing around his pillow. Kunta had yanked away a tunnel plank leading here – just big enough to send

---

[26] Pauling, pre-second millennium biochemist-ethicist and Nobel Laureate – never once, met a pirate.

Turt through to fetch fruit. He's tied a long string around Turt so he can pull him back. Dreg yanks knife from sheath and lurches for Turt. Kunta yanks. Turt slips through man's hand, arcs through the air, still clutching a mango in his beak-snout. Kunta reaches through the opening, catches and pulls him behind the wall. Victim sees only the blur of the strange flight. The dreg's leap weakens the bed. It gives way, '*smooshing*' more 'stash'. A dozen others hear the commotion, rush in, see what they conclude is a member of a fruit-theft gang. Kunta and Turt peer through thin slat and witness a strange turn: Instead of drawing and quartering the perceived vitamin C bandit, they too, delirious from the drugs, begin feasting on the vitamin- 'elixer' that looks like it would be wasted. Mad shouts, "Gimme some. I wants my share."

Turt's attacker squats, rocks, howls about a strange aerial creature flying off with the bounty.

A dozen other pirates hear his wail as they enter and see the fruit carnage.

Scowls. Accusations. Threats. Knives, swords are drawn.

The vitamin C's civil war has commenced, triggering similar battles at other stashes throughout the ship. It's a war Mariner, Buzzard, Rrrose Heather and her girls avoid because Mariner has discovered Cookie's galley stash; has hidden it where no dreg dare look – within Trumpeter shells Buzzard has spun into being haunts for Trumpeter 'haints'.

Captain Polly knows well the perils of a ship adrift. That is what she fears with both war and poisoning. Vile currents will send untended ships to unknown waters. Too many salt waves, too much sunlight will crack disregarded sails 'til they're in danger of crumbling. As if a ship's a giant reed instrument, westerlies will sound dirges, of the ominous danger of capsizing, through open portholes. Forget then the worry about sharks. All'd be dead long before sharks dined.

The worst of the to-be-imagined lot – being chained, as she, helpless to escape.

So, day, night, Captain Polly squawks, squeals "SAIL ON…

SAIL ON." Of course, the drugged, fruit-warring crew, they pay no mind to a "simple" parrot.

* * *

In the wharf-shack, Buzzard takes a break from the story, sips jack and thinks admiringly of Captain Polly's shrewdness during that long-ago tumult.
Mariner takes over when he sees fear sweep Carper's face.
"Captain Polly needn't a worried, son. Mama Lucy taught me well, how much I could dose. Just enough so the dregs could do the hard work sailen' to get us to some shore, and we slaves could laze-back and watch. Buzzard coulda' chirped that to her, but at the time we warn't sure which side 'a battle she stood with that peg-leg a' her-'en."

CHAPTER 26

A TALE OF TWO THOMASES:
Sans AQUINAS, a'BECKET; cum a KEMPIS, a-HEMPIS

"Even Capt'n don't know his ship's guts well as us, Turt," says Kunta as he hammers peg-leg totem through the slats of an isolated cargo hold. A humidor-intense pungency, damp, woodsy, sifts out. Kunta and Turt's nose and beak-buds swell with pleasure. They've discovered a cache of barely-dried, high-fibred Lindian hemp to be sold in the cordage industry.

"Here we go again partner." Kunta ties string around Turt, guides him through the splintered opening. He devises a grand plan for this plant that stalks his village: Spin a rope, as have ancestors in sacred ceremonies. Rope allows life, providing nets for their fishing, ladders to retrieve bounty of trees, traps for wild beasts. Here, it might save his life.

What drives Turt? An overwhelming desire to taste the leaves.

For hours, a scene repeats. Turt creeps in, clamps jaw onto the intoxicating treat, *'AHH!'* Sweet ecstasy instantly flows within shell. One moment he hallucinates basking on Jericho's beach, next, he fancies racing over sand, faster-ever than any Trumpeter. Kunta reels him in. Turt feels he rides an ever-so-high ocean wave. Kunta reaches through the opening and retrieves the plant. Turt anxiously returns for more. When Turt's delivered a bundle, Kunta removes string, binds plants, positions load on back, and hastens to Blithe-abwe. Turt grasps the precious cargo.

For the first time since his separation from ma and fa on Jericho, EVUUTHIING of life seems BEEUUTIFULL! He's exhausted yet oddly exhilarated. He feels like munching, something. When they pass spiders ensconced safely in webs, or titter-mice peeking from behind timbers, Turt cranes neck, chomps. Munchies quelled.

* * *

Stopping along the Lindian pathway next to a stand of the same wild weed, Turt remembers that joyful yet confusing trip of long ago. Rrrose Heather helps James dismount so he can make water behind a tree. She laughs to Turt as he sniffs the weed. 'Reminisce; don't partake.'

Turt's considering. 'Being with Kunta made the ship bearable. Just a taste could return me, just-briefly, to him. No, can't think about that. Responsibility, have I.'

James drinks from a clear stream. Turt nudges him back onto shell. Onward.

* * *

Back at Blithe-abwe Kunta goes to work. Turt sleeps. From observing village elders ceremonial use of the plant, Kunta knows contented rest always follows. (Throughout his sea odyssey, Turt will take many a leisurely stroll to that cargo hold. It would be an even more leisurely stroll back to Blithe-abwe.)[27] Kunta picks off leaves; soaks them in captured

---

[27] As a public service for the group CONCERNED AMERICA ABOUT CANKERING ABUSE AWARENESS (CAA CAA) Fiction House publication would like to pass along the following advice – "DON'T!" You see, in Lil Turt's time, product was pure. Today it is often cut with and thus

rainwater, in a makeshift trough he'd dowelled from scrap wood: He creates green paint for his artwork. Somberly he slices elastic stalks into strips, weaves, until they are one. Turt sometimes awakens and helps. He locks strands in his jaw, dangles from them and Kunta spins. *WHEE!'* Dizzy, he plops to floor; dozes.

Each of Kunta's twists add length: Five feet, ten, twenty, finally after many focused hours, a 50 feet rope; ¾ inch thick. With dull edge of knife, Kunta whacks a chunk of scrap iron he's found. Sparks leap onto a small pile of the leaves. They smolder. A white cloud rises. He breathes it deeply while chanting, "Tribute to my ancestors, for all they have taught me."

Now, as chance would have, Buzzard, Rrrose Heather and her ladies stand by the cupola covering the shaft discussing in hushed voices the mutiny's progress. The faint aroma pleasantly arouses them. "Where's it from?"

Captain Polly, far above, but with an acute sense of smell, is immediately overtaken. Instead of becoming somber like Turt, her jealousy is enflamed. She looks down longingly at her male 'bird' alongside the 'pseudo' female 'birds' wearing feathers galore in their hats. She flaps, showing-off beautiful 'real' plumage of yellow, orange, gold, and blue. She squawks, "BUZZARD!"

He glances up briefly then returns stare to the prettily rouged humans around him.

One of them glares up and jostles bosom in her low-cut dress. "You ain't got what 'e wants Captain Polly."

Feeling momentary shame, Captain Polly furls wings, bows head. 'I'm ugly. I'm hobbled by chain, disfigured with eye patch, propped with peg-leg.'

At that moment, she feels the warmth of Poppy Sol and looks up to see his encouraging wink. 'Pretty bird, you be.

---

tainted with illicit snot garzle weed; or even worse, the condensed powders dried from once-healthy but 'past-the-shelf-life' and now rife with bacteria and needing disposed of – goat scrotum juice.

Lovely bird.'

Confidence bolstered, she shouts, "I AM BEAUTIFUL!" She fluffs feathers. 'If I were free I'd fly down and gouge-out the female's eyes and claim my bird.'

Kunta pulverizes hemp seeds between palms. Secreted oils mingle with his sweat. He massages it into the rigidly bound fiber. It quivers from the friction, becoming pliable. Kunta, entranced in ceremony, vows, "To those who came before me, for all they have made possible for me, I pledge to dedicate my life to helping those-in-need."

Somewhere, midst the beliefs of Kunta's upbringing, the mystic realms of his imagination, and the stark reality of his present, Kunta's ancestors' spirits – the knowers, seers, watchers from throughout the ages – enjoin with him. 'We send to you, captive-son, Kunta – YOU, the first of many of our people surely destined never to return home – a guardian in spirit. In your hands now is that spirit. Its' strength will enable you to guide many others.'

'Who are these people?' How shall I help them?' Kunta asks, grasping the rope. He twitches; cold sweat drenches feverish body. Boy's passage to manhood commences.

THE MONK'S RAIL

Answers to his questions take root, once-upon-a-millennium-and-a-half era A.D., when there lived a German philosopher, Thomas a Kempis. He was an Augustine monk, a teacher of a gentle humanity. His words – 'Love flies, runs, rejoices. Nothing can hold it back.' They are translated to thousands of languages. His followers happen into Kunta's village. His thoughts on peace and goodwill so complement theirs, they become part of their tradition.

a Kempis's spirit now lives in the rope now known as a-Hempis. Kunta holds it, absorbing the spirit into his.

Author's note: a-Hempis would remain with him for the rest of his life. Yes, it too is on prominent display at the Fiction

House Museum.[28]

THE BAPTISM BY SMOKE OF THOMAS a-HEMPIS

There is symbiosis among plants and animals, necessitated by the brutish world. It is indecipherable to humans. So when Turt looks up, bleary-of-eyes from the smoking leaves, he sees the plant-made-rope do a mesmerizing dance. Because the seeds of anger are already growing in Turt, especially when Captain Polly squawks seemingly unendingly, these emanations of wisdom from this ancient soothe him.

At behest of Kunta's ancestors, Thomas a-Hempis allows Kunta to hear also.

THE TALE OF THE SERMON ON THE SKIFF

'Yea I tell both ye young sires. Eat ye the leaves of my yet, full green cousins. They will grow back. Do not be self-indulgent with them. In excess their goodness will do only harm, as with this tenseness of the anger I feel coming from the shelled one.

'Nibble only some of our seeds, so others may fall and future generations take root. Ye must use us for productive, gentle means. Heed these warnings:

'Never sever our permanent ties to earth by displacing us by the roots.

'Never utilize us for hateful means such as the human whip or death machine, the noose.

'When you use more of us or of anything your needs call for, know then that we are being used as a means of warring.

'People eat animals. Animals eat plants. We plants depend on our brother and sister, the soil and water, for our sustenance. All plants, animals, humans are one; for soil and water is what we all return to. It is only when any of us exceed

---

[28] Kunta's later work with the Underground Railroad tests his ability to practice peace, goodwill. (Sometimes, unfortunately, or, maybe, fortunately as you've seen with Silent and Jocular, he fails.)

our share that we overstep our bounds and begins destruction. That is when we begin to make war – on ourselves; for we are all one.'

Tired; Kunta sleeps. He feels peace though not vindication for killing Cookie and Quill Head.

Thomas a-Hempis circles into a pillow for him. Quiet, at least by human perception, a-Hempis lay still, so boy – now man – can rest following passage rites. What is quiet to you, me; to plant and animal world, is…SHOUTING OUT…to those of their world, choosing to listen.

Wisdom of a Hempis emanate quietly past ears of sleeping boy, past Mariner, Buzzard, Rrrose Heather, the ladies, and crew. Almost human, Captain Polly, too distraught with her own enslavement, doesn't absorb the emanations. 'I am SHOUTING all this out to you Turt; am shouting it to all plant and animal brother and sister – everywhere.'

Curious dolphins, surrounded by other of sea-life, have been surfacing near the ship to hear the sermon. Rodents and snakes onboard heed notice. A spider atop Turt's shell listens. New revelations come to Thomas a-Hempis. 'If these thoughts reach lowly insects, there must be a way to reach all humans. One day, I shall discover how.'

Half a world away in the Tehas desert **(a quarter-century before foster mothering Golden Boy)** is a newly sprouted Prick Lily. She is little bigger than Blythe-abwe Turt. So moved by the emanations, she dances in the sand. Although no breeze, upstretched arms wave and finger-size trunk with pin-thorns sway. A golden bonnet-of-a-butterfly lights on her. Batting wings in time to her movements, it provides tender Prick Lily shade.

'We must ponder the meaning of the emanations,' Prick Lilly whoops. Suddenly, '*snap, slurp, burp,*' butterfly disappears down the snout of a creature foreign to the desert. Grief, shock, dismay, and, a before-unknown emotion, trepidation overtakes Lily.

TALES OF THE FICTION HOUSE

Midst reverie, neither Prick Lily nor butterfly realized a craven caravan quietly approached them from behind. A dozen alligators in a double line, led, by the chomper, Huey Long. (He too hears a-Hempis, but he listens only for wizened ways to aid his gator-to-human transformatin' plan.) They escort an adolescent about Kunta's age: Lazarus Bontez Thibidioux.

HOW THE 'BOY/IT' FIRST CAME TO THE DESERT

He appears a miniature creature-person to Prick Lily. Nobility: His cape is a cold-blooded live baby alligator draped around neck to keep him comfortable in the heat. Crown for shade is another small gator. This one twists in a circle and holds tail in snout. Two of four legs spire upward; others dangle around Bontez's ears brushing away mosquitoes. Bontez's scepter-stick is three times his height, and is the kind used for killing bayou gators. Its steel point is longer than on any cactus Prick Lily's seen.

'WHOA a gol' dern minute,' she emanates to an iridescent green and violet chameleon who camouflages to gray at hearing the sloshing of sand of approaching claw steps. 'Why, that-there's a human boy!' Lily's seen others pass-by in wagons, never seen one – without a older human. And this one is bucknaked.

At first blush, most are confounded by the, not-boy, not-yet-teen's appearance: On one side is leathery face, withered arm, bottom of foot claw-like and crusted from jumping bayou logs. So, burning sand does not bother him a whit. He appears fairer than most that travel the desert. That's because Mama Lucy has packed into his bindle kit, along with dozens of protective potions, a root-blend to place under his tongue to ward off dehydration. It has effused through his skin, making him seem coated by powdery salt. It also screens light to protect his growing-ever-more-so, handsome opposite side: Full cheeks, steak neck, dominant brow, sinewy leg, and arm.

Before he journeyed out, Mama had say'ed: "I hates what you becoming Lazarus Bontez, inside-wise, not sight-wise. I'll never stop potionin' and conjurin' that ya change. Yer leavin', as a boy's oughten'-to, when his passing to manhood nears, always be the right 'ting. But I vows, you laza boned Lazarus, to never stop protectin' you, even from a distance."

Why has the youth traveled hundreds of miles from bayou familiarity? Just why, Lazarus doesn't inform Mama Lucy or closest advisor, Huey Long. "Owe no one 'esplanation, does I."

As Lily surveys desert's new arrivals, she realizes a snouted creature is sniffing one of her tiny flowers. 'Oh no!' Snout encircles her: Darkness. Certain, is she of her doom. But she's thankful that in her short life cycle she's been allowed to share in a-Hempis' emanations. Snout snaps shut. Prick Lily hears a wild scream and instantly sees again the light of Poppy Sol.

A wild, overgrown cowlick of a thorn where butterfly sat gouges gator's mouth.

Bontez calmly leaves procession, ambles to the distressed beast. It instinctively begins circling. With quick precision, Bontez gouges out the alligators eyes with his spear. Wail magnifies. Bontez rams point into brain; leaves him, barely alive, impaled on the desert sand.

"No one hep, unless wants ta meet 'eez fate," decrees Bontez. "Eez payin' fer bein' stupid."

Prime Snout and Baron Tail puff-up to scare whoever might assist the fallen.

Liege Leather grits snout, disillusioned. He'd hoped new digs might ease Laza's butchery that he and Mama'd watched escalate in Bontez as he grew. (Gruesome abuse of bayou critters, too vile to recount)

Others watch gator-mate, seeing their own fate if reckless. All will remain loyal to their king. The 'good life', he would bring them via transformation. For it, they would wait patiently – all but Huey Long.

Laza lay in the sand. Entourage entwines, semi-circling for a few feet over his head, creating shade. He would take a pleasant little nap, 24 hours or so, only then would he put the hurt gator out its misery.

'Ah, the beauty of the laza'-life 'a royalty,' he ponders: No concern for loyalty, not with the powers over them of Mama Lucy's potions; the protection of Huey Long's henchmen; and the counsel of Liege Leather. Liege Leather has traveled this desert often with two-leg circuses. He knows the oases, and streams that flow even in driest summers.

Transformation: Boy Lazarus isn't sure of its secret but when he thinks of himself as King, Creole, it matters little; he's already transformed. He'll never share it and then have competition. He's certain he is a transformed gator-to-human, not just a mangled boy, because so many superstitious bayou folk tell him so and show their fear of him because of it.

Prick Lily keeps still, hoping the strange group'll depart and she'll be shed of the varmints forever. That will **never** happen. Boy has found a quiet place he likes with plentiful water close. This is where his half-beast mind first heard a Hempis'lamentations – even if only half of them. Still the message seems simple to his adolescent thought processes: 'Do exactly opposite what a Hempis preaches. That will get you what you want.'

Thus answered, is Huey Long's unasked question – 'Why are we here?'

It is a journey of discovery, Lazarus' self-administered rite of passage; to test himself in an environment opposite his to find a place equal to his bayou liking. Not only has he found such a place but also here a Hempis' words first provided direction. It's the opposite direction, but it's the only direction he'll ever take.

* * *

Mama Lucy '*pops*' into the Lindian Woods. She's trembling: Anger, remorse, regret mix when she says, 'May-as-be I be right when first I fished Lazarus from the bayou. May-as-be shoulda' tossed him back.' She vanishes quickly as she appeared.

Rrrose Heather sees James' sorrow for Mama Lucy. She

strokes his hair and smiles. 'Mama'd not give up on one she cared for. Remember, Lad. Those truly carin' always'll be there. Take your protector. He could've chomped the wild weed and took to flyin'. He never would because he's here for you. Just like a new ma and fa will be when he gets you to them.'

* * *

Thomas a-Hempis shares his message of love with all humans — starting on the ship, hoping to spread it to distant ports, through the pirates and their slaves — a magnanimous but lofty goal.

He channels via obvious intermediary, Captain Polly.

Feathers unfurled in grand fashion, beak open-wide, she sings a-Hempis' missives squawklessly, sweet as any Gregorian chant. Bow-to-stern, clipper becomes cathedral. 'May my songs rest deep in your souls and be twisted, not. Slip not, on the road of good intentions, lest ye be bound eternally to the inferno where it leads.' Alas, her libretto is an ocean-going tower of Babel. None onboard, even those of Germanic origin, recognize the archaic 15th century Teutonic dialect from which a-Hempis springs and Polly relays.

Mariner, Buzzard, ladies, crew — confounded, entertained — glare up at the parrot. Buzzard's look is most intense. It's as if he's seeing Captain Polly for the first time and realizing her siren song is for him. He feels, as any male counterpart of the upcoming century might — whether gay, straight or transgendered — experiencing for the first time a grainy yet ever-vamping Marlene Dietrich cinema. An enchantment of spirit never before felt, whether love, lust or sweet envy, always follows. Many other partners appear in that male's life, but the beckoning image of the blue angel lingers — just as our songbird does for Buzzard.

Kunta awakens to Captain Polly's rhapsody. It helps him sense again the peace that enslavement suffocates. He feels he's again in his village, safe, near those he loves.

* * *

"Want to know what a-Hempis was FEELING, Carper?" Buzzard flaps. Carper nods.
"Yer sayin you can untangle a rope's thinking, 'asides knowin' Kunta's?" Mariner spouts.
"Only relaying what Captain Polly once whispered me. Said a-Hempis was confident he'd guide Kunta through the mutiny."
Mariner puts glass to ear. "She's sayin': Re-fill me."
Buzzard takes a conch shell from the cupboard, pours-in jack and hands it to Mariner. "Best you replace that Si-reen glass Mariner."
As Buzzard and Mariner quibble about, *facts, stre-e-e-tched* over decades, Carper speculates about what Mariner seems forever been repeating in the few days he's lived at the wharf-shack. At least a dozen times Mariner's pulled a book from the shelf, placed it before him. Fanning through the pages Mariner conveys gruff sentiments that reveal elegant passions.
"Great books a' all time, Carper – learn whats in 'em, 'n the world's yer 'erster, n' clam, all-in-one. You'st can sail the seven seas, all the whilst a book's ported 'tween legs. The imaginin', Carper. The books'll set it free in you."
Imaginin's what Carper commences – as he examines Mariner's clipper-ship-in-a-bottle. *You embark; sail from the mucky Ohio to the ocean voyage you've been hearing about. You're a new first mate, all starched-shirty, dungareed. You creep past dregs. They don't see you. Maybe you're invisible? You spy Captain Polly. You need a saw: 'Plink'; one falls from sails. You begin sawing her chain. She hears 'scratch-scrape', bows beak, gratefully nuzzles your arm.*
Suddenly, it's like any invisibility wears off.
"An interloper be aboard," a dreg shouts.
You climb up and disappear in sails. You observe battles, brutalities, joys, and tenderness – LIFE, midst unjust strife. You see a lifetime of these adventures-tragedies in the moments before, 'POP', you're back safely in the wharf-shack. You think of the friends you've made, through stories,

now enslaved onboard. You'll remember for-always their troubles and sorrows.
You shout, *"IT'S WRONG AND MUST BE FOUGHT TO BE RIGHTED!" You are so loud the wharf-shack shakes almost as much as when Turt trumpeted. Buzzard and Mariner look curiously at you. How can they know what you're thinking: Of vile things done to others that you'll remember always, that you'll read of many times in Mariner's BOOKS.*
For-always they're imprinted onto Carper's forming, to become, abolitionist conscience.

Something new, you begin imagining: Or is it real? Captain Polly's outside.
"Lover Bird," she's coos to Buzzard. *You climb a chair and peer out the porthole. On the dock: the walk-offs, seeming more humorous than scary as they march single file. Luny Mum flickers off tiny flags waving from between their toes. 'Even walk-offs bloody-well parade for your Independence Day,' Carper, Mum beams. You're convinced such a spectacle is there to be seen by anyone if they just look, yet you hesitate in calling Mariner and Buzzard over to give a gander: afraid they might say, "whatcha' tellin' us you see?"*

Suddenly, peering back at you from the darkness is someone, or something's, eerie marble eye; blinking in Mum's glint. "A MONSTER!" *You lurch back and begin to fall.*
Despite game leg and being almost two-of-three-sheets-to-a-gusty wind from the stiff jack, Mariner moves, dolphin-swift, catches Carper.

Carper looks back out – nothing there.
"Mayhaps be Monsieur Thibidioux swum up from *bayuuu* to visit you Mariner." Buzzard parodies-mangles Leeziaan Cayan. "Hearsay be, 'e's some unrequited score-settlin' wit' ya."

"No beef wif' 'im or 'issens *bayuuu* crew. Iffen e's got one from our paths crossing, it's 'is problem. Can you caw that same thing?" Mariner's mangled parody quiets Buzzard.

Mariner sits Carper on a stool. Carper's thought race with people, stories, explorins' he's been hearing about. So excited by recent adventures – imagined, *no, real!* He flails arms, and nearly topples again. Mariner knows that a boy of Carper's grit won't let talk of Laza Bones squelch his reverie, so he puts him on the safe overstuffed chair.

Carper smiles, thinks of the kindly things Mariner's told about Mama Lucy, and about how he and Buzzard make accents sound outlandish. Already Carper's put thoughts of the peering eye, if not to rest, at least down for a nap. "Tell more 'bout Mama, Mariner."

"Onna-these-days you, me 'n Ol Tom'll embark Turt: Float on down to visit ouren' sweetheart Mama. They say she lies about her age – says she's only 115: Really 135."

"You play it close the vest and stay far from the bayou, son." Buzzard's stare burns warning. Buzzard pets Tom. 'Nothing like a feline's stroke to tender good luck when you're tempting fate by talking about Thibidioux.' He hovers over Carper. "Let me tell you about what happened when I wandered to the swampland one fine spring day, and into the lair he calls his tavern. Oh, he made it look all pleasant, sweet little curtains, pretty lamps to lure weary travelers in to play some friendly hands of poker."

Mariner interrupts. "You heard easy-pickens abounded."

Buzzard ignores him and walks around with Ol Tom. "Not just '*hands*' you become worried about losing. Before you even sit, dozens of devil-gators crawl from behind bar, from back rooms, from upstairs where Thibidioux's ladies-for-hire reside."

Carper squeezes, nearly breaking the chair's feeble arms. Its rusty springs squeak '*ouch*!'

"Gators surrounded the table, so close that their snout-breath rattled our chips. You know from that moment you have to lose everything – right on past long johns – if you plan to leave with all your pieces intact."

Poster Laza Bones listens pridefully to the tale of his tavern, but thinks, 'Don't rightly cotton to word of my tactics being spread around. Ah'll have to do somethun' 'bout that.'

Buzzard hands Ol Tom to Carper so he too can earn good luck. "Why, I even seen that kindly, sweet Mama pass-by outside, shaking her head disgusted while I was stripped of my worths. Even that crafty, divining amuletter can't control Lazy Bones. That's saying something – because I heard tell she midwifed him into being."

Buzzard and Carper's stares lock throughout the telling. Mariner lights pipe: Sweet terbacky' smoke billows through wharf-shack. Carper absorbs all Buzzard says, weighs the virtues of caution against the hindrance such restrictions put on the adventure of life. His calculating intuition, though still unseasoned, weighs these thoughts, tests, weighs again.

It would be a process he'd tarry with through life.

Something thumps into the wall outside. Ol Tom screeches. Like a billiard ball he careens from Carper's arms, to against Buzzard's thigh, back to Carper's lap, to atop Mariner's shoulder, then onto the highest points in the shack – the nearly ceiling-high bookshelf where he clings to the dusty, fat copy of Milton's Areopagitica. Ol Tom never met Laza Bones, but he's heard of the gator's tales; too often. If Lazy Bones is outside, he feels safe inside. If he crawls on in, Ol Tom has it planned – from long ago. He'll tip Milton into his snapping jaw when Laza Bones lurches for him. Then he'll spring onto his snout, onto the floor, and out the door before he can spit out the classic.

Ol Tom thanks the gods of words – that Milton produced oh-so-many of them.

Mariner goes out and checks around. Some of Rrrose Heather's feather-hat ladies are marketing for clients. A blue-uniformed gendarme scritches billy-club upon palm, figuring percentage he'll get for permitting the ladies to work his beat. An irritated bird, barely visible in the starless sky, keeps dive-bombing the ladies' plumes. They shout, "Shoo, damn feathered bitch!" Their waves and curses don't deter; bird snatches feathers in beak and claws.

Mariner thinks, 'She musta' missed the whures in one of her strafes and accidently bumped our 'umble abode.' He shouts, "Honorable flyer ya be – retrieven' the remains of your own kind. Fly on over so's I can introduce you to the Carper and you can tell him all 'bout your mission."

"Nothin' *too* unusual hap'nen," Mariner reassures boy when he steps back in. He grasps Carper's shoulders. "I was quiet 'afore, so Buzzard could 'ave his say. Now's my turn. Don't you listen to 'im. He's really not a Buzzard. He's a worrisome old hen."

Indignant, Buzzard puffs, struts. Mariner ignores him. "Doin' what you want, what don't hurt others, that's the important and honorable thing. You live life and don't let the the world's Laza Bones' stop you. There's always ways around hissen's kind." Mariner gets a pouch from the dresser; pinches-out a saffron-colored powder.

Poster Laza Bones looks over, curious, wary.

"Me and you, Carper, we 'ent need worry about gators. Mama Lucy alchemey'd this to protect humans from the many other gators that blimey halfer Laza Bones drag to hissen's bad way a behavin'. So always keep this close 'n a gator's snappin' all be ne-gated." Mariner sprinkles it above Carper. Laza Bones holds breath and dips down so far in poster you can't see him. Carper's hair sparkles with the frosting. Mariner says, "There's magic in believen' boy."

Carper's glance shifts upward. The powder clings to his eyebrows. He shows no emotion. He's busy considering ALL.

Buzzard's poker face can't mask doubts about ever controlling Thibidioux.

Mariner squints at him. "You shoulda' had some of this believen' when you was swamped. Could 'a flew away with winnins' steada leavin' pluck-naked."

Peeved at being upstaged by what he considers bayou mumbo-jumbo, Buzzard swirls like he's taking to wing. For good luck, he seizes reluctant cat clinging to the security of Milton, then a lean Shakespeare, then desperately but unsuccessfully to a fat Bacon. "Yes we have powders here Ol Tom. No need to worry about Laza Bones now," Buzzard mocks as he returns to something, anything more pleasant than Thibidioux – the telling of the pirate ship's tales to Carper. "Why, when I and everyone else on board heard the Capt'n scream out, I swooped down from the deck just knowing he must be a goner."

"Twarn't *gone* though, war' he," Mariner interrupts, peace-offering Buzzard a Havana.

Buzzard's brow furrows. He wonders where Mariner got it. He pockets it – later.

You twitch nervously as you listen to Buzzard's taling; you wish that Capt'n, bad as the likes a Thibidioux, is no longer's about.

'Just one of 'that 'shar kinds is more-'en-enough'. You grin, proud of the array of Mariner-isms you're using. You hope you can invent Buzzard-isms to match. (Later in life, you would – to counter all the Bellows-schisms you'd hear 'aplenty.) As you listen for Buzzard's slow-to-come reply to Mariner, in your imagination you picture an evil Capt'n/Laza Bones duo, fightin'-it-out dockside, to see who'd be first to enter the wharf-shack to snatch you.

Capt'n' thrusts pointy false-leg, sword-like, at snapping snout. 'I'll run yer through ya scaly he/it. Then I'll 'ave Cookie fry-ya-up fer gatah-on-a-stick fer me crew."

'I'll be mountin' ya on yer falser', Capt'n; use ya fer trollin'-bait."

Or, maybe worse, they're teamin' – for all-out attack.

The leg points cannon-like at wharf shack – BOOM – blasts-off from knee-stump and knocks-down a wall. They 'commence a rapturous rampage by rioting-on-through' – 'ah', you grin. 'A Buzzard-ism at last.' You grab Harpoon. With the tip, you anchor their clothes and leather to the wall, for just long enough so's Mariner, Buzzard and Ol Tom can get away. Laza Bones and Capt'n wail-flail together. Alas, forever-stuck.

With beak and claws, plume-filled, Captain Polly can only softly coo as she lands on wharf-shack, "Lover Bird." She perches on the porthole's ledge where she first viewed the little visitor. 'Who is he,' Captain Polly wonders. 'Where's Turt?'

Despite Mariner's invitation, she's always wary of entering the wharf-shack – too many memories of Mariner wielding the cleaver aboard ship 'creatin' creepy walk-offs.' She'd await Lover Bird to come out. She hopes he isn't mad at her. She'd left him at New Orleans: Not for another fowl gambler, instead to avenge his ill-treatment in the swamps by Laza

Bones. Sweet revenge! Okay, so she couldn't touch Laza Bones. Who could? Not even old Mama. Ah, but the next best, his First Lieutenant, Huey Long. Sweet reminiscence:
There, on the muddy bank, he sleeps. You alight his head, do a two-step on his brow to awaken him. When his eyes open, you push claw into one, encircle the orb. You extricate it in one slick motion and fly off. Dangly part that connected to the rest of him trails behind. Huey Long rants, raves, growls, louder than any future statehouse steps speech you'd watch him make from your perch atop Baton Rouge's Capitol building.

You knot the danglings with beak and wear eye as necklace, as you'd seen Kunta with Cookie's walk-off. You're sorry your eye-necklace scared the little boy earlier. You hope Lover Bird will like the gift, maybe enough to give up his four queens and the riverboats and finally molt with you for life. If he doesn't like it? Ol Tom'd certainly appreciate an extra orb.

Before you present it, you have your duties to perform – so you spread-wing for the nearest forest. There, ceremoniously, you'll drop the feathers – freeing the colors of sunny-yellow, river-blue, green-mountain, and red-clay – one-at-a-time: burial. Finally, their owners' enslavement can cease and their spirits can join, and, together, forever fly.

Maybe, if Captain Polly had remained outside the porthole a few minutes more she could have warned those inside of the angry, creeping horde that was approaching; maybe helped Buzzard, Mariner, Ol Tom and the little one. Because, after all, she caused the horde's collective anger, and now its imminent onslaught. She was the one, who, by her rash deed, led them here.

CHAPTER 27

As Mariner and Buzzard rehash grizzly times aboard ship, Carper's imagination wanders – along a Lindian country road pictured in that precious, Book, Mariner had let him peek. He meets a boy his age. He's draped in silk and wears a turban. It is the wise one of long ago – Carpier.

Poppy Sol's glint reflects off the half-dozen cobras following Carpier.

Carper winks thanks to Poppy for letting him see the slitherers. He edges behind a fan tree.

'Do not be afraid,' says Carpier. 'When you are my friend they too are yours, for life.' A cobra climbs Carpier's leg, arm; coils on shoulder. His hood, like a finger, beckons Carper.

Singing hisses by a cobra chorus 'Come hither young sahib.'

'Join our journey, fellow traveler,' insists Carpier.

Buzzard's warnings about Thibidioux have taught Carper to be cautious, but the compassion in Carpier's look is hypnotizing. He approaches. As they clasp hands to wrists, as might steadfast friends, two cobras encircle Carper's ankles. Another climbs shirtless torso. They're cold, meaty. He shivers.

Carpier snaps fingers. Cobras slither off. 'That is their welcome. Too many humans accept it only as war, because war is what many, only expect.' (Carpier sees the fear, intrigue, wanderlust, adventure-lust, but most-of-all the curiosity of

TALES OF THE FICTION HOUSE

life's mysteries bound together in my great-great grandfa's eyes as they begin walking.) 'Today, new friend, we search the Lindian forest for a fellow foundling. A companion you dearly would have enjoyed knowing, but never could. Carper, because you have met me, you will get a chance to help him.'

With this puzzle of words boys and entourage, enter the woods. (So confused, of course, is Carper. For how could a four year old even conceive of me, his great-great grandson, and, being his own age. I am nearby, and in need of an aid that only he could provide: Companionship.)

* * *

Your vivid, NOW: Long-detached from it, yet hazily present in it is your THEN; the, THEN, of sitting on your fa's lap on the ferryboat and hearing stories from the Book of Carpier. But, NOW, as you are ferried on the shell of your protector you hear rustling in the woods. You think you see in the distance the turbaned boy and his cobras from, the BOOK. Someone journeys with him. You think you know him from, THEN. He's the one you'd tell about your day before you slept; laugh with him when you were happy and when you'd cry, he'd be there to make you happy again. POOF! They're gone. "Come back." You squeeze your eyes. Wish hard enough, you tell yourself, they'll return.

When James shouts, 'Come back,' Turt glances at him. He wishes he could help him relax. He thinks of the impetuous way he'd calm himself during his shelling days aboard ship, despite Kunta and Thomas a Hempis' warnings to be careful. The hemp growing in fertile clumps along their way now, reminds him how the leaves calmed then, but made him foolishly brave.

...HE FLIES THROUGH THE AIR WITH THE GREATEST OF LEAVES...

One night while Kunta sleeps, Turt, spirits bolstered by the leaves, decides to roam. Up the Blythe-abwe wall, he crawls clutching rafter crags and protruding buttresses. Reaching the cupola he seizes a slat in snout, displaces it and sidles through. One goal: QUIET THAT FOREVER SQUAWKING PARROT. He discards a-Hempis' admonition – 'Turt, baiting a creature emboldened by her enslavement be a fool's gambol.' Grand illusion – replacing Captain Polly at the helm – overwhelms Turt. But the leaves have made him too docile to wage a-Hempis' advised-against confrontation. He's certain a trumpet blare followed by an ominous hiss should work. The leaves also delude – into his feeling more power than he truly has: For his blare's still a peep; hiss, little-more than soft sneeze.

Luny Mum draws a beam across the isolated deck. Turt crawls along it. Mum brightens, 'If Sol be here, he'd so heat up things that you're feet would burn and you'd not be able to try the impossible. Just walk my calming beam til your anger ceases.' Turt'll not heed the advice.

Twenty feet up, on the poop deck, is Captain Polly. She's fallen asleep, yet, she chatters; in the multitude of languages, she's learned in her years aboard ship: French, English, Arabic, Portuguese, Italian, a Hempis' archaic German, back to French. '*Oui!*' Turt thinks; even more irritated. How could he know she suffers a sleep-talk affliction common to birds of her feather?

He climbs.

Captain Polly perches atop helm, instinctively sidestepping slick, gliding wheel to maintain her balance. She guides vessel more than the dozing night-skipper. Boldly Turt uses his arm as bridge to bird. Up it, he crawls. It tickles and the whisker-stubbly dreg wriggles his face.

When he reaches the wheel Turt wavers – so difficult to keep balanced. Captain Polly's easily three times Turt's size. His shell-top barely reaches her plump bosom. He glares up at the ever-jacking beak. '*Silencio,*' he squeaks: Nada. Another language: '*Haltenzie!*' Zilch. 'Shut up. Look at me when I speak,' Turt demands. He clamps jaw onto her claw. 'Ouch!' Claw isn't worm-like as old Cookie's toe. It is stick-brittle. He rubs beak-snout with tongue to dull the ache. He blares, hisses. Still

Captain Polly babbles.

So peeved, Turt's blinded to her magnificent plumage: Yard-long tail feathers, luminescent silver and blue, bright in Luny Mum's glow; pillow-soft tufts of gleaming trunk; radiance of her dozens of overlapping of jungle-greens, earthen-reds, ocean-grays, such colors among humans only the artistry of a Renoir, Van Gough, Seurat, could envision. Turt sees only the bizarre get-up Capt'n outfitted her. It reminds him of Capt'n, destroyer of his tribe. By association, he hates his bird as much she hates him.

To Turt, all Captain Polly's beautiful colors turn the ugliest of all, red, blood red of Jericho's sand. He rages, disregarding Thomas a Hempis' lamentations of peace. He trumpets a wild peep and dives for the only part of Captain Polly he can reach, her tail plumage. He doesn't realize her feathers are slick and he begins sliding. He looks down, knowing if he falls, he'll smash, paralyzed, into the deck. Since Kunta is 20 feet further below, there would be nothing from stopping ship rats from picking him apart.

Desperate, Turt bites hard. Feathers slip through his mouth. He thinks, 'this is the end,' but comes to a jerking stop at tail's precipice. He dangles, caught on a tiny gold ring. (During a marauding expedition along the Lindian peninsula, Capt'n had cut it off a finger. Later, onboard he sewed it to Captain Polly's feathers.)

Excruciating 'yank' awakens Captain Polly. "SCREE!" Reaching to bite-off the dangling 'thing', she spits invectives. In English, "You'll not steal my royal plumage. In French, *"Miserable, voleur, errant."* She shakes tail wildly, thumping' Turt against the helm.

She flies upward, trying to lose the interloper. Her chain stops her. Turt slams into the dreg's face, awakening him. The sharp edge of Turt's shell slices a bloody six-inch long gouge along his cheek. He screams whilst wetting pants, then bolts. The incident's terror magnifies in his thoughts – by the vivid tales Buzzard had earlier woven about fiend-Turt:

"Aces to eights I tell you men, his beak-snout can decapitate in one go

over." (Next day, seeing the gangrenous scar, hearing their mate's story of the, "12-foot-long, iff'-e'-were-an inch," creature, would add veracity to Buzzard's stories.) The whiplashing by Captain Polly seems to Turt to last hours. Then he feels himself flying.
Captain Polly screeches as if she's being tortured. Turt hasn't just 'come loose'. He still grasps feather. Captain Polly isn't, JUST, in physical pain. She's in mental anguish at being parted from a portion of her raiment.

Wail of pirate and parrot arouse crew. They rush onto the deck still in skivvies; see proof of Buzzard's antagonist-fiend. In Luny Mum's spotlight, flying Turt looks much larger than he is because he grasps bushy feather while he vigilantly flaps fin-claws and beak-snout. Luny Mum's anxious to help embellish Buzzard's legend, and later tell Poppy Sol, so her light never leaves Turt' flight. To superstition-laden, drugged, crew Turt looks combination half-sea – half-air creature.

A terrorized dreg shouts: "Now that the Trumpeter can fly 'e'll seeks revenge on every last onna' us for destroying 'is mates. But e'll not get me. I'll feed every last one 'a ya to 'im before..." A sword rams his back – shadow-gift from fellow-dreg.

"Leave 'is corpse fer the beast," someone shouts. Grumbling of agreement, but mistrust grows. Quickly they retreat to bunks – clutching knives. 'Who might align with 'it', to save 'emselves?' More-'n-ever, they'll see Buzzard as protector.

Luny Mum smiles. Sight of this scurrying scourge, which gives even sewer rats a good name, feels almost as good as the oncoming Gone Luna she's sensing. It will really send rats scurrying.

Bad as slamming the deck seems, Turt knows the new direction Mum's sly smile of, 'trust me', pulls him, arcing toward ocean. 'Please, no Mum! I don't know yet the ways of ocean creatures?' As Turt sails over the railing – '*plop*'. He lands on something soft. Turt holds onto the feather. Fear makes him clutch that something. He looks up; sees 'new' Cookie.

Mariner had reached over the railing, made a spectacular catch. (one as spectacular Turt wouldn't see for over 150 years when he mascots for the barnstorming Kansas City Monarchs for a season – oh those bus rides, bumpy, but the third baseline grass so sweet – and sees a young Satchel Paige turn a similar grab.) Whereas then, Turt would trumpet for joy, now he hisses for defense because the last two-leg besides Kunta who had held him, was the 'old' bragging Cookie – *"this lil hatchling'll make fine garnishment for the Capt'n salad."*

The words emblazon forever in Turt's psyche.

FIRST MEETING (of two lifelong friends)

Just as the others aboard the ship, Mariner awakened with the racket made by parrot and Trumpeter. He exited the galley; for Turt's sake, just in time.

Turt's manic clawing at his palm draws no blood.

"Right pleased ta meet-cha' too." Mariner's bark is light-hearted, like the amiable sea lions' Turt has heard off the Jericho shores. "We're shipmates little one; best we start workin' in tandem." Mariner takes fin-claw between fingers – miniature movement of handshake.

Turt gnaws at appendage; calms when he feels gentle, Kunta-like pets atop shell. 'He HAS kept me from ocean creatures.'

"Looks like you crossed our Captain Polly's wake. By the looks a' what yer holden' I wonder which critter sideswiped which. Or aren' you some kinda new air beast?" Mariner looks up at Luny Mum, winks thanks for spotlighting the critter for him. In her glow he examines the shell's village carvings, sees the cuts are fresh. He breathes deep knowing Kunta's still 'a-breathin', and hidin'. Ain't just-fodder for Buzzard's tales'. Mariner vows he'll find Kunta, prove, via a little chicanery at Turt's expense, that not all on board are *'ahh-gin 'im'*.

Atop helm, Captain Polly sidesteps and steers as she squints un-patched eye scanning the deck for her tormentor. The blank spot of her backside aches. Her pride, first degraded by humans, now by fellow creature, hurts more. 'This too will pass,' she senses Thomas a-Hempis communicate. 'In bondage though ye be, still, ye are always free. Only slaves to ourselves can we be. Trust these thoughts, grounded, but noble flyer.'

Captain Polly *'awks'*, *'squawks'*, unable to drown out our a-Hempis unwanted lament. She shouts, "Just wait until I see you again, crawler. I will pry off your shell and feast on your carcass."

Turt and Mariner hear her threat. Turt's eyes dart. One experience with her was enough.

"You gonna have ta find a way to deal with her, my little shelling," Mariner says as he cups Turt protectively in his palm.

CHAPTER 28

Carper watches Buzzard's nose disappear into the widemouth glass. Amber refraction crooks the protuberance to appear ever more beak-like. Carper wonders if he'll be able to extract it.

Buzzard is getting tight, but decades of poker-face trump any 'tells'.

"Capt'n warn't dead yet, war he?" Mariner prompts cotaler, to stave-off story drag.

Buzzard waves melodramatically; teeters. Mariner's prop-up keeps him from listing too far and squashing Ol Tom. Buzzard continues, mid-sway, his tale of Capt'n' and the walk-offs.

"Hallucinating the walk-offs coming for his jugular was terrifying enough for the Capt'n, but after Rrrose Heather left to change out of her fortune-teller frippery, there was Kunta standing right over him. Cookie's walk-off, all decorated-up with hemp toe rings, dangled from around his neck. Kunta was about to peel Capt'n' Adams apple with his carving knife."

Carper tenses. Mariner tempers the image so the boy won't have nightmares. "Kunta warn't out to turn Capt'n ta appley sauce. He was just passing through, checkin' on things, might say. He was headin' to pay a visit to the magic of the enchanted Polara."

"Who's Polara?" Carper asks anxiously, already forgetting the gruesomeness.

'Thanks for whacking off my cliffhanger end,' Buzzard's

glance says to Mariner.

Mariner one-ups Buzzard before he can spin anew. "I stopped Kunta. Iffen' I hadn't we wouldn't be here tellin'. Our plans woulda' sunk quick without the Capt'n for facade."

"Polara?" Carper fidgets.

"Polara. More a what, then who, but you'll see," Mariner says.

"Your memory's backward Mariner. I did the stopping."

"Polara," Carper reminds.

"Keep yer skivvies loose," Mariner chides him. "We'll hoist sail for Polara soon enough."

* * *

BUZZARD'S VERSION – Of that night so long ago in Capt'n' candle-lit hovel:

Kunta brings peg-leg totem from behind his back; points it at Capt'n.

"Keep him away, Buzzard. I'll give you half everything we get when we dock."

"Tell me Capt'n. Why should I settle, when I am about ready to rake in a whole pot."

"Save me, Buzzard. I'll forfeit three quarters."

"Kunta was using leg as a peace offering? Heeding Thomas a Hempis?" asks Carper.

"Don't rightly think so," Mariner says. "That would 'a spoilt yer hand, eh Buzzard?"

"We will never know Mariner: Because Rrrose Heather saw to that."

Was *really* Rrrose Heather did the stopping. On this, they both agree.

Rrrose Heather returns to Capt'n' after changing. She and Kunta's eyes meet. Her look of compassion says more than any admonition. Maybe Kunta senses his mother in her as decades later; Carper would sense a loving, young grandmother in her

at the whurehouse. Neither Buzzard nor Mariner remember who said, "Put down the leg Kunta; our lives depend on it."
Rrrose Heather reaches out. "Be trustin' us, Lad. We'll help you." Kunta, ashamed of his thoughts of doing more hurt, runs from the hovel. He doesn't want the beautiful woman seeing him weeping in shame for the wanton revenge slaying he'd nearly committed.

"What became of Kunta?" Carper asks, doesn't await an answer. "Poor Kunta. Alone. Forsaken like me." Carper begins taking-on storyteller melodrama of the two men – the Marinerism, Buzzardisms: Card-table sophistication of one; sea-grit of other – splintering them, creating, very own, Carperisms. He's not sure of the meaning of all the words, but they convey his emotions. "So who kilt Capt'n? Kunta? Mama's poisons? You, Buzzard? Not sweet Rrrose."

"It is not in me to destroy human life." Buzzard pontificates.

"Yer a saint 'mongst sinners, Buzzard. Tell 'im the real reason ya wanted Capt'n livin'."

Carper examines Buzzard's face for 'tells.'

"Well, son, there was a great amount of brilliant calculations about it on my part."

Mariner: "To help save yer 'ide."

"Well yes. You see, if Capt'n were kept alive – away from all humanly desires – wine, gambling, fine fair like Rrrose and her ladies, and so his crew figured him dead, he could be used as an apparition – that's what they call a ghost, boy – to spur them on to get to shore. Capt'n was going to be a mighty-useful, *ghost*." (Author's note: Something else that was going to help when the time came...Gone Luna you heard about earlier... but I'm getting ahead of myself.)

THE TALE OF THE NEON WALK-OFFS IN THEIR FINEST HAUTE-COUTURE

Capt'n' journey to insanity includes a trek down fashion's

walkway for his '*little darlins*'. No better *seamestre* than a seaman. "I'll gussy you little ones up right nice so you can parade."

From material lining Capt'n' cloak: Balloon britches, like Quill Head's, he sews onto some of them; top hats for others; gowns for the ladies — cobwebs, their chapeaus. He kisses their toes. "You darlins won't gnar me like that ungrateful Captain Polly. Hhmph! After all I done for her." He ravages a pillow; spits onto the feathers and attaches them to a walk-off, ties on a pipe stem as a peg-leg, attaches a cigar band as eye patch, prods the effigy of Captain Polly across a cigar: "Arrgh, walk the plank, bird. When I's sees ya again that's exactly what you'll do."

* * *

Rrrose Heather jokes to James, Mama Lucy, and Margaret in the Lindian Woods. 'His little darlins: Once when I peeked-in, he was giving them slimy appendages pedicures.' James and Mama Lucy laugh. James looks at Margaret. Even that sour-of-a-puss sweetens briefly.

CHAPTER 29

Mariner appraises Captain Polly's gold ring in Luny Mum's glint twinkling through the ship's mast. "I'll be jiggered," he says to Turt, motionless in his palm. Didn't know our Captain Polly wore a band, a dandy. Buzzard 'taint the engagin' kind. So I don't 'xpect her pining for 'ims brung a proposal. Maybe she's out to set a fashion trend 'mongst macaws."

Mariner and tiny Turt study each other. ('Ya can always figger' out a human or varmint's nature by glaring 'im in the lookers.' That's Mariner's philosophy.) "You'll have to return it to wherst' it came, fella. That's the only decent way to act."

Turt holds so-tightly that he bends the feather the ring anchors. Never has he seen anything so shiny. 'I earned this.'

To later use for fish bait, Mariner has dropped galley crickets into his pocket. He removes one and dangles it above Turt. "Betcha could use a tad bolsterin' after what you been through."

Turt remembers the sweet-tasting but stomach-grinding morsels he and Kunta scavenged under the mess hall. He examines treat with tongue tip. From Blythe-abwe, a-Hempis' counsel drifts to him. 'You must begin trusting your instincts about those around you. Only then can you fully live. He saved you. Why now would he destroy you?'

As Turt downs delicacy, Mariner studies Kunta's shell

lettering: T-U-R-T. "Turt – I'm supposins' yer monikor. Maybe you'll lead me to Kunta." Mariner closes fingers around him.

Turt squirms: 'Fooled!' He despises the tricks and treachery of the two-legs. He's barely able to see Mariner fish an object from his pocket he'd one day learn two-legs call 'key.' Mariner unlocks his ankle clamp. To Turt it looks like a larger version of the one restraining Captain Polly.

Turt's confused by a-Hempis' emanation, 'Some are slaves Turt, yet they are always free.'

The hemp's effect is wearing off Turt. Gut and emotions spin. He hopes he doesn't urp-up the hopper. So confused by all he's experiencing. Much to learn. No choice but to trust.

Mariner trolls the deck. It's dark, desolate. Aided by Mum's beam Mariner discovers the cupola's pushed-aside slat through which Turt exited Blythe-abwe. "I'll be jiggered again. 'Aven't I the sniffen-out snout of a sea-hound. Let's do some fishen', and see how you'll be for bait, Turt. Turt snaps. "Youch! Like catchen' me a mini-shark 'steada baiten a hook," Mariner joshes. He always carries a roll of thick string made from sea lion hide that he uses to sew torn sails. He ties it about Turt's shell. "Let's jus see if ya brings a nibble."

They are close to the ship's rail. Turt is certain this is his end – sacrifice for giants of the water. Mentally he's saying goodbye to Kunta and hello ma, fa and kin of Jericho, when Mariner brings from his apron pocket the shiniest, reddest little apple. He places it to Turt's beak-snout. Instinctively Turt bites. Sweet juice. "A little somethun' for you and Kunta to share," Mariner says, squeezing Turt through the pushed-aside slat, lowering him.

To Turt, Blythe-abwe never looked so beautiful. Mum beams through the cupola's slats, lighting his descent into Kunta's carved-wall village. a-Hempis words now feel true. Turt can trust two humans. It would be a quarter of a century until he would another – the boy Carper.

Mariner replaces slat. Line slackens. "Critter's landed..."

...on something soft – Kunta's shoulder. Kunta awakens, rises from a-Hempis pillow, and loosens line, slips apple from

TALES OF THE FICTION HOUSE

Turt's now-achy jaw. "What have you been up to little wanderer."

Kunta examines feather, ring, and line. He laughs, wondering if he'll ever know. Has his friend been visiting mischievous spirit ancestors? Do he and Turt have a friend aboard? For a moment Kunta thinks of the new Cookie they'd briefly encountered. Kunta wants to believe some magical serendipity visits them. He cuts apple and sniffs it to check for tainting.

Mariner drops the line. "Boy can use it to survive til I can prove he can count on me."

The line coils atop a-Hempis; quivers with anticipation feeling philosopher-rope vibration:

'Greetings little brother. From whence do you come?'

'From the sea line I hail.' Reply is silent to humans, who, if they could hear, would say, "It resembles its sea lion bark." 'I am sent from the hand of a gentle human to assist you.'

Turt munches fruit, instantly sleeps – exhausted from his adventure. Feather slips from his clutch. Kunta catches it; swishes it in the air. He disregards the attached gold ring. For Kunta wealth, it is the feather. It is a paintbrush to create art to somehow, pass-on lessons taught by his ancestors.

Thomas a-Hempis, to quivering compatriot from the sea: 'Young human chooses right, little Sea Line. May he follow the path of the kind human whom last you were with.' Happy as a-Hempis is about Kunta's choice, he is equally sad. For Captain Polly is squawking repeatedly in the archaic German only a-Hempis comprehends:

"I want my #*&#$#! feather back."

CHAPTER 30

This novel is printed on the smoothest #6 Lindian hemp paper – for your tactile enjoyment.
Kunta dabs Captain Polly's feather into palm-palate of grinded, wetted hemp seeds. By Luny Mum's watchful glow, he paints the scenes he's carved. Each stroke primes the waterfall. Tree leaves flutter in its mist. Blythe-abwe's walls come alive. Savannah lions chase long hair wildebeest. Within halcyon village potters throw clay, butchers slay, kinder play, spiritualists pray and elders lay.
Breathe deep and smell sweet cassava roasting over campfires.
Kunta is tireless. Joy of painting emancipates him from captivity's treachery. He goes until morning. The paint's green hue, midst Luny Mum fade and Poppy Sol awakening, is transmuted into pinks, violets, azures; shades no rainbow arc can boast.[29]
At Kunta's feet, Turt drowsily gnaws Sea Line who squirms like a worm from the tickle. So-missing the ocean, and used to the warm confines of Mariner's pocket sewing kit, Sea Line, yearning succor, coils timidly alongside a-Hempis.

---

[29] I resurrected Blythe-abwe in such a way within the Fiction House thus achieving that same lighting effect. Just one word describes Kunta's Blythe-abwe – masterpiece.

'Be not fearful little Line. You represent a mighty creature, respected by all, of the ocean. You go a new, noble way. As I aid growing boy, so will you be the shelling's lifeline, until he outgrows youth's impetuous ways.'
With these soothing vibrations, Sea Line chooses boldness over caution. His 30 feet of length stiffens to coming challenges.

THE TALE OF A SECOND SAVIOR – 160 years later

When, away from the perils of the sinking <u>Bashri Raku</u>, Turt surfs the trunk containing the child we know as James Thaddeus Fiction V, me, Raji, to safety. Belatedly and in spirit, Mariner, I thank you for introducing Turt to Sea Line. Via their tandem life-guard I am saved. It was Sea Line, bravely dangling long thin tongue from the trunk's handle for Turt to grab.

Hard as Typhoon hammered and twisted, Sea Line kept us united. Ashore Turt gave Sea Line to me. How happily we played during the long Lindian Woods trek. (He knew all the games children like: knotting, half-shank, lasso, jump rope. He had played them many times before – with my fa, grandfa, great, and my great-great grandfa Carper.)

* * *

a-Hempis binds attentions to Kunta. He senses the young artist's inspiration, that, all humanity's ideals may emanate from his brush-strokes.

Despite ever-twisting fate, Kunta's driven by a welled-deep understanding of himself. Twice he's taken human life: One who had enslaved him; other who, so unmercifully, beat him. It might happen again. 'Never,' mentally he shouts: 'Wash away all doubt. I AM KUNTA, captive of but NEVER slave to fate.'

Kunta finishes his work by accenting the highest carvings. Nothing more to do; yet incomplete. He lightly strokes the figures. He senses their life-pulse; instructing him. He cranes neck upward and feels scratchy rope beneath his feet vibrate. a-

Hempis is instructing him.

'Yes! I see what I must do.' He belts a-Hempis around his waist then knots Sea Line to a-Hempis. Turt still teethes on Sea Line's other end. Kunta lifts Turt. To the wooden hoist wheel within the cupola's bell house, he points as he places him on a wall support. "Go up and over Turt. Then just hold your line tight and lower yourself to me."

Turt's trek takes ten minutes: Kunta watches him while mixing more paint. Turt succeeds in his mission, but then his fin-claws slip on the slick hoist wheel. He hurtles downward, clutching Sea Line. Kunta lurches to catch him. Turt falls through outstretched hands: Just before crashing against floor, salvation. a-Hempis seems to wriggle and move around Kunta's waist so the fat knot Kunta made is closer to Turt's downward path. Sea Line whips Turt toward it.

'THUD!' soft landing. a-Hempis gently vibrates satisfaction at Sea Line's actions. Sea Line stiffens with the pride of proving oneself. Turt clings to a-Hempis. Dilated eyes show – his previous dozing hadn't quelled the hemp's affects, but this free-fall did.

Kunta pets Turt. "Good job feller. Thanks to you I will complete the work."

Kunta pulls Sea Line down until a-Hempis' other end comes to him. He pulls a-Hempis until he elevates himself above the carvings. He holds paint bucket under one arm and feather in hand of the other. He sways back and forth, painting, while saying excitedly to floored Turt. "The sky of my village. It is what is so special. It will make us totally free."

All day Kunta floats within Blythe-abwe. Clouds he recreates billow around him; his protectors. Some are shields guarding village, others, spear-like, not for offense but to point the way to the light peace brings. 'In this sky the spirits of my village will be free, always. Though others of my people may too be stolen, always will they be free because they have the sky in which their thoughts may forever soar.'

a-Hempis' thoughts soar too with Kunta's flight. Despite his spirit being centuries old, life is new as Sea Line's and it is exhilarating to go lashing around Blythe-abwe with his new companion.

Kunta lands – prolonged voyage so satisfying, yet so tiring. Before laying his head on a-Hempis, and going to sleep, he places Captain Polly's feather in Turt's mouth. "Do with it now as must be done, feller."

Turt knew this moment would come – when he would have to revisit what seems an insane Captain Polly babbling in the distance: "I AWAIT YOU MY LITTLE SHELLED ONE."

As Turt snips a few inches of Sea Line, a-Hempis vibrates. 'Often will you be cut, separated, and stretched, friend. With Kunta or Turt rest assured, your detachments will be used for good alone.' This, Sea Line already realizes, welcomes, as part of duty.

Turt grasps cut line and feather in beak-snout, shinnies-up a-Hempis, and exits through the cupola's slats. Nervously he crawls to meet foe.

Captain Polly is alone at the helm. She notices her feather swaying just over the poop deck railing, and Turt edging up. He shakes nervously as he offers it. She engages his downcast eyes. "Just a bit closer," she chortles. 'Slice, dice, and then toss you to the sea creatures to devour, will I.'

a-Hempis' emanates from Blythe-abwe. 'Be enraged by what has been done to you Captain Polly. Yet, free yourself from the emotional noose in which you strangle, by accepting this peace offer. Working together you can free yourselves from this death ship.'

Maybe it is a-Hempis' gentle message, or the all-encompassing power she has over the little shelling – one no different from Capt'n over her. Maybe it is the beauty of the paint-dappled feather, or, a combination of all: At that moment, something changes for Captain Polly. The devilry of Capt'n is absent in Turt. She sees the gentleness of similar petite creatures of her native Amazon. This lets her trust again. She turns her back to Turt, tail plumage seeming to reach for him. She balances on helm, looks over shoulder, and gives a come-hither beak motion.

Shell aquiver, Turt crawls up plumage and positions feather near to where he plucked it. With clipped-slip of Sea Line anchored firmly between beak-snout and fin-claw, he reattaches it.

Captain Polly watches imperiously – as a queen – one fitted in the most-royal raiment. Finally. *"Finnay! Fine'!"* Captain Polly twists, displaying it to enraptured flyers circling the ship. Who among them could be jealous of such beauty of feather?

The gold ring: Captain Polly sees it still attached and is now close enough to reach with her beak. She does what she always dreamed. She squawks wildly, tears at it; certain she yet smells the human blood still on it. It loosens. She tosses it into ocean. Its *'plunk-splash'* cleanses her thoughts. When she can rid herself of the peg-leg and eye patch, that's when she knows she'll be totally clean. As queen with scepter, Captain Polly gives Turt well-deserved thumps on noggin with pseudo pegleg. "Never again violate another creature of nature, shelling."

With that animal ceremony complete, Turt knows he has earned her majesty's forever, complete respect. It won't be for just years to come, but for centuries.

THE TALE OF KUNTA LEARNING THE ROPES

During the days, Kunta climbs a-Hempis. From behind cupola's slats, he spies on the pirates and whispers to Turt who perches on his shoulder: "Look at all the ways sailors can tie." Being from an inland village, only one-tenth of those knots are necessary for daily chores.

Kunta clasps a-Hempis in one hand. With the other, he practices tying Sea Line around Turt who wriggle from the tickle. Kunta memorizes dozens of loops, slips, twists. He whispers josh to a-Hempis. "Their knotty knowledge we will use – to bind them with their own ropes."

It's never 'twixt-and-tween' conversation with Kunta and a-Hempis: Kunta thinks something; a-Hempis vibrates reply. Kunta paints a mental picture for a-Hempis – himself and Turt at the helm, steering for land. The crew is bound and awaiting land-law's justice.

In his knotty fervor, Kunta pulls Sea Line – too tight. He loosens when Turt '*aack's.*' a-Hempis vibrates tidings from Kunta ancestors. 'Keep constant within you good humor, our son. The joy of the just will sustain you in bleak hours.'

So immersed in plans is Turt. He stares through slats, toward helm, at Captain Polly's manacled claw. 'Don't worry friend,' he wants to tell her. 'I'll come up every night and gnaw at it until you can fly free.'

TALE OF THE 'WHURE'S DELIGHT' – HOW ONE RECIPE CAME TO WOO A NATION

For nearly 75 years, an anonymously-written cooking column appears weekly in the Cincinnati Daily Opine. Its exotic fare is served on 19th century dinner tables – maybe once. Then it's a return to the basics more reflecting a society's stern work ethic. But one sumptuous fudge dessert, with a few alterations becomes culinary legend throughout the land.

"What ye sprinklin' in the Delight sauce, Rrrose Heather?"

"In the old country it'd be..." Over hot stove, Rrrose whispers it and Bonnie titters. Rrrose smiles – so enjoying these 'mother-daughter' kitchen times. "But since we cain't be gettin' that here I use, just a smidgen' mind ya, oil 'a the buckeye. It be givin' the same passionate allure. Wouldn't be surprised if our business triples after they print this; while over on the domestic side 'a the city babies begin poppin' out left and right nine months down nature's path."

Rrrose tenderly strokes Bonnie's abdomen. She can't wait until Bonnie realizes she's pregnant. 'A grandmother, Cincinnati's Rrrose will be!'

(Author's note: That original recipe, now so commercialized, so changed over time that it has lost, how might one say, its 'vigor', but the original Whure's Delight is still served – fresh-baked daily – couples make your reservations today – at the Fiction House Bed and Breakfast.)

CHAPTER 31

A TALE OF SOMETHUNS'

Night's quiet overwhelms the wharf-shack. Mariner swigs stump juice. Buzzard finger-shuffles his four queens and contemplates a return to the 'high life' when his time for 'nesting-low' ends. Ol Tom sleeps placidly upon Milton, dreaming trysts yet to come, while Laza Bones peeks from his poster and ponders dastardly deeds.

"We all need our own special somethuns' to help get us through til mornin'," Mariner tells Carper. A Golden sprout down Tehas way – bein' a writin' fool does it for him. That's what Rrrose Heather tells me. Like him, n' the rest a' us, you gotta find youren own way."

Lantern light plays softy on Carper as he shifts atop stool he's pretending is a thundering silver chariot. He's imagining what will get him through – not knowing he's doing it now; imagining. When Mariner says, "I'll tell you how Kunta got through nights aboard ship, 'cause it's a good lesson for you," Carper 'whoa's' his steeds to stop. Thoughts race onward to meet the excitement he senses is coming.

* * *

A VISIT TO POLARA
(whereon Kunta's Blythe-abwe lies; we call it North Star)

Elevator shaft Blythe-abwe's emerald sky uplifts Kunta's spirits, but he feels he no longer can endure the ship's bowels. He climbs a-Hempis, peeks out cupola, sees the deck is vacant, removes slats, crawls through, and replaces them. He breathes deeply of the elixir salt air and coils a-Hempis around shoulder then ascends mast. Kunta is nearly invisible amongst graying sails. He points skyward and whispers to Turt emerging from his pocket.

"POLARA! My special surprise for you, Turt."

Luny Mum moves behind a cloud so stars shimmer ever more brightly. Turt's eyes widen. Never has he seen such a spiraling showcase of the heavens' sparkles: Polara, the highest, brightest. Turt glances at Kunta. Kunta's look is glassy as the calm sea is in the stars' glow. Kunta, entranced by Polara magic, is meeting storied ancestors. a-Hempis is his umbilical providing the spirit-connect.

Kunta recognizes the spirits from seeing them inscribed on village totems. In their unencumbered state of perpetual being, they continually change shape. Their hazy visages beckon to their temporarily world-bound kin. 'Salutations Kunta. We come – to solace your soul and brighten your life, and teach you how to bask in life's glow so when you join us you may appreciate even more, Polara's peace-filled infinity.'

Kunta introduces Turt, but Turt feels he greets only misty night air. He goes along but quietly peeps his suspicion. 'Come now, are you yanking my fin-claw Kunta?' So sincere is Kunta that after a few minutes Turt is certain he too sees them. He senses their mystical wonder as they reach for his fin-claw and heartily shake it.

Scaling the mast, breathing freedom, becomes a nightly ritual for Kunta and Turt.

* * *

Mariner swigs. "Kunta found his 'somethun' in an 'estra special way."

"What were their names, Mariner? Of Kunta's kin."

Buzzard looks up from the ladies. Friendly jibe-challenge: "Indeed Mariner. Do tell."

Mariner doesn't hesitate; he can conjure a tale quick as he can spin. "Let's see; there be...."

"Kunta tell you all about them, huh?"

"Now Carper, you know that wouldn't be right. They're personal spirits, 'a his. But Turt got to know 'em all. 'Became right good friends 'cause he and Kunta spent many-a-night sailen' Pclara. Eventually one night he flies me up there for a meet-'n-greet."

"Names, Mariner. NAMES," deals Buzzard.

Mariner commences a 30-minute bluff – about the spirits, both Kunta and Turt *"spouted 'bout"*. Buzzard soon folds and Carper, spellbound, scoops up the winnings – coming in the form of Mariner's impromptu tales, that he would pass onto countless audiences: Tales about...

Rope-maker *Marv*, "...climbin' stiff, finished length 'a cordage then disappearin' 'mongst clouds." Potter *Penny*, "...storin' 100 descendin'-size jars in one big 'un'." Ink-man *Ike*, "...usin' own finger as dabbin' pen when he draws." Carver, *Karl*; seamstress, *Sal;* Weaver, *Winky*.

"Ya had ta speak Kunta's language ta be able to pronounce their *true* names, Carper. So's when Kunta and Turt even-tually tells me of 'em, they gave 'em ones I'd understand."

* * *

During his time within the sails, Kunta learns the crew's languages. He discerns the drug-induced division caused by the tainted food and the vitamin C wars. Abetting the trouble increases his chances of survival, he realizes. In darkness' cover he loops then lowers a-Hempis, pulls, slightly, tripping a German who blames a Dane who nearly slits the throat of a Latin who attempts peacemaking.

Kunta moves to a new hiding place; shouts in Greek: "The Turks are hoarding smoked meats." Ancient nationalist animosities flare; more division.

The only observer, an oral recorder of this, of all that happens, is Mariner. (Buzzard, Rrrose Heather, her ladies report to him of the day's activities as he cooks. At night, he's at the galley's threshold to the deck. Soon, he calculates, he will approach Kunta to befriend him, when he's sure Kunta knows they're on the same side. Then, will come mutiny's final phase.

JAW-JACKING CREATURES

When no storms mar the horizon, the night skipper abandons the helm to smoke hashish. (Auto-parrot is in force.) This is when Turt, from almost near the top of the mast, leaps from Kunta's shoulders. He's learned a trick by watching a flying squirrel a crewman keeps as a pet. He spreads fin-claws to point his direction, opens beak-snout to control flight. He sails, lands thudding, on Captain Polly's feather-bed wings. She absorbs shell's shock by crouching, at impact. He eases down to her talon and gnaws at steel shackle til his beak-snout aches.

They talk, small animal chatter, about retribution on the pirates.

'I have no reason to doubt Mariner can be trusted,' indicates Turt. 'But the Buzzard, he's a two-leg who don't know which way he'll fly if we fight our captors.'

Captain Polly rejoins defensively. "I'll make sure Lover Bir.., the Buzzard, is with us when it counts. It's Rrrose Heather and her ladies I'm suspicious of: The way they, all high and mighty flaunt the feathers of my fellow flyers in their hair." On and on continues gossip-fest about the two-legs, even after the hopped-up night skipper returns. He thinks Turt just another hallucination of his ever-so-high flight. So their animal plans of rebellion continue and they finally agree:

'All the captive two-legs will come together for their mutual good. We will never fully understand their odd ways, still they too survive in packs, flocks and herd, just as we.'

After each visit, Captain Polly's shackle gets a little thinner from Turt's gnawing. Turt climbs the mast and returns to Kunta's shoulder. Captain Polly looks up at him and shouts, for her gratification alone, in a conflux of languages only she understands. "One day I too shall have a shoulder to permanently lay my head upon. My Lover Bird's."

ON THE MAST ONE NIGHT: THAT'S WHEN TURT FINDS HIS, SOMETHUN'

Kunta's practicing rope tricks: looping, soundless snapping, knotting-unknotting mid air, twists even seamen think impossible. Turt, after jawing with Captain Polly and jaw-jinking her manacle, always returns to Kunta's shoulder. It feels good to his sore beak-snout, the vibrations of the little '*grring*' sounds he makes in answer to Kunta's whispered practices of the two-leg languages. The '*grr's*' slowly begin sounding like '*toots*', miniatures of the mighty blares of the bigger Trumpeters of Jericho.

Then one night, from deep within Turt's throat rolls, reverberates – a loud blast 'TRA-HOO!' It is the sound of a maturing Trumpeter: vibrant but not shrill, passionate and unbridled. 'TRA-HOO!' He cannot stop. So excited, tears come. He realizes he's becoming an adult. His shell, clawed fins, and beaked head haven't caught up yet – for when Trumpeters start growing they bowl rapidly upward. Turt realizes his journey, from tadpole to mighty, has begun. Proudly in his thoughts even louder does he blare: 'Now I am a Trumpeter. To you Jericho, one day I will return.'

Usually by this time of night most of the crew is drunk, asleep, or hopped-up. Captain Polly wants to squawk out accompaniment to Turt, to show support, but she knows it will call attention to him. She hears Kunta barely whisper, "Shush, Turt. Someone will hear."

Two humans do: A dreg; drugged by the shelling's Siren. He places dagger between teeth and ascends mast. Mariner is the other who hears. "Ah, my little Turt – you have found your 'somethun': The grand note of Gabriel that will carry you through lonely nights." He squints upward, sees pirate, quickly un-manacles himself and pursues.

Kunta is saying, "Let us enter Polara and tell the kin about your latest accomplishment Turt." So involved are they with their greetings, they don't see the pirate nearing.

"WATCH OUT!" Captain Polly squawks when she sees the marauder. Warning is too late. Dagger slices through the canvas sail just above Kunta.

* * *

Carper grabs Mariner's arm, stopping an invisible weapon-prop. "Don't let him die Mariner."

Buzzard nonchalantly looks up from his beauties. "Kunta had only that vain creature's trumpeting to blame for his problems. Odds are Kunta can't be killed. You should know that by now Carper."

Mariner clicks tongue to scrape some of Ol Tom's free-floating hair sticking there. "Well, your last part's right Buzzard." He knows Buzzard's mentally further embellishing his account of events, to one-day spin at the tables to distract the other gamblers. No attribution would Mariner receive; doesn't care, because, what happens next in the story he tells Carper would lead to one of the happiest times in Mariner's life.

Mariner pretends to lay down pretend-knife. "It's strange Carper, but I gotta thank that ratty pi-rat'. He's the one led me and Kunta ta bein' best 'a mates."

* * *

The rat slashes. Only Kunta's quick-thoughts, of confounding attacker by rolling in the sails as if they're ocean waves, keep the plunges from being fatal.

Guilt: 'What did I unleash,' Turt trembles. He nips at attacker as knife comes down, again, again. Kunta is stabbed a

dozen times as Mariner scales the mast.
Captain Polly flaps wings and moves talons up and down on the helm in parrot dance-cheer as weaponless Mariner suddenly overtakes, instantly snaps rat-pi-rat's neck. He leaves him to dangle in the shredded sail. (When Poppy Sol rises, a few hours from now, the corpse will wave warning to the restive crew of what awaits them.)

'The revolution will soar as high as I once again will,' Captain Polly consoles herself as she squints un-patched eye at Turt's bloodied young two-leg friend who Mariner gently lifts. 'I am here for you Turt. We slaves – creatures and humans – we'll unite to achieve the revolution.'

Mariner puts trembling-in-shock Turt in his pocket and prepares to commence Kunta's burial into Poseidon's bosom.

'Wait kind Sire.' Luny Mum peaks from behind clouds. She lights Kunta's face. His mouth quivers.

Mariner holds him to his chest; sees why he survived – the a-Hempis rope. It should have been sliced through. Instead, it protected. So tightly-bound is fiber, it shows but shallow nicks.

* * *

Carper's excited shout, '"a-Hempis saved his life," rouses Ol Tom who hisses displeasure at having his sleeping disturbed.

"They's pi-rats and stray rats," Mariner scolds. "Best you be scourin' for some, Tom."

Ol Tom dutifully prods a few corners, knowing the wharf-shack hasn't had any varmints, other than the Laza Bones poster, since he's anchored here; then he curls back down.

Mariner says to Carper, "I'm not sayin' everything was hunky-dory with Kunta. Not even close, Carper. Kunta, was bad-off as a soul can be, but the healin' potionin' Mama Lucy showed me was possible was waiten in the galley."

Hearing the good news Carper claps. A happy ending, that rousts Laza Bones' ire; even worse, it was aided by old bayou Mama who foiled too many of his schemes. 'DRAT!' He curses.

Buzzard, so fellow wharf-shackers won't see tears come from witnessing, admiring, envying the bond that developed twixt Kunta and Mariner, slips handkerchief from vest and blows beak.

* * *

A TALE OF NEW FRIENDS

"Potion – commence yo' healin' notion." Mariner chants Mama's words as he applies ointment over Kunta's body. Mariner has him stretched across the galley's worktable.

You clench beak-snout in anticipation as you watch from atop flour sack where Mariner placed you. Kunta's slight breaths deepen then lessen as time torturously passes. You see up-close the small band of two-legs you and Captain Polly have talked about. They arrive depart – Rrrose Heather, her ladies. They wipe Kunta's feverish body with cool cloths. The Buzzard – studying Kunta's walk-off pendant that he models his embellished tales after.

'What could Captain Polly possibly see in him?' His eyes are shifty, like his soaring counterparts that coveted you and fellow-shellings on Jericho's beaches; and occasionally swooped and carried one of you away. You shiver.

You can't tell, because it's so skyless, this place the two-legs call 'galley', but Poppy Sol and Luny Mum must have come and went many times since Mariner began trying to heal Kunta. You see Kunta's eyes open, suddenly. You 'toot' to get Mariner's attention – just in time because Kunta tries to raise himself. He almost rolls to the floor. Mariner holds him while petting you – to show sick boy that they have a mutual friend in you.

The old Cookie would have served-up Turt long ago, are Kunta's first coherent thoughts.

During the coming weeks of recuperation in the galley, where once continuously beaten, Kunta is cared for by the new

Cookie-Mariner, and the other ship-slaves. Buzzard brings Kunta drifting wood he fishes-up and Mariner entrusts him with a kitchen knife to carve it with so he can regain his strength and agility. (So special a box would he carve for Mariner during this time!)

Rrrose Heather and the ladies – so softly nurturing. As friendships flourish, and Mariner starts filling Kunta with hopes of mutiny, Kunta starts making forays back to Blytheabwe to see his village and villagers, even up the mast to visit Polara ancestors.

'Be careful,' you want to blare out to Kunta when he starts taking chances again. He robs from the dregs hidden chest of valuables. You only feel sad about one thing: seeing Buzzard over in his corner of the galley, stuffing, always stuffing the Trumpeter shells.

You relegate yourself: Captain Polly cares for him; he's an important part of the mutiny. This is your punishment for having given-away your friend with your toot of vanity- to suffer quietly the indignity of watching the shells of fellow Trumpeters, being stuffed.

* * *

"Why's Kunta risking robbing from the pirates when he's got you and the others to count on now, Mariner," Carper asks.

Mariner suddenly looks a little glummy, a little ecstatic, all at the same time. "He was riskin' himself for *me*, Carper." Mariner smoothes hand over bejeweled, intricately carved box for the Book of Carpier. "He was carving this for me – in secret; risking his life for our friendship by pilferin' the jewels for the finishing touch."

Carper: "You took him in just like you did me, huh Mariner."

"I 'spose I did Carper. I just 'spose I did."

CHAPTER 32

THE TALE OF THE MUTINY ON THE GONE LUNA – It comes to pass...

...just as the unpredictable giddiness of Gone Luna overtakes Luny Mum, a violent storm takes a churn at the ship. Mum's carefree beams sweep the blackened sky. Pelting rain so illuminates the horizon it appears a volley of iridescent spears is piercing the stern. That, combined with the brash, *'CRACK!'* of thunder, disorients creatures.

Flocks of sharp-billed flyers thrash into the sails, shredding them. Kunta holds tight atop the mast. Turt grips Kunta's shoulder in fin-claw and Sea Line in beak-snout. To fend off the flyers' onslaught Kunta whips with a-Hempis, Turt with Sea Line. From the helm, haplessly flapping Captain Polly castigates. "Steer clear, fool fowl. You'll destroy yourselves and us too."

Within the ocean, a barrage of creatures of fin lose their direction. Intrepid hammerhead shark and giant sperm whale are among them. They crush into the bow. They crack, weakening it. None on board knows the ship begins to leak. The tiniest of all the sea – plankton – band together by the millions – safety from the unusual in numbers. Upward they're swept, clinging to the ship's barnacles, causing a precarious list.

Turt glances down at Captain Polly and realizes this may be his last chance to free her. Squinting into the dense rain, he leaps. Wind blows him off the course he's flown dozens of times — 'plop' — right into roiling, swirling drink.

He has life-line Sea Line, old friend to the sea. The head mistress to a school of octopi grabs Sea Line. She holds him safely within her tentacle. He vibrates the direction Turt was aiming. Octopus raises Sea Line above water, spins him, releases, sends he and Turt circling toward the helm. She communicates, 'We can help your vessel for a while, Sea Line, but the ocean will have its way.' She and her school recess to slam into the stern to plug it temporarily. Sea Line lands on the poop deck and Turt crawls over to gnaw Captain Polly's manacle to try to free her.

* * *

"Ahem: Really now Mariner. You saw all that from the doorway to the galley? Midst that blinding rain?" challenges Buzzard.

Carper scales Mariner's canvas shirt and looks into his eyes. "Are your peepers THAT good Mariner?"

Mariner laughs. He holds Carper and glares at Buzzard. "Course I couldn't see. Found out about it later — from eagle-orbed Captain Polly."

Carper excitedly shouts, "Turt saved her. Captain Polly's alive!"

Knowing Mariner has once again beaten his bluff and kept the boy's interest, Buzzard grumbles, "Nothing could kill that *licentious* old bird. She's *immutable*, like Kunta."

Carper blinks twice, mentally banking those two odd words, so he can look them up when he learns letters.

"I suppose that octopi patch-job allowed time to organize the mutineers, Mariner."

"Right you be Buzzard." Mariner lifts Carper to Buzzard's lap. "You played no foul part. Fill him in."

Buzzard's eyes brighten as much as Carper's do. Buzzard

sways, part of his birdly way when he's weaving a new tale into old, until fiber of old is barely recognizable in thread of new.

Mariner crooks an eye, happily watching Buzzard sweep Carper away to the make-believe that always gussies up the '*so-so*' present; or the "*OH-NO*" memories of the past. Mariner knows, no matter what Buzzard did that day to save his own hide, it saved him and the others.

* * *

(Dear Rrrose Heather. She's the one to be telling the straight story. Maybe Luny Mum in her Gone Luna reverie took a shine to Rrrose and lit her way – so she could see all.)

Rrrose says to Mama Lucy as they travel the Lindian Woods, 'Mariner plays your potion recipes fine-as-a-fiddle, Mama, healing Kunta while keeping a step ahead of dregs with others.'

'A walk-off ahead. Dat bay what I heerd, Rrrose.'

James laughs at his muses' conversation.

Turt looks about the Lindian Woods wondering what's 'amusing. Suddenly he's picturing walk-offs. Beak-snout bobs in laugh: Hasn't thought of them for... been a long while.

'Listen, Jamie lad, this be how it all started,' Rrrose says. 'Instead of keeping vigil during his shift guarding Capt'n, Buzzard's sleeping – beat from hustling pirates. Capt'n, he's keen to the unusual storm, so, *up-'e-rises* from stupor. Musta found a hid-away key. Gets out to go direct crew who can't control the sails. I see him in the corridor carry-an' the humidor of walk-offs. Lid's off: He's stroking his slimy-appendaged little darlings: Gave me the heebie-jeebies, Jamie. Well I wasn't about to stop him – not til I get help.'

James grips Turt's shell and surveys the woods for any walk-offs just waitin'-ta-pounce.

'Capt'n, he wobbles to the deck. I follow, knowin', sure'an as St. Pat knew he could handle a snake or two, that the other ladies would see and come help take him back to his bed.

Suddenly it's too late for that. Capt'n stumbles on a rope that, somehows, slips from the mast.'

Turt's remembering: Kunta lowering a-Hempis in front of Capt'n – so long ago. *'TRR-III-PP!'* The first inconspicuous salvo of the mutiny.

'Out spill the walk-offs, Jamie, covering the deck like field-a'-clover, but with the stench-'a-peat: Capt'n' crawling, scraping, beckoning them back. But, even the most holy Patty couldn't steer them – they being so slippery and on a ship swaying to-and-fro. They take on the look of a crazed herd, I tell you Jamie: Charging right toward pirates already dead-fearful of them from Buzzard's salacious tales. Can't you just see it all? Dregs, one moment running from, and then the next doing battle with their former mates' feet.'

Mariner exits galley and sees what's happening. This isn't the right time to start the mutiny – the crew's not fully drugged, and they're still far from shore – but conditions give no choice. He unlocks himself and shouts upward through the pelting rain. "A favor, what say Mum. Ow's 'bout shedding some a yer Gone Lunacy onto the deck, so 'ens we can have a chance against these cutthroats?"

Unexpected answer to Mariner's request comes in thousands of pin-width beams lancing-through dark clouds, illuminating the ship. They seem to clamp onto the deck: micro-thin bars imprisoning pirates. Walk-offs rush through them. Hallucinating dregs seem trapped by the apparitions that, now real, appear even more hideous than they'd imagined.

Mariner signals fellow mutineers by striking the brass dinner bell with his manacle – a near-deafening clang. Seizing cleaver, spiraling the manacle as mace, he joins the walk-off charge. To play into dreg superstitions, he shouts fiercely, with all the foreboding of a soothsayer from a mythological odyssey: "No longer can ye gird yer loins, scurvy. The bootless spirits of yer drudge-mates have arrived to carry you to their nether world."

Some pirates jump the railing, choosing quick drowning

instead. Others, their swords stored in the weapons room, draw knives and look about for an unseen foe. From the shadows Mariner begins stealthily cutting, slashing, bludgeoning. Only briefly will his battle be a solitary one.

* * *

'We all hear Mariner's pre-planned clang and know what to do,' Rrtose Heather tells James.

James' puckering shows a dash of fear sprinkled with excitement when Rrrose says, 'Mi' ladies catch Buzzard high-plume-in'-it to that getaway raft he'd fashioned from the Trumpeter shells. While mi' ladies take him by his talons and pull him onto the deck to help Mariner, I go below and gather swords and some oh-so-special weapons we ladies devised for this moment.'

* * *

Two of their special weapons are courtesy of Capt'n; made from his metal navigational globes – each bored-through and inserted firmly with a harpoon. Rrrose's ladies fight savagely with these spear-shields as they did with wide hatpins, more-resembling daggers, they used against clients in Dublin alleys who refused to pay. Now, they remove multiple 'daggers' hidden inconspicuously in fluffy, bun hairdos, and, *"ooh"* – many a swipe to the groin of an adversary, or, a quick jab into an eye, *"Ay-yee."* Their swiftness beats dreg strength.

"Over here. You can get the drop on Mariner," shouts Buzzard to an unsuspecting pirate. Or, "Behind the crates, Turt hides. You can cut him open and break his spell on you and your mates." Despite drubbing them at gaming, Buzzard constantly used his wits to maintain their confidence. Again they trust, and come, and one at a time, they get a dagger to their gut – courtesy of, from up Buzzard's sleeve; or, a razor-edged metal plate, shaped as a playing card that he slips from a deck to slice through their jugular.

Nothing so devious for Mariner: Ever-present memories of the evil childhood experiences visited him by trash such as this empower him with the strength of many. His madness reflects on his contorted face. It's the last thing, more terrifying than any walk-off, his victims will ever see.

But, from Rrrose Heather who possesses the calmness of a-Hempis, and fleetness of Calico:

She removes blouse, undoes corset – she and her ladies prefer a frontal lacing style that can be removed easily when commerce calls. Her pale bosom glows in the Gone Luna's rays. Atop a barrel, she positions their other invented weapon – a bow device consisting of a few inches of wire tautly stretched between the brass end prongs of Capt'n' sexton. Rrrose crouches in shadows behind the barrel. She removes the dozen 18 inch long whalebone stays from the corset's channels. She had carved dagger tips into one end and notched the other. Arrows, she launches them from bow sexton. *'Twaang! Swiing!'*

Strong wind, heavy rain: Rrrose considers them, adjusts direction accordingly.[30]

'Pluunk!' Arrows penetrate cheeks – to the bone. When their knees get struck, some pirates collapse. Pain is lingering and deep as the agonizing sting of jellyfish most have felt. They quickly wrench out the projectiles. Blood spurts from wounds, dousing deck, making it even slicker so that walk-offs appear to accelerate their attack, further distracting the crew.

When she's emptied her corset-quiver Rrrose calls back first one lady, then the next. "Off with it," she shouts. She continues firing with their arrowed stays and they return bare-breasted to battle – sea-bound Delacroix's *'La Liberte` Guidant le peuple.'*

Rrrose is weakening their captors and keeping them off guard. Buzzard shouts to her as he backstabs a pirate who

---

[30] Luny Mum: 'Whenever my earth sister fired…If one of her arrows started going awry; why, don't you know, I'd pull or lessen my pull just enough so, *SLAM*, they'd hit their mark.'

rushes to kill her. "We're even-ing the odds." She sees his smile is a rare, genuine one. When finally she has emptied all the quivers she takes sword and joins others.

The *'hacks'*, *'whacks'* of swords into leather and canvas shirts and pants, though barely heard over the storm's howls, are vividly seen midst Gone Luna dancing light. So clearly, Kunta sees the battle from the mast. A fellow-mutineer is about to be struck. Quickly, he circles a-Hempis around the assailant, and then plops him into the sea. He uses one of his rope tricks to release. Re-noose, maybe grab two, three at a time, and again, *'plop, fizz,'* more into drowning drink.

* * *

James stands atop Turt's shell and dangles Sea Line, imitating Kunta on the mast with a-Hempis. Mama Lucy steadies him. To Turt, Sea Line vibrates. 'a-Hempis was loathe to cause a living thing to die, but how else could he perform in the presence of pure evil.'

'We played our part that night,' Turt proudly communicates, savoring the memory of the misery they inflicted on the stinking two-legs who decimated his island.

'Jamie,' says Rrrose Heather, 'what happens next is what truly turned tide permanently to our favor. For all, but one of us, that be. Oh I be one to give credit where credit's due, and though me and her 'ad differences, it was Captain Polly we can all thank. Of course Turt and the Sea Line too,' she kindly adds, in case they can hear or sense her.

* * *

"DOOMED! Like trapped rats we'll die," squawks Captain Polly. She flies crazily in the blinding rain around the small area her chain allows. Turt hangs on; tries to gnaw her free.

"DOOMED!" Her 'dooming' racket's meant to terrify the pirates even further; distract them, to help in protecting her

Buzzard and the mutineers until she can join the battle. Activity keeps her from thinking about her ultimate fear coming true – being trapped by her chain, going down with the ship.

Turt almost loses hold of blustering bird. Sea Line slips from around his neck, ties-on between manacle and talon; then inches to the helm and slipknots to it. Sea Line pulleys parrot to a forced-perched position so Turt may work unencumbered.

Octopi patch gives way to the storm's force. Sea rushes past. Ship's oak planking snaps, a deafening force, yet overshadowed by wind, rain and screeching sky and sea creatures.

Despite his insanity, Capt'n, so-highly-attuned to the ship he's commanded all his adult life, is the first to realize its imminent destruction. "Gone Luna's worser 'n any Goddam Typhoon," he curses. He hunkers by a rail and grabs a walk-off that slides near. His rants to it, a once living thing now all-festooned with clickety peg-legs fashioned from wooden cigar cylinders and pushed over the toes. "Don't fret little one. We'll have another float. One even grander. You will be my first mate."

...At that moment ten feet above them, seeming miles away midst the confusion, Turt *'cracks'* through bird manacle.

Up, Captain Polly flies. She's jittery from captivity. She is *wing-fived*, 'welcome to freedom, sister,' by other flyers. Adjusting flight to take into account wind and rain (another slight, pull-help from sister Mum), she swoops around, seeing, through un-patched eye, as none on board can, the ship's condition. She drops to the helm. "Crawl aboard."

Onto her plumage Turt climbs, and holds on, with Sea Line dangling from beak-snout. Up, she soars, then dives and talons the face of a pirate about to slit her Buzzard's throat. The distraction gives Buzzard time to end dreg. Captain Polly heralds excitedly in a confluence of languages: *'Liberte` du animaux de boucherie.* Liberty for all the oppressed! Human or creature."

Airborne trio assists fellow mutineers. Diversion is their cudgel. Captain Polly strafes battle, clawing pirates. Turt blares into ears, renting equilibrium. Sea Line's whipping-about lacerates lips. While shaking off the drenching rain Captain Polly points her wing, indicating to Kunta who on their side needs help. He and a-Hempis oblige – **'PLOP!'**

Steadily re-adjusting to being caught off-guard, the pirates begin to take advantage of their strength of number. One yells – "A dandy, a cook, some worn whures, we'll beat 'em down."

The sentiment drumbeats as they advance. "A conniving slave'll be first," adds the wiry boson, seeing Kunta, when a lightening flash exposes him. Turt notices boson scaling the mast and blasts warning to Captain Polly. She flies upward, rams pseudo peg-leg into his eye and talons his tongue to muzzle his yelp. He thrusts dagger at her. Turt flips in front of blade, his shell deflecting it. He grasps Sea Line while Sea Line twists rapidly around the dagger's handle.

Mightily, Turt yanks. He whips it away, and, with the flick of his beak-snout, he reverses its trajectory. Sea Line's leather-elasticity swings it back toward the pirate, *'fflumping'* into his heart. The boson drops twenty feet, landing on other dregs. Necks *'SN-A-A-A-P'*.

Kunta looks Captain Polly and Turt's way. Before continuing his puppetry, he nods thanks.

"*Squaar,*" Captain Polly warbles, flying off. "All-in-a-day's-work; day's-work." Her adrenalin rushes. She beak-taps Turt. (So close have they become that they understand the other's slightest subtlety.)

Glances catch; Turt responds. He tightens grip on Sea Line and whips opposing end to Polly.

When she seizes it in her beak Turt lets loose of plumage and dangles from Sea Line. Captain Polly rotates her neck, spinning Turt in wide loops. He closes his eyes. Circling low, she uses Turt to bludgeon dreg heads.

* * *

James begins spinning Sea Line above his head and says to Rrrose Heather. "A flyin' David vs Goliath. Sea Line was Captain Polly's slingshot; Turt her stone."

'Exceptin', Turt never 'a let go," says Mama Lucy. Dat what you told me, right Rrrose Heather?"

'Sure' 'n, Mama Lucy.' Rrrose Heather waves her hands. 'It be, as we say in Ireland Jamie, *iontach* – wonderful. Aerial bombardment happens over-and-again: Bomb bein' Turt. His sharp as-a-razor line, twixt top and bottom shell keeps slicing from one head to the next.

'Pirates shouting-out, as blood be gushers from their bandanas – "we'll get you Captain Polly." They jumping high as they can with their weapons. None can bring down that bird. A couple slip as they jump, laceratin' theyselves; stuck boars. One tosses a dagger. Big mistake. It whizzes beneath her, hitting fake peg-leg, knocking it off. Now she has two talons to torment with.'

James sees the saddest of looks instantly pale his Rrrose muse. He reaches, strokes her face, feels her tremble as she says, 'Then, somethen terrible 'appens, Jamie. A filthy bastart swipes one a mi' ladies across wrist. Blood leaping out, like flames in a peat bog I once see catch-fire. She drops in me arms. Try as I might I couldna' stop the gusher.'

"Dead?" James mournfully asks.

Mama Lucy braces his shoulders. 'You be forgettin. Mariner's got Mama's potions, *ami*. Shush now. Be hard enough for our dear Rrrose to tell this part, without our interrupt.'

'Bastart was readying to finish her off. But mi' other lady piked him.' Rrrose Heather lances fists sideways. 'Clean through, from 'is arse to 'is gullet.' James sees her wry, satisfying smile. He almost has to cover his ears when Rrrose whoops, 'Captain Polly to the rescue!'

* * *

Captain Polly looks over her wing, winks. Turt nods

understanding. She flies to the hurt lady who is shielded from battle by speared-globe-wielding Amazonian guard. Trumpeter and parrot make a tourniquet of Sea Line, squeakily '*st-reee-tch*', halting blood-flow. Turt holds Sea Line in place while Captain Polly swoops to Mariner to get Mama Lucy's healing potion.

She dodges Mariner's cleaver that strobes in the Gone Luna. He slashes, through storm torrent, dreg-after-dreg. From his apron pocket, Captain Polly seizes canister in talon and delivers it to Rrrose Heather who quickly applies the salve. For a moment, Captain Polly watches with compassion her downed fellow-mutineer. Color returns to the lady's face. Then, jealousy of Rrrose Heather, for dallying with her bird, overtakes Captain Polly and unctuously she squawks, "Whure! Whure!"

"I like you," Rrrose Heather responds sincerely, petting plumage. Captain Polly, in starchy disdain, nips at her hand and flies off to assist her Buzzard.

Turt remains on the deck. He's silent, to remain inconspicuous. He finds shadows, cast by Gone Luna, to attack from. He assaults enemies who've slipped on the slick surfaces or are temporarily downed by mutineers. He vises beak-snout onto ear lobes. When they shriek from the cutting pain, one of Turt's comrades hears them and finishes them off. When Gone Luna shadows disappear he crawls under a walk-off for cover and moves inconspicuously to another victim, wrenching a finger, nose, or he slides down a loose pair of dungarees and... "Ayy-eee!"

* * *

'Within minutes, Jamie, mi' lady was faunchin' to get back to the fight.'

'Magic be the potion. Always was; always will be, be my notion,' rhymes Mama.

Rrrose rolls her hands, as if she's winding wool. 'Magical too, be tourniquet whenI remove it. Slithers right into battle, it does, joining our fight.'

'Dregs towed our line, hmm partner?' Sea Line vibrates to Turt as James dangles him against Turt's neck.

* * *

STOCKHOLM SYNDROME: (The response by some abducted hostages where they demonstrate allegiance to their assailant.)
Captain Polly knows her weakness is her desire for the ever-spurning Buzzard; cares not, she, to control it. Compassion is what she unexpectedly feels for captor Capt'n, as she sees him hunkered down in insanity. Captain Polly cannot understand. So much does she want to descend, take arm in talon. "Come this way to the lifeboat oh Capt'n my Capt'n."
'No, wait.' She stops to think, to rationalize to clear thoughts. '*Freedom!* The choices it brings are most wondrous.' At this moment, hers is not a choice between Capt'n and Buzzard, but in the captive-past of the manacle, and the future's unshackled brightness.
Captain Polly sweeps through the rain. Woven with the light of Gone Luna, the sky becomes a prismatic tapestry. All the colors make Captain Polly light-headed, flighty, so full of life's joys. She glides upside down, whimsically parodies a Bard-spouting thespian Capt'n once shanghaied to entertain crew. "Buzzard, oh Buzzard. Wherefore art thou, my Buzzard?"
Looking back, just briefly, she sees the demise of the Capt'n at the feet of the walk-offs. The ship has listed. Every available walk-off charges his way, inundating, choking him. Capt'n bats them away, but the vessel lurches, tumbling him toward them. The toppled chief-dreg's end comes from just one of them though, a death-bringing little critter whose toes Capt'n had fitted with tiny daggers. Over all the other walk-offs, it rolls to him. It punctures his lungs before burrowing permanently into his chest.
Cares not, does Captain Polly. She is unfettered, finally, of

his dark mental hold. "Et tu, walk-offs?" she laughs. It's a laughter born in the adrenalin rush of complete, *freedom*.[31]

THE TALE OF SAMSON OF THE SEA

Glimpsing one of Buzzard's devious murders is Samson, the 400-pound oaf of the pirates. So naïve is he, a shipmate once convinced him to have a rat-eating-cat tattooed onto his forehead, because, "it'll get ye the gals in port, big matey."

"Back here, Samson," Mariner beckons. "Turt's roasting on the spit – ready to eat."

'Buzzart fools me at da' gambler's Monty. I'll pretend he's foolin me again.' "Samson?" Samson proudly grumbles. "No, my name Savaian de Pandeur." He lumbers to the shadowed areas behind the crates. Just as Buzzard turns to knife him, Samson grabs him by the lapels and lifts him over his head. "We'll see if you can fly, Buzzart. Or if you swim." Pirate corpses that he must step over or kick aside slow his walk to the side of the ship. Buzzard's flapping is useless. Samson just grasps his rain-saturated suit ever tighter in ham-fat hands.

Buzzard looks around, remembering seeing Captain Polly in frivolous flight. She's his only hope. "Captain Polly. Come. Your Buzzard needs you," he shouts, appealing in desperation. If only she might hear? If only he hadn't alienated her too often during the voyage? In a small way, some of his sentiments of desire are sincere; sincere as they ever could be for a bird like Buzzard whose only nest is a casino.

Captain Polly realizes this. She isn't concerned. Her passions are irreversible. She hears and comes to him. Into rat-cat forehead she slams and talons, tighter-and-tighter.

Samson drops Buzzard and flails. "Two devil birds back to hell I'll throw."

---

[31] Luny Mum: 'My thinken is...Every time a vile man like Capt'n dies, another's comin' round to replace him. Sure 'nuf, thousands a miles away in the desert Lazarus Bontez startin' manhood quest. Maybe some of the spirit of Capt'n sneaks into him. Makin' Laza Bones twice as bad as them both. Hmm.'

She flies to and perches on the railing, taunts, "Try it bright eyes. Try it. Try it."

Samson rushes. Luny Mum shoots piercing Gone Luna rays at his eyes, temporarily blinding him. Samson gropes for the sidestepping Captain Polly. She winks at Buzzard. Buzzard nods, understanding her signal, her 'high sign'. They've the same non-verbal communication ability as she with Turt. This one with Buzzard is instantaneous, as if a symbiotic relationship developed long before between them.

"Gonna strangle you bird. Think you're smarter than me, huh?" Samson shouts. Just before the ham-fats encircle her throat she flies up, hovers just beyond reach as he stretches out over the bending rail. Buzzard charges, part of their silently devised plan, and rams clueless oaf overboard into the consuming drink.

Luny Mum, compassionately pull-lifts the ocean waves from Samson's head. 'Bless the simple. No less is my task.' With the push of her Gone Luna energies, she sends, what seems to Samson, a thousand fish toward him. "Sweet joy," he shouts. Mouth stays open and contentedly he chokes on his last meal. Bloated, but 'blessed', he sinks.

Captain Polly flies to Buzzard's shoulder. His is soft, not bony as the shoulder of the Capt'n. She is here by her own choice not by the manacle. The continuing battle on the other side of the crates seems, briefly, a distant world to the human and the bird.

"We make a good team," Buzzard says, reaching to shake her talon. She nuzzle kisses his finger. Buzzard doesn't pull away, nor does he pet plumage to return the affection.

'No romantic Tom-Turkey Buzzard he,' thinks she, assessing relationship as it is beginning.

"You must shed this," says he matter-of-factly, removing, tossing overboard eye patch, last vestige of her life as hostage. She blinks away fat raindrops. For a moment he's mesmerized by her eyes, he's seeing close-up for the first time. In ever-changing Gone Luna, they sparkle as diamonds. Buzzard succumbs to an unexplainable attraction and strokes her rain-saturated head.

(Luny Mum is puzzled by the way human admires creature, yet strives not to show it.)

Touch, though brief, sends sensual rushes through Captain Polly. 'Nor is he capon,' Captain Polly coos to herself, thinking she'd do about anything for him in exchange for that touch.

"Not much life left in this old bucket ship, I'll wager," says he, quickly returning to his master-of-fact gambit. "Let's say we launch my raft and leave all this riff-raff to sink in its own stink."

"I'll tell the others. I'll tell the others." She readies to fly.

"No time Captain Polly." Buzzard seizes her leg. Suddenly his touch is cold as the manacle.

"NO! Never again." She clamps beak onto index finger of his dealing hand. One, '*snap*', would cede it from palm. Diamonds eyes turn violent red of ruby and burn into him what must be the boundaries of their relationship. Never again would she be possessed.

"Damn it. You are the captain I suppose," Buzzard says to Captain Polly. Simultaneously each releases. She flies to gather fellow mutineers. "If they're not here when I leave, Captain Polly, this first mate won't wait."

The ship lists sharply. The drenching rain almost flicks sopping Kunta from the mast. His heart races as he spiders cautiously to the deck to find Turt. Midst lightening flashes, he sees the lifeboats sinking. As he rushes between shadows toward the galley and Buzzard's Trumpeter-shell raft, he whistles a pre-arranged signal to others – '*little time left*'. Only Captain Polly hears. She flies leeward. She has her own plans.

* * *

"Whats Captain Polly do?" James interrupts.

'Don't go faunchun', Mama Lucy says. 'You leave Rrrose Heather weave the web at her own pace. More listenen' pleasure that way.'

James studies Rrrose. His muse's wry storyteller's smile reveals nothing before its time.

'Mmm. 'I mention a-Hempis lately, Lad?'

* * *

As Kunta darts, hides, crawls, a-Hempis slowly unfurls from around his shoulder. a Hempis ties onto Sea Line who's been fighting dregs by curling around their boots, tripping them into Mariner's cleaver or the ladies' globe-spears. Sea Line points to Turt. a-Hempis whips Sea Line toward him. Turt fiords a deck-puddle and clamps onto Sea Line.

Kunta sees the rope, line, and shelled-creature procession. "No better time for we warriors to re-unite." He carries them to the galley stairs, descends; is there before Buzzard. He drags raft from the pantry – easily five times his weight – ties a-Hempis to it, places Sea Line beneath so it slides easier; then pulls. So slow is its creaky, upward 'thump'.

The shells catch on the steps. Kunta wishes he had the totem peg-leg to pry them loose. No time to get it from Blythe-abwe.

Turt climbs along a-Hempis and loosens the shells with his fin-claws. He grits his beak-snout, enduring the genocidal reminder he encounters. This is the first he seeing remains of fellow Trumpeters since observing Buzzard stuffing the shells with *their* fat and *his* gold at the voyage's start. Turt bows briefly, thanking relatives for their sacrifice that would now help him and his warrior mates.

Footsteps on the stairs: Is it a friendly face Turt looks up to see? No. Buzzard. Turt *grr's*, 'Always will I hate the Buzzard for what he's done.' For now, reluctant complicity.

Despite mistrust, Buzzard and Kunta work together to get the raft to the deck.

All the more important is Captain Polly's swiftness of flight because the ship, with one continuous *'CRA-A-ACK'*, begins breaking. Her plan is to organize the flocks of birds circling the vessel. Captain Polly squawks orders, "This way I say. Keep your lines straight."

Luny Mum illuminates Captain Polly, so every flyer sees her through the rain.

"Now, DIP; fast," she orders. They do, forming a protective curtain between Mariner, Rrrose Heather, the ladies and dregs. The flocks slam into the dregs, knocking some overboard.

Luny Mum, she'll not miss out on the fun. In Gone Luna reverie, she morphs to an egg shape and seems to crack, slap, into the storm's horizon. Some confused birds take this as a sign; and want to pay homage to the 'great sky mother'.

* * *

'What comes next, Lad, be a true aberration. No one in a thousand, in a million years would believe it.' James' eyes widen. 'But happen it did, Lad. Me, Mariner, and the ladies seen it.'

* * *

Defying nature, hundreds of birds begin laying, dropping eggs on the dregs, confounding them even more, giving Captain Polly a chance to direct Mariner, Rrrose Heather and the ladies to one another amid throng. Birds' screeching escalates to piercing screams and begins superseding the storm crashes. Confusion aids in providing escape-cover for the mutineers.

The ship lists wildly. Remaining pirates slip slide into the ocean. Enormous fish, crazed by Gone Luna, batter them permanently under.

Mariner, Rrrose Heather and the ladies start for the lifeboats. Captain Polly repeatedly warbles. "Too late. To the galley. To the galley." She lands on Rrrose Heather's hand and pulls-flies her that way because she knows humans can't see through the storm. Drenched humans interlock hands and parade to the raft led by the even soggier bird.

* * *

'Never thought I'd ever see it, Jamie. When Captain Polly got us there, Buzzard was working to help someone, besides himself. With Mariner, mi' ladies and me joining the heave-hoeing, Captain Polly moving Sea Line when necessary, we got the raft up, in two shakes. In just one more, we pulled it to the side of that Satan-cursed ship. We lowered it with a-Hempis. Kunta, he leaps into the water to hold it steady for us.'

"That's when you were all saved?" James asks.

Rrrose's face freezes. She starts to cry. James can't remember ever seeing such sadness. He reaches to hug his muse who suddenly isn't there. She's disappeared into her sorrow. Mama Lucy speaks for her. 'No, chil', that's when tragedy struck – after all their good fortune.' She continues the rest of the story that Rrrose Heather had told her, heartbreakingly, dozens of times.

* * *

Kunta grasps the side of the doomed ship with one hand. He holds raft in the other via a-Hempis safety tether. Mariner helps Rrrose Heather and her ladies over the sea-sloshed rail onto it. Buzzard embarks with genteel steps. Captain Polly perches on his shoulder. Turt is on Captain Polly's back. Sea Line dangles from Turt's beak-snout. All aboard, Mariner begins reeling in Kunta. The ship lurches violently, pulling Kunta underwater, wrenching his hold from a-Hempis. The raft spits away from the ship. Water sloshes over everyone. They grip the raft and each other to keep from sweeping off.

"Kunta!" Mariner shouts, squinting through the beating rain. Turt trumpets beckoningly.

Luny Mum sweeps ocean with her beam. Everyone sees Kunta go underwater, re-surface.

TALES OF THE FICTION HOUSE

* * *

James imagines he's aboard the sinking ship, wailing, "Take my hand Kunta."
Kunta's too far away. Kunta seizes a-Hempis.
James tries to reel him in. The current is too strong. "Need help," James shouts. From where, James doesn't know, he's joined by two boys his age. One looks so much like him; the other wears a turban. Together they pull, grunt, grit teeth.
Above them: Mast cracks; crashes down. The boys – James, Carper, Carpier – scatter, quickly regroup and see that the mast is trapping a-Hempis. a-Hempis unknots from railing; knots around mast; and, with help of ocean currents, pulls at it; tries to point it – a giant finger that Kunta might seize the tip of. The boys put their shoulder to it. PUSH! It teeters. One final shove: 'If Kunta reaches it, we'll have saved him,' James tells the other boys. 'PLOP!' Into the water it drops.
Smiles of accomplishment amongst the boys.
Together they shout: 'Grab on Kunta. You can add carvings to it as you torpedo to land.'
Too late: The mast shoots past him. a-Hempis unties from it to keep from being pulled far from Kunta. James, feeling helpless that he's unable to save Kunta, blinks out what he thinks is salty ocean. They're tears, and he's no longer aboard ship. He's back in Lindia.

The current pulls Kunta hundreds of feet. He disappears between waves.
Mariner tries jumping in to attempt the impossible, to reach Kunta. The others restrain him. Rrrose Heather grasps the mighty seafarer, smothers his forlorn cries by cradling him.
Captain Polly knows the shaking, squealing, nearly insane-with-sorrow Turt will try to go after his friend. She seizes him, flies to, and drops him down the bosom of the lady who most-taunted her while aboard ship. Flying in front of her, they come – beak-to-nose. Captain Polly squawks, "Keep him warm, safe til I return; if you know what's good for you." She

flies off to search for Kunta.

Throughout the confusion, only Sea Line, one end held in Turt's beak-snout, the rest of him neck-laced around the lady, notices a-Hempis snake through the churning water to where Kunta was last seen. Sea Line communicates to mentor a-Hempis, 'Fare-tee-well, you who have taught me well. May we meet again.'

* * *

Crying, James shouts, "Kunta! Kunta!"

Turt wonders why the boy thinks of him now. He doesn't look back at James; afraid he might see a look to his eyes reminding him of the night on the raft; seeing Kunta drift from his life. So, Turt trudges on.

Misty-eyed Rrrose – her form reappears beside the travelers. 'Don't you fret Jamie. Just keep thinking about that mast. a-Hempis had a bead on it all along. You boys were right on how it could help.'

* * *

140 years earlier than James, Carper cries. He, too, imagined being aboard – alongside a turbaned boy and a make-believe boy, trying to save Kunta. Buzzard consoles Carper. "Captain Polly tried for days to find him."

There's a *too-big* lump in Mariner's throat for him to speak.

"He had to have lived, Buzzard." You said you saw him on the bank. Or were you just saying that to be shed of Turt!"

Carper can't explain why, but he feels so bad for both Kunta and Turt he just has to shout out, "You both lying to me?"

Buzzard knows his old friend is faultless. Sometimes a tale – or even the slightest fudge can harm. Normally, he'd not care. He places his hand on Carper's shoulder. Carper pulls away and walks to the far side of the wharf-shack. "Well now Carper," Buzzard says. "I *thought* I saw him. Almost certain. We were all hoping he grabbed onto the mast." Buzzard cannot do any more explaining, or wriggling out of his story of seeing Kunta, because,…

…the attack on the wharf-shack Captain Polly earlier had feared – it is beginning.

The sides of the rickety structure begin shaking as the thumps on the outside echo inside.

CHAPTER 33

EPILOG to end PART II

Rrrose Heather's brogue thickens like Irish oatmeal when her anger's abrewin'. Now it's boilin'.(Raji Singh, yet the Lindian Woods foundling James, observing his muse when she starts talking about Buzzard)

A BRIEF TALE OF HOW A PLUME BROUGHT PEACE AND PROSPERITY

"buzzard, Buzzard, BUZZARD." The screeching startles my great-great grandfa Carper.

He's certain Thibidioux's angry herd descends on the wharf-shack. Before Carper can shout, "Laza Bones is callin' you out Buzzard," Buzzard says, "That's my ol woman...I know you're there, ol woman. Stop your squawking."

Postered Laza Bones, awakened by the noise growls, 'Quite' er down er ya'll be sorry. And don't ya go wakin' me again til next month, hear!' He resumes his snooze.

Gliding above the dock is Captain Polly, her claws full of feathers. Huey Long's eyeball dangles around her neck. She watches the onslaught by the real culprits at the wharf-shack's entrance, not Thibidioux and his minions as my great-great grandfa wildly reckons, but Rrrose Heather and a half-dozen ladies from whose hats Captain seized the feathers.

"I cannot be seein' ya in this dark, Captain Polly," Rrrose shouts. "I know you're the thief, because when 'er the Buzzard comes to town, his jabberin' bird-mate's close by. I'll see to it, by the bones-a'-the-saints I swear, that your pestering notions 'ere plucked clean."

Tarp door moves. Mariner has them in. "I was just tellin' the boy about our pi-ratty cruise."

Rrrose, smiling, goes to Carper, hugs him. Ladies encircle Carper, petting, kissing. His shies up and hugs Mariner's leg. "Wish you'd be recognizin' your ladies, Lad," says Rrrose.

(The way his great-great grandson sees Rrrose Heather in the Lindian Woods all the years later, so too, does Carper now): Black hair like silk, sweeping grand neck; reddest cheeks; tight, ankle-length dress barely containing curves. At 45, she's still inviting as any of her scantily clad ladies, half her age. The same sweet perfume in Lindia James will inhale, that, too, so permeated the Cincinnati bordello, Carper cannot remember where he's breathed its come-to-me scent.

Rrrose lightly pinches Carper's cheeks. "Mariner be good company, eh Lad? And Ol Tom." She omits any compliments for Buzzard. She pets Tom. Ol Tom rolls his body into the sensuous stroke. "Come and visit me felines when we get a new house," says Rrrose. She looks about. "Where's me wanderin' Turt be off to? The Buzzard's ruffling send-'im-shuffling?"

"See here, Rrrose. Entangling me in your trivial feather problems..."

Mariner interrupts she and Buzzard's banter, that, even in a quarter-century after the pirate ship daze is often followed by shrill crowing, sometimes thorns. "Turt's gone searchin' Kunta again, Rrrose. We just been tellin' the Carper all 'bout their bond."

"Turt's a dedicated critter; but only to his *friends*," Rrrose says to Buzzard before beginning to put a 'THE END' to the dreg story for Carper. "Turt be bosomed, quite-comfortably, by mi' lady when we be aboard the raft, Lad. Suddenly, mi' lady screams, so loud it'd startle Lucifer. Turt, 'e nips her 'you-know-what'.

* * *

With beak-snout you pinch a bit-a-the-tit. Soon as she pulls you out, into the drink you dive. With Sea Line in fin-claw, you brave the waves and start the first of too many all-for-naught searches for Kunta.

* * *

Carper's excited. *Glums*, suddenly squelched by all the excitement, *are on the run*. "I'll bet Turt finds Kunta *this* time, and brings him to us. Just in time for one big wharf-shack party."

Rrrose Heather abruptly pulls her hatpin and waves it in front of Buzzard's beak. "I'll not have your bird rough-housing mi' delicate ladies." She touches slight talon marks on their foreheads where Captain Polly pushed off after seizing their plumes.

Buzzard's been confronted by many-a-distraught female and is certain he can spot an idle threat. He doesn't flinch, nor does he make a rash move. Mariner backs away, grins.

The only feather Captain Polly didn't get, seeming to have been held in place by the hatpin, falls from Rrrose's beret.

Carper retrieves it. It is sleek emerald. Sun-yellow, star-silver colors streak through it. Carper strokes it. Soft.

Rrrose senses his compassion for Captain Polly.

"I like Captain Polly despite what she thinks of me. But, see Lad. Plumes be our trademark. We're the feather hat ladies. So's all the gentlemens' know where to come… to – 'Dance'. It's like why Buzzard wears a tailcoat and fancy dudins'. So all the gamblers'll know where to come when they want to – 'Chance'. Wouldn't do for Mariner to get all duden' up. Gamblers might come to him 'steada Buzzard. Same with us: We don't want no one infringen' on our feathers."

Carper innocently asks, "What about Captain Polly and her birds? I'm sure they don't cotton to feather-infringen' either?" Buzzard smiles, wickedly, seeing that, for a change, Rrrose Heather has no Irish invectives to hurl. He wings arm around Carper. "The boy makes sense Rrrose, *Dear*, though you won't admit it. Now that I consider it, I'm a bit offended too; being partly of feather myself."

Oatmeal's really burbling now. Rrrose's wrist veins bulge as she clenches the hatpin.

Mariner, the peacemaker. "Understand Rrrose. You saw what Capt'n put her through on the ship. Those plumes represent freedom, just like the carving meant freedom to Kunta. It's simple as changing yer style. You'll set an example for the righteous fold."

Rrrose is tired of quarter-century of battle with Captain Polly.

Mariner kinda' whispers, "You go off and marry that Sinnator 'awho visits you, and he becomes Prezedent; look-see all the rich, fancy ladies you can influence to stop wearin' the hat feathers. Think of all our fowl friends who'll be spared the extinctin'; like so many critters already have because of us two-leg's selfish wantins'!"

Mariner takes the hatpin-weapon from Rrrose and returns it to her beret.

Buzzard, always calculating, gets an idea: An unselfish act; hasn't performed many of those. "Captain Polly and me, we've mutual concerns, Rrrose. Let's say I give that lovely bird the present she's always wanted..."

Captain Polly had landed on the wharf-shack's roof and, ear pressed to stove flue, has been listening to everything.

"...You stop wearing the feathers and I'll ship you the latest French-style chapeaus from New Orleans." Buzzard's calculating: 'I can get all I want from the mad hatter who never folds for a predictable straight flush.'

"You don't understand, Buzzard. "I'm expanding, franchising. This is the Rrrose Heather trademark, up and down the Ohio. I've even a few places along the Mississippi, and Captain Polly, when she follows you upriver, knows each of them and commences tormenting."

Captain Polly's calculating. 'Won't stop the taunt until you stop your flaunt.'

"Let's not quibble, Rrrose. I'll supply as many as you need." Buzzard knows Captain Polly's listening. They've been together long enough to know the others whim-and-way. Altruistic at first for Captain Polly's sake, but now another idea clicks and he doesn't want her to hear. He begins whispering, "In exchange…"

Rrrose: "Oh no. No dippen' yer beak in for any free nectar."

"Wouldn't think of it Rrrose. But you're expanding along the river. Well, I travel it. Sometimes I have to drop out of sight – quite quickly, and for a spell. Just allow me to lam it at one of your places for a time – set up a friendly game in a back room. I'll actually be bringing business your way…"

"20% of your take," Rrrose Heather says without hesitation.

Laza Bones, always an ear keen to transactins', even whilst asleep, awakes, but pretends to doze. 'I'll get in on that transactin', just you wait.'

"No quibbling among friends, dear: Deal," Buzzard says to Rrrose. They shake hands. He speaks loud, so Captain Polly hears his altruism. "Getting you to stop, *'feathering'*, is least I can do for my Lovely Bird."

Rrrose says to Carper when he offers plume. "You give it to Captain Polly when you two meet, Lad. A nice gesture, to be assuren' you become one of her best friends."

Laza Bones, ever bored by nice gestures, hunkers down in his poster; recommences snooze.

* * *

"How'd you all get back to shore, riden' on that skimpy raft Rrrose Heather," James asks.

'Well, Lad. Can't tell you how Turt made it.' She brushes

woodland insects from his beak-snout with a twig. Turt sniffs. 'Guess Turt'll have to spill his own beans to ya' someday. We had some bad days and nights, but Mariner could fish excellently and we'd catch rain in some of the shells.

'Oh how Poppy Sol baked us by day, but that gave Mariner enough heat to start a small fire and do some gourmet cooking. Luny Mum lit our way most nights. Captain Polly – mad-aroused as I got at her sometimes – she scouted every day by air – found us distant land and Mariner sailed us to it. Simple as that. Then we went our own ways.

'But, after all we'd been-through, together, those, ways, always led us back to Mariner.'

* * *

Rrrose Heather and her ladies depart the wharf-shack. Captain Polly having heard all, flies from the roof, sways above them briefly, and shrieks, "A peace offer will I bring *Dearrr* Rrrose." Before Rrrose Heather reacts, Captain Polly swoops down, brushes beak to hear cheek, coos, "friends, now", and flies away.

Inside the wharf-shack, it gets quiet. Carper's tired. Mariner lays him on the straw bed. He dozes, but he opens one eye and sees Captain Polly. Captain Polly is at the porthole.

She talons Huey Long's eyeball, and extends it as sign of friendship because she knows he initiated the sisterly accord. If Captain Polly had the time, she would say to Carper, 'I'll be giving this to Rrrose Heather. Don't you think she'll like it? I'm sure she'll let you play with it.'

Buzzard and Mariner are back at their one-upmanship, so they don't hear Captain Polly when she says to Carper. "Sorry I scared you earlier with it. Won't do it again." She leaves.

Carper's imagination takes over. Suddenly, outside the window, where parrot just was, he sees a rising turban; and then, Carpier, peering in at him, saying, 'Rest well, Carper. You'll need your strength, for soon we will be on our adventure to help the boy of whom I spoke earlier. Much will we do.' With that, Carper dozes off to the clinks of Mariner and Buzzard's glasses.

PART III
MEANWHILE, BACK ON THE ROAD TO VALHALLA

(on that almost-deadly night for
Ezekiah Bellows...)

CHAPTER 34

THOMAS a-HEMPIS – *Your strangling fibers tightened around the slave-catcher's neck, imbedding into his pig-skin. You felt: the throb of blood vessels, the deflating balloon of oxygen as it oinks through the narrowing opening. SNAP: Crackling of cartilage. For a moment it was you, only, holding up the body. It went limp. You followed it to the ground: THUD! Coiling limply atop it, you told yourself: 'You despise violence, but you must aid in destroying vileness; mustn't you?'*

A TALE OF TWO ROPES, TWO HORSES, TWO PEOPLE

Poppy Sol winks morning across the Ohio and Luny Mum stays the day. Dear Precious snouts Ezekiah Bellows awake. Ezekiah grasps bridle. Dear Precious lifts him. Ezekiah rises unsteadily from bedroll. Dusty cleric collar is dark as his parson suit. Face is pale. He avoids looking at Pig and Jocular's nearby bodies. He says to Kunta, "You saved my life kind sir."

Kunta pours him coffee and pokes campfire. "I destroyed vileness that would destroy me."

"God will forgive you."

"He will thank me."

Talk over breakfast confirms what they know about the other — from whispered conversations of fellow-abolitionists. Their aims are the same, attitudes opposite: Kunta seizes the glory of his mind's freedom; Ezekiah's imprisons his.

A common interest, rope tricks, draws them together. Barriers collapse with each twist and loop. Burdened adults temporarily turn adventuring adolescents. "Like this, Ezekiah. Right before spinning it you…"

"Try this Kunta. Tie together both ends. Now…"

Ezekiah sees Kunta clearly in the daylight. Face is clean-shaven, chiseled with broad features: elevated brow, dark eyes, wide canyon temples, creviced cheeks. Prominent nose flattens-out at base to balance iron jaw. Artist's hands are smooth, muscular. (Kunta lived by selling carvings, paintings, and gator-skin scrollwork so popular in the days when he first came to America. He taught himself to read and write the language of his new land.)

On leather-vest and chaps are tooled scenes of his village. He wears boots made of an alligator that had set out to chomp him. He killed it in the bayou with a stick and attached-slate he fashioned into a spear.

(Laza Bones' minions didn't phase the 17 year old, new to America. Once when Laza returned from the desert, he heard tale of Kunta. He was sure he'd meet up with the adversary his equal – soon enough. He'd savor the wait.)

HORSES TAILS

Kunta's Bay has wandered in from the woods and is getting to know Dear Precious not far from their riders. She blusters,

'So what brings you to these parts. Hope you'll be staying around.'

Dear Precious neighs, 'No reason not to.' (editor note: You see, a horse's life is too short to *not* recognize their, lifelong, mate-at-first-sight.) Necks brush; manes mingle; hides quiver. Into the woods they retreat.

Luny Mum beams to Poppy Sol. 'Ah, summer love.'

ROPE TAILS

Thomas a-Hempis and Ezekiah's, Trick Rope, entwine as they lay by the campfire when their ropers trick supply is exhausted.

Trick Rope: 'I am factory-made. My kind is suited for shipwork, but the Reverend melded me for showmanship. Oh-how gaily we would entertain every Sunday.'

a-Hempis: 'I am hand-weaved by Kunta. The spirit of his tribe smolders within me.' (editor note: You see, no matter the way we've come to be, we're all cut of the same fiber.)

PEOPLE TRAILS

"Where, bound?" Kunta asks Ezekiah as they break camp. (How could either he or Ezekiah know — that *they*, cut so different — destiny weaves as one, for-forever, together.)

'He has a destination in mind,' Kunta realizes by Ezekiah's hesitant answer, 'but he does not know what to do at arrival.'

"Valhalla calls," Ezekiah bellows, finally. He's unable to muster courage to tell of his mentor being killed in the church fire there.

"The hallways to Valhalla are fraught with these dangers, Reverend." Kunta nudges miscreants with boot. "After we bury them I shall escort you. I also travel there."

"But Sir, Valhalla is on the Kentucky side. I would not advise..."

Kunta kicks at the campfire coals. "My soul is free. I fear no borders." He has heavily insured his bravado with papers of manumission he carries. He'd led an African printer north to freedom, who later crafted the documents. Still, nothing is perfect: Kunta is always wary.

    Reverend's words are short, at burial. "May they have peace." When Ezekiah turns, Kunta spits on Pig and Jocular's graves. They mount and ride south and board the Valhalla ferry-raft.
    Poppy Sol: 'Odd grouping; preacher and cowboy crusader.'
    Luny Mum: 'I'm seein' a strength they give one another.'
    Upon river – mutual accord.
    Thomas a-Hempis, to Trick Rope: 'After escaping the dregs, Kunta and I floated many weeks on the broken mast. Nearing a tragic end of our line we fortuned-upon a friendly whaling ship. It took years before we finally worked our way back to his village. Burned by slavers. All; gone. Kunta held me tight. Shaking body spoke to me that his desire for life was slipping.'
    Trick Rope: 'Yes. The reverend experienced that torment all-the-day, yesterday. He would have ended, all-his-days, if I hadn't, for the first time ever, slipped a knot; noose's deadly knot.'
    a-Hempis: 'Humans are fragile. Near our end, they may dangle. Kunta found strength; departed those sad ashes. To this land he came – for this is where, was said, slavers brought his villagers. So long ago. Surely mother, father, uncles, aunts long passed on. Still, has he hope – of finding Aleka, his sister.'
    --In the steady slosh of the Ohio against the ferry, Kunta hears Aleka's humming, as when she weaved cloth when they were little. In the teetering sounds of wooden freight boxes, he hears the tapping-together of her double-loop earrings as she swayed to the motions. Often he dreams…
    …of meeting a woman, hearing a rattle. He pushes aside braids – the most beautiful face. He touches earrings. "Where did you get these?"
    "They were carved, given by brother taken from me long ago. They are all I have of him."

"Aleka! We are re-united." Kunta pulls her to him. Dream shatters as the ferry lurches against the dock on the Kentucky side.

From atop a rolling hill just-inland Kunta views the church's devastation: the charred, leaning steeple, bastion-walls, now rubble. Sorrows, deep as those of when he entered his village, overwhelm him. The deceased minister was also Kunta's friend, his only real family, clandestine partner in delivering slaves to freedom. He was Kunta's hope of finding Aleka.

Kunta's shout is wrenching, "SPIRITS OF BLYTHE-ABWE; DELIVER ME FROM THIS WORLD'S PAIN!" Bay stands rigid, hoping the shout will help calm her faithful rider. a-Hempis coils tightly against Kunta's shoulder, gently vibrates assuagement from Blythe-abwe ancestors. ('Look onward, son. Sorrows of the living, they are but fleeting.')

Ezekiah steadies Dear Precious. He musters courage to, *not*, look from Kunta's pain, as, cowardly, he did Bonnie's. That moment, though just days away, seems a lifetime.

Kunta's face, earlier, so calm, is a maze of twitching muscles, throbbing blood vessels – a look of icy death. Ezekiah follows closely on Dear Precious as Kunta strides Bay toward ruins. Ezekiah realizes – he must now be the one to stay strong, must now be the *true*-saver, not the showman-saver from Sunday services.

Turt cruises the Ohio clutching Sea Line. His search is in vain. Claim of seeing Kunta was yet another Buzzard lie to shed him from the wharf-shack, Turt feels certain. When Turt hears the sloshing of the Valhalla ferry, he sniffs. Twenty-five years: Still he recognizes the pungency of Thomas a-Hempis.

Turt follows the ferry to its Kentucky landing. Passengers leave, no a-Hempis.

A TALE OF A MATCH MADE IN VALHALLA

Just the opposite of when he was a boy, haplessly grieving lost family midst village's ashes, Kunta immediately immerses himself into tearing down – to re-build an even sturdier sanctuary for runaways. Kunta's on Bay. Ezekiah's on Dear Precious. With a-Hempis and Trick Rope looped to saddle horns and lassoed to the church steeple and walls, they pull. Faces sweat rain. Horses flex. Stretching ropes groan. Structure, weakened by the fire, teeters, and screeches despairingly, then, walls come-thundering, tumbling, rumbling-down.

The flurry of activity salves Kunta and Ezekiah's pain-of-present; mutual-way of grieving for the man they equally loved. Simultaneously they resolve, 'We will continue his work.'

This is even before they would discover – the TREASURE beneath the floor.

TALE OF TURT'S WILD RIDE

The scent of a-Hempis lingers and Turt crawls from the water to follow it. He feels jittery with apprehension as he ranges the lush, shell-high bluegrass. He bolsters his hopes by telling himself, 'Where a-Hempis is. That is where Kunta will be. For the first time in my life – I thank you for something, Buzzard.' After what feels the longest walk of Turt's life, faintly, a soft breeze brings him the voice that often plays in his thoughts. 'Deeper now but, unmistakable…

…KUNTA!' Turt hurries crawl. Tears from anticipation stream onto his beak-snout.

When he reaches hillcrest he squints into the distance, sees the comforting sway of shoulder where, as forlorn shelling he rested. 'KUNTA!' He wants to trumpet out to announce his presence. Can't. Too choked-up.

So anxious to greet old friend! Walking is *toooo* slow, too delaying of his joy. There's a better way. He crawls to the side of a rock, tips on his side, quickly retracts snout and legs, and begins rolling, disc-like, down the hill. *'WHRR! SHHH!'* He peaks out and sees critters in his path, scatter. Though Turt is woozy from the dizzying speed, he's able, continually, to adjust trajectory to stay on line to spin into the churchyard. He *'POPS!'* hollow logs he bumps over and steers-clear of bigger-than-himself boulders.

Kunta and Ezekiah look up; barely see the wheel-like object crushing downward.

Glimpsing crucifix some faraway missionary had painted onto Turt, Ezekiah praises, "A sign sent from the, *'ABOVE'.*" For a moment he sounds little different from the fanatic-proselyte he was the night of the fire at Rrrose Heather's.

Kunta's eyes spark with Poppy Sol's fire. So startling is his shout – "TURT, MY FRIEND! AND SEA LINE!" that Bay and Dear Precious rear-up; nearly throw riders.

Into the churchyard Turt rolls, lands 'up-shell down'. Midst the self-made dust cloud he teeters, and stops. Kunta hugs emerging beak-snout. Turt closes eyes, savors touch. Never would he be long from that touch again. When he opens eyes, he's surprised seeing Dear Precious and rider from Hell Street.

'I am sorry our attempt to change him was for naught,' Dear Precious whinnies.

Turt sees what, so-close-to-rider, ride, is unable. A new passion burns in rider's look. Turt's sure it's brought on by Kunta. The Kunta, of now, inspires, as the Kunta of then, Turt's certain.

Men tie ropes onto shell and horses pull, righting Turt. *'Thud.'*

Kunta strokes his shell-village, caressing memories: of the village's dry-clay scent of potters' kilns; steady *'thuck-thucks,'* of weavers; of listening to his tribe's storytellers. Kunta parts waterfall curtain and sees himself squeezing Aleka's hand as cool mist stings their faces. The loving image invigorates him, quells more of his sorrow.

Turt blares excitedly when he catches his breath. Horses flinch.

"Lo, behold, my dear friend Turt," Kunta quietly exclaims. Looks lock. Their 25 years apart – now it's just a wink-blink. "I was certain my village would live-on with you, friend." Re-found joy causes Kunta's reminiscences to ramble. "I was aided by your ancestors, Turt. I caught one of their shells as I was being swept away from you. I was able to catch rain and put fish in it. That kept me alive until I was saved."

Turt hasn't time to consider how Kunta has changed, because a muffled cry comes from beneath the church's floor. Kunta and Ezekiah pull at the marble slab: Immoveable.

"We'll attach ropes, Ezekiah."

"Nowhere to tie."

Turt claws, and Dear Precious and Bay scrape hooves at the slab. All back away to give Turt room when they see he is succeeding. Prying beak-snout budges it. He anchors fin-claws into slight opening, uses force of shell to push in beak-snout. Just when it seems legs, shell or snout might crack, the marble inches from its mooring midst other slabs.

"Slide the ropes under. Watch your fingers," Kunta shouts to Ezekiah. They tie onto saddle-horns and prod, "Give it your all, Bay, Dear Precious." Horses pull.

Turt cinches ropes into a 'V', to create leverage. Gratingly, the slab moves.

TALE OF TREASURE

A room, 12 by 12, six feet deep appears. Kunta hadn't yet been told of its construction by other abolitionists. The passageway leading to the room collapsed during the fire. Laying semi-conscious, mouth near a vent tube that goes to where, no one can see, is an emaciated black woman. An anemic infant clutches drained breast.

"Come," Ezekiah calls. Dear Precious approaches.

"You steady me," Ezekiah tells Kunta. Ezekiah grasps Trick Rope, still tied to saddle-horn. Hand-under-hand, he lowers himself into the pit. Horse's hooves are unmovable.

You've descended Trick Rope from church rafters to your pulpit –

your heaven-descent to save congregation in hell – as a stunt for sinners by week who aspire to sainthood on Sunday. The pipe organ screams to announce your coming. Its player suddenly stops when a veiled woman cradling a small bundle approaches. Twin plumes horn from her hat. Despite custom-sewn, but austere long velvet dress, you know the, 'MADAM' for 'what' she is.

Semi-conscious new mother uses empty metal canteen as pillow. Closed eyelids twitch. Cheeks are hollow; lips blue. Flour-sack dress is threadbare, grayish-brown from a week's wear through swamp and woods- running from slave-catchers. Legs are a maze of scratches and scars. Delirious, she rants as the Reverend draws close. "Please Mistress. I beg you. Don't let Marster sell my baby when he or she's born." Ezekiah eases naked boy from her. The infant's eyes:

You've looked before into such eyes of innocence, saw, God, but refused to acknowledge Him.

"Does he live?" Kunta asks.

Ezekiah strokes tiny chest. "Heart beats. Praise God." Gently he raises him. Kunta clasps Turt's fin-claw and stretches to receive.

Rrrose Heather lifts the corner of a blanket and reveals the soft eyes of a newborn. "Baptize this innocent one, Ezekiah Bellows," *she demands, raising her veil. You feel the hate of Satan's brimstone burn in her wild Irish eyes.*

You can't bring yourself to look back at the swaddled spawn. You preach loudly, in full regalia of your righteousness: "Leave Madam. And take away what is surely one of your whure's bastards."

Some in congregation flinch. Stares lock on you as she edges close and whispers so only you hear. "I pity you for what you choose to believe, what you refuse to believe, and what your pious-pretense demands. May it not be too late for your soul. When you stop by the house next week, and I know you will, we'll see what can be done to save it."

She brushes past your deacons who have risen to remove her. She marches aisle toward the double doors. She looks at men who have attended – her – services – by weeknight. Today is Sunday morning though. They divert eyes. But you do not. Never again will you worship at her house, you vow, or allow the smoldering temptation of its sweet perfume to beckon you. By God's hand – this time you will succeed: You will quit Bonnie.

Outside church. Poppy Sol melts morning clouds and prisms LIGHT – PROUDLY – reds, maroons, yellow – through the stained glass windows. The colors cloak the out-of-place woman and her charge. Poppy's Sol's wink is for Rrrose only. 'They glare at ya, me' daughter. They, dressed for church in their staid, women so *pious* in their beliefs. Are their looks those of pity, hate or sorrow? Or prayerful? Admiring? Admonishing? Never care! Though they may be righteous for they'selves, they lack courage to share that good.'

Rrrose says to Sol. "So this damn way didn't work! "One day, your Rrrose, for Bonnie and the child's sake, will *make* Ezekiah Bellows accept the son."

* * *

Memories of four years before are vivid as the infant's innocent touch leaves yours and transfers to Kunta. Wasn't that other infant too, an innocent one! 'Why did you curse him? Why did you not touch him, feel HIS gentleness, HIS fragile newness, blamelessness! Why, Dear God, did I choose not to deliver him to YOU? Forgive me! Bonnie's death, all you have been through in the last few days makes you realize your mistakes. Please Lord! Help correct them.'

Kunta, as if he knows your thoughts, holds out child.

You moisten your thumb with spittle and press it to his tiny forehead. As you do, you imagine touching the other innocent. "Be wash in the Blood," you say penitently.

Kunta lay the infant on a blanket and snakes a-Hempis down to Ezekiah. He fashions a makeshift rope-gurney. 'Fine knotsman,' Turt thinks. When Ezekiah finishes he slides mother into it. She grasps Ezekiah's arm as Kunta slowly pulls. "First you take Mama away, Master: That hurt so. Losin' my chil' will kill me."

Ezekiah tries to ease her spirits. "You are with friends. No longer must you run."

Bay approaches infant who now shivers because he's away

from mother's warmth. She *'neighs'* to mother, bends neck and breathes gently onto and then gently licks son. His shaking stops.

A sense of fullness, never-before felt, courses through Bay's flanks. She feels the life of the foal that is beginning to live within her, from her relationship with Dear Precious that first night they met, drank from the stream, far from Kunta and Ezekiah's camp; then became one as Luny Mum discretely waned to let the winks of a sky-full of stars make merry the union.

Dear Precious sees a strange twinkle in Bay's eyes as she nurtures the tiny human. He *knows*.

His *'NEIGH'* vibrates proudly.

Kunta and Ezekiah lay mother on the cinders of the burned-out church's floor. "Be strong: For you are a daughter of freedom," Ezekiah says. Her hair, braided, twisted around her head, loosens. It coils down shoulders and dances alongside a-Hempis.

a-Hempis presses to it, holds tight, wanting to intertwine with it. Fibers quiver from excitement: Never before has a-Hempis met such a weave. A zebra knows her stripes, a worm, its male from female side. So a rope knows its special twists. 'There is something special about this human. Kunta will know what it is.'

In her delirium mother hums. *It is the same song Aleka taught you to weave by. That same weave you see in her hair, you realize, nearly 25 years removed from pirate ship Blythe-abwe-hold. It is the same one you unconsciously followed while weaving a-Hempis.*

As you hoist a-Hempis, mother's double-loop earrings 'click' as her head sways. You'd never mistake these symbols of the women of your village. Aleka was this age when you saw her last. Though the mother looks so like Aleka, you are certain she cannot be her.

Your searching has led you, all the way from your village to this place called Kentucky – you were sure this is where you'd find her because of all the stories you had heard of a woman that sounded so like it could be her, living at some nearby plantation. You wanted it so to be.

Kunta's brings the child to her. He slips babe into her arms;

she tries, in vain, breast-feeding.

Ezekiah milks the old preacher's cow pastured away from the fire. He sifts it from bucket into a leather water pouch and creates a nipple by boring a small hole into its wooden stopper. He leans it between mother and child. Child heartily nurses. Nipple slips. Turt takes makeshift gland in beak-snout, holds it in place; his first go at surrogate mothering.

'Sleep, nutrition, healing: That is what this daughter needs,' Ezekiah thinks. 'Soon real breast will replace pseudo.' He pillows her head on the blanket and begins spooning her liquids.

"You will have a home; and ones who will care for you," Kunta says to her as she sleeps. He massages her shoulders, arms and legs with a healing ointment the blind bayou woman gave him when he traveled the bayou searching Aleka. (Aboard dreg ship, Mariner told him all about Mama Lucy.)

"Say chil', that rope that with you strolls; I see its
magic in my soul.
Come to my cabin and Mama Lucy exchange you somma
her potions,
for some examin' time of your hemp's twist-n-roll."

Kunta spent weeks with Mama Lucy, learning things he would have from his grandmother – his village's healer. Before bidding farewell, Mama tosses catfish bones on her floor. She runs fingers over them to read their lay. "Only of your famlee do I see." Is your sister, sweet Aleka, as she struggle in this lan' a' ours ta be free. One day, my son. I see you, with she."

Before starting to re-build the church, Kunta and Ezekiah erect a tent for mother and child. Turt guards the entry. Young mother sleeps fitfully. After many days, Turt trumpets: 'She awakens, Kunta.' Turt thinks of his family on Jericho, how melancholy he'd be when he remembered them; how, now, that is changing: From no family so recently, to two. From now on – oh how swiftly he'll swim the Ohio commuting from the one family in Valhalla to the other in Cincinnati.

What, of the others, of that new Valhalla family – Dear Precious and Bay?

Bay had broken her news beneath the same winking stars in which she and Dear Precious had conceived. Equines now tower over Turt, peaking snouts into tent, quietly blustering to one another: 'He will be about the right size to ride our colt when the time arrives.'

The so-suddenly bright-faced mother holds her babe tight and calmly says to Kunta as he and Ezekiah enter. "You be who I think you be?" she asks Kunta.

Neither speaks: Needn't verify anything. Instantly, in her uncle, anyone can see her son. Deep eyes, sharp chin, sturdy cheekbones. She twists braids around her neck with one hand as she holds child to her now-flowing breast with other. "I named my baby after the brother mother so often spoke. I named him after you, Uncle. I named him Kunta."

Tears swell. You push at them. Dreams of family, at last, are real. You tremble from this so-long-gone-joyfulness, come-again. You are hopeful of what next she will say:

Of the place where you will find Aleka.

CHAPTER 35

You ask about her mother. She weeps. Be strong for her, Kunta. Your heart pounds, yearning to rip forth from your chest and fly to be with Aleka's; to beat forever entwined.

"Ten years gone since Mistress pledged Mama'd not be sold to a devil-owner downrive'. Every day I pray she kept her word. Still, I've this of her." Fingers tremble as she brushes them over braids and earrings. Then, she caresses little Kunta.

"What is your name, child?" Ezekiah asks as he sits on a stone beside them.

"Never again will I utter name Marster force on me. Or name of man he force on me to breed one more worker for him. I am Kaneshawa: Name Mama give."

Kunta holds her as she relives escape. "Ran when birthen'-time near. Good folks come on me. Bring me to the Valhalla Reverend. He deliver baby in the hiding place. He say, 'Kunta man'll come, take you north.' That's when I knew, Uncle. Brother, Mama wished so to see, was coming. Then the fire; I hear old Reverend call – 'Save them Lord.' He was trying to get me out…Can't 'member more."

"I shall pray daily God lead us to your mother; or light her way to Valhalla," Ezekiah vows.

(In the past days, before Kaneshawa regained

consciousness, and as they worked rebuilding the church, Ezekiah and Kunta had been planning:
'HOW CAN WE CONTINUE THE DECEASED REVEREND'S CAUSE?'

Now, all afternoon the trio talks, offering ideas, honing mutual passion inspired by the deceased Reverend of how to help those still enslaved. Poppy Sol's light softens. Day slips to night; appears Luny Mum's full glow. Onward, they plan, reconnoiter, verify the others thoughts.

Turt studies Bellows' expressions. Gone, is the fright he witnessed at the parade, replacing it, earnestness of mission.

Treading near a solution – one dangerous – Reverend Bellows begins sermonizing. He grasps Kunta's shoulder, then Kaneshawa's. His stare fixes on them. "Outside of us, only God will know the truth behind what we will be doing. To the world, we three shall appear, master; slaves. Always you must trust me. Always will I be true. This, I pledge. My word is my bond from God. As sure, as steady as Moses led *his* to a promised land – so shall we lead *our*."

Kunta and Kaneshawa look to one another. For a moment a mutual hatred for Reverend Ezekiah Bellows burns. Matters little, how he swears to his God. To the world, no matter anything else – they would be HIS. How, to satisfy their passion for freedom for Aleka and others, could they succumb to false-bondage?

Each knows others thoughts. 'Can one, freed, ever live again in enslavement – of any kind?'

Kaneshawa kisses son's cheek. She passes him to her uncle then walks to the nearby woods. From travel pouch, she takes a six-inch knife she vowed to kill herself with if taken by slave-catchers. She looks past Luny Mum to the light of Polara. "Mama, are you there watching or are you still of this earth? Mama…I must…" She takes the knife; cuts off braids. She removes earrings. These things from her mother; her heritage – she buries; so she'd not be recognized by anyone who knew her. Softly she says, "It's for the good of our new cause, Mama, for the good of our new family."

She returns to the men. Hair is bristly fuzz. She demands, "Say nothing. With voices or eyes." Kunta hugs, holds her for a long time. She stares at Ezekiah. "I will be your servant, Reverend, everywhere but in my soul."

THE TALE OF ONE EARLY UNDERGROUND RAILROAD SPUR LINE

(Editor's Note: Slaves often traveled alone to do 'marster's bidding.')

Slow-as-Turt, who's even slower-than-Moses, is Bay. Harnessed to buckboard and reined by Kunta via a-Hempis, she moseys dirt road toward a western Kentucky plantation.

'Aleka will be there,' Kunta thinks, with each new plantation he approaches. 'She'll recognize me, but say nothing.'

Poppy Sol's yawning rise sparks, pinkish-red, against hundreds of acres of tobacco plants, then smolders the dew from the leaves. Kunta breathes deeply, holding in his lungs the stinging, sweet wonder of nature's humidor. He feels so free in his voluntary servitude. Duty-bound to brothers and sisters in real chains, his soul soars. Delivering runaways, to safe houses north of the Ohio for the old Reverend he rode Bay straight, proud. Gathering slaves for the new Reverend in the south, he slouches on splintery seat, subservient.

Looking at the white-pillared mansion in the horizon, he pretends not to see the rifle-wielding overseer approaching on foot. Kunta's an actor playing a part. He begins singing in a contrived, almost-yelping *Halleluiah* timbre!

"Pharoah's daughter on de bank, little Moses in de reeds. She fishes him out wid a..."

"Whoa boy! Where you think yer headin'?" Overseer grabs a-Hempis at the Bay's snout and loops the rope around his fist. He aims the gun at Kunta's pretend-flinch face. Kunta knows overseer's thinking, 'No killin' 'nother man's property lest there's might good reason.' The six-foot tall white man is clean-shaven, pristinely kempt. Creased pants and pressed vest contrast Kunta's 'slave costuming – threadbare jacket, tattered chapeau, patched pants and boots. (Constant and mortal danger on ship engrained in Kunta a perpetual sense of courage-caution.)

On Kunta's lap is a bible. Into its leather cover, he's scroll-worked 'Moses-aleadin'-'is-people'. The image of his village women's braid snakes through it and points to a northerly 'promised lan'-a-milk-n'-honey'. He inscribes it into all Ezekiah's bibles he delivers to slaves. Quickly glanced, it is a picture, pleasing. Examined, it is a guidepost to freedom.[32]

"You 'def, boy. I wanta' know where yer headin'?"

"Ah is Reverend Ezeki' Bellow shepherd-boy. I's on his mission," Kunta says with absurd argot and pretend-cower. He sees his *fools'* crescent smile in overseer's spit-shine boots.

("Boots for kicken' a relcalictrant neg' or negress who don't pick their share," the overseer loves telling newly-bought arrivals.)

Kunta raises bible and thumps it with his knuckles. "Ah's deliverin' the good word for the good Reverend, suh. For the Reverend's dark flock." He motions, eyes diverted, to an open-lidded crate of bibles behind his seat. If he came across Aleka, or maybe a runaway, he could slip them into the crate's false bottom and smuggle them to Valhalla.

Kunta clenches jaw, concealing momentary grit of the degradation he again feels – of enslavement to Cookie. He hates this overseer he knows nothing of yet knows everything of, hates him as much as he hated Cookie.

"Hey, boy. It'd save me a heap a hasslin' before breakfast if I just blow yer brains out now."

a-Hempis doesn't want to test the overseer's brag. What he does now will give Kunta a chance to defend himself if overseer's intent on firing. He tightens around overseer's hand as Bay tenses snout. "Ow. Son-of-a-bitch." He pulls away,

---

[32] At this point in the latter half of the 1820s, few, if any whites knew of the secret codes and cryptic maps woven in quilts, painted on barns, carved into trees, that runaways and their abettors utilized to successfully navigate to a free state, territory, or Canada.

lowers gun and shakes reddening fingers.

Bay becomes jittery. She kicks-up dust. 'Can't let anything happen to Kunta. He must be there when I foal to see our pony galloping beside Dear Precious and me for the first time. Must see him when little Kunta makes him his horse.' (Bay and a-Hempis have varying plans for different scenarios. If Kunta's ever set for-a-whippen', a-Hempis would convince the leathery bullwhip to soften its slashing – by promising some of a-Hempis sought-after scent. If Kunta's hung by his own rope, and, on his own horse, a-Hempis would slip from tree limb, then Bay would gallop through memorized bramble pathways she has traveled through that no hound, man, nor other equines, could figure out and follow. Each situation so different – they would observe Kunta's lead; follow it.)

"Ahm sure mistress-'a-house wouldn't want the spreading of our Savior's savin'-word be slowed." Kunta allows a mere tinge of slyness to stain his words. No matter how little the man thinks of him, he won't want black blood splattered all over mistresses '*Word*.'

Overseer rubs hand. "Gimme your papers." He examines documents that include intricately scrolled documents Kunta has created to show that body, if not soul, belongs, without-question, to Reverend Ezekiah Bellows. Kunta has, well hidden in a place not far from Kaneshawa's buried braids – equally-meticulously forged documents signed by Reverend, that show he, Kaneshawa and Little Kunta *are* free humans. Overseer drops the papers onto Kunta's lap and opens crate. "Pretty fancy covers for folks born for picken'. None of 'em read – least better not be able, or I'll see to it they never do again."

"Well suh, when Mistress not a readin' to 'em, to help calm 'em for you…they can meditate on the cover – calms 'em even more for you when they're in the field…"

"I got whippings to do that, boy." He pats the bullwhip that rings around his belt.

"Got lots a' deliveries for the Reverend today, suh!"

"Sounds like whip-lip you're deliverin'." He quickly decides against any action because his hand aches. He looks at pocket watch, gift from his Kentuck pappy; 'overseer 'afore me – and his, 'afore him – taught me all 'ah needa' to know about treatin' negs'.' "They're due to crops. Swing a wide berth from the house, head straight to the quarters and don't snail about."

Outside the shanties, shadowed gray by the white mansion, your heart, ready to burst free from your chest to fly to be with Aleka, coldly sinks. Nowhere is she among the dozens of ragged spirits, blank-eyed from the day-by-day tobacco sameness. None read, but all smooth their hands over your cover design. 'Follow its path,' you want to shout. 'You will discover routes to escape your Egypt – you'll find sympathetic Moses' ready to help.' You begin to preach-hint, as you stand amongst your people. "Close your eyes and meditate on the, PATH. You'll be delivered to the Promised Land."

You become a mandatory quiet when you see the plantation owner in his creamy suit and string tie approach, followed by overseer and the field guards. "Let me see that," owner says.

You shan't look into his face to decipher what he's thinking when he examines the cover. You realize he's interested only in leafing through the pages for contraband. Overseer and guards do the same with other bibles. He drops the book at your feet. "Yes siree," he says to the air as if you don't exist, "delivered to a promised land, of tobaccy. All right everybody. To the fields."

For emphasis, only a few feet from a dozen men and women, he cracks whip. It 'snaps', stinging ground. Overseer: "Your heard your Massah. To …"

'Does anyone here see hope?' you want to shout as they shuffle away. You pick up the bible. As you think, 'they are too beaten to see,' a burly-chest man and petite wife, with two clingy sons under age 4 and a baby, stop briefly. The only difference between him and the others: His eyes are afire – with desire to find the Path. When no one is looking, he puts hand to your shoulder. No words. But his expression says, "Thanks brother. Somehow, we will see you, and soon."

'Yes! There's always hope. Aleka! Your brother's coming for you: Have hope."

CHAPTER 36

One may wonder: When Turt's not rollin' down a Kentucky hill, strollin' a parade, helpin'-out a flounderin' Carper and founderin' James; or when he's not out-'n-about gettin' tattooed – just what, with his very long time on this earth, does he do? ...to make just a small corner of his world, right...

COMES NOW A TALE OF ONE SUCH NIGHT

Turt tugs a-Hempis. One end is in beak-snout, the other attaches to a wooden raft he pulls up the Ohio. Bobbing head is barely visible. 'Less clench please,' vibrates a-Hempis. Turt obliges. They've made this trip often since their Valhalla reunion.

Aboard is Kunta, dressed in dark colors– to be inconspicuous to trolling slave-catchers. Turt is a low-gear motor, freeing Kunta to check for sandbars with a 20-foot pole. Crowded beside Kunta is the family from the tobacco plantation. Mother cradles baby. Father grasps toddlers' hands. Gaunt looks reflect the family's turmoil, their hell-on-this-earth, of the past weeks:

Hell's eternal hours –

'Quick! Hide here': Shivering in bogs to fool the overseer's

bloodhounds.

'Hurry! Crawl here': Crowding beneath stinking manure wagons.

'Climb up; fast!' Days spent hiding quietly in haylofts without food. Slightest stomach growl or barn-board *'creak'* might be their giveaway.

'Run! Run!' At midnights they streak between safe houses, stopping only to sip crick water before reaching – 'Praise on High', Valhalla!

Kaneshawa tends their physical needs – hot baths in the safe room Kunta and Ezekiah doubled in size as they finished rebuilding the church and parsonage. She burns tattered, stinking apparel and alters second-hand ones donated by northern sympathizers. Rested, renewed, fed, the children play with little Kunta, Turt, Sea Line.

Reverend Ezekiah – he tends adults' spiritual needs: "HE came with you this far. HE shall beacon the rest of your way." Adult Kunta enters through a hidden doorway and provides an earthly realm to their journey. "I – shall take you to Cincinnati. There, others will direct you."

Before Cincinnati happens, their hazardous river journey must continue:

Luny Mum stays behind clouds so this raft part of their trek is inconspicuous. Kunta keeps rifle close. He knows the best routes to avoid slave-catchers; but, always, a risk of detection.

Turt's amphibious senses tell him what Kunta cannot know:

Coming toward them in the darkness are three humans, in a float just smaller than the one Kunta captains. Turt sniffs: Same *butcher-ous* scent of the pirates; same acrid odor of the powder that makes their killing weapons explode.

No avoiding collision; so Turt quickly devises diversion. He releases air from shell pockets with a slow, reflexive, pumping action and takes in water. Still clenching a-Hempis, he submerges, dropping to the Ohio's mucky floor. He anchors fin-claws into mire, uprooting a couple of giant sleeping catfish – nearly his size. 'Sorry gents.'

a-Hempis tenses as Turt's anchorage jolts raft to a stop. Kunta uses the pole to block the passengers from tumbling into the water. 'Something's wrong.' He grabs rifle, whispers, "Hold the children." Parents pull them closer.

Suddenly: 'THUD!' A dinghy collides with them. Luny Mum peaks curiously above clouds. Kunta notes three gun-wielding men — a threadbare trio. They're stooges for plantation owners. Kunta always has plans for encounters, but is caught-off-guard by the chance collision. Move, even slightly, he knows he'll be shot. He positions his rifle inconspicuously along his leg and hopes the darkness keeps them from seeing it.

"Looks we hit a jackpot," comes a drumble from one slave-catcher-stooge.

You wait for the moment your amphibious senses tell you the enemy float is right above you. You purge water from your shell pockets, hunker down, prepare to launch upward and ram the interlopers. 'NOW!' You push at riverbed: No go. Fin-claws lock into the mire. 'Damn the mud!' Looking like a two-leg doing push-ups — you pump, cannot dislodge. You'd finally found your old friend. Might lose him just as fast.

Now, catfish: They're dumb, but persistent. After being scooted from their place, they stay close, flopping behind seaweed. They emerge and with winks and nods agree they'll help if you return their 'spot'.

Mud swirls as they burrow beneath you. Fin-claws dislodge. You rocket. You twist; turn, unable to keep balance. It's a bullet-straight ride. Heart pounds. You tuck-in neck and beak-snout, but let legs dangle because they act as quad-rudders, helping control direction. Your nerves tingle. You feel water pressure might ratchet-away your top shell and you'll have to spend life water-bound. That notion vanishes when you strike something.

A brittle, splintering sound: Turt has slammed the dinghy's hull. It *'whooshes'* above water. The slave-catchers fly, erratically firing rifles. Bullets *'puck'* into the Ohio. "Blasted Go…Da…Son-of-a …" Vulgar shouts are barely coherent as they get dunked. Water splashes raft, soaking Kunta and the

family. Boys, "WHEE", in delight.
   The men grasp their knives and swim toward the raft. Luny Mum comes from behind clouds. Seeing one of the men in her moonlight, Kunta points his rifle at him while the father, sons seizing his legs, grabs the pole and pokes at another to keep him away. "We'll take you. Mark my word," yells the one Kunta guards. The other slowly raises his knife above the water. Just as he readies to throw, Luny Mum glints against it so the father sees. He slaps it away.
   "Ow, Goddamit," the man squeals.
   The third one had swum underwater, to behind the raft. Unseen, he boards. The baby, startled by his movement, whimpers. Turt hears. His protection instincts activate. He skims through the water. As the man readies to begin slashing their backs, Turt cranes neck and grabs his ankle, snapping it easily as a twig. He drags him, kicking, screaming, son-a-bitching – "some-un get the Goddam 'ting off me."
   He's on Turt's surf now. Turt pulls him away, looses, and then lets a current do its work. It sweeps him downstream. Turt disposes the others similarly, seeming to wave mock 'so-long chumps' with fin-claw.
   Boys cheer wildly. Mother shushes them. Her face mirrors a contentment she's never before felt. She looks onward, believing she can almost reach-out, touch the freedom her children soon will know. They pass around a canteen. Kunta takes one of the boys on his shoulder and the father does the same for the brother.
   "Look straight on, son." Kunta points. "Soon you'll see Cincinnati's lights." Kunta knows what their mother is thinking. He has seen it in so many others he's transported. He whispers to her, "Soon you'll touch freedom's beacon."
   The boys grin when they first see the city's glitter. Despite what they've experienced, they yet possess smiles of innocence, something long lost to parents.
   You tighten beak-snout to a-Hempis. You pull, and the journey continues. How many more will you make? Which might be your last? You put those scary thoughts in your shell's furthest recesses. You replace

them with the good thoughts: Soon you'll see Carper, Ol Tom, and Mariner. You can't wait for the look on Mariner and Kunta's faces when they see each other again.

* * *

The next day

THE MAKING OF THE LEGEND OF WHAT HAPPENED DOWN-RIVER

Poppy Sol watches as dockworkers seine two of the stooges to safety. Poppy listens, amused, to one of their accounting the fate of the third.

"All've sudden a Goliath catfish nabs Moe by the 'u-don't-wanna-knows. Bites herself off his prizest possession 'afore she pull him under – fer what porpoise? He didn't have the part left that coulda 'satisfied her.'"

'That's what the blimen' blow-hard tales to those that save 'ims,' Poppy Sol tells Luny Mum.

Mum remembers seeing it all, and grins. 'Twas but a mere submerged limb did the pulling on 'ims.'

'Must of drove the other stooge batty, Mum, watching his slave-catcher mate drown. Funny thing, as I blink from high-sky I see, those that done the savin', they're not buying the blowhard's sale. Instead, they're takin' a shine to batty's *true* blitherens' – about how a giant shelled creature be passengerin' humans. Maybe the ye ol blow-hard's *big fish* made it sound possible?' Poppy imitates blitherer. 'The…the shelled one's tail be hundred foot if it be an inch.'

Mum shimmers. 'Twas a taut, extended a-Hempis what seemed a hundred foot tail. Harmless as can be.'

As the smuggling of humans to freedom continues in coming decades, the legend of the abolitionist-creature grows; making future slave-catchers wary of the beast; and preoccupied, with what might appear from nowhere to attack them. Because of it, many-a-runaway gets away.

CHAPTER 37

You can't just trumpet out to Mariner, 'Kunta's alive! We're working together.' Can't exclaim, 'Kunta's found a family. Soon we'll add Aleka.' Nor josh, 'After we find all-a'- hissen kin, maybe hissen'll help dredge-up some of my lost shellatives.' It will take time. You'll find a way for you to communicate it. So – for next three years – Turt merrily stops by the wharf-shack to visit after freedom-swims, while Kunta continues freedom-escort overland.

A mini-TALE OF A CITY'S ENLIGHTMENT

Cincinnati: *noisily* growing by meets and bounds, rods, chains, and stakes that surveyors keep extending outward to accommodate the influx of populous– seeking jobs (shipping), commerce (retail), and pleasure (Rrrose Heather's). *Quietly* the city becomes hub to the abolitionist fervor our Valhalla voyagers help stir. Most-profoundly affected by this movement will be young minister Lyman Beecher's forever-scribbling teen daughter, Harriet.[33]

---

[33] Harriet's epic anti-slavery tome prompted Abraham Lincoln's greeting: "So you're the little lady who started this great war."

A 'mini-er' TALE OF A NEW LAD

Few things change at the wharf-shack, always the cryptic Rorschach test of disorganization. Mariner's books march from shelves, become fortress where Carper retreats to practice reading and storytelling on Ol Tom and Turt. Carper's calling himself Blackjack now: A miniature Buzzard slicker, wearing creased black slacks, waistcoat, and silk shirts sewn by Rrrose Heather's ladies. Sea Line is his long string tie that he bows in the dozens of knots Mariner teaches him. He sports the latest in wavy New Orleans-style haircuts given by Rrrose.

Contrast: Mariner. Dungarees seem never to change or be changed, nor, ever-graying sailor shirts. He stands them in the corner when he goes to bed and ruminates, 'Oh the troubled seas Carper'll sail iffen he keeps parrotin' Buzzard.'

THE TALE OF KUNTA'S SECOND LONG-IN-COMING REUNION

Turt and Kunta land their passengers in Cincinnati. Kunta escorts them to safe houses; Turt swims to the wharf-shack. Carper shrieks when he enters. "See Turt's shell, Mariner. There's a new addition to Kunta's village. Its gotta mean he's found…"

Mariner trembles when he sees the fresh, beautiful carving: Mother, caressing child. Mariner's shout quakes the wharf-shack, "Poseidon be thanked."

Humankind's ever-flow of slavery, so damnable, but, so far, un-dam-able, ferries *hopes* for millions of reunions. Seldom is there landing. Most of those, hopes — they break against life's rocks.

Mariner thinks of these once-in-one's-lifetime precious reunions as he props himself by leaning on Turt's shell. He swigs stump juice to calm himself.

Turt licks his arm. 'I felt the same when I saw Kunta again.'

"You're crying, Mariner." Carper begins crying too. He

knows Mariner isn't glummed. So strongly bonded are their emotions – each feel what the other does. Carper takes Mariner's hand.

Ol Tom mews and rubs their ankles. (Every alley cat senses that 'cat', something lost then found pride, like when coming upon a litter sired along-the-way but forgotten about 'til now.)

Carper pleads. "How can we find Kunta, Mariner? How would he know how to find us?"

"I wisht I could write. *Aaugh*..." Mariner growls to a stop; embarrassed. He massages his fingers and amends admission. "I means, wisht I could *right* me rhuemtasm'. I could add somethin' to Turt's shell to let Kunta know we're around."

Carper smiles – a one-of-kind understanding. "I could just write, so you don't strain your hand, Mariner: Something like – 'Cincinnati pier, come see the Mariner, Kunta.'"

"That's the last port we can dock. 'Members my spoutins' of being ship slaves."

Carper watches Mariner's stare burn with the memory.

"Parts 'a this country still no better'n one big slave clipper for Kunta. He won't want no one knowin' his comins', goins'." Fingers drum on Turt, calculatin'. "I got it Carper: The word of the drawer's ink. 'Bout the onliest one's'll know how to read it are me, Kunta and Turt."

More calculatin': rub of whiskery chin. "Don't suppose Buzzard and Rrrose Heather would – too bloody for 'em in their memories. Now Captain Polly might. But she's got too much critter-sense, 'n Rrrose and Buzzard people common sense, than to waste their times squawkin' or talkin' outta turn."

Mariner instructs. Carper draws. Turt's the canvas. The *'scritch, scritch,'* of pen tip against shell is soothing to Turt. He cranes neck, nodding approval that the rendering – an all- 'ariggly-toed, blood-oozin' walk-off – is accurate. It is leashed. A stick figure of Capt'n heels it. "Squid ink yer usin', Carper. Last long enough so Kunta'll see, be led here by Turt when the time's right."

Ol Tom one-eyes the work, as a critic. He *'hacks'* acclaim.

Mariner says, "Right good, Carper. We three decree: Yer a storyteller in any ocean a' words, pictures, or rhymes you might choose to sail. Now, we wait."

The day comes: Kunta seems continually to strain neck upward in anticipation as he walks beside Turt to the wharfshack. When Mariner comes out, Kunta's gaze shifts downward. The towering man he remembered is a foot shorter than he is.

Mariner's look moves, from just above the pier, toward the sky. Thin boy-of-sea, is now, strapping man-of-land with a determined face. Gleaming leather attire grasps snugly to his muscular frame that explodes, with each movement, total self-assurance.

Turt watches Mariner and Kunta's faces as their looks meet at a mid point, just before their arms and bodies lock. Turt will always remember the crescent smiles of their eyes – the same smile he saw in Kunta and Kaneshawa's eyes a few years before; one he hopes to see again – if Kunta finds his Aleka. It's a smile he hopes someone sees in his eyes, if he finds another Trumpeter.

Turt's beginning to get the desire to go looking again for one of his tribe, that itching burning want to just depart, spend months, maybe years, searching.

That Day will come. Now he is busy with his Valhalla to Cincinnati commutes looking after Kunta; and at Valhalla seeing to Little Kunta, Kaneshawa, even Ezekiah at times, and the runaways; then Mariner and Carper when he reaches Cincinnati. *Whoo!* Humans are fragile; need such care. Lucky there is Bay, Dear Precious, a-Hempis, Trick Rope, Sea Line, Ol Tom, and Captain Polly to help: And down Tehas way, Prick Lily and Liege Leather for Golden Boy.

Mariner pulls Kunta inside. Kunta breathes deep the cooking. "Ahh! I haven't smelled those sweet scents since the galley days, Mariner."

"Dock yer weary river-legs in me' stateroom, Kunta. I've a carafe of stump juice to toast the returning hero." Mariner introduces Carper as he emerges from his book fortress. "Calls 'isself Blackjack. I call him Carper 'til he 'kin come up with a right-proper name. Carper and Turt, they go way back."

As Mariner excitedly yammers, Carper shakes Kunta's hand and stares wonderingly up at the artisan of whom he's heard dozens of ship stories. He remembers each. He tells them to dockworkers often as they gather around him at lunch breaks. A cup, to catch coins for the entertainment fee, is always at his feet. *('You keep reminding yourself: Tell Kunta's tales, but NEVER give away his comin's-goin's.')*

Kunta says, "Still hard for you to catch a breath midst all your spinning, eh Mariner."

"Jaw-jackins' me 'n the Buzzard's nature, Kunta. Man's gotta have 'least *one* vice." He swigs, pours; swigs again, again. "We kept those pie-rates off guard with the walk-off tales."

"Were not always exactly tales though, were they?"

Mariner grins. "Nope, 'spose oh-so-bloody-foot not."

They sit at small table throughout the afternoon visiting ship times – what happened since – finding Kaneshawa, Little Kunta, sadly, not Aleka yet. Decades may have passed; tens of thousands of miles both Mariner and Kunta have travelled, but so close in spirit they have stayed. It is like only seconds-ago that they were man and boy in galley, trusting completely the other.

Almost nightfall: They arrive at Kunta abetting runaways. Mariner's thoughts sail to the realms of freedom he dreamed of during their enslavement. He imagines captaining to those very same realms, the *anonymous* souls of whom Kunta tells.

* * *

'What comes next twixt the Mariner and Kunta,' Rrrose Heather tells James, 'be somethin' bound to happen – knowing the Mariner's sense of right and wrong.' Hardly has James time to hear Mama Lucy echo those sentiments, because, he's so-curious to know, that he is leaving Turt's shell, exiting the Lindian Woods, and entering the wharf-shack.

TALES OF THE FICTION HOUSE

* * *

A TALE OF LONG-AGO MUTINEERS JOINING AS CIVIL WARRIORS

Mariner stomps the planked floor. Shelved conch shells rattle. Unseen James steadies them. "Riitch' here in this spot Kunta: We'll install a trap door to the river. Poor souls can ascend from the raft unseen, up to the wharf-shack's glorious freedom."

"Even when Luny Mum and Polara shine their brightest," speculates Kunta. "A perfect port!"

Though Carper plays with Turt and Ol Tom in his fortress, he's listening to Kunta tell of the transport of living souls, from bond to freedom; of safe, kept-secret places for them, right in his city. Carper's imagination races when they mention making their wharf-shack a *'safe-place'.*

You eavesdrop on Carper as he whispers to critter-mates of expanding his fortress.

"I could sleep the little boys here. I'd tell 'em tales they'd never forget. Ol Tom, you'll act out the animal parts and me the human. Turt, you'll need rest after your journey so you'll join the audience. I could teach the little girls to tie Sea Line into bows. I'll Dude-up the young fellows in my duds so they look keen on their journey further north. I could… I could…"

It is the beginning and you, the future Raji Singh, the former James, are here seeing the person, Carper, becoming James Thaddeus 'Blackjack' Fiction – future abolitionist publisher – mover of men, woman and children already free in their souls, to be free in their bodies. You are here, where your Fiction line begins – to see why your great-great grandfa's long-in-coming chosen name has such respect here and at other points of freedom along the road of history.

Cherish it. Never forget. It is a gift, from all those, real, imagined who have watched over you, and still do.

Satisfied now, back to the woods for you – to find out how Rrrose Heather knows so much about this important day. But wait, just one more whiff of the wharf-shack — ahh! The smell of freedom; fresh as the woods.

"This Reverend you work with, Kunta?" Mariner questions, "Sounds like a good, honest man. Whyen't he ever come back up Cincinnati way?"
"Never says. *Something* keeps him at the church. Like he is doing some penance. His being there, it's good for Kaneshawa and little Kunta, and he's present to hide arriving runaways."
Mariner leans over, interrupts, whispering so Carper doesn't hear. "Is his name...?"
Mariner's look diverts to Carper. Kunta's follows. Kunta hadn't taken time to study the boy. Now he does, and sees, Ezekiah: same black eyes, hair, gently arching brow, flattened chin; same diligence with many books, as Ezekiah with his, just one. As resemblance and mannerism told of Kaneshawa being Aleka's daughter, so to, does Carper's, as Ezekiah's son.
What will you do with that information, Kunta? What must you do for a son and father? Even though son has had the best father for him for years. You know what you will do.

And now, three know his lineage.

Comes-a-rapping from the wharf-shack's outside wall. Enters the first person to see Carper-Blackjack — on the day she delivered him. "Beautiful Rrrose Heather," gushes Kunta.
"K...K...Kunta," she stammers in a shock of joy, excitement, wonderment. Barely visible wrinkles web from sides of her eyes as she smiles up at him. They grab and hold each other tight. Tears streak her rose-petal-pink face; his, fall atop thick bouffant of still jet-black hair of surrogate ship mother. But, oh-so-low-cut silk gown she'd just purchased in Memphis shows she is mother only to her 'whures.'

'Odd lit-'el family,' reflects setting Sol as the last of his daylight disappears from one wharf-shack porthole. 'Think Kunta and Turt will unite them with Valhalla kin, Mum?'

Luny Mum, rising, glints through the other porthole. 'Indeed, hmm. Then Turt'll extend it down Tehas way, to include our Golden Boy and complete the circle.'

BEGINS THE STRANGE TALE OF RRROSE'S WITHERING? NEVER!

To some, in the coming months and years, Rrrose' actions are a puzzle "for a woman of, *business*". "It flies in the face of logic," someone comments.

"Hhrrmph!" from another. "Where's the profit? She's lost her senses."

They see only consequences. Rrrose veils her actions. Even she doesn't fully understand her motives for suddenly, fully, embracing fate. 'Hang the consequences; it's for the sake of what is *right*.' Maybe it was from experiencing, seeing, the worst that could happen – (on the ship, then later with Bonnie); that she joins Kunta and Mariner in a new, hardly talked-of façade of flesh trade: This one – *"no charge for the service."*

* * *

Rrrose's brogue morphs to Tennessee drawl: "Ya all be gettin' in, gettin' to work, hear me."

Kunta herds a husband, wife, dressed as butler, maid, to the back of Rrrose's white-pillar *'high society'* Memphis bordello. 'Just-in'-from-the-delta couple wears white gloves to hide field-worn hands. Kunta snaps a-Hempis, who is today, a pseudo-whip.

a-Hempis cracks lightening-swift and loud against the sidewalk as Kunta shouts. "Serve Miss Rrrose well or you'll be hired-out to share-croppers." Whenever he performs this fake ill-work Kunta thinks of Quill Head – an enslaver of his *own* race – and he despises himself for appearing, to most of the world, the same.

"Always stay two bluffs ahead of your 'marks'." Rrrose Heather thinks about what Buzzard always says. "Keeps them off-kilter. Buys you time to continually adjust your flight path."

To help insure none would ever expect her to be a "damned *abolitionist*," time for a Buzzard-like bluff: Boldly Rrrose strokes the cheek of this, her muscular and all-in-leather cowboy-ish pseudo head servant – for all passers-by to observe. Hang the consequences for a white woman in south, America, 1830's – if it comes to that: Appearance, only matters. She has prepared for, and is prepared for any fate her chosen thorny path may lead.

'Special favor to herself,' some sidewalkers wickedly think. Others; brows furrowing: *'Welll!* The audacity. The temerity. Any other woman and neg in Dixie 'd be strung up. Why's the law-keepers allow such...' But the more pragmatic: 'One may pleasure oneself as one chooses when the poly-tissions are in her purse.' (That Kunta might receive a bullet in the head at any moment; Kunta had prepared for long-ago – aboard ship.)

What less-conspicuous safe houses for runaway slaves south of the Ohio and along Mississip, than Rrrose's string of whurehouses? Also, she can observe firsthand Ezekiah's actions when she travels through Valhalla. Queen-like, she will decide his fitness for his sons in the future. But, so un-Rrrose-like; not taking into consideration future changes in the sons.

CHAPTER 38

A TALE OF TWO STALKERS

James reclines atop ever-wary Turt. Despite the protector's shushing trills, James chatters incessantly – to Carpier who walks nearby. The soothing '*scrish*' of his fin-claws brushing the ground relaxes Turt, enables him to concentrate on the half-human – half-beast stalker who appeared on the beach at his journey's start. (That it could be Lazarus Bontez Thibidioux, Turt never dismisses.) He considers those in the past who have plagued generations of Fictions: *Gator-man; Kidnapper; Buggerer-man, Thief.*

Poppy Sol winks: 'I'll be sayin' goodnight to you soon, blokes.' Surroundings begin to darken.

The last of the food given our travellers by Rau and Rue is gone. This poor section of the Lindian Woods, so picked over by creatures and humans, bears little to sustain travellers. Turt hears rustling sounds and is certain a second stalker, that recently joined their parade, a starving tiger, will sooner than later attack.

Sea Line stiffens around Turt's neck in anticipation.

Turt can only keep moving and stay ready. He nears a bark-stripped tree. Up high; cherry-like berries. He butts the trunk.

A dozen fall. He tests – pit-less, sweet. He calipers some in beak-snout, twists neck, and slowly drops them in James' hand so he won't gorge.

"Mmm. Good. Like one?" James asks Carpier.

'You enjoy. A most important errand have I.' With a barely-audible, *'pop'*, Carpier disappears. Calico is in his place. She flits behind a tree, becomes temptress tigress – orange, smooth, sleek – to try to lure away ravenous male.

Berry juice streams James' cheeks, *'plips'* onto shoulders.

Turt scans the forest-scape. He knows the eerie lore of the region they enter. *Can things get any worse?* It's said, amongst animals, that some of the two-legs here pleasure in holding their catch, skinning them alive, especially turtles and terrapins and the like – which Turt is, the like – and the bigger the better, which, Turt is. Turt pictures hundreds of hands lifting him, digging into his fresh-cracked shell.

They approach the outskirts of a village. A sign meaning nothing to Turt or James reads, 'KALAMBA: ½ km'. Luny Mum casts her soft glow on thatched roofs. James crinkles nose and savors dinnertime's spicy scent. Turt knows he must ignore lore and enter to get James help.

Close-by tiger knows he can't let meal get much closer to the lair of the dangerous two-legs. 'Be gone FEMALE,' he tells Calico, ignoring her purring, pawing overtures. He turns his back.

'POP!' She's butterfly again, flitting onto another plan.

Tiger's suddenly piercing scream, warning, 'THE PREY IS MINE,' vibrates saplings.

Turt flinches. James wails. He crouches, clutching Turt's neck. Turt sees the lithely stalking, 400-pound beast emerging from the underbrush. Cushiony paws caress twig floor. Joint muscles flex beneath creamy yellow fur. It wrinkles with every move.

40 feet away. 30. 20. 'AH, HOW I DO LOVE TENDER YOUNG TWO-LEG MEAT.'

Turt's nature is to fight any comers, but his first duty is to the little Fiction, so he creeps on. Suddenly there is no choice. Tiger pounces. Turt bucks-off screaming child and bares his fin-claws. Sea Line whips-outward, to help, in some way or other.

* * *

"A LONE CHILD WILL ARRIVE FROM THE SEA; BRINGING PEACE AND HEALTH."

Some say Carpier relayed this prophecy from Nardesha to the Lindian people moments before he died. Rau and Rue believe it. Most do. The TIGERMAN believes.

TALE OF THE TIGERMAN

On the beach – 72 hours before
– just after Turt surfs James to shore – the stalker watches from behind Bashri Raku wreckage. 'It's Turt,' he says to himself, certain the land-sea creature doesn't know he's there. After Turt and the boy enter the woods, he rifles through the trunk's soggy contents. With the Bowie knife, anxiously he cuts away the plastic that kept the box containing the Book of Carpier dry. Kunta's tigress grrs. Pachyderm toots. He opens it.

Calico flits out. 'Blessings to you who bring release from cocoon.'

She flutters against his cheek as he says, "I shall protect this for you, old friend Calico, until the time is right to present it to the young Fiction to protect – as only a Fiction can."

'Indeed. That is most appropriate,' Calico flutters. She flies to join Turt and James entering the woods.

The Book's pages are crisp, its leather-cover ever gleaming. He clutches it, kneels. Wiry, gaunt of face 70 year old Balu Baiku does this to praise the one Glorious, Always-Good, Goddess Nardesha. 'SHE has sent boy and creature,' Balu Baiku is certain.

There are thousands of religions throughout Lindia. At the nearby village of Kalanza, where Balu departed at 16 and never returned - it's barely an hour walk from ½ km Kalamba - there is Nardesha. One of Her many gentle messages is 'co-exist, all living things'.

'Of a child...' she prophesied. 'He shall arrive, alone, on the shell of a monstrous sea creature.' Village elders always interpreted this to mean the "ONE" would arrive in their village cradled in a large sea shell washed ashore alongside a giant albacore, or swordfish, "during the most-powerful typhoon ever" – since no ordinary typhoon could ever reach their inland village.

Balu Baiku holds tight to boyhood beliefs though he has lived on six continents, seen, experienced what would take most a dozen lifetimes.[34]

Now, so near the village of his youth, he's certain this is the "ONE" chosen by Nardesha to affirm Carpier's words: 'A LONE CHILD WILL ARRIVE FROM THE SEA...' 'HIS JOURNEY MUST BE MADE WITH THE BAREST OF ASSISTANCE.'

While still on the beach, Balu strips shirt, pants, sandals; slips on skin-tight golden shorts: No wrinkles on hairless frame. From knapsack, he takes a can of theater paint. He yellows himself. Erratically shaped cranial plates on his baldhead, akin to canyon ridges in miniature, he shades to resemble that geography – to captivate audiences: for he is an entertainer. He believes his performing honors Nardesha.

Balu Baiku, last remaining of Lindia's ancient, once revered, TIGERMEN. For centuries, Lindia's troubadours, they made-up as tigers and roamed the country.

Poppy Sol looks down on Balu's almost-ceremonial transformation, ever amazed by its grandeur – man becoming both man, animal. Balu inserts gnashing false teeth that protrude from his mouth. He lines on cheek whiskers with a pencil, attaches six foot long silken rope tail, glues on dagger

---

[34] Dined, jibed with rotund Kings, and cunning Prime Ministers in palatial surroundings. "You never pass, or pass on the venison, eh, Farouk." "Look to your own belly, Winston. Our friend Balu, even if he did partake of it, his still could not expand. For it would never make it past yours."

prosthetics fingernails, and dons claw-foot moccasins. He rehearses and Poppy Sol summons Luny Mum to watch: Movement, ballet; growls, operatic; a beautiful melding, not a halfway grotesque Thibidioux transformation.

Throngs have seen Balu Baiku – in massive arenas, in village gatherings.

"GIVE US YOUR POUNCE, TIGERMAN!" Crowds' shouts reverberate.

He rockets – just above them and seems to hover. Children *stre-eetch* to touch; adults become quiet.

None can tell: Is it allusion-real? Tigerman dances a lithe air-tiger ballet, sings-out roars that transcend animal-human communication barriers, so two-legs will understand-share a four-legs' anxiety, ease, or ennui. To audience time stands still; a minute? hour? – Then, instantly, Tigerman is tiger-reclined on a tree limb or atop a light pole. Deafening explosions of applause, shouts.

Through his art Balu transcends human and cat; creates mystical levels of human – non-human existence; inspires in viewer a depth of calmness, most never have felt. Audiences are certain: It is the same peacefulness Carpier, through his tales, provided audiences.

All the grandeur ended abruptly for Balu; at age 36 – when circuses begin bringing real tigers, and movies came, the celluloid REEL thing. Audiences' desire-for-peace, are replaced, by cravings for unceasing scintillation.

TIGER TRIBULATION

Unneeded, unwanted in his own country, feeling displaced, disgraced by progress, Balu stalks depression-era America, trying in vain to resuscitate dying Tigerman; whether it's for an audience of 2 or 200.

BEDRAGGLED TIGERMAN

He continues Carpier tradition of lifting spirits of those

most trodden-upon; tent-city families, homeless veterans, beleaguered vagabonds: A toothless smile or a bowl of stew is his pay. Always, he performs. From HIGHEST SOCIETY to lowest burlesque, middle of America vaudeville, even a Hollywood movie bit. Almost gives up, defeated by reel-real tiger. That changes one night:

A VAUDEVILLIAN'S TALE

Balu's in costume, waiting to go on. Clap and clatter of theater don't exist in his inner world of remorse. He looks about. One person in the theater's crowded backstage stands-out. Balu's drawn to the elderly man, James Thaddeus 'Blackjack' Fiction- as his ancestors were drawn to child Carpier. Blackjack watches his magician grandson James III, onstage, readying to make a giant shelled sea creature, swimming in a rectangular glass water vat, disappear.

When Blackjack sees Tigerman he says, unhesitating, "Your burden cannot be masked sir. It is well we meet for I carry the antidote to make the *glums-be-gone*. Someone from your country, and of your training, will understand."

Balu feels the aura of Carpier's peace in the presence of Blackjack. The lines of the old man's face gently sway with contentment as he speaks.

"I was led to Lindia to walk its paths nearly a century ago. I met Tigermen. Perhaps they were relatives of yours. Undoubtedly, kinsman." Blackjack keeps two things close to him in his later years: Bowie and the Book of Carpier. More important than seeing the, 'ultimate claw', for Tigerman, is seeing, the Book, when Blackjack opens its box slightly and hands it to him.

Kunta's tigress growls welcome to human counterpart-in-stripes. She bids, 'Enter'.

Pachyderm toots, 'Blow into my trunk, and I shall remember you always.'

Calico flits out and lights on his shoulder. 'Partake of the peace we bring you, Tigerman.'

Briefly, she morphs into the body of Carpier, opens book; turns pages.

Balu weeps joyously, basking in Carpier's peace as he reads almost-forgotten stories written in Lindian. He hears a voice. "Tigerman, listen. Heed my words." At first, he believes it is countryman Carpier, who lived over a thousand years before. It is Blackjack Fiction, soothing, calming, instructing, as if he channels the saint.

"As Carpier's words live on to inspire and soothe, you, the last Tigerman must continue on. So the bridge of harmony between humans and nature may continue."

These *relayed* inspirations of Carpier: They steel Balu's desire to carry on.

Hundreds of two-legs clap for you as you swim in the see-through container. You doff fin-claw to them as James III waves a cane, stirs the water, and says the magic two-leg words.

"Voila!" Container begins to smoke, then smashes to bits.

Water floods out and you ride mini-Typhoon oh-so-close to gasping audience. Again, you doff fin-claw. As you do, James III, face, octopus-serious, drapes a cape in front of you. He lifts it. "Voila!" Two-legs again gasp.

You hear them, but you are no longer before them, but backstage, back in the container of water that somehow didn't break after all; and you are beak-snout—to-face, with just-about the strangest he/it you've ever encountered. The Tiger-Man. He will become close, maybe closer to your Fiction family than any other he, she, or it.

Balu befriended Turt — by showing him the imperative of slow movements to Turt's goal of ultimate relaxation. Turt lets Tigerman carve his image into his shell.

From then on Balu was as family to Turt and the Fictions: He helped James IV establish the Lindian clinic in Cincinnati; convinced poor Lindian immigrants to seek medical assistance there, after his performances as Tigerman in their neighborhoods.

Before Typhoon destroyed the <u>Bashri</u> <u>Raku</u>, Balu was to meet the Doctor and his family and escort them to his village. Now, after seeing Turt save James, the only Fiction he'd not met, he's convinced, 'They are part of Nardesha's prophecy. He can only watch – and assist, but just in the direst case.

"Nardesha: Assist me in protecting your chosen one."

As he brushes on the last of the Tigerman paint Balu says a prayer to Nardesha for Dr. and Mrs. Fiction and all others who were on the ferry. He lifts Bowie, the mightiest of forest-claws. It seems to meld with his hand. He bows, thanking Nardesha for the gift. "I shall do your bidding Nardesha – my ultimate calling; my greatest performance – or I shall die in my duty of protecting your 'ONE'."

He raises up, sweeps sand from knees, and from a distance trails the slow-moving pair. 'Turt does not know it is I who follows. Best not tell him. His instincts are keenest when he travels solitaire. Let all his thoughts be those of protecting the 'ONE'.[35]

THE TALE OF WHAT RAU AND RUE SAW THEIR FATED NIGHT

The monster of their *hallucination* – man-tiger – speaks succinctly. "Alone must the boy journey. He must fulfill Nardesha's desires. I alone shall follow; help only if the need be most pressing. The boy must continue to prove his foundling grit-compassion. You must go your way. You will help him; by now doing Nardesha's work."

Rau and Rue, strangled by the smoke of their little huuka man, believe the 'figment-monster' is sent by Nardesha. To each other they say, "The child truly is the 'ONE'."

"How could we have doubted?"

---

[35] For the next 72 hours, Tigerman often is tempted to intercede. During the cobra attack: Witnessing James' repel them, stopped him– because developing that keenness for survival would serve James well; make him stronger to face future challenges of being a foundling. Other experiences: They prepare James for the yet-to-come benevolent work of Nardesha.

"And we tried enslaving the 'ONE' for our benefit."
"Dear Nardesha: forgive us. We will do as your emissary says." Some of their butterflies flit back to them. The sweet-sounding sitar strains of their wings – mystical and beautiful – are all Rau and Rue hear, as if Nardesha speaks through them:
"BLESS YOU. GO NOW! UNITE YOUR FAMILIES."

* * *

Tigerman sees tiger in mid-air, flying straight for Turt and James. Calico flits near Tigerman's ear and Tigerman believes he hears the peaceful voice of Carpier:
'Rightfully, you did not help earlier; but Balu, NOW you must!'
Time has arrived for Balu's ultimate performance: Tigerman verse Tiger-beast. He has gotten James *so close* to the destination and the people he had planned to deliver Doctor and Mrs. Fiction. So, today, he would battle his nemesis for the life of the 'ONE'; the *final* Fiction.

CHAPTER 39

Turt sees something-someone, torpedo parallel to the ground, toward the mid-pounce tiger. Another tiger? A man? No its – Tigerman. He's spinning like a bullet in a gun's chamber to keep his direction straight.

Tigerman-Balu thanks Nardesha for providing him Bowieclaw, but human pride – 'a two-leg needn't a crutch to defeat four-leg nemesis.' He throws Bowie. It sticks into a tree. Whether he lives or dies, he would do so with the honor of a Tigerman, and Turt would now have time to get James safely to the village.

Tigerman slams, *'thump'*, into the creature nearly four times his weight. They meld into a roiling yellow mass.

Calico flits above them to try to distract the tiger. Turt, elated at seeing old pal, wanting to help, but pragmatic, scoots to the shaking boy he bucked from his shell moments before. All that is happening mesmerizes James. He can barely move. Turt must scoop him up and onto his shell.

ONE CAGEY CAT ENTERS THE RING

Woodland creatures gather to watch the battlers midst Poppy Sol's setting glint.

Tiger pride – Tiger rises to haunches to show his height equals any two-legs'. He swipes claws. Tigerman, his face drawn in concentration, dodges. To other humans the claws would be razor blazes. To Balu, with six decades experience in the mystic art of 'tigermanning' that melds motion and thought, they are slow-moving stumps.

Like a seemingly overmatched boxer, Tigerman dodges, weaves. Stirred dust shadows around his opponent. Tiger sneezes. Refereeing squirrels and rabbits scatter as tiger phlegm gushes past them. A treed carrion crow, anxious for morsels of human remains he's wagering Tiger will provide, shrieks new rounds every few minutes.

Something unprecedented suddenly happens.

Tiger halts offensive, balances upright, and glares at two-leg. 'Only guile can defeat this ultra-endowed two-leg.' Next, the thing animals who edge backwards, to watch safely from behind ferns and hollow logs think unfathomable, occurs: A wild one begins *talking* to tame.

WILD: "Foolish Tigerman; you cannot defeat me without your claw."

TAME: "Need only tire you, woodland sire. I have no desire to harm any creature – be they two-leg or four."

Creatures of all legs chirp, squawk, and in general bellow approval. None likes the idea of being chow for the ones above them on nature's ladder. At this sound of woodland anarchy-in-the-making, of which Tiger is the chief despot, Tiger roars, silencing all.

Turt is inching toward the village. 'If any human can buy the time for us, it is my old vaudeville compatriot.'

Still upright Tiger points Turt's way. "Fight me, Tigerman, like a true Tiger would, or in two leaps I'll get to your shelled friend, and in two bites I'll dessert on his tender cargo."

Tigerman curls pseudo-claw hands. They sweat. He wipes them on his silk tail. Luny Mum glistens off his tiger-like whisker face that reveals no emotion.

Tiger states in cat scr-eam-casm. "After the count of three *Tüggeerrmaan*, I'll be enjoying cub and picking teeth with shards of the domed one if you don't flight me with your real claw. Go ahead, get it," he growls temptingly. "One..." he counts slowly.

Turt inches on.

"Two..."

James screams as if he knows, from the quiet around him, what his fate will be.

"Thr..."

Tigerman lurches toward the tree twenty yards away where Bowie lodges. Never before had Tigerman harmed human, animal, reptile, or insect. Now, he is forced.

"Human sucker, fool," Tiger roars. He lights on all fours and bounds toward Turt and child.

* * *

In the forever-poor village, less than 500 feet away, people brought in children and shuttered windows when they heard the first tiger growls. Inside her tiny, but nicely appointed hut – for she is the wife of the village's doctor – Indira Singh kneels on a tightly woven 500-year-old prayer rug. Dr. Singh is napping after a sun-up to moonrise routine of treating patients.

('He works so hard, Poppy.' 'Yes, Mum.')

Indira lights a candle in front of a two-foot high gold and crimson porcelain statue of Nardesha. The flame flickers against a silver tea service sitting on an intricately carved teak stand, and then reflects into Nardesha's green eyes. She seems to stare down at the tears flowing along Indira's delicate brown face.

Indira strokes the statue. "Dearest Nardesha. Allow your daughter to bear life's fruit."

Nardesha is Goddess of fertility in the nearby village of Kalanza from which Indira came. Already 26, twelve years into an arranged marriage in which she has grown to love, Indira has no children. She has been hearing the cutting whispers of other village women for a few years – at the market, roadside, in the temple – "BARREN".

And their jealousies. Helps little that her husband, from a wealthy city family, has vowed his life to helping the poor; and, whose only extravagance is seeing his wife dressed in the fiery red, yellow and lavender sarongs his mother sends. In them, and with her petite, cobra-smooth-moving frame, and pearl smile, Indira seems herself a Goddess midst the Kalamba sameness.

"Unacceptable for a mere human," Kalamba hens cluck of the 'Kalanzan'.

If only she could bear a child, Indira prays, she could *bear* the prattle. (She had been looking forward to meeting the American doctor and his wife and their son, who were to be coming, but rumors of Typhoon capsizing the ferry dashed that brightness.)

As she prays and weeps quietly, another growl shakes the village.

In nearby huts children cry out. They are hushed by parents who are used to the caterwauling beasts. From the next room Indira hears husband mumble something sleepily then turn over on the rustling, straw-stuff mattress.

A SCREAM: Indira thinks it is that of a child.

'Will any of the village men check? But the bell sounded earlier; telling that everyone is accounted for.'

Midst wonder, sadness, longing, Indira wants to be certain.

As she twists the doorknob she begins thinking of, but cannot understand why, her world-traveled uncle she'd heard so much about, never met – Balu Baiku – mystic-man, Tigerman. Maybe somehow, unexplainable, maybe he's thinking of her and this triggers the thoughts. Or, maybe the tiger triggers them. Maybe her desire for a child is causing all these strange notions, she thinks.

Has Balu died somewhere, reincarnated and is coming to visit as the Tiger? Even stranger, are her roiling thoughts of, 'Is the baby scream, along with that of the tiger's, an answer to my prayers – from Nardesha?'

Luny Mum retreats behind black clouds, unwilling to see Tigerman mauled by the tiger.

Indira opens the door and steps into that ominous darkness. 'Trust all to Nardesha.'

Indira's thoughts roil. 'Whether to be eaten alive, or, to become a mother? Barren for all time, or will Nardesha's power be visited upon me, via tiger, and allow me a return to Ben, to become impregnated by him this night? Would the spirit of mother's mystical brother, Tigerman, guide my destiny?'

* * *

Tigerman dislodges Bowie claw from the tree, and throws. A fly in the pathway scrams upward. *'Whoosh'*. Tip barely misses the fly's rear. The air current from Bowie's handle pushes the fly into a moth.

'Plaw-ease suh,' moth states officiously to its perceived underling. 'DO beg my pardon.'

A blackbird swoops down and eats moth as it brushes off fly stickiness.

Bowie nears destination. Then, all those who'd ever thrown it – maker Bowie, compatriot Davey Crockett; and Golden Boy, Carper-'Blackjack', and all the Fiction line, appear in the night sky to Tigerman and relay thoughts without words – 'Save our Turt, and the last of the Fictions, Dear Tigerman.' Tiger roars, as if sensing the apparitions and disavowing their desires.

'THUD!' Bowie finds mark; twixt Tiger's rear paw. Beast is heeled, mid-pounce; anchored to a tree stump. Stump dust, stirred by his landing, seems sparkles in the light of re-appearing Mum. Tiger is stopped, inches from Turt and James.

Tigerman didn't want the creature to bleed, so when he threw Bowie he added a wrist-flick, so its momentum of flight twisted downward, over paw. Tiger growls and lurches forward impotently. He rears. Front claws scratch skyward.

Tigerman approaches. Woodland creatures follow and gather just beyond Tiger's reach. His growls heighten as a taunting mockingbird lights on his tail. He reaches to slap it, but forgets bird when he sees paw, expecting it to be the blood red. Nothing. There is only a grinding sharpness if he moves. If he tries to pounce, paw will sever. He crouches, trying to appear menacing. Eyes lower as if he's scowling. Murmurs seep through clenched jaw.

Curious boy slips from shell. Sea Line's reach to try and pull him back isn't long enough. James toddles toward tiger. Tiger pretends not to notice.

Tigerman gleans ruse, just as Turt blares warning. Tiger lurches. James smells and feels his fetid breath, screams. Tigerman pounces, rolls, swipes James away as Tiger's jowls snap shut where James' head was.

Tigerman places James on Turt's shell and places Sea Line reins in his tiny hands. Tigerman and Turt's eyes briefly meet. No words needed; their Vaudeville days were full with such silent understanding of the other. This, just another shell game for them Turt knows; one he's *naturally* good at, but a Balu-Tigerman/Turt combo – is unbeatable. Ah! Their shell games in the alleys behind the Orpheum circuit theaters:

With squinted right eye, you follow walnut shells, miniature of your own shell. You always keep your left eye on palm and pea. Con-artist stops; you point fin-claw. You win every time. Balu watches, making the cons pay-up. Balu gives the winnings to hungry, shelterless two-legs.

You realize now that Balu-Tigerman, had a shell game-type reason for invisibly trailing you and James; for not helping when you were in peril; and for even now, not just carrying James to the village himself. You plod onward, trusting that reason.

* * *

On the village outskirts, Indira Singh screams as she feels an icy pawing at her shoulder.

* * *

Tigerman crouches near Tiger. Says Tiger: "Hear that; I am not the only of my kind here."

Says Tigerman, "Unfortunately, I believe you are, sire, the only of your kind in these parts. We are both becoming extinct." Tigerman, melancholic, preens pseudo-tail with pseudo-claw. Tiger, equally-glummed by that reality he's loathe to admit, preens ensnared paw with tongue.

* * *

Dr. Ben Singh's hand is cold, as if he's been autopsying cadavers all-the-day. Indira Singh's heart, races. She turns, barely seeing her husband in the darkness. She pulls from his cold touch, then, as quickly, strokes his cheek and kisses graying temples.

He wears only boxer shorts. (Awakening from his nap, he discovered Indira gone. Fearing for her, he came looking.) Luny Mum reflects off his only body adornment – a tattoo of the universal medical insignia on his broad hairless chest. The foot-long staff is crimson, the serpent curling up it, gold, colors of Harvard where he attended medical school. A tan rugby helmet sheaths the serpent's head. Rugby, his passion before his desire to help others replaced it.

"Woman! What is this craziness? You know the warning bell has sounded. You must come inside."

She resists when he takes her arm. "I heard a cry, Ben. May be, a baby."

"There will be no children out, Indira."

He's glad for the darkness. It hides the wrinkling-up of his face that mirrors exasperation – at his wife's desire for a child that he is certain feeds this hallucination-dream-desire. He shares the desire. But he willingly accepts fate. "For own safety, we must go in dear."

"A child, my husband," she weeps. "Goddess Nardesha may be bringing us one." Indira knows her pleas are fruitless. She succumbs to Ben and he leads her back to the hut.

More tears streak his face than hers. He loves her so.

If they remained a half-minute more they would have seen

Turt and boy-cargo arriving.

* * *

After he retrieves the boxed Book of Carpier from where he dropped it before battle, Tigerman paces thatch, patiently; Tiger claws it, impatiently. 'Turt will succeed,' Tigerman assures himself. Neither Tigerman, or Tiger, or any of the encircling creatures make sounds for what seems half the night. It is only hours, as they all notice by Luny Mum's continuously rising orb. The thought *'extinction'* so dirty a word in their world – weighs heavily on them.

Extinction – It comes quickly, randomly. This time it appears to be their predator's turn. How could the creatures, not, feel sorry for him? Yet, their thinking, 'Would we be sorry for him if midst his jowls?'

Turt feels torn as he arrives at the village outskirts: Giddiness; that the little Fiction would be safe and continue the line of his old friend, the once-upon-a-time- also little, 'Carper'-James Thaddeus 'Blackjack' Fiction, who had given Turt such a full life. Trepidation – that he himself may be ripped limb-to-shell, at the hands of those who take delivery of James. Turt breathes deep; trudges onward.

Tiger's muffled roar ends a long silence. "So Tigerman, your friend has the morsel well-away. I guess you taught me who is King about these parts. What say you pull the thorn, from now on, I follow you, eating only leaves and vines as do you. We'll live happily-forever-after in our woodland paradise."

Animals edge away as Tigerman reaches for Bowie. 'What is he thinking?' Tigerman pushes Bowie down ever so slightly.

"Ouch. Geez, Androcles."

"We'll await Turt's return," Tigerman says. Immediately he feels guilty for the hurt he's imposed. It is the same guilt-like pleasure when he watched the shell game's cons sweat whenever alley-dwellers began betting with Turt, and against them.

Time passes – Not our time, animal time...

...The snap of a human finger can be time spent in having a meal for some creatures.

A double episode of Lassie for us – for them is a final spawning trip up the Colombia, or the soaring, in-flight mating then departure of Rocky Mountain eagles...

...For us, a Santa Monica to L.A. freeway commute to reach a tropical fish specialist to treat our ailing guppy; for some of them that time equals the change of many seasons.

So, some creatures around Tiger and man are nodding drowsily... long day.

A growl of hunger from Tiger's stomach churns the night air. Impatience, desperation for grub, brings trivial talk.

Tiger: "That two-leg lair eats turtles; any shelled creature."

Man: "Since when."

"Since always: They slice, dice; fry thrice." He motions with paw, scowling: "I am surprised you sent him on his own. Good friend you are."

"For your information: I came from there. Not one turtle or terrapin did we eat."

"None-the-less. It is fact. They do." Tiger looks for animal confirmation.

Critters nod agreement.

Tigerman shrugs. He hadn't been home for over half-a-century, still he couldn't imagine it. "You can't get me to leave so easily, my furry friend. Even if I did, even your vise-jaw could not remove the claw. No sir. At Kalanza, vegetables and fruit are the fare."

Tiger laughs. His jaw curls wickedly. Other critters look away, silent, fearing for the 'passing through' shelled creature. "Kalanza," Tiger, bellow-laughs. "Why that's a good half-a-hundred pounces beyond. You have been away too-long Tigerman. You do not remember the difference any longer between Kalamba and Kalanza lair." (Tiger's seen tv through hut windows. He knows how the hip cats sway.)

Tigerman pales. How could he have forgotten the location

of his birth? What has he done to his friend? He rises and quickly runs, in tiger-like pounces toward village. "Don't let it be too late for Turt," he prays to Nardesha.

Tiger turns slyly toward woodland critters. "Any here strong enough, desiring from me, AMNESTY, from this night forward: APPROACH!" He adds garnishment to his lie – so that some strong-jowl wart hog or beaver might believe him. "Remove the claw, and it will be granted to not only you, but your family." Tiger waits.

As Turt enters the shelled-up village, he looks for a sign. 'There. It is there.'

He approaches the only thing that looks familiar: a four feet high white cane with a snake made of red rope curling up it. It mirrors the insignia on the front door of the Fiction medical clinic in Cincinnati. James holds onto Turt's stiff neck and looks up at it; trying to remember.

Turt trembles as he hears the banging open and close of a door, and a voice. He closes eyes and inches toward the hut, wondering if the voice is saying, "That one will make a plentiful meal." Sea Line slips from around his neck. Turt retrieves, slips string in James' pocket, and communicates to long, skinny pal: 'Anything happens to me; you will be his lifeline.'

Moments before: Indira sits inside hut at easel painting an elaborate Nardesha.

"Goddess, show me happiness." Brushing sounds outside: Indira looks out, sees in Luny Mum's glow the largest shelled creature ever, riding him – a boy. "Thank you Goddess. All praise your power to fulfill your Carpier's prophecy." Her heart is suddenly, joy-filled.

A woman, beautiful as Rrrose Heather, but dressed in a rainbow of colors, emerges through glowing line of light of opening door. She kneels. You dismount shelled creature-your protector, and run to her outstretched arms. You've yearned-for that softness; to be s-'mothered'; warmed.

Turt watches. Thoughts flash back, over 150 years, to the day of the dregs on Jericho – to the last time he saw his mother. The same love encompasses this gentle human face. Turt knows, finally, all is well. Slowly, in bittersweet melancholy he turns to leave.

She cradles you; puts softest of cheeks to yours. Her whispers are sweet. Suddenly you're so tired. You don't know if you're asleep or awake as you see Calico, 'blip' into Carpier and say, "Trust her. She shall love you with all her heart." Carpier 'blips' back to Calico but you don't see Calico – yet you sense she's there – always will be.

Indira carries James to Turt, and leans so they are beak-snout to face.

"Dearest messenger of the Goddess. How might I thank you?" She sees Sea Line slipping from boy's pocket. She braids the string into the halo that symbolizes Nardesha and encircles it around Turt's neck. (Anyone coming upon Turt will know he is 'blessed by Nardesha' and won't tear him limb-to-limb and eat him.) She sprinkles holy powders, thanking Turt, "for all Lindia," for fulfilling the prophecy.

Everything is happening quickly. Creature-protector rubs beak-snout against your cheek. You feel moisture from his eyes roll onto your face and mix with wet from yours. Your human-protector rises, takes your hand. As the three of you walk toward the village outskirts, creature-protector begins, so-slowly, fading from your thoughts.

You try to hold onto him tight in your memory. 'Come back.'

Suddenly, appearing beside you, 'blip, blip, blip'; your three muses. They speak, but you can't hear them. Rrrose Heather and Mama Lucy kiss you. Even Margaret looks a little sad. As quickly as they appeared, 'blip, blip, blip', gone.

Creature-protector continually fades; will soon be gone – for forever?

Now, appearing beside you – you reach out and touch him – he is real – the Tiger-man from the woods. His arms stretch around you and your new protector.

"Uncle Balu. This is all Nardesha's miracle," Indira cries, no doubting that it is him on this miraculous night. They lock arms; walk to the Singh hut. Together they lift and hold James.

Indira can't contain the torment she's endured for so many years. To this uncle – gushed lovingly of by her mother – and whom Indira instantly trusts, bonds to, she whispers quickly of mistreatment, jealousies by Kalambans. Then, Indira *gushes* – passionately – about the 'son' Nardesha *'wills'*.

"I have the words to convince your husband to take you and your new son away, niece."

You look back at your creature-protector. All you see is the darkness that leads into woods you, already, barely-can, even now, remember being in. You squint between trees. Who do you look for? Memories hazily fade. Completely gone? Forever? You tremble. You're held, tight.

CHAPTER 40

A QUICK TALE OF HOW EASY IT CAN BE TO MAKE A LIFE-ALTERING DECISION

James sleeps on a pad inside the hut. Balu-Tigerman, Indira, and Ben talk for hours of leaving, of the Cincinnati clinic.

"We *must* go my husband. It will be said because I am barren I am unfit to keep this child."

"Traditions of this village are barbaric," agrees Tigerman. "They'd have torn Turt apart."

"None will cede Nardesha's miracle from my bosom. None, Ben."

"We must stay and change such ways and superstitions. I am needed."

"Kalanza doctor handle it before we came. I tell you, Ben, it is Nardesha's will that we go."

The more Balu speaks of Doctor Fiction and Imah's ideas of bringing a Lindian physician to Cincinnati, the more Doctor Singh is convincing himself they are correct. 'The shelled creature has fulfilled the prophecy – Fiction son, is the 'ONE' sent by Nardesha, that Carpier foretold.'

"Not to *save* our people," Balu suddenly says, reading Ben's thoughts in his expressions. "But to bring you to Cincinnati to help them, so they can go on to help others of ours there, or return to Lindia to do so."

"A thousand, a ten thousand fold of giving; not just by the 'ONE' – is Nardesha's desire, Ben. She does not want us to rely-always on her for solutions, but for us to provide them. I came to realize this as I followed him and the shelled creature's woodland pilgrimage."

Indira holds her husband's hands. Ben now plans, more than listens. 'I can do much for our people at the clinic.' Stone face reveals none of the rhapsody, the ecstatic, spiraling ever-higher of emotions – emotions he never thought he could feel – when he looks over at the sleeping boy. 'We've a son, Indira. Nardesha has provided your miracle. Forever blessed, $I - us$.'

'This village can be served by the Kalanza doctor. We can leave before daylight. No more will my Indira be victim to Kalamba's pettiness. Nor, will my son.'

Decision; set.

TALE OF YET-ANOTHER DARING-DO ADVENTURE OF CAPTAIN POLLY AND TURT

"Prick Lily signaled me of the trouble. Got here. Soon as I could. Long flight from Cincinnati," squawks Captain Polly, panting.

'Just delivered boy to new ma, fa. Tigerman is inside hut – arranging.'

"How now can I help, Turt?"

'Here is the Tigerman's and my plan,' Turt tells Captain Polly as she perches atop his shell.

(Turt and Tigerman, are able to, sense the others thoughts; dating from the vaudeville shell-game days. They quickly relayed them as Tigerman, entering Kalamba, passed departing Turt.) 'Tigerman will keep the, Book, safe until James is ready for it. I will see to Bowie.'

They approach pinned tiger. He begins roaring 'for show'. Animal onlookers scatter.

Tiger waits, contemplates, 'The land-sea creature desires the

Tigerman's claw. They saved the young two-leg, but they must fight me for this. I shall grab his beak-snout. That will be the slowest part for him to re-shell once battle commences.'

Turt needn't tell Captain Polly why he is doing this, freeing beast to go in peace, retrieving Bowie to safe-keep for James until he's prepared to balance the instrument-of-war with the Carpier Book-of-peace; so, in James' boy conscience, Book and Bowie become one, for only good.

As Turt gets within Tiger reach, Captain Polly, knowing what Turt expects, drops to the big cat's head. She talons into his furry crown; holds tight. Woodland king screams, shakes head, bites upward.

Turt snatches Bowie, throws it straight up, and quickly re-shells.

Moments before Tiger can swipe her, Captain Polly takes flight and talons Bowie in mid-air. She taunts, "Can't catch me, yellow-cat. So re-seat in defeat." She circles just-above him.

He pounces atop Turt to try to snag her. Unable, he violently claws Turt's impenetrable shell. He stops when Turt begins to almost, '*purr*', enjoying the scratch-massage. With a final woodland-shaking growl, Tiger leaps away and stalks proudly off, as if he didn't really want to bother with the odd duo in the first place. He'll not let fellow-creatures know his thoughts, 'Gotta-be easier ways to get a meal.'

Turt exits shell. Captain Polly drops Bowie to the ground beside him. Another battle won. After mutual congratulations, Turt says, 'You go be with James, Captain Polly. You can be useful to him in his new surroundings, as I cannot. The two of us can hook up when he's again home.'

"Usual meeting place?" squawks Captain Polly.

Turt nods. 'The wharf-shack: Been so for over 150 years. Don't see need to change now.'

Captain Polly takes flight, noting, but unable to stop, the GLUMS of leaving the boy, she senses is overcoming Turt. Captain Polly knows where Turt is bound – to be with Prick Lily in this time that is absent a Fiction in his life. She knows what Turt is thinking,

'Maybe James will remember you, Turt. Only time will tell: Mustn't think of that now. Think only of the joys you've had together; and one day will again.'

Turt takes Bowie in beak-snout and leaves for America.

THE TALE OF AN OH-SO-DIFFERENT BOY

So-quickly, you become Raji Singh in the coming year: assimilating to Lindia City's bustling life; leapfrog with newly acquired cousins in the sprawling, curry-scented, Singh house; listening to philosophizing, beetle-nut chewing uncles in the lush gardens. Your butterflies love the gardens.

New ma beams as you're fussed over by chattering, silk-draped aunts. "Most handsome are you, Raji. So treasured a son Nardesha has sent our Indira." The aunts dress you in satin balloon pants, and rhinestone-encrusted dhotis. You feel you walk a tightrope as you get used to pointy togs. So many different ivory nose-rings tried on. Mascara lines from your eyes to ears, symbolizing the family's honoring of Nardesha.

New fa says proudly as he passes boudoir where the transformation happens, "Carpier must live in you, you look so much like him, Raji."

You so-like all this attention.

Raji, is olive-skinned, burnished by Poppy Sol during the woodland ride, as *James*.[36]

When soothing sitar sounds cease and house sleeps, Balu comes to your room. He dresses as Tigerman and he performs calming Tiger dances. The dances help ease the lingering nightmares of Typhoon and trek. Tigerman takes you on his lap, as Mariner did Carper. What comes next is the same magic for you as it was for great-great granfa, Carper.

'CLICK.' Tigerman opens Kunta's box. Tigress and pachyderm whisper, 'Greetings Raji. Come. Travel with Carpier. You will visit his stories through Mariner's drawings.'

---

[36] LKFFF: I remind you, gently, who I became; because becoming another can be so confusing. New ma and fa planned-on telling me who I was – sometime? When? *Carper comes to you: 'One day you will choose who to be, if you don't want to be Raji.' Carpier appears beside Carper. 'Remember: Raji will you be to survive, thrive. This is all is asked of you, as Raji.'* Then comes Golden Boy; dressed, so silly by Marr-grrr-ett. *'In Cincinnati you'll look different than most. Never let that affect who you are. Whether that boy be Raji, or...'*

"When you learn the words, you will traverse ever-newer paths," Tigerman says.

A world *James* once knew well, *Raji* learns afresh. Unlike Mariner with Carper, and James' fa for him, who would *tell* the tales as *told* to them – Tigerman *reads* to Raji, as written, in Lindian.

Author's note: Though I knew Lindian from my earliest memory, learning from the Cincinnati Lindians, my Lindian vocabulary grew during this time. Outside my bedroom window constantly was Captain Polly. Whenever I had trouble with a Lindian word – she would parrot its English counterpart. How could I not become most proficient with such a multi-lingual mentor?

And also: Now, as I write these reminiscences as an adult, I must reveal that – three of those who played such a large part in the care and well-being of me and, before that, my Fiction ancestors for over a century-and-a-half – they are still alive. I cherish these oh-so-still active, ultra-elders: Captain Polly, Turt, Prick Lily.

THE PAPER TRAIL

Dr. Singh, so incurable a workaholic – morning kisses wife and new son goodbye. *(Bye-bye Fa.)* Off he goes with Balu Baiku: De-Tigermanned; in suit, tie, and feeling caged by Lindia's sprawling bureaucracy; determined to claw through to capture adoption papers.

One day, tiger-quick hands of Tigerman-Balu, as in the vaudeville shell games with Turt, succeeds in conniv...convincing one department after another, 'nother, 'nother, that the previous one had discovered the 'papers'-pea under-the-shell and shuffled it over to them. So,

...off to America – where Fiction Clinic staffers greet new physician and family who join others residing on the premises. *(This bedroom you're given; these toys; all are so-familiar.)*

No one recognizes the boy, so changed after well over a year away; so Lindian-like in clothes, haircut, and darker

complexion. He looks, speaks, *so* Lindian. They picture a sister or a cousin's son; or the image of themselves or someone they knew growing up: almost everyone they picture, but not – the poor lad thought-lost with a thousand others. *(Maybe they see, you; but mentally deny it, because of how bad they felt about your fate.)*
  The Lindian patients in the clinic see something so-different – they see a boy, not quite a Lindian, but 'ONE' touched by the blessing of Nardesha; swarmed over by butterflies, as Carpier. "All praise," silently they chant; and they feel their healing hastens in his presence.

TALE OF REMEMBRANCE

  Balu Baiku has travelled to Cincinnati with the Singhs. As Tigerman, he acts out bedtime stories for Raji from the Book of Carpier. "…then the big cat leaps from tree. Not to eat Carpier: To blanket and keep him warm. Many are the nights he does this when Carpier roams the mountains, searching ever-enlightenment."
  Tigerman thinks you sleep.
  Tigerman sees a silver, ruby and gold shimmer in Luny Mum's light: "Calico." *Through open window, she flits; lights on BOOK. You listen to Tigerman say to her. 'I remember when I met his great-great grandfa, Blackjack. He had to have been 30 years older than I now. He showed me your, Book. Out you flew."*
  Your imagination drifts. You think butterfly says to Tigerman. 'I remember meeting Blackjack long before, as young Carper; shivering under the wagon.'
  For a moment, you remember: 'I know that boy! How much don't you remember? Will you ever know?' you wonder, as Tigerman and Calico both tuck you in. You sleep, so deeply.

CHAPTER 41

Four years pass for each boy. For Carper it is 1830. James, now Raji, 1970.

You awaken to Luny Mum's whispering twinkle, 'Peek outside.'
Comes, your muse, 'Was passin'-by Jamie; wanted to see how you be.'
Indira and Ben love you, Lad – just like Mariner loved Carper,' Rrrose assures. She fades when your mother enters.

"I thought I heard voices. Is everything all right, Raji?"

"I love you, Mother, like Carper loved Mariner," *you say as you hug her. Her gentleness says, 'I love you.'*

"Who are this Carper and Mariner of whom you dream, Raji?"

How can you tell her? 'They're real, Mother. Maybe one day you'll meet them – after all, you heard Rrrose and Mum speak.'

* * *

Just a few city blocks away, yet 140 years separated, Carper lives 'happily ever…' with Mariner in the wharf-shack. Mariner, touting tales, sails a tattered globe with his index finger. Carper's 'all aboard' for the cruises.

"…It was the biggest squid ever was saws, Carper. Follered us day-n'-night. Kept tryen' ta pull hisself onto deck. After 'bout a week, well, he musta' figgered out our pile of netting twarn't some sorta' 'eexotic female squid.'"

TALE OF A FICTION-IN-THE MAKING

Rrrose Heather's ladies 'doll-the-Carper-up' – in latest boy fashions from Rrrose's New Orleans contacts – as Indira's sisters-in-law will, with his great-great grandson. Neither boy minds the nips, tucks. During the fittings, James-Raji reads Carpier. Carper has new fiction-friends that the ladies bring along: Ivanhoe, Ichabod Crane, most-importantly, "Uncas", Carper reads to Turt from *The Last of the Mohicans.* "But you'll not be the last Trumpeter, eh Turt."

"When are you and Carper going to clean this hold," ladies, who look for an uncluttered seat, ask Mariner.

"Carper 'n me gotta feel to home. No use messin' about what's already ship-shape."

You don't mind them calling you Carper. In your mind you are, now-always, 'Blackjack'. You stroke the silk shirts and imagine yourself at riverboat tables eyeing, like the Buzzard, for an ace and queen. You like even more – the reading. "Tell me this word," says a lady. You tell her. "...Wow. That's a whopper, Carper."

Sometimes Captain Polly decides to stay with you and Mariner when Buzzard's on short gambling trips. She perches outside an open porthole. Her peace accord, with the now-featherless ladies, holds. As they help you hone reading skills, Captain Polly parrots the harder words so they'll be recorded in your thoughts.

The ladies do a lot of winking of those long eyelashes: Both at you and Mariner, but not Buzzard, when he's in town. You're sure that's because Captain Polly won't let them.

Ah, so fun, your life.

Time passes. Soon you are reading, ever more 'lickety-split'. This ever-increases your passion for storytelling and transports you even further into imagination's euphoria. It becomes hard to, not read, not tell others who come to the wharf-shack, or passers-by on the dock, all about the stories living in 'BOOKS'.

Almost every free moment, you read to Mariner. His eyes spark as he sinks into the word sea.

He says to you as he nets you into his lap, as he's done hundreds, maybe thousands of times now, and hugs you. "These times offer us just the best 'a catches, Carper. Cherish 'em."

You want to imitate all he does. You hug and cling to him.

Mariner points at the globe. He begins recollectin'-storytellin'. "Durned straits a' Bosporos, boy. That's where Captain Polly finally gave Buzzard the ultimatum after our mutiny:

'SQUAWK! 'Eyether chose me or Rrrose Heather.' Of course he chose Captain Polly."

Captain Polly peers in through porthole; looking proud.

"Though Buzzard pined for Rrrose, Carper, he knew she'd never have 'im — seen too many card-birds fly in 'n outta her life. Rrrose's planted earthy-deep. Nothin' flighty for 'er." Mariner adds with a quaver of forlorn. "No sea-legged swabs for 'er 'eyether."

On another fine day: Beside Captain Polly outside the porthole: LOOK!

THE TALE OF RRROSE'S VOW

Peeking into the wharf-shack, unnoticed by old man and boy immersed in their own waters...

It's Rrrose Heather: Bless her. Be it 1830, 1970; she never changes. Kind. Calculating. Always beautiful, crowned by black tresses. Ol Tom leaps from roof onto her shoulder. "You be doing an extra mighty heap of strutting-out lately, Tom," Rrrose purrs. "Me Angorra's getting worn out. Takes to hiding under the bed when she hears your paws brushing the railing. I'd have to charge you double if you be a two-leg."

Ol Tom joins Rrrose in squint. Rrrose whispers to the spirit of Carper's mother. "Your Bonnie's boy's home for good, lassie. He grows so, hmm? Can ya see his broad shoulders? Don'tcha worry, Bonnie. I'll always be keeping me' promise. He'll always be watched over."

Rrrose winks to Calico. Calico enters wharf-shack through

a crack, lights on Carper's shoulder. Rrrose shares wizened mothering observations with that other wizened female. 'Much as he tries bein' like Mariner, Calico, he's more everyday his fa, be'int he. That marble honesty of expression showing in those Blarney Stone-hard cheekbones. Nary once did it crack in Ezekiah in his house visits. Pity: If it had, he'd be the better.'

Rrrose imagines Calico's response: 'Just pray to Nardesha, my dear, that its weight does not sink son, as did it father. But even marble can re-surface, if one pulls hard enough.'

Rrrose smiles, seeing the growing love between Carper and Mariner. 'Ah Ezekiah – the one you've left behind. Will you ever prove man enough to raise the marble to deserve me telling you someday of that gift – no; GIFTS!' She thinks of Carper's brother, William, the Golden Boy. Carper has Mariner. And Golden Boy; Captain Golden. Or does he? Her letters are returned, un-opened. She's not heard of Captain Golden's death – and of whom fickle, Margaret has chosen for his new fa.

* * *

After school, Raji explores the neighborhood around the clinic. He's drawn to the docks. Sometimes he sees an object looking like the tip of a round steppingstone in the river. It seems to move, following him. Kinda fun; mysterious. Every so often, a once pal parrot, now lost and forgotten in a foundling mist, is sitting on it – watching him.

Plot's kinda' fun-thickening. In his wanderings Raji sees Cincinnati's mix of old – new: Glistening steamers pass-by rotting, but still-afloat piers of the city's founding.[37]

In his room at night, the sloshing of the Ohio beckons Raji.

---

[37] LKFFF: One of the city's legends proves fact. Raji discovers a moss-covered stone plaque at the water's edge, proving, the city really was founded by twin foundlings, Cincinnatus and Cincinnatum – suckled to survive by a wild pig – the city's mascot and later made famous in the mid 20th century by a Kay Kaiser big band song.

In his imagination, he's standing on the dock: A memory flash. *OVER THERE! It's Carper. From a distance, you watch him. You're entranced by the stories he weaves to the dozens of tattered dockworkers during their break.*

* * *

Like his namesake Carpier, and the thousands of master-storytellers in the thousands of years of human history that came before him, Carper's tellings, coddle, scare, warm, and spellbind his audiences all at once. He leaps onto a post, spreads arms, and becomes a skulking buzzard.

"I' swoop down and..." He hides leg behind back, covers eyes to become patch-eye, peg-leg romancing parrot. "Oh Lover Bird. How I... *squaaack.*"

Carper's clothes are the dapper of Buzzard. His demeanor is the amenable salt-of-the-sea of Mariner.

In tales, he sways like a cobra; lurches as mongoose: Then, simultaneously, he becomes both – battling each other back and forth. "All who fall in the jungle are mine." "Never, cobra. Carpier is the exception."

All-the-while Carper spins, knits, and embellishes yarns told him by Mariner and Buzzard, and other stories *hidden away*, in BOOKS, for all to find if they'd only, read. These men, poor of spirit, mind and body can't read. They're happy to "drop-a-dime-in-the-lad's capper."

'Carper has the pulpit theatrics of Ezekiah,' Rrrose Heather *'tsks'* when 'er she passes. 'But oh his wonderful risk, living life!' A pair or Rrrose's ladies are always about at the shows, watching o'er their Carper and drumming up business for later, via Rrrose's array of methods.

"...Ichabod Crane thought the punkin' flyin'-by he and his galloping horses was a head – a human head, I tell ya," tales Carper. One of the ladies screams, feigns a faint – into quickly outstretched arms of a group of seated men – a trick always guaranteed to get three or four of them to, later, escort her back to the house.

Carper's audiences are men who sweat as much from anticipation, excitement and fright from the boy's spins, as from any heavy lifting. They see a bleeding head in their imaginations, not a punkin'.

"Wait'll he starts tellin' about the walk-offs," the *'fainted'* horizontal lady whispers to them.

On any of Cincinnati's docks, workers can set their clock by Carper's appearances. He knows exactly when each crew 'breaks'. Owners don't mind. Whistling, chatting, more productive workers return after a show. Carper leaps from atop post, slides to dock, begins crawling, spitting, howling like a man-alligator. His audience laughs as he turns the character into a laza bones buffoon who can't stand straight. So violent is his air clawing, men monetarily flinch.

* * *

NO, CARPER! You shout. Don't go telling about Laza Bones. His senses are so keen he might hear you all the way down the bayou or in the desert. Might take out his angers on the Golden Boy, then come lookin' for you.' But Carper can't hear you because the audience around him are laughing, clapping. You try to run to stop him. That invisible wall of time that's been between you before is appearing again.

As it grows higher, and thicker, the dock gets darker. Everyone's disappearing. Slowly you return to your room, hearing only now the words of some drifter who's stopped to listen to the tales. "Why I know a feller who looks just like that. If I see him on my next trip down the Mississip', I'll just bet he'll pay hefty a good price to find out who's disparaging his image."

A TALE OF HOW A WRITER COMES UPON A SCENE

Dear Charles,

I again saw the boy from the Independence Day parade when we visited Cincinnati just before papa moved us here. I think of it now because I am working on a scene…. I'll just tell you what that boy did: Leaped from his storyteller post; grabbed the hat in which the workers put coins in payment for his wonderful tales, jumped *'ONTO'*, and *'RAN'*, across the river.

Charles, I know not if it was miracle or magic. (Papa would rebuke me if I claimed the latter.) If ever the boy's stories' villains were to chase him, woe to them for they would drown.

Charles, I also thought of the little slave girl I saw at that Independence Day parade. A miracle or magic as that I've often wished for her, nay, prayed, for. That she'd be able to run across her Jordon to her very own independence day. Oh Charles. I do hope Papa would think such a prayer would be appropriate, or, that you wouldn't think it just fal-de-ral…

For, barely a second, Carper is out of sight of his audience when his feet hit the water – hardly a sound of splash to be heard because he's whooping so loudly. He *'thumps'* as he lands, unseen, atop a speeding-past, stepping-stone, Turt. Carper's weight pushes shell underwater and he runs fast as he can, on the water. He gets back within sight of his audience. They gasp at what they see, then, suddenly begin cheering-wildly. Turt cruises toward the middle of the Ohio. It's an easy jaunt for Turt, but Carper must run in place, *full-bore*, to keep up.

Turt slows and drifts. Carper catches breath by doing a little dance for clapping, hooting passengers on passing steamboats; and then he and Turt float downstream: *Outta-sight!* Running's easy; timing the jump; hard. (Rehearsal's always at night; so only a peeking Luny Mum sees. 'Wait til you watch him do it Sol. Wow's all I can say! *WOW'S!* But, many-a-cold dunk 'e took before perfecting it.')

The land Drifter: 'Gator-man'll want to know about that running on the water gambit.'

'Did Carper ever have to use his water-running trick?' You asked

your fa, once-upon-a-time, when you were James.
'Many-a-time,' Fa replied.
'Did it always work?'
'Well, we are here. So it must have.'

TALE OF THE PREACHER'S DAUGHTER MEETING THE WHURES

Midst cheers for water-*'legging'* Carper, Harriet shouts, "RUN, LITTLE ONE RUN!"

Rrrose Heather and her ladies look over at the prim teen. Competition for them: In *that* bonnet? *That* flour-sack-of-a-fashionless ankle-length dress? No! Rrrose comes over to befriend her, the beginning of a lifelong friendship. Rrrose and some of her friends relay some of Harriet Beecher Stowe's best 'underground railroad' notes.

CHAPTER 42

"And for that bit 'a infoam-ation, how much you say you be needin?" Before the drifter can answer, Thibidioux, while picken-'is-pocket, tips him into the bayou. He's so skinny his splash into the murk's barely a, '*plunk*'. "Well, I sees ya can't run across a bayou like that youngen' can across the 'Hio."

"You Goddam, low-down, somva-bitchen..." The drifter's soliloquy of curse ends in scream as Baron Tail and Prime Snout yank him under.

Poppy Sol glints through Spanish moss. 'If he be *so* dim to try shake'n down Laza Bones – no amount of me' shinin' ray would ever 'av 'im seein' the light.'

Thibidioux tells his resurfaced, burping minions. "Look after things here. I'll git ti' Tehas to make certain the Sergeant and *Hizzoner* cash-cur Austin are keepin' things in hand. I'll check-on the *'Will-a-meenie'*, then head Cincy-way and take care that sitia-ation. Never been north. Might find us some ripe opportunities."

Lazarus Bontez Thibidioux never stops thinking he has the power to resurrect and see another day, (who wouldn't – *living* the legend as the babe plucked from gator's jaw) but his Mama Lucy, appears she'll never die.

That frail, old, *blind-old*, so-old midwife, strangely, her hearing gets even better with age. From her distant cabin, she listens to what transpires. She blows dust and sprinkles a potion – westward – toward Tehas and north to Cincy. "From strafes, keep the two brothers safe." Mama Lucy's beautiful dear young friend, Rrrose Heather has told her all about Carper and Golden Boy. Protect them with all her magical powers – that's Mama's plan.

* * *

Galloping away on Jesse, Golden Boy shouts, "Ya hoo!" Just out of sight of the outpost, the eight-year old strips off *Willamina* dress. He stuffs it in the saddlebag.

Squints Poppy Sol, 'There's me' William, me' Golden Boy, priden' in his secret cowboy attire.'

The dark Hell of William's six-days- a-week as Willamina, cooled and lit only by constant writing, disappears in the bright of the seventh – *Heaven* of being allowed out. The reprieve is against Margaret's wishes, but stone-face step-fa Sergeant Miles Peabody insists,

"Steed needs a workout Margaret, and boy needs some daylight."

Margaret stomps. Their living quarters shake. "No! No! No!"

Peabody knows of William's secret clothes but he doesn't tell her. He's vowed, 'when she eventually figures it out, I won't let her take them away.' He shouts back at her, "YES!" He'll have his way – or, for the insecure Margaret it's the 'bye'-way. He knows she'll not travel it.

Peabody's not soft hearted, altruistic, loving as Captain Golden was. Thibidioux has ordered him to *allow* William these outings – so the boy will be strong, fit – so he'll 'MAN–UP' for when the time comes to either lead him to the maps; or, as keen as the girl-boy seems, Thibidioux figures, he'll decipher them, then lead him right to the treasure. The only work Laza Bones'll have to do is seize it – then 'KEILL 'IM!'

As Golden Boy sees Prick Lily on the horizon, he believes he sees a young cowpoke sitting on her shoulder. 'No. Just a desert mirage,' he reckons, then vows with a whoop, "One day I'll ride away and never again be Willamina." He's tried this dodge twice; was thrashed when Peabody traced him. Golden Boy breathes in the desert's sweet sage and expunges those memories, because today is his special day.

He leans forward and says excitedly to Jesse, "Maybe Turt'll be back from his travels and be there. Maybe Liege Leather will have come over from the bayou. What will today's surprise be, Jesse?" *You see the surprise, as you get closer. It's not a mirage, but Seventh day's Heaven-sent miracle that comes whenever your duds tighten up on you as you grow:* It's a shiny, new cowboy outfit hanging from Lily's shoulder.

As you ride up you imagine Lily says, "I've been takin' right good cara the duds."

Whoosh! Jesse bucks you up to the soft spot on her shoulder as he always does. You quickly change, and leave the too-small outfit on Lily's prickers. "The doves'll carry them to some other young buckaroo in needa' duds, just like you" you imagine Lily say.

(Not doves that deliver attire: But Thibidioux, via Peabody, to make certain William remembers he's on his way to being a man; that he'll need to be strong – to one day quest out and seek his fortune – but, *their* treasure.)

One of the few fragments of sanity in William's life comes crawling over the sand, stops at Prick Lily's trunk, and looks up: Liege Leather. Nose-bone bounces up and down and the tattooed lady mambos as he opens snout. His cries say to William. 'Sharp duds, Golden Boy.'

Prick Lily tips over a pod of rainwater. It washes down Liege's gullet. 'Ah, many thanks, Lil'.'

'Yer right welcome my Liege.'

This will be a leisurely afternoon of conversation-relaxation between plant, animal, and imaginative boy.

Liege Leather blinks in surprise as he looks up, to beside William, and asks, 'Who is the boy Calico's brought down for you to visit with?'

"What boy?" You ask, noticing that Calico is suddenly beside you, but nothing and no one else. "You must be seeing the same mirage I saw earlier, Liege Leather."

(How could Liege Leather know William has a great-great

grandnephew, me, Raji, who magically returns from the future?)

You try to warn Golden Boy about the danger to his brother. You flail your arms, and shout. Glass wall is thick as the one on the dock when you tried warning off Carper. You fear, what you want to believe is so, is impossible: That one day all these friends you, more-than imagine, may be gone forever. The glass wall is getting thicker, smoky. You can't see through it. Whoosh! Back in your room. A voice, calling, "Raji, suppertime."

"Coming Mother." *You look down at the picture you've been drawing. Can't remember... Why were you drawing a giant cactus? Oh yes. It's for Mother.* "Mother", *you shout as you run to the dining room.* "See what I have for you."

* * *

EPILOG

Saturday morning: playing in your room:

Restless. You try to escape into the happy-go-lucky of imagination. It's become harder to do because you're so content in your new life. Yet, you have the GLUMS. Your butterflies comfort on your shoulders. Maybe you're just missing something! What?

Your woodland adventures of four years before, they fade as time passes. 'NO! DON'T LEAVE ME.' You browse the Book of Carpier. Fun to romp through its tales. But what of your own? You want to slow their disappearance, but because you're so loved by your parents and Tigerman, so cared for by the staff and patients, the desire to be whoever you were, lessens.

A rattling sound. You look up, smile at someone you haven't seen in so long: Rrrose Heather! She's at your desk picking up marbles, tin soldiers, spinning the top. 'I remember other boy 'aving fun with these; right at this spot. This be where his bedroom, be – ages back.'

You think of his name, and for a moment – glums-be-gone.

433

"Carper."
'That be the right lad.'
"Sometimes I almost forget him. I don't want to, Rrrose Heather?"
'Then get to the wharf-shack. Surprise be waiting.'
"Nothing but a big restaurant there."
'Go, Lad. You'll discover what you must.' Suddenly Rrrose Heather's gone. You feel so alone. You want to return fully to your imagining and lose these come-and-go glums. (Ma, fa are in bed til noon Saturdays: It's their special time.) You slyly imitate Rrrose in your thoughts. 'They'll not be missing you Lad. Go now.'
You push Sea Line into your pocket. Through the window you sneak.
Barely light out. Dew moistens the deserted pier. For a moment, you think you see an old sailor holding the hand of a young boy. They're entering...
Wait! You're imagining. No wharf-shack there; only the restaurant. You go behind it – on the murky Ohio River side. You hear a slap against the water. Emerging from beneath discarded catfish heads – the *creature*. You'd almost forgotten him – your *protector*. As his shell rises above the water revealing Kunta's village, Poppy Sol rises over the horizon and greets Luny Mum. Their winks prod, 'Do the brash thing, me' tad one. Go wi' 'im.'
You step onto protector's slippery shell, rein Sea Line around his neck, and hold tight.
Suddenly you're being swept across the river. Sitting just far enough above slapping water, you stay dry. Every so often fish surface to *i-u-up*. If fishermen squinted from the shore, they would think a boy was riding a helmet.
It's not long before you enter a wide cove, than, narrower ones. Overhanging trees on the banks quilt the sky. You wonder who could ever find their way in, let alone, out. It feels night – until Poppy Sol and Luny Mum peek through. "Thanks for the flashlights Sol, Mum."
You hear ever-so-slight cries that grow louder. There! Just

ahead, onshore. You see them: Hundreds of cats. Cat-wails seem a human chorus – *"He's coming. Get ready."*
You see shadowed forms: People? Maybe animals? Their moldy, worse-than-any-animal stench overwhelms the woodland's pine-nut perfume. They sneak behind bushes to watch you. Is the felines' siren-call summoning them? You're wary, so as the river arrows to an end and creature-protector crawls onto land you remain on his shell.

A memory figment swoops from the sky: No figment. "CAPTAIN POLLY! YOU'RE, *'REAL'.*" You'd thought you'd heard her outside your bedroom window sometimes at night.

She squawks; points wing at the felines. "They're all related to Ol Tom! They keep dreg rats and snakes away from the..." To some sort of structure, she swoops. So twisted-up in vines, but by its 'carbungle onna back-ass-side 'a...' perpetual look – you know its Mariner's wharf-shack. The bottom foot of it is brown and rotting, from where, for decades, it was sinking into the soil. Mature trees growing close slowly lifted it out and now their trunks provide a sturdy dock.

(You smell Rrrose's sweetness, hear, but don't see her. 'Told you you'd be findin' it, Lad. Likely you're first person been here – in oer' a century.')

"This is *the* special meeting place," squawks Captain Polly.

('Always true to his word – the Mariner,' – comes Rrrose Heather's voice again, 'he set sail from Cincy in that wharf-shack ship of his; 'e did. Found new peace here. You'll be re-finding yours here, too Lad; iffen ya try.')

Creature-protector ventures to the cracking, oilskin tarp door. When he pushes it aside, it's as if the magically healing calmness of the inside suddenly jogs your memory. *Creature-protector* – he's *TURT*, your, for-always, friend.

An avalanche of memories – all but the *one* most important – seem to roll into your thoughts. They break through the mental block of being a foundling. (The most important one: that you had a 'ma' *Imah*, 'fa' *James*. A wonderful, yet ironic paradox not understandable to an eight year old – that you are so-loved by 'fa' *Ben*, 'ma' *Indira* – that is the reason you do not, cannot remember ma, *Imah*, fa, *James*.)

Luny Mum brightens through one clean-as-a-whistle porthole, Poppy Sol, other. It is as you visited in your imagination, but oh-so-cleaner than you remember Mariner keeping it.

A voice gruffs, 'Don't lolly-gag. Embark or jump ship, mate.'

You enter. "MARINER!"

He hugs you. 'Yer sailen' the right course by venturin' yer imaginin'here to visit us, Mate. Ya might have to tie yerself to the mast a time or two because-'a rough waves, but mark it – it'll pay off in mighty-full nets-a-liven'.' Carper's to his starboard; Ol Tom portside. Carper takes your hand, leads you around as Tom leaps to your shoulder.

Carper says, 'Captain Polly and Calico keepin'-up the inside. That'll be yours to do one day.' *Books*, are neatly shelved. Harpoon sentry stands straight, with Bowie sharp and glistening beside. Scrimshaw, conch shells, telescope are dusted. On the table are Buzzard's playing cards.

The wharf-shack darkens as cats, crowding outside the portholes to see patriarch Ol Tom, block Sol and Mum. Huey Long's eye, mounted on a little stand, glows in the pitch. It finds you; burns it hatred for anything joyful. Turt trumpets; 'scat cats', and cats do. New light reveals Laza Bones'acrawlin' from poster. 'I got me uh right to know what and who be awakin' me from my long sleep.'

A sudden ruffling-sound – like feathers flapping – then, a wager Laza Bones cain't rightly refute: 'One round Tehas hold 'em...' challenges Buzzard. (He's at the table: When'd he fly in?) Buzzard wings arm protectively around you. '...you lose, Lazy Bones, then you just slime your way back into that poster and no pestering this young gent.' 'Ah, but if you win, I'll be your, personal, for-all-perpetuat-in' bottom-dealer.'

'De devil marks the bet,' Laza grunts. He chomps his own thumb and swipes a bloody image of crossbones across Huey's eye.

"Can't let you make that deal for me, Mr. Buzzard," you shout.

Buzzard grips you. 'Son, I have been waiting long to prove I can live up to the Mariner's righteous expectations. None may deny it. If I lose – 'I'll 'ave 'ad me voyage, as Mariner'd say.' Mariner's, Buzzard's looks lock, and you understand how much they'll always mean to one another.

Captain Polly flies near, whispers to you, "My bird's not foolin' Mariner. Mariner knows he's got feathers up his sleeve Laza Bones *only* thinks he can pluck." Captain Polly hovers over Buzzard's shoulder and winks as if saying to him. "Let's fleece this pigeon. This time he won't have his minions to bail him out."

Game commences. Coinage, cards slap back-forth, to-fro.

The door flap moves. Turt moseys in and Mariner says, 'Whole crew's aboard. Let our odyssey, commence!'

"Where we bound?" You and Carper simultaneously ask.

'Parading, mates. Grand Marshall Turt'll lead the way.' Ol Tom leaps to Turt's shell. You expect to exit. Mariner must be reading your thoughts. 'Plenty of route to parade right here. He gyrates arms, commences captaining: 'Hoist sails, mates.'

WHOOSH!' Wharf-shack roof magically, vanishes. Poppy Sol's and Luny Mum's rays intersect, creating translucent sails, hundreds of feet high. Wharf-shack morphs into a triple-mast-rigger, expands, to as long, wide, as any deck. Mariner beams: 'My ship! Ain't she a beaut?' He shouts-out, 'PARA-DEERS: EMBARK! Room enough fer all. Two-by-two.'

Boarding from a *suddenly-there* gangway is Rrrose Heather, her ladies, Mama Lucy.

When Thibidioux ignores Mama Lucy's order, 'Drop zee stashed King a yours, Lazarus- *et si vous plait, Monsieur, et parlay,'* she yanks the card away.

Laza Bones growls, lays down hand. Buzzard caws victory as he spreads his four Queens. They curtsey with gentility to Bones' fallen three Kings. Captain Polly squawks; ever jealous of the belle-queens yet glad they chose this ball to attend. You sense that both Captain Polly and Buzzard know that Laza

Bones Thibidoux'll sidle up to the devil, eventually slither out of the pact; just as they know some Fiction, Golden, and now a Singh, will always push 'em back.

Rrrose Heather tells you, 'We ladies'll be suren' the Laza Bones don't disrupt our parade.' She waves hatpin at him whilst ladies arch backs, bowl-out chests at him; looking like opera divas of the greatest of bosom. When he slithers away they sift out beaded necklaces from bottomless pocketbooks and place them around yours, Carper's, Mariner's Ol Tom's and Turt's neck, and kiss your cheeks. 'A Mardi Gras be our goal fellas.'

Parading starts. They toss necklaces that *'clink'* every-which-way.

Margaret arrives. She huffs, seeing Golden Boy riden' up-high in a sail like it were a bronco, 'Why I never… and in your new dress, at that! 'Climb down Willamina before you tear it.'

Golden Boy ignores her, smiles. He has all eternity to pleasure in ignoring her now.

A gathering, like you never before seen, appears and joins the parade. Cat boxer royalty in satin and lace – and riding in lavish palanquins carried on cat shoulders – peer-out at bowing cat subjects. All, even royalty bow, when they see Ol Tom.

Shouts of: *'Horray! He's finally here!'* You don't know who is doing the shouting, or why, but you just know you're the one being shouted about. Why, you?

THE GOOD, THE BAD AND THE SMELLY

The *'good'* – that's Captain Polly, Turt and the butterflies – they lead the parade. They step and fly to brassy cat-wail cadences that sound a marching band. The *'bad'* – Capt'n, Quill Head, Cookie – they rope-down from sails. Pig, Jocular sneak-up the gangway. (Now you know who was trailing you when you arrived. *Eww!* They stink.) Rrrose, and ladies and card-queens madly wave their fans.

Mariner sees you're frightened by the *'bad'* and leans your

way. 'Even Laza Bones' ilk is welcome to parade. That's just the way 'a life, son. All us been waiten' on ya for a long while, so none's about to harm you.'
You know that your face shows how confused you are. Mariner grasps your shoulders. 'Listen; catch what I say and reel 'er in: Our stories'll all end if they're not told. All we've ever done: the gooden', badden', even the mediocre blanden'.'
Mama Lucy adds-rhymes. 'Poof! Our lives'll've been for naught if we're forgot. 'As flyers in a Gone Luna night. We'll disappear – forever outta sight.'
Rrrose Heather puts her soft cheek to yours and the brassy cats quiet briefly so you may hear her whisper, 'Up to you alone Lad to do our taling.'
Mariner, Rrrose, Mama all hold you tight. Their words seem to come as one. 'If you don't tell our stories, it'll be like we never lived. May-be this last grand parade will keep you from forgetting.'
A chant rises among all the *para-deers*. 'LET US ALL LIVE, RAJI! SO OUR MEMORIES WILL LIVE ON. YOU MUST TELL OUR STORIES: SO WE MAY REST IN PEACE.'
More appear on gangplank and join-in: Charles escorting Harriet Beecher, Stephen F. *gal-launtly*, offering arm to Harriet Tubman. Green of jealousy paints Margaret's face: '*Fashionable Mr. Austin should be mine!*' Quill Head leaps to take Margaret's arm and grins wickedly. She can't pry loose.
'Clip-cloppity.' Ezekiah's riding in on Dear Precious. Are you imagining what you see: In *this* parade, the starched Reverend reaches down; scoops up son. You want that to be true in real – as it is now in imagination. 'Ne Hee,' neighs Dear Pre…No, wait. That's BAY's neigh greeting Dear Precious!'
"Hey everyone," you holler. "Look! Kunta's here. He's on Bay and Kaneshawa's riding with him."
'And see,' shouts Carper from Dear Precious on high alongside Ezeki, 'on Dear Precious and Bay's colt – it's Little Kunta.' Trick Rope and Thomas a-Hempis dance from Ezekiah and Kunta's quick hands to entertain Little Kunta. Sea Line waves wildly to mentor a-Hempis.

Seems thousands of multi-colored banners begin waving as millions of migrating-north butterflies arrive. Their flutters, echoing like a gale on the wharf-shack-ship, shout, 'Prick Lily was grounded but sends 'YA-HOO'S!' Prick Lily's emissary is the Golden Boy. In a blink he's changed from Willamina to all cowboyed-up, William, and he's 'ariden' Jesse. His spurs are jinglin', janglin'. He's hoopin', hollerin', 'Wouldn't miss one of Turt's parades. No siree!'

'Get down Willamina,' Margaret repeats. Remove those horrible clothes Captain Golden should never have allowed you to wear.' William looks sorrowfully at her. You just know he must be thinken', 'A good parade will get her laughing; and she'll spit out that sour lemon she's always sucking.' You see a smile sweep William's face. You realize it's because...Captain Golden's arrived! He pushes aside Quill Head, takes wife's arm and looks up to son. 'I'm proud of you, *William*. You've been through more than you deserved. Going far will be your reward.'

Laza Bones saunters to Golden Boy. Golden Boy dismisses him with doff of his ten-gallon. "You'll not be sheddin' me easily Golden Boy-Willa-*menii*. I's own all the time there is: Eternity. You find that treasure, and sure as I stand here, I'll be there to collect it – even in hell.'

'The treasure...' G.B. says slyly. You blink; suddenly see the turbaned boy, Carpier, has arrived. He finishes Golden Boy's sentiments. '...most of us here Sahib Thibidioux, have already found it. Oh how they would love to share it with you now. Just search for it deep in your...'

Thibidioux ignores him.

Carper looks down proudly from Dear Precious – at all of you who have found it. You are so hoping, that it isn't just your imagination that Carper's in the arms of his fa, that even Ezekiah has found the treasure.

For what appears to be 'show', Jesse, Dear Precious, Bay and the colt, who've been neighing in time to cat-brass, rear-up in unison. Quickly you see the reason:

Huey Long, Prime Snout, and Baron Tail, swummed-up

from the bayou, are crawlin'-screamin' from the Ohio for the purpose of doing some chompin'. Just as the other '*bad*' hustle over to help Laza Bones' minions rabble-up the parade, from the water appears cunning Liege Leather. He chomps first one, then, another of the gator's tails, making it seem for a moment they are turning on one another. For a moment, they do – just long enough for equines to kick them back into the Ohio –
– they kick so hard that the gators are sent 'plopping'-skipping out of sight – well on their way back to the bayou. Ezekiah and Kunta lasuu' Pig, Jocular, Capt'n, Quill Head, Cookie, and elly-vate 'em. They let the bellering squirmers parade, but from on high. Laza Bones keeps a distance. He wants to walk into the immortal-ness of being remembered.

Liege Leather stands on hind legs. (That's one trick his circus captors taught that serves him well.) He extends claw to escort Mama Lucy. She takes it, bows reverently. 'None more determined to *obleege* has ever swum or walk this world than thee, *mon liege*.'

You blink. Carper's become an adult, James Thaddeus 'Blackjack' Fiction. He walks beside you as the parade plays out: Cat-band starts sounding shrill; most butterflies aim north. Though the portrait of confidence with his intense stare, and dashing in his waistcoat and meticulously trimmed beard, Blackjack is misty-eyed forlorn. Sadly, he says, sounding like a frightened child. 'Everyone's here…but one.' Then he speaks as wizened elder: 'You are the last of the line, James. It is for you to tell our stories; so our spirits will know contentment.'

'James? Who is James?' you ask yourself. The paraders, they begin disappearing one-at-a-time. Cats go about cat business. Finally, only Turt, Captain Polly, and some butterflies remain.

"Better get me home," you tell them. You know that you're already starting to forget things.

"PLEASE! DON'T LET ME!" you shout. You touch everything on the wharf-shack-ship, assuring yourself it is all real. How you wish everything, everyone else was.

JAMES? Will you always wonder who he is?

"Don' let them all go and never come back!" you plead.
"Don't ever forget this place."
You're so tired. You lie down on Mariner's sea trunk and drift to sleep thinking of all the tales you've heard.
You open your eyes. You don't know if you're awake or dreaming.
Luny Mum and Poppy Sol fade behind trees and clouds. Swept away are the sails.
Shadows, seeming long arms with gentle hands, reach to lull-a-bye you. 'Don't you be ever forgettin' me Bonnie Boy,' a voice softly whispers.
The wharf-shack's flap door moves. "Carper, you've come back! Your ma, she was here all along, watching over you," you assure your great-great granfa as he comes and sits beside you.

The end

OTHER WORKS BY RAJI SINGH

'Tell our stories, Raji. If you don't, it will be as if we'll never have lived.'
These whispering cries of joy and sorrow rise from the bookshelves and portraits in the Fiction House.
I cannot refuse.

No. 38: 'sss- SO WE MEET AGAIN, SHELVA,' SAYS CECILY THE SNAKE
By Raji Singh (the further adventuring of my great grandmother, Shelva Fiction)

Last Week: Not far from the Fiction House, Shelva enjoys a warm soak in a just discovered hot springs inside her hired hand's, Efraim Ephraim's, man-cave. Efraim partakes. Their mule, Sir Winston leaps in. Big 'ol Turt figures it's something too akin to what humans use to make turtle soup. He relaxes along the water's edge. The soothing bath is just like the ones Shelva often visited in her native Russia. Except, little does she, or any of them know until after they're in, this one comes with its very own cobra.

...I freeze in the hot water as the snake slithers up my body and looks me in the eyes...

Believe me, these seconds seem hours.

Not mere coincidence is it that we are, face to face, again, thousands of miles and an ocean apart, after nearly twenty years. Let me explain. I was a little girl in Moscow then. The Crimean War and serfdom was ending. Czar Alexander ruled. It was the 1870's.

Safely inside mama and papa's house, (or so we assumed) away from the turmoil of Mother Russia, so many screams of fear did mine brutter Ivan and I make – in a seemingly perpetual scared anticipation. It was all because Papa and his visitor had kooky idea to have our visitor's pet cobra, Cecily, roam free to catch mice.

"Everybody in Lindia does it," said the visitor.
Mama went along. She hated mice, more than anything. (aside from the Czar, Cossacks, serfdom, and wars.)
Visitor, tell Ivan and I, "Don't be afraid of Cecily. She likes children..."
"For lunch," our cook, Vampira, whispers to us as the visitor educates us in Cecily's diet. "If it swallows big rabbits, like he says, it could open just a little wider for little children." (Ivan and I nicknamed her Vampira because of the spooky stories with which she tormented us.)
"Well," you're probably asking yourself as you read this. "Why not get a cat? Your Mama's not allergic, is she?" No. It's just that cats were hard to find in Moscow at that time. The reason for that becomes evident as this story progresses.
The visitor and his Cecily spent a few months in Moscow. I hadn't seen Cecily, since then. But the visitor, him I see a great deal. He is James Thaddeus 'Blackjack' Fiction, my kindly father-in-law. I am glad the father is the snake charmer, and the son the Shelva charmer. I'd never asked Blackjack what became of Cecily. Now I know. He brought her to America, to roam the Fiction House environs. Hmm. I wish he would have gotten around to informing me.
"*sss*Shelva," it sounds like Cecily is saying to me. Her eyes glow like bright silver bars as the steam of the hot springs sifts past her. Her trunk continuously slaps the water, echoing like drumbeats in Efraim's man-cave. Efraim, Sir Winston, Turt, I, none of us move. I tense even more than I think I am able as Cecily circles my shoulder, necklacing me. How, ever til the day I die – if ever I should live that long, as my koo-koo Uncle Vanya would say – could I forget the sensations of this experience? Breathing becomes hard, but the brushing of Cecily's hood to my temple creates a slight, briefly refreshing breeze. Her fork tongue kisses my cheek. It feels like two tears rolling down. The round of her fangs traces – like a pair of *shushing* skis – over my nose. Her steady breath is volcanic hot, and the medicinal balm of an apothecary. *Any second now, Shelva, will be your last.*

TALES OF THE FICTION HOUSE

A voice from the past, and the present, suddenly thunders out in the man-cave. "Here now, Cecily. There's a point where you risk being too friendly."

I am hearing the voice of Efraim Ephraim. But I recognize the words of Blackjack, years ago in Moscow. At this most traumatic of time, it seems both the present, and memories of the past, intermingle as one.

When Cecily was loose, back home in Moscow, I believe she had a mind of her own. She seemed to take a pleasure in tormenting Vampira often as she could. Vampira was a moody, solitaire woman. She acted and seemed ancient and gray as the Carpathians from whence she came. Looking back though, I believe she was probably not more than 25 or 30.

Cecily loved traversing the open rafters, and resting on the one in the kitchen above Vampira's ever steaming cooking kettles. Cecily moved so quietly, you never knew where she was. She would dangle down, right over the jungle-like humid kettle, just in front of Vampira's face. Vampira's scream was a dozen times more blood curdling than mine and Ivan's ever could be. She'd stand petrified, as if hypnotized, not by Cecily, but by the superstitions and fears, her own horror story creating had instilled in her. Everyone came running to the kitchen.

Blackjack, always a well-dressed man in a black suit, with a red rose in his lapel, says, "Here now Cecily. There's a point where you risk being too friendly." Blackjack takes a long stirring spoon from a rack, and slowly lifts the snake. "Don't move an inch," he tells Vampira. You've already frightened Cecily enough with your caterwauling."

Ivan and I smile at each other. We sense what the other is thinking. 'It's Vampira's resemblance to a *smushed* poisoned toad that quakes the snake.'

"Now back away slowly, Vampira," Blackjack says. Ever the diplomat, he adds. "Those lovely spices you cook with must have attracted her." With snake on spoon, he tastes what Vampira is cooking; and so does Cecily. "Ah delicious." Cecily reaction is different. She spits it out and hisses at Vampira. A

445

team of mice races across the rafters and Cecily abandons us to rampage after them.

Past is suddenly present when Efraim slowly reaches for his shovel that looks like, to me, for a moment, that spoon Blackjack curbed Cecily with so long ago. Efraim says. "Cecily's not hissing, Mz. Shelva. She must just be welcoming us to her version of a snake-cave." Efraim uses the shovel handle to let Cecily climb on, and off, of me.

Cecily slithers to atop Turt's shell and coils into a relaxed position. Sir Winston leaves the water, gets a carrot from the vegetable basket, and gives it to her.

Seems everyone, but you, dear Shelva knew she was around.

After a few minutes, when I regain my composure, I confront Efraim. "Why did you not have the courtesy to let me know she was here?"

Efraim stammers. "I...I..."

His eyes suddenly twinkle. I know he's just now invented an excuse, or at least taken a semblance of the truth and *str-e-e-e-e-tch-ed* it into some concoction of the truth.

"Well, Mz. Shelva. It's like this. Blackjack always wants his dear Cecily to be a free-ranging snake. That comes from his long ago abolitionist activities. You can understand that. You saw the same hurt, back there in your land with the serfdom. So Cecily comes and goes. I guess Blackjack either forgot to tell you about her, or was afraid you might pack up and leave if you knew she was here, and he didn't want that. It's all conjecturin' on my part, Mz. Shelva, but that's my guess."

Exasperated, trembling now, I look at him contemptuously.

"I swear to you Mz. Shelva. I had no idea she was makin' a home in this water. I swear it. Well, what the heck. Cobras do like the warm. The spring's big enough for all of us, right?'

I won't say Efraim is right. I won't say anything. Of course, I won't just pack up and leave. I love mine sweet *druzhyna*, mine husbant, too much. Though, I'll sure give Blackjack a stern talking to about Fiction House rules concerning letting a person know what is what.

"Hmm," I say to myself. "So it is Cecily, dear Cecily is the reason I see no rodents around the Fiction House. Thank you so much Cecily."

"Why do I thank Cecily so profusely?" you may ask.

Because. I hate mice as much as mama did.

NEXT WEEK: Where the cats of Moscow disappeared to following the Crimean War. (and, no, they weren't eaten.)

(Join me every Sunday night at my blog: talesofthefictionhouse.com, your place for short story, lark, whimsy, and merriment. Meet the many residents as I archive their lives and centuries of adventures.)

©2013 Raji Singh

Index to the Tales

The Foundlings	1
The Carper's Tale	3
The Tale of a Love Forever Lost	9

PART I
The Fiction Line

Chapter 1	'Call Me Turt	13
	1966	
	Portrait: A Calm Before the Storm	15
Chapter 2	Unsafe at any Knot	20
Chapter 3	A Typhoon's Tale	26
	The Trunk	29
	Now Beginnith Your Days of Daze	
	Catch a Wave	
	Old Age	30
	And, At Last, Death	
	Ol Doc Turt Delivers	31
Chapter 4	1826	34
	Ol Tom's Epic Tail	38
	A Tale of Carper, a Crud, and Near Carnage	39
Chapter 5	The Tale of the Tellerman	43
	Begins the Tales from the Lindian Woods	44
	Limerickin' Leeziana Governor Long	46
	The Butterflies	47
	The Tale of the Beauty	
	Tales of Our Hero's First Grandiosity	48
	1826 – The Tail of the Beast	50
Chapter 6	Now Comes the Tale of James' First Muse	52
	The Unshackling	54
	"No Good Deed Goes Unpunished"	55

	A Superstitious Tale	58
Chapter 7	Jungle Voyagers	60
	The Tale of Carper Greeting Poppy Sol…	61
Chapter 8	The Tale of Poppy Sol, Luny Mum	65
Chapter 9		71
	The Tale of Rau and Rue, and Turt and You	73
	Rapscallion Rau and Rue	76
	Alas, Achilles	77
Chapter 10	1826 – The Tale of a Golden Boy's First…	79
Chapter 11		84
Chapter 12		87
	Begins The Tale of Lazarus Bontex…	88
	The Legend of Transformation	91
	A Rare Tale of Gator-Honor	92
	The Conclave	
	Ol King Creole Sings No Merry Ol Soul	93
	A Sub-Tale: Kingfisher, Huey Long…	98
	The Tale of Gone Luna	99
	Tale of the Long-Ago Witch Hunt	107
	A Petite Legend of King Creole…	
	The Tale of Lucy and Her Son, Lucius	108
	The Tale of the Little 'Huuka' Man	113
	The Tale of the Spawn	125
	Come James' Second Muse	130
Chapter 13	1826	133
	Valhalla Calls	137
	Horse Sense	140
	Tale of Tom's Passion	141
	Tale of Two Harriets	144
	Tale of Rapture	146
	The Tale of Carper's Woe	148
Chapter 14	Revelations 6:18 Ominous Portents	151

TALES OF THE FICTION HOUSE

	A Tale of a Mum-Lit Night	159
Chapter 15		162
	The Glums	163
	A Treasure for the Ages	167
	The Book	169
Chapter 16	Eighth Century: Begins the Journey of...	175
Chapter 17		185
	Just Seconds	191
	Publisher's Insertion	
	A Squirrel's Tale	194
Chapter 18		203
	Epilog to End Part I	207

PART II

	Introduction	208
	Portrait of a Man Who is a Legend...	
	The Brothers	213
Chapter 19		213
	Four Years Earlier (just what went on...)	
	The Tale of a Gentle Rrrose for Two Brothers	215
	Now Comes James' Third Muse...	218
	Lily's Royal Tale	225
Chapter 20	The Tale of Captain Golden's Dream	230
	The Tale of Golden's Greed	
	The Tale of Golden's Fleece	231
	Lindian Woods Gossip	232
	A Tale of Re-Birth	234
	A Short Tale on the Spirits of Entrapenuarin'	236
Chapter 21	A Lesson in His-Turtry	237
	Last of His Tribe?	238
	The Tale of the Lad Who Becomes A Legend	239
	He is My Savior. He Baptizes Me, 'Turt'"	241

Chapter 22	The Tale of the Embellishen' Buzzard	255
	Tale of the Unweddeds - Unbliss	259
	Tale of Capt'n Romancing the Buzzard	
	Tale of the Near-Wife's Jealousy	
Chapter 23		266
	Buzzard's Belles	269
Chapter 24	A Tale of Blythe-Abwe	275
	The Disputin' Rasputins of the High Seas…	276
	The Tale of Mama L's Secret Slickens	278
	Tale of a Sail	279
	Tale of How the Walk-Off's 'Really' Came…	280
	The Tale of a 'Good' Life for Some	
	The Tale of a 'Worse' Life for Others	
Chapter 25	The Tale of a Birth and Re-Birth	282
	Kunta's Tale of Life in the *'Hold'*	283
	The Tale of the Vitamin C Wars	284
Chapter 26	A Tale of Two Thomases: Sans Aquinas…	287
	The Monk's Rail	290
	The Baptism by Smoke of Thomas a-Hempis	291
	The Tale of the Sermon on the Skiff	
	How the 'Boy/It' First Came to the Desert	293
Chapter 27		304
	…He Flies Through the Air with the…	305
Chapter 28		311
	The Tale of the Neon Walk-Offs in…	313
Chapter 29		315
Chapter 30		318
	The Tale of a Second Savior – 160 Years…	319
	The Tale of Kunta Learning the Ropes	322
	Tale of the 'Whure's Delight' – How One…	323
Chapter 31	A Tale of Somethuns'	324

	A Visit to Polara	325
	Jaw-Jacking Creatures	327
	On the Mast One Night: That's When Turt...	328
	A Tale of New Friends	331
Chapter 32	The Tale of the Mutiny on the Gone Luna	333
	The Tale of Samson of the Sea	345
Chapter 33	Epilog to end Part II	354
	A Brief Tale of How A Plume Brought Peace...	

PART III

	Meanwhile, Back on the Road to Valhalla	361
Chapter 34		
	A Tale of Two Ropes, Two Horses, Two...	
	Horses Tails	362
	Rope Tails	363
	People Trails	
	A Tale of a Match Made in Valhalla	366
	Tale of Turt's Wild Ride	
	Tale of Treasure	368
Chapter 35		374
	The Tale of One Early Underground Rail...	376
Chapter 36		380
	Comes Now a Tale of One Such Night	
	The Making of the Legend of What...	384
Chapter 37		386
	A mini-Tale of a City's Enlightment	
	A 'mini-er' Tale of a New Lad	387
	The Tale of Kunta's Second Long-in-Coming...	
	A Tale of Long-Ago Mutineers...	391
	Begins the Strange Tale of Rrrose's Withering?	393
Chapter 38	A Tale of Two Stalkers	395
	Tale of the Tigerman	397

	Tiger Tribulation	399
	Bedraggled Tigerman	
	A Vaudevillian's Tale	400
	The Tale of What Rau and Rue Saw…	402
Chapter 39		404
	One Cagey Cat Enters the Ring	
Chapter 40	A Quick Tale of How Easy It Can Be…	416
	Tale of Yet-Another Daring-Do Adventure…	417
	The Tale of an Oh-So-Different Boy	419
	The Paper Trail	420
	Tale of Remembrance	421
Chapter 41		422
	Tale of a Fiction-in-the-Making	423
	The Tale of Rrrose's Vow	424
	A Tale of How a Writer Comes Upon a Scene	427
	Tale of the Preacher's Daughter Meeting…	429
Chapter 42		430
	Epilog	433
	The Good, the Bad and the Smelly	438
	Other Works by Raji Singh	443

Made in the USA
Charleston, SC
20 August 2013